A PLUME BOOK

VELVA JEAN LEARNS TO DRIVE

Jennifer Niven's first book, *The Ice Master*, was named one of the top ten nonfiction books of the year by *Entertainment Weekly*, has been translated into eight languages, has been the subject of several documentaries, and received Italy's Gambrinus Giuseppe Mazzotti Prize. Her second book, *Ada Blackjack*, was a Book Sense Top Ten Pick and has been optioned for the movies and translated into Chinese, French, and Estonian. *Velva Jean Learns to Drive* is the author's first novel, and in 2009 Simon & Schuster will publish a memoir about her high school experiences. Niven has conducted numerous writing seminars and addressed audiences around the world. She lives in Los Angeles.

JENNIFER NIVEN

Velva Jean
Learns to Drive

A PLUME BO

PLUME
Published by the Penguin Group
Penguin Group (USA) Inc., 375 Hudson Street, New York, New York 10014, U.S.A. •
Penguin Group (Canada), 90 Eglinton Avenue East, Suite 700, Toronto, Ontario, Canada
M4P 2Y3 (a division of Pearson Penguin Canada Inc.) • Penguin Books Ltd., 80 Strand,
London WC2R 0RL, England • Penguin Ireland, 25 St. Stephen's Green, Dublin 2, Ireland
(a division of Penguin Books Ltd.) • Penguin Group (Australia), 250 Camberwell Road,
Camberwell, Victoria 3124, Australia (a division of Pearson Australia Group Pty. Ltd.) •
Penguin Books India Pvt. Ltd., 11 Community Centre, Panchsheel Park, New Delhi – 110
017, India • Penguin Group (NZ), 67 Apollo Drive, Rosedale, North Shore 0632, New
Zealand (a division of Pearson New Zealand Ltd.) • Penguin Books (South Africa) (Pty.)
Ltd., 24 Sturdee Avenue, Rosebank, Johannesburg 2196, South Africa

Penguin Books Ltd., Registered Offices: 80 Strand, London WC2R 0RL, England

First published by Plume, a member of Penguin Group (USA) Inc.

First Printing, August 2009
10 9 8 7 6 5 4 3 2 1

Copyright © Jennifer Niven, 2009
All rights reserved

Photo of truck interior courtesy of Brian Griffin. Photo of Mama McJunkin on p. 401
courtesy of Jennifer Niven.

 REGISTERED TRADEMARK—MARCA REGISTRADA

LIBRARY OF CONGRESS CATALOGING-IN-PUBLICATION DATA

Niven, Jennifer.
    Velva Jean learns to drive : a novel / Jennifer Niven.
       p. cm.
    ISBN 978-0-452-28945-1
    1. Appalachian Region, Southern—History—20th century—Fiction. I. Title.
PS3614.I94V45 2009
813'.6—dc22   2009006254

Printed in the United States of America
Set in Granjon • Designed by Eve L. Kirch

For Mom, who first gave me the keys and taught me how to drive,
and who showed me that I could go anywhere

And for John, who was with me on the journey

~

For Granddaddy Jack—gentleman, magician, hero, friend—
who gave me the mountains

And for his parents, Samuel Jackson McJunkin,
one-eyed buck dancer,
and Florence Fain, player of the autoharp,
who filled those mountains with music

Something is calling her homeward—
Bidding her spread wings and fly
Up from the valleys and hillsides
Into the bright golden sky.

—Words and music by Velva Jean Hart

Acknowledgments

Thanks to all the folks who believed in Velva Jean, in the story, in me, and who hopped aboard that yellow truck. Velva Jean has found a wonderful home at Plume with some amazing people: Clare Ferraro, Kathryn Court, Cherise Fisher, John Fagan, Liz Keenan, Joan Lee, and the fabulous sales team. Thanks to Eve Kirch for designing such a beautiful book, and Melissa Jacoby for creating the perfect cover. Thanks to Everett Barrineau for his enthusiasm, and the superb Norina Frabotta, for all her work in helping Velva Jean take shape. It was a joy to work with my fantastic editor, Carolyn Carlson, who enabled Velva Jean to make her journey. My agent and friend John Ware remains one of my greatest supporters, and his guidance and wisdom are invaluable. Huge thanks to my family, especially my mom—sage editor, best friend, all-knowing mentor—who first gave me the story, and John Hreno, who drove miles and miles to see that it was told. To all my McJunkin relatives, who shared laughter, pictures, and tales of my daddy's people. And to my friends, too many to name, but particularly Joe Kraemer, Angelo Surmelis, and Scott Berenzweig who, along with the Jonas Brothers, Disneyland, snacks, and BGS moments, helped me stay sane, and Sheryl Monks and Valerie Frey, who swapped stories and cheered me on from the outset. Further thanks to literary kitties Lulu, Satchmo, and Rumi; classic truck wizard John McClellan; photographers Stephen Hunton and Brian Griffin; the Foxfire Museum & Heritage Center; the Blue Ridge Parkway and the U.S. National Park

Service; the Southeastern Railway Museum; Bit Creek Primitive Baptist Church (for Sacred Harp singing); Brushy Mountain Prison; and gold panning champion Johnny E. Parker, buck dance champion Thomas Maupin, and wood carver Charles Earnhardt for inspiration. Lastly, I'll always be indebted to the American Film Institute, where Velva Jean made her debut, and to Jack Angelo, Yoram Astrakhan, Larry Chew, Beth Shea, and Lars Wodschow, original passengers in the truck.

Contents

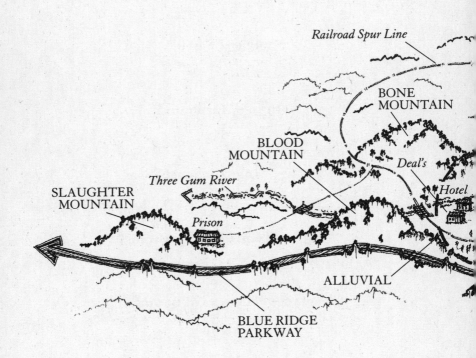

Railroad Spur Line

BONE
MOUNTAIN

BLOOD
MOUNTAIN

Three Gum River

Deal's

SLAUGHTER
MOUNTAIN

Hotel

Prison

ALLUVIAL

BLUE RIDGE
PARKWAY

*Velva Jean
Learns to Drive*

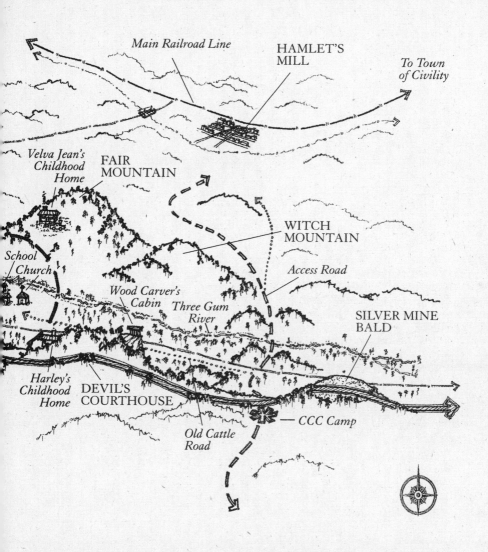

~ 1933 ~

I am saved by his love,
Saved by his light,
He has filled me with joy,
Changed dark into bright,
He has showed me the way to the great Glory Land,
Oh Jesus, my Jesus,
Beside you I stand!

—"Saved"

ONE

I was ten years old when I was saved for the first time. Even though Jesus himself never had much to do with religion before he was twelve, I had prayed and prayed to be saved so that I wouldn't go to hell. Mama had never mentioned hell to me, but the summer after my tenth birthday, on the night before the yearly Three Gum Revival and Camp Meeting, my daddy told me that I might have to go there. He said that's where sinners went, and that everyone was a sinner until they were saved.

"Have I been saved?" I asked him.

"No, Velva Jean." He was polishing the handheld pickax he sometimes used for gold mining. The front door was open and a faint breeze blew in off the mountain. It was still hot, even at ten thirty at night. Somewhere, far away, there was the high, lonesome cry of a panther.

"Why not?"

"I don't know. Maybe you ain't opened yourself up to the Spirit." Daddy's face was quiet and blank so I couldn't read it. His one good eye—the one that wasn't blind—wasn't dancing like it normally did. It was always hard to know if he was mocking or serious on the subject of religion.

"How do you know I ain't saved?" I asked a lot of questions, something my daddy never had much patience for, especially in the heat.

"Because you'd know it if you was."

I thought about this, trying to remember a time when I might have been saved without knowing it. I couldn't think of one and suddenly this worried me. "What happens if I don't get saved?"

"It means that you're 'astray like a lost sheep,' and that after you die you're going straight to hell." Daddy laughed. "That's why your mama and me prays every night for our children."

For a moment, I couldn't speak. What did he mean, I was going to die? What did he mean, I was going to hell? I didn't want to go to hell. Hell was for the convicts down at the prison in Butcher Gap or the murderer who lived on top of Devil's Courthouse. Hell wasn't for decent people. I was sure my mama wasn't going to be there or Daddy Hoyt or Granny or my sister, Sweet Fern, or Ruby Poole or Aunt Bird or Uncle Turk or Aunt Zona and the twins. Probably my brothers, Linc and Beachard, weren't going to hell either, but I wondered about my youngest brother, Johnny Clay. And then I began to cry.

Later that night, when me and Johnny Clay were lying in our beds pretending to sleep, I whispered, "If you was to die, would you go to hell?" I had shared a room with Sweet Fern until she got married, and then Johnny Clay moved in with me.

There was silence from his bed and for a moment I thought he might actually be sleeping. Then he said, "I guess."

I sat straight up and looked at him, trying to catch his face in the darkness to see if he was fooling or not. He rolled over and propped himself up with one arm. "Why you want to know about hell, Velva Jean?"

"Daddy says if we ain't saved, that's where we're going because we're all sinners till we been born again."

Johnny Clay seemed to consider this. "I guess," he said again.

"I'm going to get myself saved," I said, "if it's the very last thing I do. I ain't going to hell."

"Even if I'm there?"

"It ain't funny, Johnny Clay. I'm answering the altar call at camp meeting and I'm going to pray and pray for Jesus to save me."

"You don't even know how to pray, Velva Jean." Johnny Clay was smart. He was twelve years old and he knew everything about everything. He'd been an expert gold panner since he was nine, he'd been driving since he was ten, and at school he was the marble champion three years running. He was also the bravest person I knew. I just worshipped him.

"I know, but I'm going to start praying anyway. I'm going to start doing it right now." And I got out of my bed and kneeled down beside it and closed my eyes tight. I tried to remember how Mama always began. There was a sigh and a rustling from Johnny Clay's bed, and then he was beside me on the floor, hands clasped.

"Okay, Lord," he said. "Please be merciful on us sinners. Please don't let us die anytime soon. And if we do, please don't send me and Velva Jean to hell. We just can't stand it if we die and go to hell."

"Amen," I whispered.

~

The first day of camp meeting I could barely sit still. "Stop fidgeting," Sweet Fern hissed at me across Beachard and Johnny Clay. Sweet Fern couldn't stand for people to fidget, most particularly me, her own sister. She said it wasn't something that ladies did, even though she knew I wasn't one bit interested in being a lady. Still, I decided it wasn't a good idea to talk back while I was on the path to salvation, so I sat on my hands to keep from picking at my nails and my dress. Johnny Clay kept poking me in the leg, trying to get me to thumb wrestle, but I stared straight ahead and waited for the altar call. Reverend Broomfield, the Baptist preacher, said he wanted only the backsliders—those who had been saved already and then lost their way. One by one, they went up to the altar and rededicated their lives to Jesus, and then everyone sang and Mrs. Broomfield announced the serving of the potluck supper.

On the second day, Reverend Broomfield said he wanted all the feuding neighbors to come forward so that he could talk to them about forgiveness and put them on speaking terms again, and afterward we all sang and Mrs. Broomfield announced the supper.

On the third day, Reverend Broomfield and Reverend Nix, who was the preacher at our church, asked for all the sinners who wanted to be saved. I sat straight up and paid attention. Reverend Broomfield promised salvation to anyone who needed it, and all you had to do was come up to the altar and kneel down and say that you loved and accepted Jesus and would live your life for him now and forever. I wondered what that meant exactly, if I could live my life for Jesus and still be a singer at the Grand Ole Opry, with an outfit made of satin and rhinestones and a pair of high-heeled boots. To sing at the Grand Ole Opry and wear an outfit made of rhinestones was my life's dream.

One by one, I watched the other sinners take their places at the altar. I did not want to go to hell. But I did not want to give up my dreams either. I sat there, my toes pressed into the sawdust shavings, my legs tensed up, my hands gripping the edge of the bench. Even Jesus must like the Opry, I told myself, and I stood up.

No one in the congregation was supposed to look at you—they were just supposed to sit quietly and close their eyes or stare at the ground—but when I got up to answer the call, Johnny Clay grabbed the back of my dress and tried to pull me back into my seat. I kicked him as hard as I could and marched right up to the altar with all the other sinners and got down on my knees and closed my eyes and thought about how much I loved Jesus.

To my left, Swill Tenor, one of the meanest and crookedest men in the valley, suddenly let out a shout and jumped to his feet and began jerking in the Spirit. His eyes were closed and his body was twitching like he was being pinched and pulled all over. Not to be outdone, Root Caldwell, who was so mean that he fought roosters on the weekends, let out a shout and started dancing all around, up and down the aisles. To my right, Mrs. Garland Welch swayed and quivered and spoke in tongues. I just sat there on my knees, watching like a person struck dumb, like a person without any sense. I didn't jerk or dance or speak in tongues because the Spirit hadn't touched me one bit.

The congregation sang "Just as I Am" and "I Surrender All," but when I lay in bed that night I felt exactly the same as I always did. The next day, I answered the altar call again and watched as all of my fellow sinners were overcome by the Spirit, speaking in tongues or jerking, running or dancing for the Lord. They fell to the ground and wept and shouted his name, while I sat there on my knees, my hands folded in prayer, and wondered what was wrong with me that I couldn't be saved. I answered the altar call the day after that and the day after that, but nothing happened, which meant, if my daddy was right, I was still doomed to go straight to hell.

On the sixth morning, just one day before camp meeting's end, I stayed in bed while everyone else got ready to go to services.

"Come on, Velva Jean," Johnny Clay said from the doorway. "You're gonna make us late, goddammit." He had taken up swearing when he was eleven. He grabbed my foot, but I yanked it back under the sheet. I didn't want to go because I didn't have anything left in me to pray with or about. *I give up, God,* I thought as I lay there, the sheet up over my head. *I just give up right now. If you want me to go to hell, that's fine. I'll go right to hell and I hope you're happy.*

But then Mama came in and told me to get out of bed in that tone that meant she wasn't fooling.

"I can't," I said. I didn't like to disobey Mama, but I knew I was not getting out from under the sheet.

The bed sank a little as she sat down. "Why not?" Mama was a good listener. She was shy around most people, but she always wanted to hear what they had to say, and she always asked you things instead of just ordering you to listen to her.

"Because I'm a sinner that can't be saved. I'm astray like a lost sheep. Even Swill Tenor got saved, and everyone knows he keeps a still."

She didn't say anything, just sat there quietly. It was hot under the sheet and a little hard to breathe, but I wasn't about to come out.

"Daddy says I'm going to hell."

Mama coughed and then tugged the sheet back, just to under my chin so that she could see my face. Her voice was soft but something in her eyes flickered. "Since when have you known your daddy to be wise about religion?"

I thought about this. Daddy never went to church if he could help it, and whenever Mama said the Lord's Prayer, he just moved his lips and pretended to say the words along with her. I wasn't even sure if he knew them.

"You, my baby, are not going to hell. You're a good child, true and pure, and the Lord will call you when it's time. You can't bloom the flowers before they're ready, Velva Jean." Mama was referring to the time I got into her garden and opened up all the flower buds because I couldn't wait till spring. "They got to be ready to open on their own."

"What if they never open?" I said.

Mama sighed a little like she did when she was praying for patience. She didn't seem upset, though. She seemed sad. Her eyes were clear and blue with gold bands around the irises, like sunflowers against a blue sky. "They'll open when it's time," she said.

"They'll open when it's time." I repeated it to myself later that morning as I sat waiting for Reverend Broomfield to call up the sinners. They'll open when it's time.

Once again, he called us, and once again I walked up to the altar, and once again I kneeled, my knees buried deep in the sawdust shavings. I tried to clear my mind and not think so much. I tried to remember Mama's words, and I pictured her flowers and how they had died after I bloomed them too early.

After the laying on of hands and the singing, the people around me stood up and dusted themselves off and returned to their seats. But I didn't get up. I stayed right where I was, eyes closed, hands knotted up together in a fist, and told the Lord I was done with him if he didn't save me right then and there in front of everyone, with everybody I knew watching and me humiliated. I knew I'd never be able to show my face again down at Deal's General Store or at school if he just left me sitting there like a heathen while sinners like Swill Tenor and Root Caldwell got their souls saved.

My knees started to burn in the sawdust. I knew everybody was staring. "Velva Jean," I could hear Johnny Clay hissing at me. "Dammit, Velva Jean."

I didn't care. I was not going to leave that altar until I was saved. I didn't care if they all went home and left me. I didn't care if I had to spend the night there, on my knees, with the woods closing in and the panthers coming down out of the trees to eat me.

The congregation began to sing. If you've never heard shape-note singing, you should know that it can sound a lot like thunder when enough people join in together. The music was loud and raw, and it took over the air and the trees and the earth. The power of all those voices was so great that the ground shook below us like a tornado or an earthquake. There was a trembling in the shavings around my knees. My bones rattled. My teeth jittered in my mouth. My fingers and toes began to tingle, and I lost my breath. Something was growing from down deep inside me, starting somewhere in my stomach—a feeling of light. I felt dizzy like I did right before I took sick with something, and I felt shaky like I did when I got too hungry. I wanted to lie down on the ground and hold on for dear life, but I wanted to spring up into the air at the same time.

It was like the sky had opened and the sun was beaming down only on me, warming me from the inside. I opened my eyes. When I stood, my legs were wobbly and I had to hold on to Reverend Nix's arm. I felt the cool, dead half-moon of a snakebite up near his elbow, a place where long ago he had been bitten and nearly died. I rubbed the scar, even though it gave me chill bumps, and then I brushed the sawdust shavings from my knees.

Everyone was singing and watching me. I looked at my mama and my family and at all the people I loved and even the people I didn't like very much, and they were all, each and every one of them, beautiful and shiny—even Sweet Fern. Everything around me seemed brighter and prettier and suddenly the only thing I wanted to do was dance. My feet began tapping against the sawdust floor and they carried me all over the tent until I was dancing in the Spirit. I started singing too, and then I started crying because I knew, at last, that God had listened. Even though I was just Velva Jean Hart, ten years old, from Sleepy Gap, North Carolina, high up on Fair Mountain, he had listened to me and granted my prayer—I was born again.

~

Just two months later, I was standing up to my waist in the calm and peaceful waters of Three Gum River, getting myself baptized in the name of Jesus, and I surely wasn't going to hell after all. I was relieved that my old, sinful self was gone forever. I imagined I wouldn't ever feel like talking back or fighting anymore, and I would never feel envious again. I would do my chores without complaining and stop wishing for things I didn't have, and, most of all, I would get along with my sister. I would only be good and upright and brave from this moment on.

The water was dark and cold. I was floating, then sinking, then choking, then drowning. My lungs felt full and tight and I gasped without thinking, swallowing the gritty, cool water of the river. I should have taken a breath before the dunking. Johnny Clay had warned me, but I'd been too proud and thrilled by what was happening. Maybe I would die now because I hadn't listened to Johnny Clay. At least if I did, I would most certainly go to heaven.

The sounds of crying, shouting, and chanting above the surface disappeared. There had been the congregation singing and clapping from the shore. There had been Reverend Nix: "I indeed have baptized you with water: but he shall baptize you with the Holy Ghost." With his left hand on my heart and his right hand lifted heavenward, he had raised his voice so that all could hear: "In obedience to the command of our Lord and savior Jesus Christ, we baptize this our sister, in the name of the Father, in the name of the Son, and in the name of the Holy Ghost."

And then there was only the darkness of the river.

Hands pushed and pulled me back to the surface and I came up coughing and dripping, blinded by the water and the dazzling sun. My white dress floated up around me like foam.

"Thank you, Jesus! Somebody lift your hands and praise the Lord!" Reverend Nix hop-skipped in place, jerking his head back with a snap and raising his hands toward the congregation gathered on the shore.

"Hallelujah!" they said.

"Praise the Lord!"

Mama wailed, waving her hands in the sunlight. My brothers stood in the shallows, clapping and praising Jesus, except for Johnny Clay, who thumped the guitar and closed his eyes to the sun. Sweet Fern, twenty years old and already expecting her second baby, stood off a ways up the river with her husband, Danny Deal. Daniel, Sweet Fern called him, even though no one else did. One hand was pressed to her forehead to shade her eyes; the other was curved against her belly. And our daddy was nowhere to be seen.

Reverend Nix helped steady me, and Brother Hiram Lee brushed the damp hair off my face where it stuck to my cheeks and chin. I had seen the others baptized and knew I should say something or cry or fall back into the water. I thought of Jesus and how when he was baptized the heavens had opened and the spirit of God flew down like a beautiful dove. I squinted up at the sky, which looked white hot and empty, and then I stared down at the snakebites on Reverend Nix's arms, the ones he'd gotten from years of taking up serpents at the Bone Valley Church of Signs Following, over on Bone Mountain. "If you're to lead our church," Daddy Hoyt, my mama's daddy, had told him years ago, "you will not be handling snakes." Reverend Nix had agreed, but the scars were still there—welts and bruises up and down his arms, disappearing into his shirtsleeves, which were rolled up over his elbows. I wondered what the rest of him looked like, if the bites covered his whole body.

> *Oh, they tell me of a land far beyond the skies,*
> *Oh, they tell me of a land far away*

My mama stood on the shores of Three Gum River, in her faded blue dress. I had always loved it when she sang, but I'd never heard her sing alone in public. To Mama, her own voice was a private thing, a sacred thing that she didn't go around sharing with everyone just to be proud or to show off. It was something special to be reserved for God.

There was a rustling from the crowd, a stirring that meant people were catching the Holy Spirit. They talked over each other—"Amen," "Praise God," "Praise Jesus"—hands raised, clapping, strumming banjos or fiddles or guitars.

Mama stepped forward into the water and began wading toward me. Her beauty was as faded as her dress. Her thick, tangled brown hair was shaded with gray. Her high apple cheeks had thinned lately: Her face had turned pale. But her sunflower eyes burned bright and her voice was sweet and pure like a girl's. The tired lines of her face seemed to disappear as her singing filled the holler. There was only her voice now and the gentle splashing of the water rising as she walked, to her ankles, to her shins, to her knees.

I wanted to sing with my mama, to hear my own voice mix with hers. I love to sing more than anything else in the world, and Mama said I had the prettiest voice of anyone on Fair Mountain, just as pretty as anyone we heard on the radio. She said I had a gift and a duty to use it, and that's why I'd already made up my mind that one day I was going to be a singing star at the Grand Ole Opry with a Hawaiian steel guitar and a costume made of gold satin and rhinestones.

Now I felt my heart bursting and the words rising in my throat. Maybe I was filled with the Spirit, too. "Glory," I said suddenly, very small, so that no one heard me. It was what came out instead of singing. "Glory," I said again. I felt the light and the warmth on my skin and I saw my mama's face. There was a surge of joy from way down deep. I couldn't tell if it was the Holy Ghost or just happiness, but my voice grew strong: "Glory, glory, glory." I couldn't seem to stop myself.

My twin cousins, Clover and Celia Faye, were singing now, joining hands. Their dresses had been worn and washed so many times that you could barely see the flowered prints. Their hair was gathered off their necks; their round faces were sweet and unpainted.

"Praise God!"

"Praise Jesus!"

There was swaying and stirring and prayers sent up to heaven. Daddy Hoyt smiled his kind, distracted, faraway smile. Granny danced along the shore, arms waving like a wild bird.

I wanted to run to Mama and wrap my arms about her, but my dress was heavy from the water, pulling me down toward the river bottom, and I couldn't seem to move my legs.

Oh they tell me of a home where no storm clouds rise,
Oh they tell me of an unclouded day

Others joined in—Johnny Clay and my other brothers, Linc and Beachard, and Daddy Hoyt, who was a ballad singer and fiddle maker and healer—but I couldn't sing. Suddenly the urge was gone. Maybe the Spirit had left me. Or maybe it was that I wanted just to stand there, the water lapping at my waist, listening to the voices of the people I knew best and watching the love in their faces.

~

Everything changes when you're born again, but not in the way that you think. If I'd known all that was going to happen after I was baptized in the waters of Three Gum River, I never would have prayed for God to save me. I would have risked going straight to hell no matter what my daddy said about me being a sinner astray like a lost sheep. The funny thing is that until I was saved I never knew what it was like to be lost. Afterward, I could point on the calendar to July 22, 1933, as the day when everything changed.

TWO

When we got home that night from Three Gum River, my daddy was gone again. There was a note this time, and Mama seemed to be expecting it. She stood to one side of the kitchen and read it, and then she folded it up and slipped it into her dress pocket. She didn't say anything to me or my brothers, just set the table for dinner and went about fixing the food without saying a word.

After we ate, she had me and Johnny Clay clean up the mess, and even though it was warm she put on her shawl, the one that hung by the door, and went out into the night with Daddy Hoyt.

"Where's Mama going?" I asked Granny, who'd come over from next door to sit with us. All of us—Mama's parents, Granny and Daddy Hoyt; my brother Linc and his wife, Ruby Poole; Mama's sister Zona and her twins; Great Aunt Bird; Mama and Daddy; Beachard and Johnny Clay and me—lived within a few feet of each other up in Sleepy Gap, which sat high up in a holler on the side of Fair Mountain. Mama and Daddy's house was a narrow weatherboarded two story, painted yellow, with a tin roof and a porch on the front and off the back. There were two rooms downstairs—a kitchen and a main room with a stone fireplace—and three small bedrooms upstairs.

With the rest of the family we shared a big red barn, a chicken house, a smokehouse, a springhouse, a root cellar, and a hog scalder, and we'd lived there all my life and all Mama's life and all Daddy Hoyt's life too. That mountain had been in our family for generations.

It was named for us, even though the family name was Justice. My great-great-great-granddaddy had named it Fair Mountain when he first arrived in 1792 because he liked the sound of it, liked that it was another word for *just*, and liked that it had more than one meaning.

Granny, who was one-half Cherokee, said the Indians believed Fair Mountain was sacred. Only our mountain made its own music; only our trees told stories. The music was like the humming of a thousand bees, only it never happened in bee season and was always loudest before a thunderstorm. The air shook so you could feel it through the bottoms of your feet. The stories were left there by the Cherokee, those sent west on the Trail of Tears. They carved out holes in the trees and left messages for each other inside of them, and they bent and shaped the trees along the trail so they could find their way back someday. They called these "day stars" because you could see by them.

"Where's Mama going this late at night?" I asked again.

"Down to use the telephone at Deal's," Granny said. Deal's General Store and Post Office was the only place within miles that had a telephone. It sat just off the railroad tracks, down by the river, in a small oval-shaped valley called Alluvial. Surrounding the valley were mountains forged together in a high dark circle, with names like Blood and Bone and Witch and Devil's Courthouse. With our mountain, they stood in a tight ring around Three Gum River and the stubborn lines of the railroad and looked out over high, lush green hollers tucked here and there—Sleepy Gap and Snake Hook Den and Bearpen Creek and Juney Whank Cove and Bone Valley and Panther Hole and Devil's Kitchen, a place so horrible they named it after the devil himself.

"Who does she want to talk to?" I said.

"She's just asking around after your daddy."

"To see where he went to?"

"Yes."

We lived in the wildest part of the North Carolina mountains, up in the Smokies—the oldest mountains on earth—where winter and summer the clouds and the mist settle down over the hills and hollers and cover up the valleys. The peaks are the steepest here, the most rocky and wild. The colors are the deep brown-black of the stone and the soil, the burnt red of clay, and the darkest green of the balsam firs that cover the mountaintops. Daddy Hoyt called it the land of the wild things—the last place where the wild things could roam untouched. We lived near the Indian nation, near the Cherokee. Waterfalls. Thick forests. Rich soil. A river in the valley, which is why Daddy Hoyt's people had settled here in the first place, all those years and years ago, when they came from Ireland.

I thought the whole world was right there inside the Alluvial Valley. There weren't any roads that came into our part of the country—just the old cattle path that got you started toward Hamlet's Mill, the nearest town, ten miles away, and a few old Indian trails and footpaths. The other roads we made ourselves, by walking or driving on them. If you wanted to leave Alluvial, you walked or left on one of the three trains that came in every day on the spur line from Hamlet's Mill. Daddy Hoyt said you could barely find us on a map, that we were hidden, that no one would ever know we were up here, out of sight beneath the smoke and the trees.

Now I sat up listening for Mama and Daddy Hoyt because I knew full well all the bad things that could happen at night, that there were things to be afraid of in the dark, not the least of which were bears and panthers and haints. I wanted to make sure my mama and granddaddy got home safe. When Daddy was gone, I worried in a way I didn't when he was home. He had a way of filling up a house so there was no room for anything bad or scary to get in.

I was in bed by the time Mama came back. When I heard Mama and Daddy Hoyt walk up on the porch, I got up, quiet as I could, and went to the window. It was already wide open and I kind of leaned my ear out so I could hear.

"He'll turn up, Corrine," I heard Daddy Hoyt say. "He always does."

Mama hugged her daddy then and clung on to him for a long time. When she pulled away, I got back in my bed and yanked the covers up over my head even though the room was hot as a Dutch oven.

"Did they find him?" Johnny Clay asked from the other bed, yawning in the middle of his question.

I didn't answer. I just pulled the covers up tighter and tucked my whole self under them, snug as a bug.

"Velva Jean?"

I was born again. I'd been saved at last. I wasn't ever going to hell now. I tried to feel the water on my skin and hear the singing and tell myself I was brand new in this world. But all I could think of was Mama's face when she read that note and the way she'd held on to her daddy.

~

The next day, Mama took to her bed and stayed there. I tried to imagine what was in that note that would make her so sick that she couldn't get up. She just lay there, her face feverish, her eyes closed or turned toward the wall.

"I knew from the start that your daddy was going to be a project," she liked to tell us. "We was at a candy pulling, and there he was, playing his mandolin and dancing the back step, long legged and nice looking. The prettiest thing I ever seen." She said she fell in love with him right off, and he fell right back in love with her.

Daddy was what Granny called "charming," something I knew to be bad by the way her voice turned flat when she said it. He could barely read or write, but he carried hundreds of old songs around in his head, and he could buck dance and play every musical instrument he picked up, especially the harmonica. He could make it sound exactly like a steam engine, right down to the whistle and the wheels on the track.

Mama said she knew that Daddy drank too much, fought too much, that he was a wanderer who didn't like to live in one place for long, a blacksmith like his daddy and a part-time gold and gem miner, with talent but no real ambition, and that he had only a passing belief in God. Mama loved Jesus and she knew the Bible front to back. But she loved Daddy too. She couldn't help it. She said she had enough faith for both of them.

Back when it was just the two of them, before any of us children came along, they would pick up and go when Daddy got work. He may not have worked hard, but he was a good blacksmith and people would ask for him. He and Mama went all the way to Murphy, and then to Tennessee—Copperhill, Ducktown, and up to Johnson City. They went to Waynesville, North Carolina, and then to Asheville, which Mama hated because she didn't like so many people. She missed her mountains. She said the Black Mountains weren't the same—that they left her cold. They went to Bryson City, then to Cherokee. Then they came back to Sleepy Gap. When Sweet Fern was born and then Linc soon after, Mama told Daddy she was done moving. She didn't plan to raise her children like gypsies. So Daddy came and went just like he always had, and Mama stayed put. She called him Old Mule because he was stubborn. He called her BeeBee, but we never found out why.

I supposed Daddy was off now chasing another gold vein or hunting gems or maybe doing some blacksmithing work for someone. Just to be sure, I went outside and looked over on the back porch and there was a stack of wood, just as high as the house. We could always tell how long he'd be gone by the height of the woodpile he left behind.

"How come she won't get up?" I asked Johnny Clay. We were supposed to play on the porch and be quiet about it because Daddy Hoyt was looking after Mama, and Granny said Mama needed rest and that we weren't to get on her nerves. Johnny Clay had some marbles he'd won off Lester Gordon, so we were shooting them back and forth. "What do you think was in that note? Daddy's left before. Daddy always leaves."

Johnny Clay pointed at the wood stack. "It ain't never been that high before."

"Is she gonna get up and fix lunch?" I didn't tell him that I was worried about her. Never in my life did I remember Mama staying in bed past sunrise. It made me feel nervous to think of her in there with her face turned toward the wall.

"I don't know, Velva Jean," Johnny Clay said. He flicked a large green marble into a smaller blue one and they rolled off the side of the porch.

~

Daddy Hoyt didn't leave Mama's side all morning. Later that afternoon, he took Johnny Clay and me out to find the mayapple plants that grew on the floor of the forest like green umbrellas. They smelled so sweet that they made my stomach turn, and I held my nose as we picked the leaves. Daddy Hoyt said they had something in them that might help Mama get better.

"What's wrong with her?" I asked him. Mama had been sick before, with a chest cold or headache, but she never took to her bed. She always just worked right through it.

"Your mama's ailing," Daddy Hoyt said. "And I'm doing my best to fix her." But that's all he would tell us.

"You'll fix her," I said. "You fix everyone." Daddy Hoyt could heal anything because the Cherokee had taught him how. When he was eighteen years old, he had left Sleepy Gap and walked all the way over to the reservation on the other side of our valley and our mountains, two ridgelines away. He went to live with the Indians and learn from their medicine man, and while he was there he met Minnie Louise Kinsley, or Granny, whose daddy was a Scottish missionary and trader living on the reservation and whose mama was a full-blooded Indian. Daddy Hoyt stayed with the Cherokee for ten years and learned how to heal people from the land and the trees and the plants, while Granny became a midwife. When he felt he had learned enough to go back home and help his own people, he took Granny with him. By that time, the Indians called him *didanawisgi*, which means medicine man.

I pinched my nose and stuffed the mayapple leaves into my apron pockets. "There ain't no one you can't heal," I said again. "Right, Johnny Clay?"

"Right," he said, his head bent toward the ground.

Daddy Hoyt didn't say anything to this, just stooped over and pulled up an entire plant, roots and all, with one hand. He pulled this leaf off and another and another, and left the ones he didn't want. Each time he pulled up a plant, he dropped a bead into the hole left behind in the earth and covered up the hole with dirt. He carried red and white beads in his pocket just for this purpose. It was something the Cherokee had taught him. They said it was like a thank-you—a way of giving back—for what the earth was providing.

Back home, Daddy Hoyt ground the mayapple leaves into a powder and added small doses of it—barely enough to taste—to Mama's food and drink. He gave Mama snakeroot tea to bring down her fever and ginger root boiled and rolled in sugar to help with her stomach trouble. He made her a poultice of ground up poke root and laid it across her chest to ease the pain, and when that didn't work he made one out of comfrey root and cornmeal.

While Johnny Clay and Beachard worked with Linc out in the yard and the chicken house and the barn, I sat outside Mama's door and waited to go in. Linc was tall and handsome and looked like a darker, quieter version of our daddy. He and Beachard had gotten a touch of Cherokee, both of them brown-eyed and lean, but Beachard's hair was copper instead of black, exactly the color of North Carolina dirt. At twelve Johnny Clay was nearly as tall as Linc, but he was bright gold from his skin to his hair. None of them had freckles like me.

Finally, Daddy Hoyt came out and said I could go in for just a few minutes and hold Mama's hand or read to her. Inside the room, Mama lay still with her face turned toward the wall. I wanted to ask her what was in that note Daddy wrote that made her take to her bed, but I was worried that asking about it might make her worse. So instead I opened the *Grier's Almanac*, which I'd taken down off its nail by the fireplace, and read her the weather forecasts. And then I read her a story from *Farm and Home*.

Mama didn't move or say anything, so I went over to her chest of drawers and got the family record book, which she kept displayed on top, right beside her brush and comb and the silver-plated hand mirror Daddy had bought her years ago. The record book had a red leather cover and listed every important date and event to ever happen to us. It went as far back as Ireland, to the family of Nicholas Justice who first escaped France from the Huguenots. It was a complete history of our family on Mama's side.

I read some of my favorite entries to Mama: "1766: Nicholas Justice and his wife move to the United States. 1781: Ebenezer, fourth son of Nicholas—Revolutionary War soldier, hero of Kings Mountain—is run through with a sword at the battle of Cowpens and nearly dies. 1792: Ebenezer Justice arrives in the Alluvial Valley of North Carolina and names Fair Mountain."

I couldn't get over the fact that if Ebenezer Justice had died way back then, none of us would be here—not me or Johnny Clay or Mama or Daddy Hoyt. I loved to read the family record book. It told about modern things too, like when Mama was born and when she and Daddy were married and when all of us children came along.

I was just reading about Linc and Ruby Poole's wedding day, when Mama rolled over a little and looked at me. Her eyes were kind of half-open and she said, so soft I could barely hear her, "That's enough, sweet girl. Why don't you sing me a song?"

I said, "Mama, what's wrong with you? Why don't you get up? Do you have a headache?"

She said, "Sing me something you wrote. Have you written any new ones I don't know, Velva Jean?"

I said, "I wrote one about a giant that lives in a cave." This was based on Tsul 'Kalu, the giant that lived at the top of Devil's Courthouse. His mother was a flashing comet and his daddy was the thunder. He could drink streams dry with a single gulp and could walk from one mountain to the next. His voice could make the heavens rumble and his face was so ugly that men ran from him in terror.

She said, "Sing that one." And she closed her eyes.

I sang:

> *He comes out when you're sleeping*
> *Creeping on all fours*
> *Creeping down the mountain*
> *Bar the window, block the doors*

Sad and lonely giant
Living all alone
Steal you from your bed
So that he can take you home . . .

I sang the whole song, and when I was done I felt a hand on my shoulder. Daddy Hoyt was standing there and he said, "Let's let her sleep for a little while, honey."

~

After supper Johnny Clay and me ran off to play along the tree line, where Granny and Sweet Fern and Ruby Poole could see us. We gathered the leaves that always seemed to cover the ground, even in summer, Johnny Clay kicking them into a pile, while I collected them in my dress and threw them in.

"Let's make the stack higher," Johnny Clay said, and grabbed a long stick that was split off at the top like a fork. He began using it as a rake.

"And then we can take turns burying ourselves in them," I said.

"And being born again," added Johnny Clay.

Playing like we were being born again made me feel new and light, like I didn't have anything to be worried about. It took me back to being baptized, back to that happy moment before everything changed. When I played being born again, I could pretend that it was all happening all over again, only the right way, the way it should have happened the first time, without Daddy going away and Mama getting sick right afterward.

When the pile was high enough, Johnny Clay let me go first. I crawled into the leaves and lay flat on the ground, closing my eyes, while he covered me up till I was invisible. "Ready," he said at last when he got the pile just like he wanted it. His voice sounded muffled and far away.

I lay there for a minute more, smelling the earth and the mustiness of the leaves. I opened my eyes and forced myself to stare up at the blackness. There were only tiny specks of sunlight showing through here and there. As flimsy as they were, the leaves began to weigh on me, as if pushing me down, down into the ground. I wondered if this was what it felt like to be buried alive.

I pretended that I wasn't buried in leaves but was standing to my waist in Three Gum River, getting saved in the name of Jesus, while my mama walked toward me, singing. I listened now for the first line—*Oh they tell me of a land far beyond the skies*—until I heard her voice in my head. I closed my eyes and folded my hands over my chest and prayed. *Dear Jesus: please help Mama feel better.*

Then, when I felt my breath going and didn't think I could stand it another minute, I jumped up and out of the leaves toward the sun. "Praise Jesus!" I shouted. "I am born again!"

~

On the third day Mama stayed in bed, I woke up and went into her room to check on her. There was an old woman standing over her, up near the headboard. Daddy Hoyt sat in a chair against the wall with his hands on his knees, and Granny stood with her arms crossed, frowning.

The old woman was waving her hands back and forth over Mama, who lay there sleeping. The woman looked to me like a sort of elf, small and delicate, but sturdy, with an ancient little face. She wore her white hair pulled back in a bun at the nape of her neck and a pair of black-rimmed glasses perched on the end of her nose. Her hands were working over Mama as if searching for something.

"What's she doing to Mama?" I said.

"Why don't we go outside?" Granny said, and she shooed me toward the door.

"I don't want to go outside." I ran away from her to the other side of the room. "I want to stay." Suddenly, I was mad at Granny and mad at Daddy Hoyt and mad at this woman I didn't know. "I want to stay right here with Mama." I was practically yelling. I didn't trust this old woman, didn't want her putting her hands on my mama.

For as long as I could remember, Granny had talked about the bandits and the panthers and the haints that roamed the woods, about the giant who lived in Devil's Courthouse with the devil himself, or the cannibal spirits that lived in the bottoms of creeks and rivers and shot children with their invisible arrows and afterward carried the bodies down under the water and ate them. She'd told us of the Nunnehi— fair-skinned, moon-eyed people who were invisible except when they wanted to be seen. In the thick of the night, you could hear them drumming and see the lights of their fires or lanterns through the trees, and sometimes they guided wanderers who had lost their way, and sometimes they played tricks on them and led them deeper off course. She'd told us about the runaway murderer—half-man, half-giant— that lived at the very top of Devil's Courthouse, not leaving his house except at night when he crept down the mountain to climb on rooftops and scratch on windows, looking to rob from widow women and steal babies from their cribs. He was known only as the Wood Carver be- cause he carved things out of wood with his killing knife all day long and he still had blood on his hands. Granny said it would always be there, try as he might to wash it off, because once you'd shed the blood of another, you could never wash your hands clean again.

She had also told us about Aunt Junie, the witch who lived alone in the woods, up on Devil's Courthouse, raising sheep and bees, and con- juring spirits. Me and Johnny Clay used to dare each other to go up there and spy on the witch. Everybody said she could look at you and say a spell, and if you were bleeding, the bleeding would stop, and if you had a headache, it would go away. They said she could turn people into sheep or dogs and that the bees she kept worked magic.

People said this Aunt Junie looked about a hundred years old, maybe older, and I knew that she probably was at least as old as that because witches lived longer than regular people. And now Daddy Hoyt had let that witch woman into my mama's room.

"Velva Jean can stay," Daddy Hoyt said to Granny.

Granny just shook her head at him and stomped out. I knew she didn't trust her baby to this witch woman either, and I didn't blame her. What if the witch turned Mama into a sheep or an old brown dog like Hunter Firth?

Daddy Hoyt waved at me to come over, and then he pulled me onto his lap. I sat rigid and waiting, ready to jump up and knock that witch down if she started saying spells. We watched as she fluttered her hands in the air above Mama. She closed her eyes, and then she began moving her lips with no sound coming out. I jumped then, but Daddy Hoyt drew me back and wrapped his arms around me tighter.

"How do we know she won't hurt Mama and make her worse?" I said. I was thinking I could knock her down if I had to, and then I would yell for Johnny Clay. While I waited for him, I would say an old Cherokee spell that helped you kill a witch.

"Because she won't, Velva Jean. She saves people like I do, only she can do it without plants and herbs. She can do it all on her own because God gave her a special gift."

Aunt Junie bent over Mama, her hands hovering above her, her eyes closed. Her mouth was moving but there was still no sound.

"There is a verse in the Bible that only healers know," Daddy Hoyt said in my ear, "and that they never reveal to others for fear that their powers will be lost forever. That's why she doesn't say the words out loud."

I sat very still and watched her. I knew that normally Daddy Hoyt didn't hold much stock in faith healers, but he trusted this woman, and I trusted him.

"There," Aunt Junie said several minutes later, nodding at Mama. "I done what I could for now, Hoyt." She sat back, staring at Mama's face. "I don't know. I just don't know." Her voice faded off.

"Can she heal everyone?" I asked Daddy Hoyt, very low so that Aunt Junie wouldn't hear.

He sighed and his arms tightened around me. "Not always, Velva Jean. Not all the time."

~

That night Johnny Clay and Beachard and me were sent over to Linc's house to eat supper with him and Ruby Poole. Usually, this was cause for celebration because Ruby Poole—who was born and raised in Asheville and looked just like a doll, with her lips painted red and her dark hair curled so that it bounced on her shoulders—would let me try on her perfume and her lipstick and let me read her movie magazines, but I knew this time they were just getting us out of the way so that the witch lady could sit with Mama.

"You want more slaw, Velva Jean?" Ruby Poole got up and carried the bowl over to me herself instead of just passing it down.

"No thank you," I said. I couldn't eat a bite. I just sat there thinking about Aunt Junie and the way she had shook her head and said, "I don't know. I just don't know."

~

By the next morning, the witch woman was gone, but not long after she left we heard a rattling and a quaking, and there came a truck right up our hill, and out of that truck stepped Dr. Keller with his black bag, all the way from Hamlet's Mill. Daddy Hoyt met him on the porch, and they went upstairs and into Mama's room together and shut the door.

I knew it was a big deal for Dr. Keller to come—that it was a far, hard way to come from town—and that the only time folks called him was when someone was hovering at death's door. Once a year, Dr. Keller sent his nurse up to Alluvial to give us our shots at school, and the night before she was supposed to arrive Johnny Clay and I would lie in bed and pray to Jesus that she would die so that we didn't have to get stuck with a needle. But Dr. Keller only came in the case of emergency.

I stood with my ear against the door, trying to hear what Dr. Keller and Daddy Hoyt were saying. I heard Daddy Hoyt say, "I should have known." And Dr. Keller said, "You couldn't know if she didn't want you to." And then he said the word "hospital." I listened as hard as I could until Granny found me and made me go outside.

No one would tell me what Dr. Keller did for Mama or what was wrong with her. He stayed for hours, and afterward he came out of Mama's room with his black bag. I watched him climb back into his pickup truck and bump and rattle down the hill, and after I knew he was gone, I went in and sat with Mama.

We held hands and didn't talk. I didn't read to her or sing, and for the first time I thought: What will happen to me if Mama dies?

Mama didn't say anything, just squeezed my hand and kept her eyes closed and her face turned toward the wall.

I left her then to go try to eat dinner, and afterward, while Johnny Clay and Beachard helped Linc with the farm chores, I crawled under the front porch and sat there. I'd been doing this every afternoon for the past four days. Sometimes Hunter Firth, Johnny Clay's old brown dog, joined me and we would sit, curled up tight as we could, and not make a sound. In my head, I thought about Mama in Three Gum River, walking toward me, and how I'd wanted to run to her and go to her and sing with her like the others did but how I hadn't. I felt sick now that I hadn't.

I know you're busy, Jesus, and maybe you haven't had time to answer my prayers. But I need you to help me now. Mama is just a very little part of this world you made, but she's the biggest part of mine, and if you would just spare her and let her stay here with me, I will be good and grateful forever and ever.

I remembered what Mama once said about how we shouldn't bargain with Jesus. She said this was something everyone did, promising him things if only he would help them, when what you should really do was ask him to help you help yourself. And then I heard Daddy's voice, which always sounded scratchy, like he had a sore throat, and laughing, like he'd just been told a joke: "You got to be willing to give up things to get things."

I'm being as good and as true as I know how to be and am living my life for you, just like you asked. But if I can be better or do better, I will. Just please fix Mama and make her well. And please bring Daddy home to make things better. Whatever he said in that note, whatever he wrote, I know he didn't mean it. Amen.

From the house above, I heard Daddy Hoyt's footsteps, heavy and lumbering. I knew he was leaving Mama's room to get a cool rag with fresh water. He would soak it through and then wring it out just a little, and then he would go back in and place it on her head. He would sit with her then, and Granny would chant some of her Cherokee spells, and Mama would lie there with her eyes closed and her face fading into the pillow.

I liked to go with Daddy Hoyt to gather his plants and herbs and help him to mix up his medicines, and I liked to talk to his patients and hold their hands and tell them it was going to be all right because Daddy Hoyt was there and he always made everything better. But this was different because this was my very own mama, and because I didn't know if even Daddy Hoyt could make this okay.

"Hunter Firth," I whispered, "you listen to me." Hunter Firth didn't look up. One paw lay across his nose and he stared straight ahead. "Everything changes when you're born again. But not in the way that you think."

THREE

When Daddy Hoyt told Johnny Clay and me that he was sending us to a bootlegger in Devil's Kitchen, we understood how important it was. First, he was sending us to a dangerous place filled with moonshiners and panthers—home of the giant Tsul 'Kalu, where the Devil himself was rumored to hold court, and, most of all, home of the runaway murderer. From up there you could even see Butcher Gap Prison—sprawled outside of our valley, off in the distance—where only the lowest, wickedest convicts were sent.

And second, Daddy Hoyt only treated people with a whiskey potion as a last resort. We knew then and there that Mama was even worse off than we had thought. She had been in bed five days. It was three miles to Devil's Kitchen and three miles back, some of it by the old cattle road, some by woods, some by Indian trails, now overgrown. Daddy Hoyt said he would go himself, but he couldn't leave Mama, and then Johnny Clay said me and him could go just as well.

"Why're we going all the way over there?" I said. "There are plenty of bootleggers right here." I didn't much like the idea of going to Devil's Kitchen.

"Because," said Daddy Hoyt, in his deep calm voice, "there's a man there that makes a corn so fine and pure that it doesn't leave a hangover."

Johnny Clay whistled at this like he knew what in the world it meant.

"I can drive us over," Johnny Clay said. Linc had a creaky old tractor truck that he'd let Johnny Clay learn to drive on before he was even ten. Sweet Fern hated it because it was big and loud and dirty, but Johnny Clay and I just loved it.

"Not this time," said Daddy Hoyt. "There's no road from here to there. You'll have to cut through the woods for most of the way." He handed Johnny Clay a small coin purse. "There's money enough in there. He may not ask for it, but you offer it just the same."

"Yessir."

"I want you going straight there and coming straight back." Daddy Hoyt looked hard at both of us. "No stopping at Deal's."

Deal's General Store had been there since Mr. Deal's granddaddy built it in 1841, and was the only place on the mountain to buy anything.

"Yessir," Johnny Clay said again.

Daddy Hoyt placed a large hand on Johnny Clay's shoulder and the other on mine. "Be watchful," he said.

We didn't talk as we set out. I walked backward, waving to Daddy Hoyt. We always waved until one of us was out of sight of the other. He stood on the front porch, frowning into the sun and raising his hand so I could see it. I hadn't let on, but I was nervous. I thought Devil's Kitchen must be a dark, dangerous place to have such an ugly name. I didn't want to see the giant and I didn't want to see the devil and have him sit in judgment on me, even if I was sanctified. I prayed that we wouldn't run into haints or panthers or escaped convicts or, worst of all, the Wood Carver. They said he used his knife, the one he'd killed his own family with, to carve things out of tree limbs and branches—strange and evil masks, and deadly slingshots, and canes like the one Daddy Hoyt sometimes used. Only unlike Daddy Hoyt's canes, these were carved from sourwood shoots in the shape of a rattlesnake, right down to the scales, the flat head, the tongue, and the rattle, so lifelike that it made people gasp. I thought it was just exactly the kind of thing a murderer would carve.

As we made our way down the hill from home, Daddy Hoyt began to disappear until it was only his shoulders, then his head, and then his hand, and then nothing. I started walking forward again.

"You reckon the Wood Carver ever comes out in the daytime?" I asked Johnny Clay.

"Nah," he said.

"You reckon Junior Loveday's locked up? He ain't broke out in a while." Junior Loveday was the meanest man ever to come from Alluvial. He had been rounded up and sent off to Butcher Gap Prison three years ago but every now and then he escaped. I was thinking maybe I'd like to see Junior because it was interesting to look at crazy people, but I was also hoping that he'd be locked tight in his cell where he couldn't get me.

"We'd have heard the whistle if he was out," said Johnny Clay.

~

It didn't take us long to reach the valley. Alluvial—a twisty, twining walk down the mountain from our house—was just a tiny leftover spot of what used to be a town that had grown up in 1840, when gold was discovered deep in Blood Mountain. The hills around Alluvial were spotted with diggings, and old mine openings sat empty. There was still a working mine up on Blood Mountain, but most men had given up on gold except for Johnny Clay. He said there was still gold to be found. You just had to look for it.

All these years later, the dirt of Alluvial still glittered with gold dust. It was the only place I knew where the earth sparkled. Sometimes on a windy, dusty day, I came home shining like sunlight on Three Gum River. You had to wash the gold dust off you after you walked through town.

Before Alluvial was Alluvial, it was a stockade where Indians were rounded up before being sent west on the Trail of Tears. Granny loved to tell the story of how her granddaddy, a brave warrior and medicine man, had escaped into the mountains with his wife and baby—her mama—and how they managed to disappear so that no one could find them and send them far away from their home.

At its peak, Alluvial was a regular town with stores and hotels and banks and a doctor's office, but when the gold rush died out, Alluvial died with it. The spur line came through years later and saved it from dying all the way. But all that was left of Alluvial now was the Baptist church; the school; three houses; Deal's General Store and Post Office, where we went to buy food and supplies and candy; the jail; and the Alluvial Hotel, which had once been grand but was now faded and gray and empty of customers.

As we passed the Alluvial Hotel, I stared at the windows, hoping to catch a glimpse of the woman who lived there. Her name was Lucinda Sink, and she was supposed to have hair as red as a barn and a beauty mark on her cheek that wasn't even painted on. Even though I'd never seen her, I knew that sometimes she sat out on the wide hotel porch and rocked in one of the twelve straight-backed rocking chairs, which had been set there long ago for guests, and waited for men to come visit her. She was, according to Granny, "ruined," although Granny never would explain why or how.

"Stop your staring, Velva Jean," Johnny Clay said.

"Is it true what they say?" I asked him in a whisper. "That she charges men money to look at her bosoms?" I liked saying "bosoms." It made me feel like I was doing something I shouldn't be. Sweet Fern said I should be expecting my own bosoms soon, like this was something to be happy about, but as far as I could see there was nothing good about them. They would only get in the way of things because they kept you from climbing trees and running fast. Sweet Fern's were so big, she never ran anywhere.

"Where'd you hear that?"

"Rachel Gordon. She said her daddy and Swill Tenor come down here regular." Johnny Clay didn't say anything to this.

I looked with longing at Deal's General Store as we walked past. Usually, we went inside Deal's to look at the candy selection. Seeing how Danny was married to our sister, Mr. Deal sometimes gave us a free sample. Sometimes he even gave us a bottle each of orange Nehi or Cheerwine, and then we hung around outside to watch the train come in as long as Sweet Fern wasn't around. She and Danny lived above the general store in an apartment she had decorated herself, and the one bad thing about Deal's was that you were always running into Sweet Fern.

We crossed through Alluvial, over the railroad tracks, over the river on the old wooden bridge that had been there as long as anyone could remember. Normally, we liked to bounce up and down on it, to try to make each other fall off. Today we didn't because it wasn't that kind of day. We started up Devil's Courthouse, making our way along the unfamiliar hillside. Soon we were swallowed up by thick, green woods.

Johnny Clay was following an old Indian trail that wound around the mountain like faded red ribbon. He was good at tracking. He could find his way anywhere. I collected fairy crosses from a creek bed and put them in my pocket. These were stones shaped like crosses that protected you from witchcraft and sickness. I thought I would take one back to Mama.

Usually, we would have played Spies on a Mission, our favorite game ever since Johnny Clay had thought it up last summer. I was Constance Kurridge—detective, spy, pilot, and sometime movie star. And Johnny Clay was Red Terror—fierce code breaker and member of the Russian secret police. He'd made up Red Terror all by himself and had given him super strength; the ability to speak ten languages; and, best of all, a limp. We had a series of hand signals we'd worked out over the winter—things to mean "stop," "wait," "hide," "retreat," "run." But today we weren't spies on a mission. We were just Johnny Clay and Velva Jean Hart, gone to fetch moonshine for our mama who was too sick to get out of bed.

We climbed up and down hills till I wasn't sure where we were or if we'd ever find our way there or back. We crossed the river—now a creek—fifteen times.

I didn't know what would happen once we got home. I didn't know what would happen tomorrow. But for now, Mama was here and the sun was out and Johnny Clay and I were together and the giant hadn't shown himself and the devil was staying away. I wanted this trip to last forever, because right now Mama was still with us and everything was in its place.

~

The moonshiner lived in a two-story house in a clearing halfway up the mountain. You had to cross a little stream on a wooden plank to get to it. The house was white with bright blue trim, the color of a robin's egg. It had a great, slanting roof that made me want to slide down it, and a wide porch that wrapped around the front and one side. Beyond the house there was a big black barn, a chicken house, a springhouse, a cornfield, and a small open meadow. Johnny Clay whistled. I figured there must be good money in moonshine because these people had to be rich, almost as rich as the Deals.

"You looking for me?" a man shouted at us. The moonshiner had a fountain of white hair and a hollowed-out face and a fat wife who sat on the porch fanning herself and watching the woods. Daddy Hoyt said the old man was crazy, due to the metal plate in his head, which was put there by World War I army medics after the top of his skull was shot off by a German soldier. Daddy Hoyt said the moonshiner claimed to communicate with Jesus through that metal plate, but that he was kind and fair and would give us a good price for the whiskey, if he charged us at all.

I was too scared to go any further than the woods that surrounded the house, so Johnny Clay left me at the tree line and marched forward to where the fat woman and the old man sat. A boy not much older than Johnny Clay was feeding the hens that clustered at the side of the house. He was tall and dark haired and covered in coal dust, and there were two white rings rubbed around his eyes. He didn't even bother to look at Johnny Clay as my brother marched past him and up to the old man.

"Hoyt Justice sent me for some whiskey," Johnny Clay said.

"What he need it for, boy?" The fat woman leaned forward in her chair and fixed her eyes on him, her gaze moving up and down over his face and clothes and his bare, dirty feet.

"My mama's dying." He said it matter-of-fact and straight and looked her in the eye without blinking.

The old man got up, joints cracking. "Come on."

The woman stared after them narrowly. "Mountain trash," I heard her say. She sat back in her chair again and kept on fanning herself. Then she turned to the dark-headed boy and called out, "Baby boy. Baby boy, get you over here."

The boy was facing the woods where I hid. I saw him square his shoulders and say something under his breath before emptying the rest of the feed onto the ground. The chickens fell on it in a noisy pile. The boy watched them for a moment and then looked up and out at the woods like he knew I was there. He pulled a pistol from his back pocket and aimed it at a tree not far from me. I thought I was going to faint right there, and then he surely would kill me.

"Baby boy!" his mama said. She leaned forward and smacked her hands together and the sound was like a crack. "Baby boy!"

He shoved the pistol into his belt and turned toward the house. "Yes'm." He hitched his fingers in his belt loops and shambled over to her, looking like he wasn't in any hurry to get there.

"You fetch your poor old mama somethin' to drink and then wash up for supper."

The boy's eyes flickered over to where I was standing, pressed up behind the trunk of a tree. He stared in my direction for a moment, as if he could see me. Then he turned his eyes back to the woman. "Yes'm." He wiped his hands on his pants and walked into the house, dragging his feet. I thought he moved more like a young-old man than a boy and that he was probably the wickedest, most miserable boy I had ever seen.

"And change out of them filthy clothes," the woman called. Her gaze slid over to the right of her and lingered. She seemed to be looking directly at me, even though I was hidden behind the tree. I shivered. The fat woman spooked me. She seemed to see right through that tree, past my face, and straight into my brain. This might be the devil himself, disguised as a woman—a devil woman—or Spearfinger the witch, who could take any form, so, just in case, I made myself think nice, clean thoughts about Jesus.

When I saw Johnny Clay come back with the old man, I thanked

God. The fat woman was still staring in my direction. Johnny Clay shook the old man's hand and came to get me, not caring if the woman saw us or not. He was holding a jar painted white so that it looked like buttermilk.

"Daddy Hoyt wasn't lying," said Johnny Clay as we headed back home. He stopped and shook the jar. "Look at this. Look in the top, just here under the lid, right above the paint. See how the whiskey climbs up the glass a little? This is the purest corn I ever seen."

I wondered when my brother got to be such an expert on corn liquor.

"He said he sells it as far away as New York City."

"No wonder he's so rich," I said.

Johnny Clay started walking so fast that I had to do a kind of run-hop to catch up.

"Did you see the still?" I said.

"At first he made me wait in the woods and close my eyes," Johnny Clay said. "I think he had to make sure I wasn't a branch walker." Branch walkers are snoopers who get ten dollars for each still they report. Just such a one had moved over to Sleepy Gap from Wrongful Mountain back in March, and one after another he got six or seven stills shut down. Two months later, Elderly Jones, the old Negro who lived in Alluvial, was fishing down at Three Gum River and found the snooper floating face down near the shoreline, shot through the head.

"Oh." I was disappointed.

"But I followed him and I told him what Daddy Hoyt said, about how he's known as making the best corn liquor for miles. That warmed him up enough to let me see it."

"What did it look like? Was it big? Was it loud?" I'd never seen a still before, and I was sorry now I hadn't gone with Johnny Clay. I thought about the boy with the dark hair and the raccoon eyes and wondered if he drank whiskey or helped his daddy make it.

"It was the biggest thing I ever seen, hid in a cave behind a waterfall. You got to go through the Devil's Tramping Ground to get to it." The Devil's Tramping Ground was a bare circle of earth where no plants grew. Old Scratch was supposed to go there in the dead of night and walk round and round, thinking up his evil plans. "He's got a rock furnace in there that he built himself. He said the waterfall hides the sound of the still, which is loud, real loud. He said he's up there every day because you got to go up every day to stir the whiskey. He had barrels to catch it in and cases of half-gallon glass jars. You should have seen it, Velva Jean. The steam raised up out of it. I almost got drunk just standing there."

I could tell he was proud of this. "Let me smell your breath."

Johnny Clay put his hand up to his face and then blew into it. He shook his head. "You're too young."

"What else did he say?"

"Just that some revenuers have been up on the mountain sniffing around." I knew from Johnny Clay that revenuers were even worse than convicts because revenuers worked for the government and carried guns and came onto the mountain and got rid of the stills and took people to jail and sometimes killed them. "He said Burn McKinney's been closing up stills left and right, every which way, ever since they found that branch walker in the creek."

Burn McKinney was famous in the Alluvial Valley. He was filling the Hamlet's Mill Jail and Butcher Gap Prison full of shiners, and chopping up their stills, selling the copper for junk, and burning the wood so that there was nothing left but a pile of ashes.

"He also said his wife thinks he's going to hell for making whiskey, but that it don't seem to stop her from living off the money he makes or trading down at Deal's with a jug now and then. He said she tells him all the time that his soul is doomed to hell, but he don't seem to care. He said if he *is* going to hell, he might as well do all he can to earn it."

This was the most shocking thing I had ever heard. After all the work I put into praying to be saved, I couldn't imagine a man who knew he was going to hell but didn't even care.

"The son's just as bad. He's been to jail once already and he ain't much older than me." Johnny Clay seemed both jealous and impressed. He kicked the dirt up as he walked. "Shit."

All the way home, past Alluvial and Deal's General Store, I thought about that moonshiner who didn't care that he was doomed to hell and his son the convict.

As we reached Sleepy Gap, the sun dropped behind the trees, turning the sky pink and orange and red. We walked the last half mile staring up at it.

We got near to the house and could see it up in the distance with the lights through the windows. Granny was sitting on the front porch, and when she saw us coming she stood and waved.

I brushed the gold dust from my skin. I said, "You think Mama's going to die?"

Johnny Clay didn't say a word, just took my hand with his free one and kept walking.

FOUR

On July 28, six days after Mama took to her bed, Daddy Hoyt and Granny sat me and Linc and Beachard and Johnny Clay down. Sweet Fern stayed upstairs with Mama, with the door closed. Johnny Clay told me he had a bad feeling when he saw Sweet Fern come up from Alluvial without Danny or her baby.

Daddy Hoyt did the talking while Granny sat, stiff as a post, and stared angrily at the floor. Every now and then she blinked her eyes real hard as if there was something in them.

"I've done all I could for your mama," Daddy Hoyt said. "Me and Granny both have done everything we know to do."

"What about the whiskey potion?" I said.

Daddy Hoyt shook his head.

"What about Aunt Junie? Dr. Keller?"

"She's too far gone," Daddy Hoyt said.

My brothers and I just looked at him.

"You children need to say your good-byes."

I didn't understand what he was saying. Daddy Hoyt was the best healer on the mountain and he had been working on Mama all week. We had prayed, all of us, to God. How could that not have saved Mama? Hadn't God heard us? If he heard us, why wasn't he listening? Why wasn't he doing something?

Linc stood up. He was the oldest boy, and although he was quiet, he was stubborn and liked to take charge. "We'll take her to another doctor. We should have took her long ago. We'll take her to Hamlet's Mill or to Waynesville. We'll take her to a hospital."

Johnny Clay looked like he was fixing to punch something. Beachard sat with his eyes closed, and I knew that he was somewhere far away because even when Beach wasn't out wandering, he was wandering in his own mind. Beach was just like our daddy that way. He liked to ramble off and go exploring all alone, and although he didn't talk much, he wrote messages to God and about God on rocks, trees, and walls: "Look for the Lord." "Search out God." "Where Is Jesus?" Mama said it was his very own way of communicating.

"Dr. Keller said the sickness is too widespread." Daddy Hoyt sighed. His face looked sunken, as if it might fall in at any minute. "It's taken her over."

We all just sat there and Granny blinked fast and hard, and I stood up in the middle of them and shouted, "How am I supposed to tell Mama good-bye? What am I supposed to say to her? How can you tell someone good-bye like that?" And then I ran outside and crawled under the porch.

The tears stung my face but I didn't wipe them away. I just sat there and rocked back and forth, back and forth, and thought how much I hated being born again. This is what you get for giving yourself over to Jesus, I told myself. Nothing like this had ever happened to me before I was saved.

~

Later that night, after everyone had gone on home or gone to bed, I crawled out from under the porch and went inside. I'd heard Granny and Daddy Hoyt arguing earlier. "Let her be," he'd said to her. Granny had wanted to pull me out and make me go in there and talk to Mama like my brothers were doing. "She'll do it when she's ready," he said.

"What if Corrine don't hang on that long?" I could tell by Granny's voice that she'd been crying.

"Corrine ain't going anywhere until that child comes to see her."

So they let me be, and I sat out under there through supper. I sat there and listened to Sweet Fern as she came out of the house crying and walked across the porch, and I watched her as she ran down the hill. I sat there listening to Linc go home to Ruby Poole and Johnny Clay run off to the woods, Hunter Firth howling after him. I sat there while Granny crouched down above me and peered at me through the slats in the porch floor and called out to me and told me she loved me and to come on over to her house if I needed her. I sat there until the night was quiet and still and I didn't think anyone was around to see me come out.

I pushed open the door to Mama's room and saw Daddy Hoyt in the corner, wide awake and watching. When he saw me, he just stood up and walked past me. He laid a hand on my head and then went out, closing the door behind him.

Mama was sleeping. I sat down beside her and watched her face in the light of the oil lamp. I pulled a fairy cross from my pocket and rubbed it, just like I'd been rubbing it ever since I picked it from the creek. I had already placed another one under her pillow. I tried to breathe soft and quiet so that she wouldn't hear me, and I didn't touch her because I was afraid I'd wake her up. I almost prayed that she wouldn't wake up because I didn't know what to say to her.

While I sat there, I tried to remember the words to the song I'd started the day before.

> Sweet young Sue, eyes of blue
> Don't be mine cause I ain't true
> I'll only leave and make you sad
> I don't want to make those blue eyes mad

I went over it and over it in my head, but that was all I could remember. The song wasn't finished yet, but there had been more yesterday. What if I didn't finish it in time? What if Mama never got to hear it?

After ten minutes or so, Mama opened her eyes and saw me. Her eyes, wide and blue, were hazy at first and then sharpened as they looked at me so that I knew she was really seeing me. She held up her hand so I could take it. I wanted to cry and throw myself on her and tell her to get better, that she had to get better, and have her wrap her arms around me and tell me it was all going to be okay, just like it used to be. But instead I sat there and held her hand and bit the inside of my lip so that I wouldn't cry.

"How's my girl?" Mama's voice was just a whisper. I had to lean in close to hear her. She still smelled like Mama but there was another smell, the smell of sickness. She smiled at me, a small, gentle smile, the corners of her mouth barely lifting. "I will always be here, Velva Jean. Big things will happen for you, and I'll be there to see them."

I couldn't help it. I cried, even though I fought the tears as they came out and cursed myself blue for letting them show. I didn't want anything big to happen to me, not if Mama wasn't here. "Don't go. You can't go," I said, and it sounded like a baby thing to say. "I love you."

"I love you, too," she said. She squeezed my hand just a little. "Go to the window now." She let go of my hand. "Go and look out there and then come back and sit by me."

I walked over to it and stood there. The window was half-open and I rested my chin on the sill, my forehead against the pane, and looked out, wondering what I was supposed to see. I looked back at Mama, who just watched me. I opened the window more and stuck my whole head out and gazed at the dark sky, the stars, the moon just disappearing through the trees, the long slope of the hill, black in the night, as it rambled down toward the bottom of the mountain. The blackness of the horizon where I knew other mountains grew. In the daytime, they would be there, layered in the distance, one after another, separated by narrow valleys and hollers like ours, with clear, cold springs and wide, rushing streams, and wildflowers. The crickets were humming and the lightning bugs were blinking here and there. I took a long, deep breath of the heavy honeysuckle air and closed my eyes. Then I sat back down by Mama and took her hand again.

"Live out there," she said finally. "That's where you belong, Velva Jean."

I had no idea what she meant, so I just looked at her.

"Promise me," she said, and her eyes were watery.

"I promise." I was scared not to. I wanted to promise her whatever I could.

"My daddy heals people with plants," she said. "You do it with your singing voice. It's a power, just like healing."

And then she squeezed my hand once more and pursed her lips so I could kiss her. "I wish I'd never been born again," I whispered into her ear. "I want everything to go back the same way it was."

We prayed together then, one more time, and I wondered how Mama could speak to Jesus when he was letting her die and leave us all alone. "Look after my babies for me," she said. "Amen."

I kissed her again and watched her drift off into sleep. She looked peaceful, like the pictures of Mary, the mother of Jesus, that were painted on our church fans. I thought about the promise I'd made to her, how she made me look out the window and told me to live out there. Did Mama want me to live outside on the porch or under the stars?

I thought about her prayer to Jesus. Just one week ago, I thought he had smiled down on me and chosen me to be saved, to be lifted and to begin again. But now I wondered where he even was to let something like this happen to Mama and to me and whether I really wanted to live my life for him after all.

And then I thought of my daddy, somewhere out in the world, not knowing that Mama was lying here like this and that he had done it to her. If only he had been here and not gone off again, I thought. If only he hadn't written that note.

FIVE

Mama had been in the ground for a week when Daddy got home. We heard his footsteps on the porch sometime after supper. Johnny Clay and me were shooting marbles, Beachard was reading, and Sweet Fern was cleaning up from the meal. Even though Sweet Fern and Danny Deal were living in their apartment above Deal's General Store, they had come to stay with us till Daddy got back.

He walked in and grinned that big grin of his and we all just stared at him like he was a ghost. He was dusty and tan and there were sweat stains under his armpits. He smelled like apple brandy. Johnny Clay left the room and Beachard looked back at his book and kept reading, or pretended to. Sweet Fern slammed a dish down on the counter so hard that it broke, and Daddy looked confused but happy and said, "I'm home."

When Sweet Fern told him about Mama, Daddy ran out of the house and up the hill to the cemetery, and Sweet Fern followed him, and then he sat right down on the dirt, right on top of Mama, and just cried and cried. I stood on the edge of the cemetery and watched him. I'd never seen Daddy cry before and it made me nervous. It sounded like a dog or a panther, this wild, lonely sound, like he was turning inside out.

"Go back to the house, Velva Jean," Sweet Fern snapped. She was standing over Daddy with her arms crossed, the breeze blowing her hair. She was crying too, but not making any noise. As I turned back down the hill I saw her lean in and put her arms around him.

Thank you, Jesus, for sending Daddy home, I thought. I went home and sat on the settee, the one my mama had inherited from her grandmamma, and waited for him to come back in and make everything right again. *Thank you.*

~

Daddy always said he knew in his bones when it was time to set off again. He told us he didn't know why he couldn't sit still like other men and be happy right where he was. Sometimes he tried. A path still led from our house up to an old mine he had dug himself. The mouth of the mine was dark. An animal had built a nest there. All around the opening, the ground shone like a rainbow—black and blue and reddish pink and yellow, depending on how the sun hit it. This was from the gems that weren't good enough, the ones he'd tossed aside and that were now a part of the dirt—garnet and sapphire and beryl and black tourmaline and gold. Just past the mine was the little cabin where Daddy sorted the gems and where he did his blacksmithing. It was overgrown now and falling in on itself. One corner of the roof touched the ground and the floor had rotted away. One wall was completely gone.

Daddy had tried to be a gem miner in that little cabin. He had tried to set up a blacksmith shop. But then he would feel the urge start to well up in him, and he said he just had to follow it. Sometimes he was called to work and sometimes he just went because the urge was too great. He traveled up and down North Carolina, across the line to Georgia, and all over Tennessee.

Mostly he did blacksmithing. But sometimes he picked up work digging wells, laying railroad ties, farming, mining for gold and gems, to earn money to bring back home. While he was away, Mama and my brothers took up whatever work they could find. Linc farmed, Beachard did chores for the neighbors or did blacksmithing or took work on the railroad, Johnny Clay went panning for gold, and Mama took in washing and sewing. She never asked where Daddy wandered to.

Whenever he came home, I searched his pockets for the gold dust that always seemed to be there, and even though Mama never did, I always asked where he had been. He started telling me: "I've just come from London, England, where I talked with the king," or "I've just got back from Constantinople, where I met with the prince."

Afterward I would pull out the map of the world that Daddy Hoyt had given Beachard on his tenth birthday and look up the places Daddy had been. I put my finger on North Carolina, right toward the very bottom left corner of the state where I knew we lived, and then followed the route to England or France or Egypt or wherever it was with my other hand. I tried to picture my daddy in those far-off countries, doing important work that kings and whole governments needed him for.

"Do you think Daddy is in Africa by now?" I had asked Sweet Fern one day when Sweet Fern was seventeen and I was seven. I'd been lying on the ground, trying to see pictures in the clouds. I was supposed to be helping Sweet Fern with the wash but I'd gotten sleepy because me and Johnny Clay had stayed up all night catching lightning bugs in a jar and watching them till their lights went out.

"What on earth are you talking about, Velva Jean? Daddy's not in Africa."

"Oh yes he is. He told me so."

"Daddy is over in Copperhill or Waynesville."

This made me mad, and I thought Sweet Fern was mean for saying so. "He is not. He told me he's in Africa. He's going to bring me back a real live nose tusk like the natives wear."

"Well, he isn't. He's right over there on the other side of the mountain or in Hazel Bald or somewhere else around here that he can get to by walking."

"I don't believe you."

"Velva Jean," Sweet Fern had bent over and looked me straight in the eye. "Sometime you got to learn that what folks says and what's the truth ain't always the same."

That was when I learned that Daddy didn't go anywhere far or interesting or important when he left us. He barely even went past our own mountain. And all those things he brought me back from his trips—from Africa or China or Ireland—were just things he'd picked up over the hill or down in Georgia or across the line in Tennessee, things that suddenly had no meaning once I knew where they were really from.

~

Daddy was still crying when he walked in the door. He sat down next to me and took my hand and gathered me close, and for a few minutes we cried together. Then he wiped his eyes and stood up and ran his palms down the fronts of his pants to dry them. I watched him as he walked to the front door, just as calm and quiet as you please, and went out into the night. He took off faster and faster, his long, buck-dancing legs pulling him down that hill. Sweet Fern followed after him, yelling, "Where do you think you're going?" But he didn't answer. We all knew he was going to get his hands on the meanest third-run sugar liquor he could find, the kind that made you drunk fastest and hardest.

Hours later—along about three o'clock—Sheriff D. D. Story came up to the house from Hamlet's Mill. He said, "We found Lincoln Sr. down in town, liquored up and causing trouble outside Baskin's Bar. He got into an automobile with a woman he didn't know and scared the wits out of her."

Johnny Clay said, "You can keep him."

Sweet Fern said, "Johnny Clay."

He said, "I mean it. Let him stay overnight and sleep it off. It might do him some good. One of us might come for him tomorrow. Or we might not."

Beach said, "I think Johnny Clay's right. Leave him in there." Beach was already on his way back to bed.

The rest of us looked at Johnny Clay. He said, "We'll most likely see you tomorrow, Sheriff."

~

The next day, sometime after lunch, Johnny Clay rode down to town with Linc in Linc's old farm truck. It took them nearly two hours to get there and back over the old bumpy cattle road, but finally they came home with Daddy. When he got out of the truck, he didn't say a word, just went into the woods and then came back later and got Linc and

Beachard. They disappeared into the trees, and when they came out again, they were dragging the biggest boulder I'd ever seen, even bigger than the one Beachard had left in front of the porch on the day of Mama's funeral. They pushed and pulled that boulder out of the trees, across the yard, and up the hill to the cemetery. Then Daddy walked back down, his face wet and red, and went into the house and came out with his tools. He went back up the hill and sat there for the rest of the day and the rest of the night, and when I got up the next morning, he was still there, carving that stone with his chisel and hammer.

Two days later, it was clear what he was carving—a cross. An enormous, raggedy, rugged old cross, just like the hymn.

With Linc's help, Daddy moved the cross to the head of Mama's grave, where they worked for nearly an hour to dig a hole deep enough for it in the dark soil. In the end, Daddy sank down on his knees and dug with his hands. When he had dug as deep as he could, he and Linc lifted the cross into the hole and packed the loose earth around the stone so that it finally sat there like a sad, mournful soldier.

Daddy stood there a long time, fingers bleeding, head bowed, tears streaming down his cheeks, and then he walked back down the hill— as slow as an old man—and went inside the house and got out his traveling sack, the one he used to carry all his things in, and dumped the contents onto the floor.

He saw me staring at the mandolin, the one he gave me years ago and that I gave right back to him. When I was eight, Daddy had ordered instruments from a mail-order catalog—just up and purchased an entire band from money earned on what he called a healthy vein of gold. Our whole family—for six generations back—was musical except for Sweet Fern, who couldn't carry a tune in a bucket, but even she went down with us to Deal's to pick up the instruments when they came in. Everyone from Sleepy Gap turned out to see, and for the first and only time in my life I was proud of something my daddy had done. But when I asked him where my instrument was, he said I was too young to have a new one, and that instead I could have his mandolin. He'd got himself a new guitar to replace it.

No one on the radio played mandolin—they all played guitar or banjo like my brothers. "I don't want your old mandolin," I told Daddy. "I want a new instrument like everyone else or I'd rather have nothing." So he said fine, have nothing, and when it came to all of us playing music together, I was expected to sing or just bang on something like a drum.

Daddy handed me that mandolin now, and then he went through the house and picked up things that had belonged to Mama, books and a brush and her silver-plated mirror and some handkerchiefs, and he stuffed them into the sack and tied it tight. Granny had saved Mama's wedding ring for him, and he put it on his pinky finger, right beside his own.

That night, when he was sitting on the front porch, staring off toward the mountains, his hands folded in his lap, I sat down next to him and said, "Tell me where you've been."

He didn't say anything, just sat there, so I said it again.

Granny passed by the door and said, "Come inside, Velva Jean. Let your daddy sit in peace."

I said, "No, I will not. I want to know where he's been."

Daddy sighed. He said, "I've had an adventure," but his voice was flat. He said, "I was in Weaverville. I walked from there to Virginia, across the top of the mountains, with a man who's building a road. He's building it right across the mountains, right across the tops of them. That road is going to reach from Virginia all the way down here, right down through these mountains we live in. It's going to be the greatest scenic road in the world. A road of unlimited horizons."

I listened until I couldn't listen anymore. I stood up and said, "A road across the mountains? From Virginia to here? Does it take you to Africa or England too?"

Daddy stared at me.

Granny walked onto the porch. She said, "Velva Jean."

I said, "Did you bring me something from the mountaintops? From the horizon?"

Daddy said, "I brought money. I worked hard to get it, to bring it back." His voice caught, and he cleared his throat. He said, "There's something for you in my bag."

I said, "I don't want it."

And then I pushed past Granny and walked straight upstairs to my room and shut the door.

~

When we got up the next day, Daddy was gone and so was the sack of Mama's things. But Daddy had left an envelope, fat with money, and he had left me something as well—an emerald, big and uncut. Johnny Clay whistled. He said, "You can't get that kind of rock down here. Only place you can find emeralds is up there at Linville or Little Switzerland, up in the Black Mountains. What was Daddy doing up there?"

I didn't say anything. I was turning the rock around and around in my hand so that it caught the light and made the green come alive.

Sweet Fern said, "A gem that size is probably worth some money."

Ruby Poole said, "You ought to have Uncle Turk cut and polish it for you. He could turn it into a pretty ring or necklace." Uncle Turk was Mama's brother who lived down on the river banks like an Indian, cutting and polishing gems and camping along the river, living off the game he caught.

I looked at the rock as I turned it around, and I liked the feel of it— rough and raw, so sharp it could cut my hand. I thought I just might keep it that way.

I took the emerald upstairs and slid my hatbox out from under my bed. The hatbox was left over from Sweet Fern's wedding hat and was where I kept all my treasures, little things I'd collected and that Mama and others had given me—a painted thimble, a silver whistle, my Little Orphan Annie secret decoder ring, some pretty stones, my fairy crosses, and clover jewelry me and Mama made. I had papered the insides with pictures of Buddy Rogers, the handsomest man I had ever seen, and Carole Lombard, swearing that I would one day be that glamorous. When I told Mama, she said of course I would, that I could do anything I put my mind to and not to forget it.

I opened the hatbox and set the emerald inside it, and then I closed it back up again. Then I went downstairs for breakfast. No one ate or talked, and when I walked outside afterward to give the leftovers to Hunter Firth, I saw Beachard's stone—the one he had brought from the woods after Mama's funeral. It sat, large and blank, still completely bare and empty—which was somehow worse than any message he could have written. Up on the hill, at the head of Mama's grave, sat the enormous cross our daddy had carved. It was so heavy that it had started to lean a little, tilting forward over the earth as if it was bowing to Mama.

~

That night I lay in bed thinking about my daddy's note—the one he'd left for Mama—until my face grew hot and my chest felt dull and heavy, like someone was sitting on it. When I finally fell asleep, I dreamed about my daddy and the little slip of paper he had left behind for Mama. He would hold it over my head, just out of reach, and wave it back and forth, laughing.

"Where you reckon that note is now?" I asked Johnny Clay, but he said it didn't matter, that Mama was gone now and finding the note couldn't bring her back. But I wanted to find it. I had to know what it said.

The next night, when everyone was sleeping, I got out of bed and went into Mama's room thinking I would go through her things till I found it. But when I walked in and shut the door behind me, I forgot why I was there because everything was just the way Mama had left it. Granny had made up the bed with fresh sheets and a coverlet, just the way Mama always did. It looked like Mama might walk in at any moment to fold back the covers and get into bed, like she'd just gotten up for a minute and would be right back. There was still a hollow in the pillow where her head had been.

I took Mama's nightgown off the bedpost and held it up to me. It smelled like Mama, only the sickness smell was gone. It was just Mama now—a mix of lavender and honeysuckle and the lye soap with spices in it that Granny sometimes made. I sat on the very edge of the bed so that I wouldn't disturb anything.

I spread Mama's nightgown across my lap so it was covering my knees and my legs and hanging down to my feet like I was wearing it. I put my hand in the hollow of the pillow. I sat like that, watching the moonlight come in through the window, and thought how Mama was just here, and how just over a week ago I'd held her hand and talked to her and promised her I would live out there. And now, just like that, she was gone.

Toward morning, I hung her nightgown on the bedpost and went back to my own room, forgetting all about my daddy and his note. I climbed into bed and curled up in a ball and cried myself to sleep, and when I woke up I couldn't remember dreaming at all.

~

The first thing I saw when I rolled over was Johnny Clay sitting up in his bed. I said, "What are you doing?"

He said, "Hush, Velva Jean."

I could hear Sweet Fern and Danny talking downstairs. Johnny Clay had opened our door just a sliver and closed the window, even though we might suffocate from the heat, just so he could hear better.

"We can bring them home with us," Danny said.

"No," said Sweet Fern. "After all they've lost, those children will pitch a fit if we make them leave their home. Besides, there's no room in the apartment."

They were talking about Beachard and Johnny Clay and me. Linc was eighteen and already married to Ruby Poole and living on his own, but Beach was fourteen, Johnny Clay was twelve, and I was ten. I sat up in my bed.

Danny had promised Sweet Fern a beautiful house of her own, which he was going to build with the help of his brothers and his daddy. Sweet Fern had picked the house plan herself from a catalog and she was mighty proud of it. She got it out all the time to look at and show people.

"It don't mean we have to give up the house," Danny said now.

"I know." We could hear her sigh even from downstairs. "I guess the thought of that house makes it easier to move back here for a while."

I imagined her looking up at the newspapers on the walls—the ones Mama had put up to cover over the cracks, the ones my brothers and I had learned to read from by studying the articles, advertisements, and cartoon strips—and at the old-fashioned kitchen, which was cramped and not at all fancy, not like the one Sweet Fern would have one day.

"We could ask Granny and Daddy Hoyt," Danny said.

"No."

"Or Zona."

"No," Sweet Fern said again. "Granny and Daddy Hoyt are too old to take on these children, and Zona's not strong enough. Besides, Daddy asked me. He said I was the one to look after them. I'm to be their mother."

I started to cough. I coughed so hard that my eyes began to water and I couldn't get my breath. Johnny Clay jumped on me and put his pillow over my face to get me quiet, but I felt my whole world spinning away from me. Sweet Fern and I didn't get on at all. She was barely even nice to me, and that was only because Mama used to be around to make her act civil. I couldn't deny that Sweet Fern was born to be a mother, but I knew without a doubt that I didn't want her to be mine.

For ten years, Sweet Fern had been the only girl—Mama and Daddy doted on her; Daddy Hoyt named her himself because she was his first grandbaby—and then I came along and she hated me right from the crib, no matter what Mama said about her loving me from the start. When Mama wasn't around, Sweet Fern used to stand over me and just stare. Sometimes she would look mad and sometimes she would look sad, and one time she leaned down over me and said, "I wish you had never come." Granny said there wasn't any way I could know something like that, being just a baby at the time, and she said not to make up stories. But I remembered it.

And now she was going to be my mother.

"I'll never leave you, Velva Jean," Johnny Clay whispered. "Don't you ever worry about that."

"Promise?" For some reason, I felt more scared now than I'd ever felt in my life—more scared than I'd ever felt over Junior Loveday or the devil or the Wood Carver or even Mama dying.

"Promise." We grabbed hands and shook, and then I lay back in bed and tried to conjure Mama's face and her voice and her smell before the sickness. It was hard to think of her lying alone outside in the deep, dark earth, while we were inside where it was cozy. I lay there and pieced her back together as best I could—her bright smile; the way her eyes lit up when she sang; her long, curling hair, the color of winter leaves; the way her face was shaped like a heart, just like mine. I waited till she was fixed in my mind and then I shut my eyes. Just like that, her face was gone, but I could still feel the cold of the river water on my flesh and I could still hear her sweet, pure voice filling the holler down by Three Gum River, alive with the spirit of God.

Granny said Mama had answered the call of death's angel. I wasn't exactly sure what that meant, but I thought it sounded wonderful and grand and brave. It sounded just like my mama.

~ 1934 ~

No sweet and tender mother
Cheering their dark home,
No strong and loving father
Watching over them below.

—"Orphans"

SIX

It was the hardest winter anyone could remember. January filled the Alluvial Valley with snow until it was covered. The weather turned so cold and mean that we had to stay inside. There was sleet that cut your skin and fog so thick you couldn't see two inches in front of you. We were closed off from the rest of the world and even from parts of our world—from Alluvial and from our own neighbors. We read and sang and slept and tried not to get on each other's nerves. We crowded around the radio at Daddy Hoyt's and listened to the news reports. That's when we heard about the inspection party the government had sent out across the mountaintops to make a survey for the road they planned to build there. It was going to be a road from Virginia to North Carolina or Tennessee. The inspection party got as far as Grandfather Mountain but was forced to turn back because of the weather.

So it was true. There was going to be a road on the mountaintops, just like Daddy had said.

When the weather cleared and we were able to get down the mountain, we walked to Deal's. Everyone was buzzing about the news. Linc bought a copy of the *Asheville Citizen*, a few days old. It talked about this scenic road that would open the mountains to tourists while saving the poor, downtrodden people who lived there: "These primitive mountain folk, these rural mountain poor deserve help. This scenic road will be the biggest thing that has ever happened or that can be expected to happen for them. It is essential if their economic needs are to be met. It is their only salvation."

Everybody had something to say about this and none of it was good. No one liked being called "poor" or "primitive." No one liked the idea that we were a people in need of saving. No one liked the idea of out-landers coming here and trying to change things. And most of all, no-body wanted that road coming in. Johnny Clay said if those road builders wanted to come to our mountains and cut a road through, they could just try. He'd like to see them do it.

I said, "I don't want a road coming in here."

Daddy Hoyt said, "We don't know that it will, Velva Jean. But it's a funny thing about a road. It's not just an incoming road you know. It's an outgoing road too."

~

By May the sky had cleared and the sun was out. I was sitting on top of the mountain, up on the highest point. I liked walking to the top of the mountain, to the bald spot, where I sat by myself and sang. I did this year-round, in the daytime when the panthers and haints were asleep, because it was up here that I could really hear myself. I was working on the words to a mean song. It was a song about a murder because lately I was in a murder sort of mind. I knew I had turned wicked since Mama died, that I was backsliding, but I didn't care. All the songs I wrote now had murders in them.

I was staring off into the distance, toward the layers and layers of mountains, thinking that if I was a giant like Tsul 'Kalu I could step on them, from one to another, on their very tops, and walk across the earth. The air was clean and I breathed it in. For a moment, I almost felt like writing a pretty song. But then I saw, off toward Reinhart Knob, a line of automobiles and trucks. There were maybe twenty of them in all. They were stopped, men standing around. Some of the men were staring out into the valleys, hands on hips. Some of them stood with their eyes shielded from the sun, looking out toward me and my mountain.

I got to my feet and looked right back at them. I stared at them so hard I hurt my eyes, trying to look as fierce as I could. Maybe they would think I was a witch woman or a haint or a spirit from the mountain or an Indian princess. I thought I might scare them off and let them know we were a force to be reckoned with, not poor and primitive mountain folk who wanted them here. At the same time, I was trying to see their faces, trying to see if any one of them was my daddy.

~

On Memorial Day, we dressed up in our best clothes and climbed the hill to the cemetery. I carried merry-bells and Indian pink and the little white daisies that Mama loved, but not as much as she loved asters, which weren't yet blooming. Sweet Fern and Aunt Zona had stayed up all night, making bright paper flowers. We sang hymns and, one by one, we remembered the dead. When it was time to talk about Mama, I didn't have anything to say. Granny said, "Go on, honey." But I just stood there, holding the flowers so tight that they turned my hand green.

~

By the time he was thirteen, Johnny Clay had been the youngest gold-panning champion in North Carolina for four years running. He was nine when he first entered a competition at Blood Mountain Mining Company—where our daddy and his daddy and his daddy before him had worked when they weren't doing blacksmithing—and beat men more than twice his age, ones who had come to Blood Mountain from far and wide to work the mines. They lived up in shacks on the mountain, and Johnny Clay always pointed them out and said, "You won't catch me living in a shack, mining someone else's gold. By the time I'm as old as them, I'll have my own mine and my own mountain."

He knew that the best place to test for gold was at a sharp curve in a stream. I sat on the bank of Sleepy Creek and watched him and didn't say a word because this would have distracted him and made him mad. He didn't like anyone to talk while he was panning.

I didn't mind because I liked the woods in the daytime. They were peaceful and quiet and I could think there, out of sight of our house and Mama's grave. I liked to lie there and stare up at the sky and think about how I lived in the center of the world because there was the sun right above me. These were the moments I would listen to the creek and to the mourning doves and I would breathe in the sweet, clean smell of the pines and think that I always wanted to stay in Sleepy Gap and never leave in all my life.

Johnny Clay was bent over the water, shirtsleeves rolled up, arms wet and red from the cold, shaking the pan away from him and toward him. Buried in the grains of sand there were tiny flecks of gold, glittering now and again in the light.

Johnny Clay worked the water like he was part of it. He was smooth when he panned, not wild or urgent like some of the other gold panners. He could do it faster than anyone if he had to, but he didn't believe in fighting the water. If you fought the water, you ended up losing the gold and being left with nothing but a dirty panful of sand. This was the most peaceful he ever was—when he was panning. Unless he messed up and lost some gold. Then he got mad at himself and brooded and fell into a silence so deep and distant that you couldn't go near him for hours afterward.

I was half-asleep in sunlight when I heard a step behind me. I sat up and turned and looked just over my shoulder to see the moonshiner's boy standing there. He said, "What are you doing?"

I said, "None of your business. Go away."

He said, "There ain't no more gold up here."

I said, "That shows how much you know. He's a champion."

Johnny Clay said, "Shut up, both of you." He kept working.

The moonshiner's boy sat down beside me. He was smoking a cigarette. He held it out to me like an offering. I shook my head. Smoking was dirty.

"I seen you before," the moonshiner's boy said.

"No," I said. "I don't think so." I didn't want him to think he had any reason to know me.

He shook his head. "I have. You and your brother come over to my house once to get some whiskey for your mama."

"You got me mixed up with someone else," I said.

"I don't think so," he said. "How is your mama?"

"She died."

"That's too bad. You loved her?"

"Of course!" I thought to myself, what kind of question is that?

"Don't get offended, sister. I can think of worse things happening than losing my mama."

"I think that's an awful thing to say."

The moonshiner's boy just shrugged.

Johnny Clay tilted the pan toward him and the sun caught the gold that was there. He counted the nuggets and then wrapped them up in a handkerchief and stuffed the handkerchief in his pocket. He looked at the moonshiner's boy. "What do you want?"

The moonshiner's boy said, "I just wanted to see what you all were doing."

There were voices moving toward us in the woods. Three boys appeared. One of them was skinny, one of them was fat, and one of them was short like a child. They looked as wild and dirty as the moonshiner's boy. They all three had knives hitched into their belts. The skinny one carried a bottle that he was drinking from. The little one was smoking. Each of them looked right at me.

Johnny Clay bristled just like a dog. He went rigid all over like he was expecting trouble.

The short one said, "Who's the girl?"

The moonshiner's boy stood up. He said, "Come on." He went off with them and didn't look back. We heard them whooping and hollering in the woods even after they disappeared from sight.

I said, "Let's follow them and see where they go."

Johnny Clay said, "They ain't nothing but trouble."

I said, "Don't tell me you're scared."

He stood up. He picked up his gold pan. He said, "Since when in your life have you ever known me to be scared?"

I didn't say anything to this because he hadn't been scared a day. We started after the moonshiner's boy, careful not to make a sound. My heart was beating so loud that I was sure everyone on the mountain could hear it. I was trying to prove that I was strong and brave, which I wasn't, and that I wasn't afraid of everything, which I was.

In the months since Mama died, Johnny Clay and I had taken to doing every bad or wicked thing we could think up to do and had got ourselves an impressive reputation as terrible children who couldn't be controlled, something folks were always complaining about to Sweet Fern or to each other. "Those children are running wild," we heard them say to her. "Sweet Fern needs to keep better hold of them," we heard them say to one another.

We smoked rabbit tobacco and stole snuff from Hink Lowe, and Johnny Clay taught me to spit long-distance. We talked back to Sweet Fern and stayed out past supper so that she had to call and call for us to come. We lay down in the high grass outside the True house, waiting for Miss Martha or Miss Rowena to set fresh-baked pies out to cool on the windowsill, and then we took the pies and ran off to the woods to eat them. We trapped snakes—water snakes and garter snakes—and wrapped them around our waists and necks just like they did at the church where Reverend Nix preached on Bone Mountain. We went down to Alluvial and hung around outside the hotel to spy on the whore-lady. I colored my cheeks and lips with red clay and paraded up and down Sleepy Gap until Sweet Fern caught me and gave me five lashes with an old switch of Daddy's.

Being bad was nothing new to Johnny Clay and me, which was why we decided to follow the moonshiner's boy and his friends down the hill toward Alluvial. They drank and smoked and sang dirty songs and chewed tobacco and just as Johnny Clay said, "There ain't nothing to see here, Velva Jean," the moonshiner's boy pulled out his pistol. He held it up over his head and put one hand on his hip and said, "I'm Clyde Barrow. I'm a wanted robber. Come out with your hands up." Johnny Clay and me ducked into the woods, down behind some mountain laurel. The moonshiner's boy pointed the gun at the trees just east of us and pulled the trigger. My heart jumped up into my throat just like it did when I was homesick and couldn't swallow, but the gun didn't make a sound.

"It ain't even loaded," said Johnny Clay.

The moonshiner's boy shoved the pistol into his belt. He said, "Let's go. We're the Barrow gang. We got a bank to rob. Time's a wastin'." And then he walked over to where I was hiding. "I wish I had a Bonnie," he said. "You can't be Clyde without a Bonnie." He pulled the branches of the laurel bush apart and stood there grinning. He said, "Well, looky here."

Johnny Clay stood up and said, "Let her alone."

The moonshiner's boy said, "I ain't bothering her. Am I?" And then I felt a strange tingling in my heart. Underneath all that dirt, he wasn't bad looking.

I said, "Yes, you sure are."

He shrugged. "Okay. I guess that's why you been following me all over this mountain then."

He turned around and started back down the hill. Johnny Clay shook his head at me. "Shit," he said under his breath.

~

We followed the moonshiner's boy and his friends down to Alluvial, sneaky as spies. Johnny Clay said, "Hang back. Don't let them see you. And if it looks like trouble, I want you to run, Velva Jean."

On the way down the hill, the moonshiner's boy and his gang tipped over outhouses and stole clothing off of clotheslines and helped themselves to whiskey from a still hidden in the woods.

When we got down to Alluvial—Johnny Clay and me careful not to be seen—a small crowd of men was gathered on the steps of the general store, waiting for the train to come in, waiting to look at the railroad passengers, to find out if anyone was actually staying in Alluvial or just getting right back on and going somewhere else.

The moonshiner's boy said, "We should go into Deal's and get some candy and cigarettes, as much as we can walk out with." He started up the steps and the short boy and the two taller boys followed him.

I said to Johnny Clay, "What does he mean 'walk out with'? Does he mean steal?"

Johnny Clay handed me his gold pan. He said, "You wait here." He was up in front of them in a flash, blocking their way. He said, "Mr. Deal's son is married to our sister. You ain't robbing his store, and I ain't standing by while you do."

Johnny Clay and the moonshiner's boy were practically nose to nose. Johnny Clay won every staring contest he ever entered because he didn't believe in backing down. The moonshiner's boy said, "You better get out of my way."

Johnny Clay said, "No."

The moonshiner's boy gave Johnny Clay a mean look and then walked to the edge of the porch and jumped off. He stood there in the dirt and looked around him, one hand pushing his hair back, the other on his pistol. He said, "Why don't you come down here and fight me like a man? If you ain't too chicken." He laughed at this. The rest of the Barrow gang laughed, too.

Johnny Clay was on him in a minute. They were rolling all around in the dirt and there was blood mixed in with the red clay. Someone from the front porch of Deal's let out a yell. I ran over and tried to kick the moonshiner's boy but kicked Johnny Clay instead. He yelled, "Goddammit, Velva Jean!" I started screaming.

Suddenly Mr. Deal was outside with his three sons, Jessup, Coyle, and Danny. They were in the middle of everything, pulling those boys apart. The moonshiner's boy had a scrape on his head and one on his chin and he was bleeding from his nose. Johnny Clay had a bloody lip. But the moonshiner's boy looked worse. I couldn't help it—I was proud of my brother.

The moonshiner's boy was mean. He was maybe even as mean as Junior Loveday, who sat over in Butcher Gap Prison for murdering six men. When they asked Junior why he did it, he said he guessed there was a meanness in him and a meanness in the world that just couldn't be heled.

~

Mr. Deal sat Johnny Clay and me down on the hard bench in the Alluvial Jail, a one-roomed building in back of the store. This was where they held drunkards and other folks who broke the law while they waited for the sheriff to come up from Hamlet's Mill. My own daddy had been here too many times to count. We watched while Mr. Deal locked up the moonshiner's boy and the rest of the Barrow gang in the one and only cell. The moonshiner's boy was saying, "You can't lock me up. No one locks up Clyde Barrow."

Mr. Deal said, "You get in there right now, Mr. Barrow, and shut your mouth. I don't want to hear another word." He slammed the cell door shut and then he wheeled around to face Johnny Clay and me. He said, "What do you think you're doing? Since when do you start hanging around with that sort?"

I said, "We are that sort. We're just as mean and bad as they are."

Johnny Clay kicked me.

Mr. Deal sat down on the bench beside me and said, "I'm tempted to lock up the both of you right now and send you down to Hamlet's Mill, down to the real jail. You'll wish I had once Sweet Fern gets done with you." Mr. Deal was one of the kindest men I knew. He had never in his life spoken to Johnny Clay or me this way. He said, "Do you realize you all are almost convicts? That you're just a step away?" He pointed to the jail cell. He said, "Look how far. Just a couple of feet, by my guess. Do you realize once you become a convict you can't ever take it back?"

He stood up. He set a hand on my head, just briefly. He said, "I don't want to hear that either of you has been hanging around with them anymore." He nodded at the moonshiner's boy and his friends. "Is that understood?"

I thought it was shameful to have to agree to something like that in a jail in front of hard criminals like the bad Barrow gang, just like we were children, but Johnny Clay and I both said, "Yessir."

When Mr. Deal left, I leaned over and whispered to my brother, "This is the most exciting thing to ever happen to me."

Johnny Clay said, "We're almost criminals now, Velva Jean. Did you hear? Mr. Deal almost sent us to the jail in Hamlet's Mill. You know what's next after that—Butcher Gap Prison." Johnny Clay was watching my face for a reaction. I kept my expression blank on purpose even though my heart started racing at this, and I hoped that Johnny Clay wouldn't somehow notice.

I was now officially a wicked person. I had backslid so far that Jesus himself couldn't save me. I almost had a prison record. I was almost a convict. I was practically like Bonnie Parker. People would write songs about me and sing them for years to come. I tried not to think of what Sweet Fern would do to us. I tried not to think of Granny or Daddy Hoyt. Instead I concentrated on Jesus and how upset he must be, especially since I had pledged myself to him. For months, I had been trying to upset Jesus. I wanted him to feel betrayed, just like I did because he had taken my mama away.

We heard Sweet Fern before we saw her. "Where are they?" she said. She wasn't using her company voice, the one she put on for other people. She was using her everyday voice, the one she used all the time for us. And then the door to the jail was thrown open and there she was, her face a round, white cloud, smoke swirling up and out of her like the mountains on a misty day. She said, "If Mama weren't dead already, this would be enough to kill her."

She looked us over from head to toe and then turned on her heel and walked back outside. As we passed by the moonshiner's boy, he came to the bars and leaned against them and said, "See you soon, Bonnie."

I didn't say anything. I wondered if anyone would come to get him and take him home, if anyone would care that he was here, or if they would even miss him at all.

~

When we got home, Sweet Fern marched right into the house and said, "Johnny Clay, I want you to get your things and move them back out to Beachard's room."

It was the most horrible thing she could have said or done. It was worse than the switch or getting hollered at. Johnny Clay said, "No."

"I'm not going to tell you again. You're getting too old to share a room with Velva Jean. You're as tall as Linc now, and Velva Jean's practically a woman."

"I am not," I hollered.

"Hell no," Johnny Clay said.

"Johnny Clay Hart. Don't you swear at me." Sweet Fern led Johnny Clay and me up the stairs and into our bedroom. She and Danny had moved right in after Daddy left, taking over the room he'd shared with Mama.

"Dan Presley will move in here with you," she said to me.

"He's only three!" I said. "He's a baby!"

"I want your things out of here by supper," Sweet Fern said to Johnny Clay. When we just looked at her, she said, "You all are about to kill me, the way you run around. Every single person I know has an opinion on how I should raise you. Every single person thinks I don't know how to be a mother."

She spun out of the room, leaving Johnny Clay and me to look at each other. "What are we going to do?" I said.

"Nothing, I guess. We got to listen to her now." Johnny Clay looked like he wanted to spit.

"She ain't our mother."

"She's the closest thing we got, though, ain't she?" He mumbled something under his breath. "Like it or not, we live in her house now. Not Mama's house, not Daddy's house, not our house. Sweet Fern's house. And that means we got to do just what she damn well says." Until we're old enough to leave, I knew he was thinking.

I watched as my brother packed up his clothes and his few belongings and stalked out of the room. In a minute, I heard him next door, moving around in his old room. I sat down on my bed until Sweet Fern called us to supper.

~

That night I lay in bed listening to Dan Presley sleep and concentrating hard on a Cherokee spell. It was a spell to drive away a witch and get her to do your bidding. I thought I would use it on Sweet Fern so that she would let Johnny Clay move back into my room. Even after Mama dying and Daddy leaving, I had never felt so lonely. Why did things always have to change? Change was almost always bad and I was tired of it. I just wanted things to stay the same for a while.

I tapped on the wall beside my bed. "Johnny Clay?" I sat up on my knees and leaned over, putting my face to a crack between the planks. "Are you there?"

From the other side of the wall, I heard a rustling. "I'm here."

"Is Beach asleep?"

"Yeah."

I leaned forward on my elbows and shook my hair down so that it covered my face. I pulled one of the strands out and tried to straighten the wave so that it lay flat.

Johnny Clay said, "You okay?"

No, I wanted to say. I'm not. I want Mama and I want Daddy, and if I can't have them, at least I can have you, Johnny Clay. He was too far away on the other side of the wall. I needed to know he was there in the same room, just an arm's length away.

"I'm okay," I said.

There was silence. When he didn't speak, my heart skipped a beat and I sat up. "Johnny Clay?" Had he gone to sleep already?

"I'm here," he said. "I was just thinking."

"What about?"

"Going to jail."

I hunched over again and pulled the blanket up around myself.

"I reckon we're different now," said Johnny Clay. A chill crept up my spine all the way from my toes and I pulled the blanket tighter. "I reckon we're changed forever, Velva Jean. There's no going back to the way we used to be. The old us is gone."

The thought of this made me sad because so much was gone now and I had liked the old us. "How so?" I said. I whispered it. "You think we're mean forever now?"

It took him a minute to answer. "Not mean exactly. But not soft either."

There was a lump in my throat as big as a bullfrog. We both sat there in silence, on either side of the wall.

"If you want," Johnny Clay said finally, "I'll stay awake till I know you're asleep."

My eyes teared up at this, and I squeezed them shut so that the water stayed in. "Okay," I said. I lay back down and rolled on my side so that I faced the wall. I pulled the covers up to my chin and closed my eyes. I thought about the moonshiner's boy, about the meanness that was in him. "See you soon, Bonnie," he'd said. I thought about the meanness that was in me. I wondered if I would be able to sleep at all.

~

One week later, Johnny Clay found me under the porch, playing Daddy's mandolin, pretending it was a Hawaiian steel guitar and I was Maybelle Carter, the greatest guitar player that ever lived. I sang a song I'd just made up that morning. It was about a girl who had no parents and went to live on the moon with a race of moon-eyed people who could only see at night.

I saw Johnny Clay's feet before I saw the rest of him. He came up from the direction of the creek, where he'd been panning for gold with Hunter Firth. He squatted down and looked at me and I ignored him, went right on singing.

"I'm afraid the meanness in me has taken over," he said.

"That's okay," I said. "I reckon I'm mean, too."

"We been sneaking over to a still in Devil's Kitchen. The one you and me went to last year. Daddy Hoyt was right, Velva Jean. It's the purest corn liquor you ever tasted, and it don't leave a hangover. Not even a headache."

I felt sick and excited all at once. I wasn't sure I wanted to start drinking regular. But I also wondered if I had a choice now that I was on a wayward path. I said, "You just want to steal from the moonshiner's boy."

He ignored this and said, "I'm going back over there now, and you can come with me if you want or you can stay here."

I sang a little louder to make it clear that I was busy and not to be bothered.

"Velva Jean."

I stopped playing. I lay there looking up at the sky through the slats in the porch floor. I thought that this particular moment felt a lot like the night before Dr. Keller's nurse came to give us shots—that same feeling of dread sat like a weight in the bottom of my stomach.

~

I could hear the pounding of the waterfall long before I saw it. Then suddenly we were there, and the water was pouring down the face of the rock, fifty feet or so, and it all looked so peaceful. You would never have known there was a still hidden back of there. Johnny Clay and I sat down in the laurel bushes at the side of the falls. Behind the water was a narrow ledge that led to the mouth of a cave, which you could barely see.

"What now?" I said, and I tried to whisper it but still be heard.

Johnny Clay said, "You wait here." He pulled a watch out of his pocket—an old gold watch of Daddy's. He rubbed his nose. The skin had healed nicely from his late summer sunburn and was now as brown as the rest of him. He checked the watch and said, "The moonshiner just went home for lunch."

While I played lookout, Johnny Clay slipped across the ledge and into the cave. He was gone for five minutes. I was holding the watch and didn't take my eyes off it. I jumped at every sound—every bird and creature that rustled by in the underbrush—sure it was the moonshiner come back to catch us.

Finally, Johnny Clay came out of the cave, jar in hand. He grinned, his hair wet from the spray, and edged back to me. He shook his hair like a wet dog, spraying me with water, and unscrewed the lid of the jar. He held the jar out to me. My head swam. It smelled like gasoline. He said, "We've got to be men about it, Velva Jean."

I took the jar from him and raised it to my lips. I took the smallest sip I could. The liquor tasted better than I expected, but it wasn't good. It was strong and sharp and it hurt my throat. I took a bigger drink, and this one burned going down. I started coughing so hard that my eyes watered.

At that moment, we heard a gunshot. I screamed and dropped the jar.

"Run, Velva Jean!" Johnny Clay hollered, and I did. I ran so hard and so fast that I didn't pay attention to where I was going. All I knew was that I had to get out of there and get away as fast as possible. The moonshiner was after us. He would kill us if he caught us. He would kill us and then he would take us up to his cave and bury us in there or burn us up in his still and turn our blood into whiskey. I wanted to get home to Daddy Hoyt, who I knew would take care of me and keep me safe and who wasn't one bit afraid of bootleggers.

I ran so hard that I couldn't breathe. I ran up and down and this way and that and here and there until I didn't know where I was anymore. I turned back to look for Johnny Clay, but he was nowhere to be seen.

"Johnny Clay!" I began to shout it over and over again. "Johnny Clay!"

The woods were still and silent.

"Johnny Clay!" I knew I should keep my voice down because I didn't want the moonshiner to hear me. My heart was beating as fast as hummingbird wings and as loud as a drum, so loud I couldn't hear.

I threw my head back and shaded my eyes from the sun. I was high up Devil's Courthouse, near where the giant lived, near where the devil held court. I could see the dark, jagged peak of Tsul 'Kalu's cave, above and to my left. Up here you could see as far away as Georgia and South Carolina and Tennessee. Some people said that on a clear day you could even see the ocean.

The trees around looked dead and black. Their limbs reached up and out like witch hands, skeleton hands. Smoke was rising from the ground. Sixteen years before, a man was murdered on this very same path, higher up Devil's Courthouse, and some said he still wandered this trail. I prayed that the haint of the trail wouldn't come out just then, that he was somewhere far away, wherever haints went when they weren't spooking people or searching for their killers. I prayed that the devil and the cannibal spirits and Spearfinger, the great witch of the woods, and Tsul 'Kalu the giant wouldn't find me, and that the Nunnehi, or little people, might help protect me and get me home, even though I knew they only came out at night. I prayed that Mama might somehow guide me to safety from heaven.

I turned around and ran forward, and suddenly I hit something. I hit it so hard that I fell down. Then two great hands lifted me and set me on my feet. A man stood in front of me—so tall that he blocked out the sun. His hair was long and black and his beard was wild. He wore a hat that was pulled down over his eyes. My first thought was that it was Tsul 'Kalu himself, but this was a man, not a giant.

"Slow down," he said. "What are you running from?" I couldn't make out his face because the sun was behind him. But I knew exactly who he was: the Wood Carver. I had run from one murderer right into the hands of another.

I stared up at him and didn't say a word. I looked down at his hands, still holding my arms. They were nicked up and scarred and he wore a bright gold wedding ring on his left one.

He dropped his hands and took a step back. I turned around and ran.

~

After supper Johnny Clay and I stood on the front porch with Hunter Firth. The door to the house was open and there was the sound of Daddy Hoyt starting a tune on the fiddle; of Linc strumming his guitar; of Granny beginning a song in her thin, raspy voice; of Sweet Fern and Ruby Poole washing the supper dishes; of Dan Presley banging on a pot lid; and of Danny laughing and playing with baby Corrina.

"The bootlegger's probably forgotten all about it by now," Johnny Clay said. There was a question in his voice. I knew what it was—we might not have gotten away with his moonshine, but that didn't mean the moonshiner would forget that we tried to steal from him. In his eyes, we would be as bad and as hated as branch walkers now. We would never know where or when the moonshiner might find us.

We could hear the stomp of Granny's shoes as she danced and Beach-ard's shouts as she whirled him around. He was staying away from home more and more lately, no matter what Sweet Fern and Danny told him to do. Beach was fifteen now and said they weren't his parents and he didn't need to mind them. He didn't mean anything unfriendly by it— Beach never did—he said that's just the way things were.

I wrapped my arms tight around my waist and shivered, even though the evening was warm. I thought about the moonshiner over in Devil's Kitchen and the bitter taste of his whiskey and about his son who was a bad and dangerous criminal. I thought about the Wood Carver—tall enough to block out the sun—walking the haunted trail. I wondered if he was out there now in the dark.

Johnny Clay caught a lightning bug in his fist and then slowly opened it so we could see the light. "It's late in the season for him," he said. "He should be dead by now." He let it go and we watched it wobble into the air and then light up, go dark, light up, as it headed away from us.

I never wanted to go back to the jail ever again or get chased through the woods or shot at, and I knew Johnny Clay felt the same way. Still, someone had to say it out loud, so I told him I was bored rigid leading a life of crime and, what's more, that I was swearing off liquor. He said he was too. I think he was glad I said it first.

SEVEN

School started on a cool day in early September. I was in the sixth grade now. I had two more years at the Alluvial School, and then I would be done forever. Johnny Clay was in his last year, but he threatened to quit every day, just like Beachard had when he was almost fourteen.

We went to school according to the planting cycles. We were there through December, then out again until March while we picked peas, dug potatoes, and rounded up the free-roaming cattle from the woods. Then we were back at school again until summer when we waited for the crops to grow.

The school itself was a one-room building, painted white, that sat between Deal's and the Baptist church. The classroom was one large room with a blackboard along one wall and desks for thirty-six students, ages six to fourteen, in eight grades. Our teacher was Mrs. Avery Dennis, and her husband was Charles Hampton Dennis, nicknamed Dr. Hamp because he was a doctor, but a doctor of books not medicine. They lived on a hill above Deal's General Store, in a house that Dr. Hamp had built himself, filled with bookshelves floor to ceiling and old books from the library in Philadelphia, where Dr. Hamp and Mrs. Dennis were from. Everyone on the mountain was allowed to come in and borrow what we wanted and take the books home or read them right there in the fat overstuffed chairs that could fit three of us if we sat close and snug.

On the first day of school, Johnny Clay found a seat in the back with Daryl and Lester Gordon and Hink Lowe and the other boys who were older and liked to stretch their legs out into the aisle and stare out the windows, and I sat up front behind Rachel Gordon and Alice Nix and the others in the sixth-grade class. Everyone buzzed and chattered and Mrs. Dennis let us talk on and asked us how our summers were.

Then she walked up and down the aisle and passed out lined pieces of paper, laying one on every desk. "I want you to write down your life dreams," she said. Some of the kids just sat there staring at the paper, like Davey Messengill, who never thought much beyond lunch or recess; and Janette Lowe, who couldn't read or write even though she was a year older than me; and her brother Hink, who couldn't seem to pass the seventh grade and who everyone knew would be a down-and-out just like his daddy. The Lowes had been mountain trash for generations and, according to Sweet Fern, they weren't about to change when it suited them so well.

At the back of the room, Johnny Clay was bent over his paper, writing. When he was old enough, I knew he planned to hitch a ride on the rails and travel around the country, picking fruit and mining gold. He was going to be a cowboy out west, and when he got to California, he was planning to look up Tom Mix and William S. Hart and get a job riding horses in films. Johnny Clay said Mr. Hart would have to hire him because we had the same last name and were probably family. When I asked to go with him, he said I was too young but that maybe he'd send for me one day.

Rachel Gordon and Alice Nix sat side by side, as always, matching blue ribbons in their hair. I guessed they would write something about being dutiful wives and mothers. And I guessed that aside from my brother, I would be the only one who didn't write "to be married and have children," or "to help my daddy with the farm," or "to buy that new bait line I saw down at Deal's." Personally, I thought these were stupid dreams, but Daddy Hoyt was always saying that what was ugly to one was beautiful to another, and it was a good thing or else we'd all want to live in the same place and do the same kind of work.

I picked up my pencil and wrote, "I would like to one day be a singer at the Grand Ole Opry." Afterward, I crossed it out and wrote, "I *plan* to one day be a singer at the Grand Ole Opry."

I sat and reread the line over and over again. It was one thing to dream it; it was another thing to write it down where someone else could read it. By now everyone knew I had been to the Alluvial Jail and that I was a bad and wicked person, that I had backslid so far that it didn't matter if I was saved or not and that I was surely going straight to hell, just like my daddy had warned me. I wondered what Mrs. Dennis would think of what I'd written and if she would laugh at it. I thought of Mama and how she never laughed, no matter what I said. I thought of writing something else instead, but I didn't know what it would be. I folded up the paper and shoved it into the pocket of my dress.

Everyone else passed their papers forward and then Mrs. Dennis told us what a good class we were and how much she was looking forward to the months ahead.

One week later, as school let out for the day, everyone ran for the door and freedom. I collected my pencil and my lunch bucket and hurried to catch up with Johnny Clay, who was already outside with the Gordon boys.

Mrs. Dennis called to me. "Velva Jean? Do you mind staying after?"

I watched the others leave, running out into the sunshine, screaming and wrestling, those that could afford it heading over to Deal's for candy or an ice cream. I searched for my brother and saw him go off with the Gordons without even looking to see where I was.

Mrs. Dennis asked me to sit down at my desk, and then she sat down next to me. "Velva Jean," she said, "why didn't you hand in your paper?"

"I wasn't sure what to write," I said.

She tilted her head to one side. In a few moments, she nodded. "I see." I was now used to her voice, which had a slight northeastern twang to it, but when she'd first arrived we all thought she sounded very strange. Her dresses were always neat and nicely starched and she had a smart-looking nose, long and straight with a bump in the middle.

I glanced at the open doorway and beyond to the sunshine and the crowd of my classmates gathered at Deal's. I saw Johnny Clay come back out from the store, holding an orange Nehi and wondered where on earth he'd got the money to pay for it or if Mr. Deal had given it to him for free.

"I'll let you go in just a minute," Mrs. Dennis said. She stood up and walked to her desk and then came back. She set a blank piece of paper down in front of me and tapped it with her fingers. Her nails were painted a soft pink. "I'd like you to write something down for your life dreams."

I stared at the paper. "What if I don't know what I want to do?"

"I'm sure there must be something you've thought about." Her voice was bright and she was smiling, but she was looking at me the way Granny did when she knew I was lying.

"What if I write something down and then I change my mind later and decide on a different dream?"

"If you change your mind later, there's no harm done. It's never too late to change your mind."

She left me alone then and returned to her desk. She sat down behind it and picked up a book and began to read. I pulled out my pencil and held it over the paper, rolling it round and round between my thumb and fingers. I thought about writing something simple and acceptable like "to one day get married and have ten babies," or "to be a missionary and help save the heathens." But I didn't want to write those things when they weren't true.

Although I still wasn't sure what my mama had meant about living "out there," I was beginning to think it had something to do with not making my life's dream buying the new bait line down at Deal's. Ever since Mama died, I'd felt the need to do something outside myself, so that people would know I had been in the world and so that they wouldn't forget me. Mama had made an impression. Everyone still talked about how good and how special she was. I wanted people to remember me like that. But my daddy had gone away without anyone paying attention. We never mentioned his name and we never discussed him. I figured he was as good as dead, and now he was forgotten. I didn't want that to happen to me.

"I plan to be a singer at the Grand Ole Opry," I wrote. "And play Hawaiian steel guitar as good as Maybelle Carter. And wear a costume of satin and rhinestones and high-heeled boots. I plan to go to Nashville just as soon as I save up enough money."

I sat back and reread it and considered folding it up and slipping it into the pocket of my dress, just as I had done with the first one. I read it again, and then I stood up and walked to the front of the room and handed it to Mrs. Dennis. I didn't even look at her, just turned around fast and walked out of school as quick as I could. By the time I got out, Johnny Clay and the others had already gone.

~

I avoided being alone with Mrs. Dennis in the following weeks, running out of school just as soon as she dismissed us, not even waiting for Johnny Clay. One Saturday in October, I got up early and did my chores, and then I crawled under the porch and read the books I'd brought home from Dr. Hamp's: *The Little Prince*, which was written by a Frenchman, and *Roughing It* by Mark Twain. When I got tired of reading, I watched Beachard. He was carving "Where Is God?" on a rock the shape of a pumpkin that he had dragged out of the woods.

"What are you going to do with that one?" I called to him.

He didn't even look up. "Carry it to the top of Old Widow's Peak and leave it there where everyone can see it from three states." He had just come back from the peak not two days ago to report that he'd met a man up on the mountain named Getty Browning who had walked from Virginia across the mountaintops. Mr. Browning told Beach he'd had some help when he first walked that route from a man from our mountains, a man named Lincoln Hart. Beach didn't tell Mr. Browning that Lincoln Hart was his daddy. He just shook the man's hand and left.

"God's in heaven," I said.

"How do you know?"

"Because it says so in the Bible. He lives there with Jesus."

Beachard didn't say anything to this. He just went on carving.

"They live up there with Mama," I said, although I secretly wondered if this was true.

Beach's chisel went *tap tap tap*, *tap tap tap*. His hair caught the sun and looked more red than brown. "Are you sure?"

I hesitated. I wasn't sure about anything that had to do with God or Jesus anymore. But where else could they be? I said this aloud now.

Beachard stood up straight, tapping the chisel against his leg. He stared up at the sky and then off toward the woods. He rubbed his eyes with his free hand and then he bent back down over the stone. "They could be anywhere, I guess. If they're anywhere at all."

"Well where do you think God is?" I asked. I felt a slight creeping in my heart. It was one thing to know where God was or Jesus, and to know they just weren't listening to your prayers. It was another to think they might not be anywhere.

"I don't know," he said. "That's what I'd like someone to tell me."

I watched him for a while until I couldn't think about it anymore, and then I lay on my back under the porch and thought about my life dreams. Suddenly, I wasn't sure about these either. What if, when all was said and done, I didn't have what it took to sing at the Opry? What if, when it came down to it, I wasn't that special and had an ordinary voice and was normal like everyone else?

What would happen to me if I got to Nashville and discovered that I wasn't very good? What if I returned home "ruined" like Lucinda Sink? Would I have to live at the Alluvial Hotel and rouge my bosoms? What if I never grew any bosoms big enough to rouge? I felt my chest where my bosoms should be, but where there were only two little bumps, barely bigger than quarters. What would I do if I couldn't sing? What would my life's dream be then?

EIGHT

By November the air was turning cool and dry, and the floor of the mountain was covered with leaves and then snow. The sun went down a little earlier each night, leaving us in darkness. My bedroom turned cold from the new chill in the air, which came in through the cracks in the walls, and every night I heated up one of Beachard's cast-off stones in the fire, putting it at the foot of the bed to keep me warm.

When I went to sleep, the Wood Carver was all I dreamed about. It was the same dream over and over. In it he stood so tall that he blocked out the sun, turning the sky as dark as night. His hair was wild and almost touched the ground, and he would pick me up and hold me over his head so that I was as high as the trees and the clouds and the stars, and then he would spin me around and around. I never saw his face.

I wanted to get a look at his face. I wanted to watch him and study him just like I'd been studying my own face in the mirror ever since Mama died. Was I marked? Could people look at me and tell that my mama had died and my daddy had just as good as killed her? I figured the Wood Carver, of all people, would understand what it was to lose something precious, like the people you loved most in the world.

I hadn't said a word to Johnny Clay about meeting him. It was the first thing I ever wanted to keep completely to myself. So when I decided that I was going up the mountain to spy on the Wood Carver—in the bright light of day—I didn't tell Johnny Clay that either.

~

"Velva Jean?" Mrs. Dennis said one afternoon as Johnny Clay and me were running out the door after school. "Can I see you a moment?"

I walked back into the school and stood by the door, hoping Mrs. Dennis would figure out that I was in a hurry.

"How would you like to earn some money?" she said.

I wondered if Mrs. Dennis could read minds like the man Johnny Clay and I had heard on the radio at Deal's. The man could predict the weather and tell you what number you were thinking and how many fingers you were holding up without even looking at you. And then I remembered that in my life-dreams paper I had said I was saving up money for Nashville.

"I can pay you twenty-five cents a week to help me in the mornings before lessons—cleaning erasers, washing slates, collecting chalk. Just help me tidy up a bit and keep things in order. Are you interested?"

"Yes, ma'am," I said. I would put every penny I earned into my Nashville fund.

I began arriving at school thirty minutes early. I stacked books and wiped down the blackboard and sharpened pencils. Sometimes I stayed late and walked home with Mrs. Dennis. I even helped Dr. Hamp sort and shelve books and keep track of the ones that were loaned out and the ones that came back in. He taught me to repair them and to rebind them. And I always chose a new book to take home with me, something Sweet Fern would approve of because she wanted to know the name of any book I brought into the house. I loved *Little Women* and *Alice's Adventures in Wonderland* and *Through the Looking Glass* and *The Tenant of Wildfell Hall*, which was so beautiful and sad that I wanted to throw it at the wall.

At the end of each week, Mrs. Dennis gave me a brand-new quarter. On the walk home, I turned it round and round so it caught the light. When I got home, I went straight to my bedroom and hid it away in my hatbox. After four weeks, I had four shiny quarters—one entire dollar saved for Nashville. I figured I was on my way.

~

It was one week after I got the idea to spy on the Wood Carver before I was able to get away from Johnny Clay. He was going down to Alluvial with the Gordon boys on a Saturday. When he asked me to come along, I told him I was going to stay behind and work on a song I'd started, since Sweet Fern was visiting the Deals and wouldn't be around to hear me and to tell me to save my voice for the Lord.

The place where the Wood Carver lived was at the very top of Devil's Courthouse, about an hour's walk from Sleepy Gap, and there was no way to get there but to go through the forest and the gullies and the streams, and to climb up hills, some of them so steep that I had to pull myself up by one tree and then another.

To get to the top of Devil's Courthouse, you had to follow a path that wasn't really a path. For a while, I went along an old Cherokee trail, but when that disappeared I broke through the rhododendron and the laurel, which grew thick and wild even in winter. I crossed the river by stones and then by an old footbridge that someone had built and abandoned long ago. I walked over strawberries and cranberry shrubs and rattleweed and tangles of wandering Jew. The spruce pines grew thicker the higher I climbed. The air became cooler and sweeter.

I passed the Toomeys' house, set back in the trees, and, farther up, old Buck Frey's place. As I reached the very top of the mountain, I walked through long tunnels of rhododendron that hung down over the path. The devil's cave, the one he shared with Tsul 'Kalu, loomed nearby, dark and craggy. I tried not to look at it, tried not to think of what or who lay inside. I walked away from it, not sure where I was going exactly. I passed a little log cabin with sheep in the yard. I waited, watching, but when I saw Aunt Junie come from the house, bees swarming around her, I kept walking.

I wasn't even sure where the Wood Carver lived. I knew he lived at the top of the mountain, in a cave or in treetops or in his wood cabin. I hadn't thought it through before coming. I just wanted to see him.

The trees got thicker—dark balsam firs, ash trees—until I came to a clearing. Close up, close in, from all sides, you could see Witch Mountain, Bone Mountain, Blood Mountain, and Fair Mountain. Further on there was Silvermine Bald, Richland Balsam, Waterrock Knob, Wrongful Mountain, Cold Mountain, and, in the far distance, Mount Pisgah, the Blue Ridge Mountains, Mount Mitchell, and the Black Mountains. I knew the names of each peak, thanks to my daddy. Since I was a little girl, he had been making me learn them one by one. It looked like you could step down onto one of those other mountaintops and walk your way across them until you ended up in Tennessee or Georgia or South Carolina or beyond.

When I got to the highest point, the ground flattened out. The mist settled down here, the smoke rolling in and out through the trees. I tiptoed quiet as a mouse across the floor of the mountain and stopped just at the edge of a thicket of laurel bushes that grew in a circle. In the middle of them, within a ring of fir trees, was a small wood cabin, and on the front stoop sat a man with long black hair.

I hid myself behind a tree and held my breath so he wouldn't hear me. I huddled there, every now and then taking a gulp of air, and just watched him. What if I saw him using his killing knife and there was blood on it? What if he caught me and used it on me?

There were those who believed he was the son of Tsul 'Kalu the giant or that he had lived with the bears and taken on their nature, becoming one of them. Others said he had come to Devil's Courthouse from the city, that he used to be a rich man, and that he'd been educated right through college. Some said he had gone away to war where he had been a hero or, others said, where he had killed his own men, and when he returned home he had lost everything. His wife left him and took their children, and he ran away to the woods. But the story most everyone believed was that he'd killed his entire family, and maybe even some other people, and had come to the mountain to hide.

Whenever anything on the mountain went missing, people blamed it on the Wood Carver. Whenever the weather turned strange or the crops failed, they said it was because of him and the curse he had brought with him. There were rumors that he hid in the caves of the mountain, that he stole from helpless women and children or orphans, like my brothers and sister and me, and that he walked on all fours when the moon was full.

Right now he sat on the stoop of the small wood house, whittling a long branch. Every so often, he'd lay down his knife and prop the branch between his knees while he smoothed the wood with his hands. I tried to get a look at his knife, to see if there was blood on it, and I tried to see his hands, but I wasn't close enough. So instead I stared good and hard at his face.

He had a full, overgrown beard and wild black hair. He wore an old battered hat and a flannel shirt with the sleeves rolled up and a pair of dark green work pants. His legs were long and stretched out in front of him, and he was kind of whistling to himself as he worked. He didn't look at all like you'd expect a murderer to look. He didn't look marked in the least. He actually had a nice kind of face—almost handsome. I stood and watched him for a long time and then, quiet as I could, I headed back down toward home.

~

Whenever I could, I made the long hike up Devil's Courthouse to spy on the Wood Carver. The laurel bushes that surrounded his cabin were sturdy enough and thick enough, all twined and braided around each other, and I was light enough that I could climb on top of the branches and walk from one to another, never touching the ground. There, I would sit or stand and watch him. He was always on his stoop when I arrived, sitting with his legs stretched out in front of him, carving something. I would watch for an hour or so, and then I would turn around and go home.

One day I was sitting behind a large stickery shrub, staring at him through the leaves, when he said, very low: "I wish I had someone to talk to." He never looked up, just kept working, using his killing knife. "It surely would be nice to have some company right now," he said a little louder.

I sat there telling myself to run back down the mountain before he could get me. I told myself to just back right up and turn around and go home as fast as I could. I watched to see if he was going to get up and come after me, but he just kept on with his carving.

Finally, I got up and brushed myself off, and then I walked out from behind the shrub and went over to him. I stood there, feeling terrified and excited and thinking that I had no idea what to say to a murderer because I'd never actually met one face-to-face before.

"You're Hoyt's girl, aren't you?"

"Granddaughter." My voice sounded thin and far away, the way it did sometimes when I was nervous, so soft that people had to lean in close or ask me to speak up. I wondered if he could hear me over my own heartbeat. I wondered if he recognized me from the haunted trail.

"Zona or Turk or Corrine?"

I cleared my throat and spoke louder. "Corrine." It was the first time I'd ever said my mama's first name out loud to a stranger. I wished I had belt loops to hitch my fingers through, but instead I tried to jut my chin out like Johnny Clay so the Wood Carver would know I wasn't to be messed with.

He just nodded and kept on working. I squatted down a few feet away, ready to run if I had to.

"It's nice of you to finally come say hello," he said. "After all the times you've been to see me."

I didn't say anything to this. How did he know I'd been spying on him? Johnny Clay and me were expert spies. We used to hide all the time from Sweet Fern and she never knew where to find us.

"I don't get much company up here."

"Do you want company?" I looked down at the ground and pretended to study my toes.

"Sometimes."

I kept my head down but raised my eyes just enough to watch the knife as it cut into the wood. The blade was sharp and fast, but I didn't see any bloodstains. I looked at his hands, but they seemed clean. Maybe the blood was on his palms.

"What kind of wood is that?" I asked, and wrapped my arms tight around my knees.

"Serviceberry. The tree of many names. Sometimes called Juneberry, sarvis, shadblow. It's the first to bloom in spring."

I nodded like this wasn't news to me, like this was something I had known all along. "What are you making?"

"I don't know." He held it out in front of him. "Usually I know before I start." He waved his hand behind him toward the open door of his house. "But today I'm just seeing what comes out of the wood." I looked into the house and saw there were shelves along the walls. The shelves were lined with things carved out of wood, but instead of masks and deadly slingshots, I saw birdhouses and toys and dancing men on strings.

"You made all those things in there?" I said.

He didn't even look up. "Every one."

I squinted at him, the sun in my eyes. I wondered if he knew about Mama dying and about Daddy coming home after she was already cold and buried. I wondered if he knew my daddy was a murderer, too, that he had killed Mama by going off and not being there to help her and take care of her. I wondered if he knew my daddy didn't love me enough to stay around and if the Wood Carver would still want to talk to me once he figured it out. I wondered if my marks were showing.

"It's all in there, inside," he said, holding up the piece of wood. I watched his hands, large and blackened, as the knife cut and peeled and sliced. "Carving comes from looking at the wood and seeing what it can become. You see what you can make out of it. You can feel it before it's even begun."

"How'd you learn to do it?" I asked. My legs were beginning to ache, but I didn't want to sit down.

"I didn't," he said. "I've never had a lesson."

"A traveling minister taught my granddaddy how to play fiddle."

"Is that true?"

I nodded. "He was fourteen. Later, after the Cherokee taught him to become a healer, he started making his own fiddles. He carved them out of curing woods because he thought they'd be able to heal people with their music. He makes one a year and gives it away to someone he knows. People try to give him money for them, but he says, 'You can't put a price on a man's soul.'"

"Your granddaddy's a wise man." He twirled the piece of wood round as he carved, little curled up shavings falling down on the ground by his feet.

"So if you never had a lesson, how'd you learn?" I said. I tried shifting my weight from one foot to the other to stop the ache.

"I just tried it one day and I discovered that I knew how to do it, like it was in me all the time."

"Mama always said that singing was like praying twice," I said without meaning to. I was thinking about how singing was like that for me, how ever since I could remember I'd been singing and making up songs in my head and planning my outfit for the Grand Ole Opry— a gold skirt and jacket with red trim and rhinestones, and a matching cowboy hat. I knew where Nashville was on Beachard's map of the world, and that it was almost three hundred miles from Sleepy Gap. I had already saved up a dollar and seventy-five cents to help get me there one day, money I'd earned by working for Mrs. Dennis and her husband.

The Wood Carver had stopped carving. He was rubbing at the piece of wood. I pointed to a tree that stood directly in front of the porch. Its trunk was dark and straight; its arms spread wide toward the sky. It was the only one like itself in the middle of all those firs and ashes. "What kind of tree is that?"

"It's a Jesus tree," he said and looked up for the first time. "More commonly known as a dogwood."

"It don't look like a dogwood." There were dogwoods up and down the mountain, but I'd never seen one like this. Its trunk was nearly black and it grew up tall and full like it couldn't wait to get to heaven. When the breeze blew, the leaves trembled so that it looked like the tree was dancing.

"I planted it myself to carve from," the Wood Carver said, "but its brace roots are too strong. If a tree has enough support, I don't cut it because it needs to become a tree, which is what it was meant to do. But a tree with one root—even one large root—will never be supported, so I make something else out of it, like a cane or a toy." He paused, his knife still working. "You've got good brace roots. Your mama, your brothers, your sister, your grandparents. Even your daddy."

Suddenly, I was sorry I'd come. He was nice and easy to talk to, but he was a murderer after all. I should have just sat still when he called to me or slipped back down the hill without saying anything.

I stood up. "My mama's gone," I said and kicked at the dirt with my bare foot. And my daddy killed her, I added in my head. I had never said it out loud, not even to Johnny Clay.

"She's not gone in here." He tapped himself on the head with the piece of wood. "Or here." He pointed at his heart.

I wondered if this was true. Mama felt gone. Completely gone. Mama felt nowhere to be found. I thought about Beachard asking where God was and wondering if he was anywhere and if Mama was anywhere, too. Suddenly, the loneliness came over me, so sharp and fast that I almost lost my balance.

"Yep," the Wood Carver said. "Good solid brace roots." He continued to carve and I stood watching him until I knew Sweet Fern would be worrying and it was time to go home.

Before I left, I could see that the piece of wood he was working had become a little girl with long, curled hair and hands folded as if she was praying. It's beautiful, I thought, but I didn't say it.

He closed the girl's eyes and opened her mouth so that it looked like she was singing. He blew off the loose shavings and smoothed it with his fingers, and then handed the figure to me.

"I can't take it," I said, thinking Sweet Fern would tan my hide for taking something from a runaway murderer. But I wanted it very much, more than anything.

He touched his knife to the brim of his hat in a kind of salute. It was then that I saw his eyes were a dark midnight blue, the color of a starless sky. "Yes you can," he said. "She was waiting, you see. She was in there all the time."

~

When I got home, Johnny Clay was leaning against the front porch railing, his hands jammed into the pockets of his trousers. When he saw me, he stood up straight and waved me on. I thought I would tell him about the Wood Carver and how I'd talked to him and watched him use his killing knife. I imagined Johnny Clay would be proud and also jealous that I'd spent the day with a murderer. I might even take him up there with me one day so that he could visit the murderer, too. I ran up the steps, my right hand wrapped around the wooden girl that I was carrying in my pocket.

"Where the hell have you been?" Johnny Clay looked mad as a hornet. He talked so low I could barely hear him. "I been looking everywhere for you."

"Why?" I said.

"Keep your voice down," he said.

"No I will not. Why don't you speak up? A person can barely hear you."

"Hush, Velva Jean!" He looked toward the house and then back at me.

"What're you so mad about?"

"You'll see."

"What's that supposed to mean?"

I was getting good and angry now. I couldn't believe he was being so hateful. Just for that, I decided I wouldn't tell him about the Wood Carver.

"Velva Jean?" Sweet Fern opened the front door and stepped out, shutting it behind her. Her face was pink and rigid, which was how it looked when she was upset. I waited for her to yell at me, too. "Velva Jean," she said again. Her hands worked at her hair, as if searching for loose pieces. Her hair was neatly wound into a braid and pinned off her neck, just as it always was. I thought about how she was never messy and how she always smelled just like a daisy, even when it was hot as Jupiter out, and how her hair never came down like other people's. "Daddy's here."

"What?" And then I looked down and saw the sack lying by the door. It was large and brown and just like the one my daddy always carried when he was traveling. I shot Johnny Clay a look to kill. "You couldn't tell me?" And then I shoved past Sweet Fern and opened the door. There was Danny and Aunt Zona and Granny and Daddy Hoyt, all looking grim and serious, and there by the fireplace was my daddy. It had been one year since he'd left us with Sweet Fern.

His face brightened when he saw me. He walked over to me and I thought he seemed shorter than I remembered—and older. "What do you think? I'm back. I got myself a job on the Scenic. Did you hear? They're building that road and your daddy's going to help them. From Virginia through North Carolina, even though Tennessee wanted it bad, they did. But Carolina got it. The government just announced it, made it official. 'Will need labor,' they said. That's me. I'm going to work on it, do whatever I can do. I came back to tell you. They're moving mountains up there, Velva Jean. You can't believe what they're going to do."

Daddy always did talk fast. He talked like he buck danced—hard and quick and excited and joysome. It had been a long time since we'd had that kind of energy around here. He didn't say anything then, just held out a hand as if he was going to pat my head, and then he pulled it back. "Is that my little girl?" he said, and he tried to smile, but it seemed strange on him, like the rest of his face didn't want to. "Is that my baby?"

I could feel Johnny Clay and Sweet Fern behind me, feel the look Johnny Clay was giving Daddy, the dislike that he didn't even bother to hide. I thought I should be nice to Daddy because he was my father and deep down he was still sad, but he'd left us and he'd killed Mama, and I realized that after all this time I had nothing to say.

"Is that my baby girl?" I could tell he wanted me to say something, to reach out, to somehow make it better.

Where have you been? I wanted to say. Why did you leave us with Sweet Fern? What did you write in that note? What did you say to Mama to make her so sick like that? Why did you leave her and go away?

"No," I said instead. "It's not." And then I went into my bedroom and shut the door and moved a chair in front of it so that he couldn't get in. I waited, but he didn't try. My heart was racing and my face was hot. I was not his baby girl. I wasn't a baby at all. I was a grown-up person who had been to jail and drunk hard corn liquor and visited with murderers.

How dare he come back? I thought. How dare he come back here?

I sat up on the bed by the headboard, with my knees squeezed up tight against my chest, and listened to the rise and fall of voices. There was Johnny Clay yelling and slamming out of the house, Sweet Fern sounding cold and upset, and Daddy Hoyt, like always, trying to calm and soothe. And there was another voice, the voice of a stranger. The voice of my daddy.

~

I lay in bed that night, turning the wooden girl round and round in my hands. When my eyes got used to the dark, I held the little figure up in front of my face and studied every angle. I thought about what the Wood Carver had said about brace roots and how I had good ones.

"Your mama, your brothers, your sister, your grandparents. Even your daddy," he had said.

I thought about what kind of world it was where you could ask God to save your Mama, but he wouldn't listen and would just let her die. And what kind of world it was where a daddy was so heartless that he could leave his own children, but a murderer was nice and kind. I thought about Johnny Clay and how sometimes he went away from me, too, just like Mama, just like Daddy. I thought about brace roots and weak roots and what made some trees grow one way and some another. I prayed that this new road might take Daddy away forever so that he didn't have the chance to come back and hurt us anymore.

I tucked the wooden girl under my pillow and kept one hand on it as I rolled onto my side. I felt the anger begin to wash away and my body start to go limp and my brain grow fuzzy. Just as I drifted off into sleep, I heard the Wood Carver's words again: "You're Hoyt's girl, aren't you?" "Zona or Turk or Corrine?" "Your mama, your brothers, your sister, your grandparents. Even your daddy."

Even your daddy.

How did he know my mama's name? How did he know Daddy Hoyt and Aunt Zona and Uncle Turk? Not from anything I'd ever told him, because I had never, not once, talked to him about my family.

~

Daddy left the next morning before I was awake. I looked outside and his traveling sack was gone. There was a fresh bouquet of witch hazel on Mama's grave, but otherwise there was nothing to show that he'd even been here at all.

I opened the family record book and wrote, "November 30, 1934: Daddy left." The book was just as full of bad things as good ones.

~ 1935 ~

Sing on, sweet voice, in storm and calm,
In grief and gladness sing . . .

—"Sing On, Sweet Voice"

NINE

In the middle of April the damp lifted, and Danny Deal and his daddy announced that they were taking the train all the way to Asheville to buy a truck. They were buying it practically new from a man Mr. Deal had known for ten years, a man named Lenny Philpot, who owned two drugstores and a movie theater. They were going to stay the night at Mr. Philpot's house and then start back in the truck early the next morning. Johnny Clay and me thought we should be allowed to go, too, because he was fourteen and I was twelve, but Danny said we had to stay at home.

Sweet Fern was so on edge, all you had to do was walk up behind her and say boo and she jumped about ten feet. She did not believe in trucks or cars or driving, especially since she had heard about a woman in Swain County who was run over by a car that was "out of control." The very fact that a car could run out of control was enough for Sweet Fern. She would have none of it, especially with young children to think of. She told Danny he had another think coming if he thought he was going to bring that truck up there to her house.

It was the first time I ever saw Danny stand up to her. He said, "With all due respect, I am getting this truck, Sweet Fern," and then he just walked out and left the front door wide open and walked right down the hill to Deal's. Johnny Clay and I ran after him, fast as we could. We didn't want to miss a minute. Danny banged on into Deal's and hollered to his daddy that he was ready to go, and then he banged on out and stood there, hands on hips, squinting off into the distance.

"The train's not even here yet," I said to him, and Johnny Clay punched me.

Danny looked down at me like he didn't know who I was. "It'll be here soon," he said finally.

"She's a piece of work," Johnny Clay said to him, and I pinched him hard because I thought he was talking about me.

Danny looked at him and one corner of his mouth crooked up like he was trying to keep it back but couldn't help it.

Mr. Deal appeared, and I looked instantly at his hands for candy or soda pop, but all he had was a rough brown satchel, which he pulled up over his shoulder. In the distance, we could hear the train coming.

Coyle Deal stood in the doorway, the oldest and not as good-looking as Jessup, the baby, who had one green eye and one blue eye. Coyle smiled. Maybe we could get some candy out of him. I could hear my mama's voice: "All those Deals are nice boys."

~

The next morning, Johnny Clay and I got to Deal's early so as to have good seats. We woke up at dawn and left the house before Sweet Fern could catch us. First we sat on the edge of the porch outside the store, and then on the Coca-Cola cooler that was pressed up against the window, then on the bottom step, and then finally on the middle of the top step.

Little by little, everyone started coming. Almost everyone on the mountain came out to wait for Danny Deal and his daddy to get back with that truck. Everyone but Sweet Fern.

I was tired of sitting, but I didn't want to move for fear I'd lose my seat. I had the feeling that something very big was about to happen, and everyone else seemed to feel it, too. It was a warm April day, clear and blue. Birds. Butterflies—yellow on blue sky. Except for where my hair was heavy and hot on my neck, except for where my right butt cheek had gone to sleep, except for where my leg was itching from an early mosquito bite, I felt I could sit here forever.

~

The truck was the brightest yellow you ever saw. It was the color of goldenrod or dandelion or black-eyed Susan or the burnt gold of birch leaves in fall. Granny said it looked like Aunt Bird's secret mustard recipe, but Martha True said it made her think of summer squash.

"That's the damnedest color I ever saw," Dell Haywood said.

"Why is it painted like that?" Mr. Lowe said.

"Because Len Philpot is a man prone to the blues," said Mr. Deal. Danny kind of hung around the truck, like he didn't want to leave it. He leaned on the front end like he was saying, Hey, this is my truck. "When he bought the truck, it was a dark navy, the color of the reverend's shirt." Mr. Deal waved at Reverend Broomfield. "He tried to live with it, but it just depressed him. He's not a cheery man to begin with, and he said he needed something to snap him out of his funk, to keep him happy." Everyone was staring at the truck, afraid to touch it, afraid to run their hands over it. Danny was grinning fit to beat the band. I'd never seen him look so full of himself. Sweet, nice Danny Deal. Shy and quiet. He was as puffed up as a balloon.

"That's the damnedest color I ever saw," Dell Haywood said again.

"He wanted a truck you could see coming or going," Mr. Deal said.

"Well," Granny said. "He got it."

Behind me, Johnny Clay snorted. I turned to look at him. He was snickering and shaking his head like an agitated horse. He looked like he was about to get carried away with himself.

"What's wrong with you?" I said.

He pointed at the truck. "Sweet Fern is going to have a fit."

~

Along about four o'clock, Danny climbed into the truck and said it was time to be getting home. Johnny Clay and I stood there and stared at him until he waved us over. "You want to take a ride first?" he said.

I climbed in and sat in the middle, tight between Danny and Johnny Clay. Inside, the truck was navy—the seats and the dash. Everything looked so shiny, I was afraid to touch anything. There were some dials on the dashboard and two long sticks coming up from the floor.

"That's the shifter," Johnny Clay said. "And that's the hand brake." He was resting one arm on the door. He had a smug look on his face because he'd been driving Linc's farm truck for years.

"Where you want to go?" Danny said.

"Anywhere," I said. "Let's go to Waynesville." Or Nashville, I thought.

"Before supper?" Johnny Clay rolled his eyes.

"Hamlet's Mill then." I wanted to go someplace far. Now that I was in the truck, I didn't ever want to leave. "Let me sit by the window, Johnny Clay."

"No."

"Why not?"

"My legs are too long to sit in the middle. I got to stretch them out." He stretched his legs out in front of him as much as he could.

Danny started the truck and I nearly jumped out of my skin. For one moment, I thought about that car that ran out of control, killing that woman in Swain County. Then we started to drive. I gripped on to the seat with both hands. "Whoa," I said. Johnny Clay leaned around and waved to everyone still standing outside Deal's. I stared at the road ahead—just an overgrown cattle road with weeds and grass growing over it—concentrating on staying alive. I thought if I concentrated hard enough, that yellow truck wouldn't go out of control.

Danny picked up speed. Johnny Clay rolled the window down halfway and his hair started whipping around. Danny went faster and faster down the hill till the speedometer said thirty. We flew past Lucinda Sink's, down around the curve toward Hamlet's Mill. I shut my eyes and started to pray to Jesus right then and there to get me off the mountain safely. The truck rattled and bumped and at one point it flew up in the air a little and kept right on going.

"Open your eyes, Velva Jean," Johnny Clay said. "For criminy's sake." He swore under his breath.

"Shut up," I said. But I opened my eyes and kept them open. We hit level ground then. Trees raced by, a green blur, and streaks of dark black-brown, the railroad tracks. I watched them till I got dizzy. We left our ring of mountains and came out into a valley, and suddenly there were our mountains behind us and we were surrounded by little houses and barns and cows dotted here and there. The road became dirt and I liked the feel of it under the wheels. There were other valleys, other hollers—like ours, only out here in this other world— sweeping up toward the mountains, our mountains, as we drove around them from this other side. The land out here was wider and more open and the mountains looked different, sheer and steep and wild and sharp. I felt a sudden rush of homesickness. I wanted to go back.

Then suddenly we were in Hamlet's Mill, which was a pretty little town of old brick buildings, just three blocks long. Danny slowed down and the needle went to fifteen, and we cruised through at a respectable pace. The main street—with its drugstore, diner, café, bank, grocery, two churches, motion picture theater, and department store—grew up around a neat town square, and in the center of that was a courthouse.

Everyone on the street stopped and stared at the truck. Their mouths fell open and their eyes popped wide, like they were looking at a naked lady or a man with three heads. Danny slowed down to ten so they could get a better look. I picked up one hand, leaving the other gripping the seat below me, and waved. I waved at everyone the way Ruby Poole said the queen of England did, moving only my hand back and forth, but keeping my arm perfectly still. I turned from side to side and waved to everyone and not a single person waved back.

"Well," I said.

Johnny Clay started laughing then and wouldn't stop. Soon Danny got started, and that got me started—the sight of my quiet brother-in-law behind the wheel of his bright yellow truck, just laughing till the tears rolled down his face. We all started waving. We just waved and laughed, waved and laughed, driving through town. And then we turned around and headed on up the mountain, back on up toward home.

When we got there, Sweet Fern said, "Daniel Deal, what on earth?" And then her mouth fell open so wide a bird could have flown in there and made a nest.

Johnny Clay laughed so hard he fell down. He rolled and rolled all over the ground until Sweet Fern noticed him.

She snapped her mouth shut and ordered us both inside. Then she held out an arm and pointed at the truck. I noticed that her finger shook a little. "Park it behind the barn," she said to Danny. "Out of sight of the house."

That night I couldn't sleep a wink. I had decided Danny Deal's truck was the most exciting good thing to ever happen to me, more exciting even than almost going to jail. I lay in bed and thought about a Greek woman from the fifth century that Mrs. Dennis had told me about. Her name was Hypatia and she was a philosopher and an astronomer who dressed in men's clothing and drove her own chariot through the streets of Alexandria. I thought about a story I'd read about a woman named Genevra Mudge who, in 1899, became the first woman driver in the entire United States of America, and another story about Bertha Benz, wife of Karl Benz, the father of the automobile, who was the world's first woman driver and the first person to drive an automobile over a long distance, more than sixty miles in Germany in 1888.

I was going to be just like all of them, I decided, only instead of men's clothing I would wear my costume with rhinestones, and instead of a chariot I would drive a car or, even better, a truck. That way I could leave whenever I wanted and go far away from Fair Mountain and, most of all, Sweet Fern. I could come and go just as I pleased, like Beachard, who disappeared now and then and wandered like our daddy. I could see the world and there wouldn't be anything Sweet Fern could do to stop me.

TEN

*E*very June folks came down from each of the five mountains for the three-day Alluvial Fair. They arrived in buggies, on horseback, in trucks, or on foot, carrying baskets of food, which the women spread on tables with white tablecloths, underneath a tent in the grassy area between Deal's and the Baptist church.

On the third day of the fair, the day of the singing, I put on the only pretty dress I owned. It was one of Ruby Poole's hand-me-downs, almost too small because, at twelve, I was already as tall as her. It was pink with a green sash at the waist and a green satin collar, and inside the collar there was a label that said "Bon Marche." While Sweet Fern was getting the children ready, Ruby Poole dusted my lips with lipstick and squirted my neck with Irresistible Perfume ("It stirs senses . . . thrills . . . sets hearts on fire!"), and then I sat in front of her mirror, looking at my reflection from different angles, and decided I didn't look half-bad, even if I did have freckles and curly hair.

With the help of Mrs. Dennis, I had saved up nearly five dollars for Nashville. I kept it tucked away in my hatbox, wrapped up in one of Mama's old handkerchiefs. I had decided to sing a solo at the fair, all by myself, without my family. I thought it would be good practice for when I got to the Opry, plus I wanted the prize money, which, if I won, would be an additional five dollars.

When we got down to Alluvial that morning, everyone was abuzz because some men from the Scenic had come. One of them was in front of the school talking to Shorty Rogers and Wiley Butler. He was kind of medium height and medium build and had thick brown hair and glasses. I thought he looked a little like Buddy Rogers. He was handsome like a movie star. A group of old men stood up on the porch at Deal's and picked "Bringing in the Sheaves" on the banjo, guitar, and washtub bass.

When we came walking up, Wiley Butler waved us over. He said, "That's the one you want to talk to—Beachard Hart."

We all stared at Beachard in surprise. Beachard was shy and didn't like to be singled out. He looked like he might want to run and hide. He said, "Excuse me?"

Wiley said, "This man's asking about you."

The man with the glasses nodded a greeting at Daddy Hoyt. Then he looked at Beach and said, "Beachard Hart?" That man frowned at Beachard like he was expecting someone older than sixteen.

We all looked at each other. Beachard said, "Yes."

"I'm Stanley Abbott. I'm working on the new scenic road. You had a conversation with Getty Browning a few months ago. He enjoyed meeting you. He was mightily impressed. He said he knows your father and that your father is a good worker who's been of help to him already on our project."

We were all staring at Beach, staring at Mr. Abbott.

Beach said, "Yes?" like this was the most usual thing in the world, like people said this to him all the time.

"We need men to cut survey lanes to locate the final path of the road so we can incorporate it into a map and Mr. Browning suggested we talk to you. This country is so isolated that it's hard for us to find our way. It's the largest unbroken wilderness area in the proposed path. We want to protect it, but we also need to put this road in. Mr. Browning is in the wild, flagging lines right now, but we need help. Do you think you'd be willing?"

"Where's my daddy now?"

Mr. Abbott's eyebrows drew down. I could tell he was trying to remember. "Hard to say. I believe he's helping scout and survey the areas north of Linville Falls."

Beach studied Mr. Abbott like he studied all people, really taking him in. It took Beach a while to decide on folks. Beach said, "I don't know."

Mr. Abbott looked uncomfortable. There was a fancy air to him, like he was from a city, like he wasn't sure how to talk to people who weren't from cities, like he thought you had to talk to people like us different. He said, "It's my responsibility to decide which trees will be sacrificed, which cliffs will be blasted, which lands will be purchased and used as overlooks. We could use your help as someone who knows the area—not just this immediate area, but beyond."

Beach said, "That's a lot of responsibility they've given you. That's an awful lot for just one person." He looked like Daddy Hoyt when he said it. I thought that he had just about made up his mind about Mr. Stanley Abbott. I almost felt sorry for the man, standing there looking so hot and nervous.

Stanley Abbott realized he was losing Beachard, and it was clear he didn't want to do this even if Beachard was only sixteen, so he started to talk. He told him all about his plans for the road and about how he planned to cause the least amount of harm to the mountains and the trees and the hollers (he called them "hollows") and the landscape as it was. He said, "I want to fit the road into the mountains as if nature had put it there." He could see Beachard cared about this, that this was important.

While Mr. Abbott talked, a quartet of men was singing "Jesus, the Light of the World." Afterward, the True sisters sang "Blest Be the Tie That Binds," accompanied by Pa Toomey on dulcimer and his son Claude on autoharp.

Beach didn't say yes, no, or maybe, and Mr. Abbott was still talking. Finally Beachard said, "I have to go play banjo now," and walked away. Beach was like that. When he was done with a conversation—that was the end of it.

Daddy Hoyt, Linc, Beach, Johnny Clay, Aunt Zona, and me played and sang "The Girl I Left in Sunny Tennessee" together while Granny danced. Granny could buck dance as good as any man in Alluvial Valley, as good as Daddy. She kicked her feet up, her back straight as a rod, hands at her side, holding her skirt, and moved with a rhythm and grace you wouldn't have expected from someone so old and wiry.

I had never thought twice about singing in public, but when our song was ending and folks were clapping and I suddenly pictured myself singing up on a stage by myself, I felt washed over by a cold wave of fear. The stage of my imagination was enormous, and I saw myself as just a tiny speck in the middle of it, barely visible in my satin and rhinestones and my cowboy hat with red trim. I pictured opening my mouth and nothing coming out but a squeak.

Earlier that day, Johnny Clay and me had our fortunes told by the Cherokee fortune teller. She told Johnny Clay that he was destined for greatness, which made him almost unbearable to be around. She also told him to be careful with his heart and his temper. She told me that I was charmed and that this could be both bad and good. She said I needed to be careful I didn't lose my way, because that would be easy for me to do, especially because I had a long way to travel. I asked her how I would do in the singing contest, but she said she couldn't answer things like that. I told Johnny Clay as we were leaving, "Some fortune teller."

"Look at me," Daddy Hoyt said now. His eyes were blue with gold around the center, like Mama's. "Just sing right to me. Or to your mama."

And then I was alone on the porch at Deal's, where I'd stood one hundred times or more. I looked out over the crowd at all the faces. Some I recognized; some I didn't. I hadn't expected to see my daddy, but I looked for him just the same. It was hard not to, even though I knew it was my own fault for helping to send him away.

The song I chose was a murder song, "Pretty Polly," because that was how I felt inside. It was a song Mama had taught me not long before she died, about a girl who was stabbed in the heart by the man she loved and buried in a grave he had dug for her.

As soon as the words were out of my mouth, I felt like the bravest person in the world. Even though I was singing about murder, I felt lifted. Music did that to me, just like God was supposed to, because music seemed both magic and holy. Just like the Wood Carver knew what was in the wood, I knew what was in the music. Whenever I sang, I forgot about being an orphan and having freckles and how much Sweet Fern hated me and how I wasn't right with God or Jesus. I forgot that I was singing in front of friends and strangers or that I had ever been afraid. I just wanted to open my whole self up and sing as full as I could.

When I finished, there was silence. I stood for one horrible moment wanting to disappear. Then people began cheering and one woman was crying so loud, you could hear her over the clapping.

I had never seen or felt a ghost before, although Lord knows I'd tried my mighty best. But as I stood there singing underneath the trees and the sky, to folks in their hand-me-down clothes and bare feet, I could swear I felt my mama beside me.

~

I made my way through the crowd to where my family was waiting. Strangers stopped me to say congratulations or to tell me how much they loved my voice. They said they couldn't believe that such a little girl, just twelve years old, could sing like that and that I seemed much older than I was.

Suddenly, a tall, dark-haired boy stepped in front of me. He was covered in coal dust and had two white spots around his eyes and held a lit cigarette in his hand. The moonshiner's boy. He had to be fifteen years old now, almost a grown man. I looked but didn't see his friends anywhere.

"You sing good, Bonnie," he said.

"Thanks." I felt my cheeks turn red.

"I sing a little, but not as good as you. My mama don't believe in it. She says singing is an insult to the Lord and swears I'm going to hell."

"That's a horrible thing to say."

"Yeah, well." He took a puff on the cigarette and kept his eyes on me. "You still living a life of crime?" His eyes were a pure, light green made even lighter by the black of the coal dust on his arms and face.

"No," I said. "I gave it up."

He kind of smiled. "That's too bad. You'd make someone a real good partner."

"I'd rather save myself for the Grand Ole Opry," I said.

"The Opry?"

"Yeah."

He nodded. Then he pinched the end of the cigarette so that it burned out and took a handkerchief from his pocket. I watched as he wrapped up the cigarette butt, very carefully, and placed the handkerchief back in the pocket of his trousers. "You know what, Bonnie?" He smiled, sweet as could be. "You're the prettiest girl on Fair Mountain," he said.

That's a fresh thing to say, I thought. I was shocked and thrilled all at once. "Why're you so dirty?" I said.

He dropped his smile. He looked at me like I'd slapped him. And then he walked away.

~

Mrs. Dennis and Dr. Hamp stood with Sweet Fern and Danny under a tree. When I walked up to join them, Mrs. Dennis put her arm around me. She said to Sweet Fern, "My husband and I promise to look after her and keep her safe and to ensure that she returns home in one piece. I think the National Singing Convention could be a wonderful opportunity for Velva Jean—not only a chance for her to gain more experience, but a chance for others to hear her."

"Atlanta is a far way to go," Sweet Fern said. Her voice was cold but polite. "I'm afraid we don't have that kind of money."

"I was thinking that Velva Jean could earn the money for the train ticket herself," said Mrs. Dennis. "Perhaps by working for me in the mornings or after school." I looked at her in surprise, afraid she was going to give away our secret, but she gave my shoulder a little squeeze and kept looking at Sweet Fern.

When Sweet Fern didn't say anything, Mrs. Dennis said, "She will be one of the youngest people there, singing with people who are far older and more experienced, many of whom are well known. Even some who have performed on the Opry."

Mrs. Dennis was quiet then, and we all looked at Sweet Fern and waited. I held my breath and prayed to Jesus. *Jesus, if you are there, please hear me. Please let Sweet Fern say yes. Please. Please. Please. Please.*

"No," Sweet Fern said.

"Mrs. Deal, perhaps . . ."

"No," Sweet Fern said again. She smoothed the front of her dress. "I'm sorry."

Johnny Clay walked up. He said, "What's going on?"

I said. "Why not? Why can't I? Sweet Fern, please . . ."

"No," she said again, this time to me. Danny looked at me and shook his head. The way he did it, I could tell he was on my side. "Velva Jean," Sweet Fern said. "It's time to go home."

~

We all went back to Daddy Hoyt's to churn ice cream. He and Granny lived in an old log house connected by a dogtrot—one side of the house for cooking and eating, the other for living and sleeping. We sat outside—on the porch, on the steps, in the grass—and Granny and Sweet Fern and Ruby Poole served the food. Dan Presley and Hunter Firth played chase while we watched, and Corrina, who had just started walking, picked flowers, her bottom up in the air.

I sat on the steps, drinking Cheerwine and ignoring Sweet Fern. Every now and then I patted the Gold Queen crown that sat atop my head. It was made of wire painted yellow. Little gold nuggets shone like stars at the very tip of each point.

You're the prettiest girl on Fair Mountain.

Rachel Gordon had sold greeting-card subscriptions to earn enough money for a china doll she saw down at Deal's. It cost $2.75 and she made enough in two weeks to pay for it. I was thinking I might start selling greeting-card subscriptions to earn money to get to the National Singing Convention, no matter what Sweet Fern said. If there was any left over, I would buy that Hawaiian steel guitar and save up for my trip to Nashville. The guitar cost fourteen dollars and was the prettiest thing I'd ever seen. Once I could afford to buy it, I planned to get rid of Daddy's old mandolin for good.

"One day when I get out of school," I said, "I'm going right up there to Nashville and get me a job at the Opry." I didn't feel one bit shy anymore. I felt like I couldn't wait to sing again, and not just in front of people here on Fair Mountain.

"You don't even need school," said Johnny Clay from where he sat on the porch railing. He didn't think school was worth anything, even though he was so good at it. "Granny didn't go to school, did you, Granny?"

"Not like you children do," she said, setting her glass of sweet tea on the floor by her foot. She rocked back and forth in her rocker. "But I still had lessons."

Johnny Clay waved his hand at this like he was slapping away a bug. "You don't need school if you're going to be a famous singer like Velva Jean."

I liked wearing a crown. When Mama died, I never thought I would feel happy again. A part of me felt guilty, like I had no right to feel happy now, with Mama gone. I hoped she knew that I was still just as sad over her death and that I missed her just as much. I hoped she understood that this good feeling didn't have anything to do with not missing her.

~

After the last pie was eaten and we all went home, I slipped up the stairs to my bedroom and opened the family record book and wrote down the date followed by: "Velva Jean sings at the Alluvial Fair. Wins first place. Crowned Gold Queen." I slid my hatbox out from under my bed and added my new five dollar bill to the money I was saving for Nashville. I wrapped it up, good and tight, in the handkerchief and closed the hatbox away. Then I stood in front of the mirror that hung over the chest of drawers. Was I really the prettiest girl on Fair Mountain?

I knew that vanity was a sin, but I leaned in close to the mirror over the washstand and examined my face. This time I didn't look for the marks of being an orphan or losing my mama. I tried to see past them and past the freckles and the hair that got too curly in the summer heat. I tried to look past the fact that my nose was straight and didn't have a bump on the bridge and that my eyes were more the color of Three Gum River than sunflowers against a blue sky.

I looked up and Sweet Fern was standing in the door, watching me. "You sounded real good today, Velva Jean," she said, and her voice was so low that I almost didn't hear it.

"Thank you," I said. I was afraid to move because I was afraid if I did she might take it back or change her mind and go away.

She touched the back of her neck, which was clean and bare because her hair was pinned up on her head like it always was. "Mama would have loved that song. I remember when she taught it to you." Her face was closed up and hard to read.

I felt the tears spring up then, and all of a sudden I forgot about being mad at Sweet Fern. I wanted to run to her and wrap my arms around her. But I stayed still, barely breathing, because she didn't like people flying at her and surprising her. "It was just a few months before she died," I whispered.

Sweet Fern nodded and then looked up at the ceiling. She blinked several times, like she had something in her eye. "We'll be having another baby next year," she said finally. She rested her hands on her stomach. "This house is too much for me to keep on my own as it is. I'll need your help with the babies and the chores."

I said, "Is that why I can't go to Atlanta?"

"That and other reasons. I was thinking that this next year of school should be your last. You already got a good education, more than most, and I need you to stay home and help me here. You can finish the seventh grade, but after that I need you home."

"The convention is only two days," I said. "Plus one day there and one day back. I'll be home long before you have the baby."

She picked at a loose thread on her dress and then she smoothed it flat. She cleared her throat. "Sometimes you got to learn, Velva Jean, that not every dream is supposed to come true. Mama and Daddy coddled you so much that you think you got more right to dream than anyone else, but you don't."

I didn't know what to say. I felt like I'd just been slapped across the face, like the time Johnny Clay accidentally hit me in the nose with his elbow and gave me a black eye.

"It's nice to dream, but you can't dream too big," Sweet Fern said. "It was a real nice dream to go down to Alluvial to sing at the fair. But it's unreasonable to think you're going to ride a train to Georgia." She sighed so deep that it was like all the breath went out of her. "And it's unreasonable to think you're going to go all the way to Nashville to sing at the Opry."

I felt the handles of the dresser pressing into my backside. I thought they felt just as cold and hard as Sweet Fern.

"Besides, there's other kinds of dreams," she said. "Someday you'll meet a nice boy and get married and have a family of your own. Then you'll see what I mean."

"And get old and die here on Fair Mountain without ever having seen anywhere else," I said. "That's not *my* life ambition."

"Don't be dramatic, Velva Jean. Mama's not here." Her voice had that final tone that meant she was done discussing it. "But I am. Daddy left me in charge of you, and as long as I am, you'll listen to me."

I was mad. Good and mad and hurt. I said the only thing I could think of. "You're not my mother!" Sweet Fern's face turned as red as Ruby Poole's lipstick. And then I pushed past her and ran down the stairs and out of the house.

"I wish to God that was true," she shouted after me, and her voice sounded tired. "More than you know, Velva Jean!"

~

"So Sweet Fern doesn't understand your dreams." The Wood Carver stopped in front of a tall balsam fir. He tipped his hat back and studied the tree, and then reached out and chopped off one of the long and knotted limbs. He patted the trunk of the tree and then walked back to his house, the branch over his shoulder, and I followed him. For the first time, I noticed that he favored his left leg and walked with a limp. We sat down and I tried not to stare at his leg.

"No," I said, "she don't. She don't even want to. I'm so sick and tired of her telling me what I can and can't do all the time. I want to run away and be a hermit in the woods, just as far away from her as I can get. Just as far away from everything and everybody." I glanced at his face. I was hoping he might invite me to come live up here with him. No one would bother us and he could teach me to carve and I could teach him to sing. We would be two bad, evil outlaws, out of everybody's way.

"And you think running away will fix it?" the Wood Carver said. He picked up his knife and held it over the branch.

It was the kind of question Daddy Hoyt liked to ask, one I knew I had to be careful answering because it had a hidden meaning. "No, but it will help me feel better. I'm not sure I'm fit to live down there." Ever since I was saved, I thought to myself. Ever since Mama. Ever since Daddy.

He looked at me, and I wondered if I'd answered correctly. "'And I shall be a fugitive and a vagabond in the earth.'" I waited for more, but that was all he said. He held the balsam branch this way, then that. He had told me how important that first cut was, finding just the right place to start carving the wood. He was quiet for a long time.

"Nature doesn't deal with straight lines," he said finally, setting down his knife. "Everything is a curve. Nothing is what you expect. There are no straight lines anywhere, and that goes for pathways too. You can look and look for them, but they don't exist."

I sat staring out into the laurel thicket where I used to hide and spy on him. I thought how long ago that seemed. "'Whenever God closes a door, he opens a window.' Mama used to say that. Is that what you mean?"

"I'm just saying look at this piece of wood." He handed it to me. "Look at the way it twists back and forth and goes this way and that. Some people might think there's only one way to make a cane or a crutch—the straighter the better because you have to be able to lean on it. And if I handed them something like this, they'd say, 'Oh, that can't be a crutch! It's too crooked! It's not at all what a crutch should be.' Because they think there's only one way, you see." He took the branch from me, "But I say you have to expect nature to curve and have bumps, and that's the thing you can count on. Life is that way, too."

Like when I was born again and thought it would make everything right forever, only it didn't—it made things wrong. "Are you saying that I could still get to the Opry?" I said.

His fingers rested on a knot in the wood. He wore a gold band on the ring finger of his left hand. It was nicked and scratched, but it shone like the sun. I wondered where his wife was and what had really happened to her.

He picked up his knife again. "I'm saying there are plenty of other ways to get there." He touched his knife to the balsam branch, and I watched as he made the first cut.

ELEVEN

The day after the fair, Beachard got up at dawn and did his chores and ate his breakfast. As soon as he was finished, he picked up his plate and glass and carried them into the kitchen, and then he told us he was leaving. He had packed a small bag, which he threw over his shoulder. He walked to the doorway and even when Sweet Fern hollered at him, he didn't raise his voice. He said, "I'm going to make sure the men building the Scenic don't do anything horrible to these mountains."

Sweet Fern followed after Beachard as he set out across the porch and into the yard. She said, "When will you be back?" I stood behind her and from what I could see of her face, I was worried she was going to cry. Beach was sixteen, almost seventeen. He was getting old enough to be on his own, but he was still her responsibility. Already I wanted him to come back. I wanted Sweet Fern to do something, but I knew there was nothing she or any of us could do because once Beach made up his mind about something there was no moving him.

Beach said, "I don't know. I'll write if I can. This has nothing to do with you, Sweet Fern."

Her face fell in on itself then and she covered it up with her hands. I crept forward and laid my hand on her back, light as could be, and watched Beach go. He had the bag up over his shoulder and he was heading down the hill toward Alluvial, where I guessed he was going to meet Stanley Abbott and the rest of the men from the Scenic.

"Beach will be okay," I said. I was still wearing my crown, which was bent from where I had slept on it. Johnny Clay and Danny came out onto the porch and I looked around at them. I patted Sweet Fern a little, but not enough to make her mad. I said, "He'll be back."

She took her hands away and her eyes were wet. Her face was fixed in anger, and she stared off toward the mountains and didn't say a word. I knew it would be a bad day for the rest of us.

~

That night, Johnny Clay came to my room and sat on the foot of my bed. The moonlight fell on his face and the gold-brown hair hung down over his eyes. "We got to run away from here," he said, low enough so as not to wake Dan Presley and Corrina, asleep in the other bed. Sweet Fern and Danny had turned in an hour ago. "I can't stand it anymore, the way she treats us."

I laid my book aside and propped myself up on my elbows. I was almost too upset to read *The Motor Girls on Waters Blue*, which I had borrowed from Dr. Hamp's library. The Motor Girls was a wonderful series of books. In each one, Cora Kimball and her friends drove off on different adventures in their automobiles. Cora Kimball also had an older brother named Jack who drove a red and yellow racing car that Cora called "giddy and gaudy." I wished Johnny Clay had a car. I wished I had one too, just like Cora. We could drive far away from Sweet Fern and she would be sorry.

"Where can we go?" I said. I'd never been anywhere in my life except down to Hamlet's Mill. I wasn't sure what all was out there, but I knew I wanted to go see. Maybe there were other ways to get to the Opry, like the Wood Carver said.

Johnny Clay considered. He was even more fed up than me because he was almost fifteen and already thought of himself as a man. "We could just jump the train and see where it takes us. Beachard used to do it all the time. Hundreds of kids our age and younger are riding the rails from one state to another."

I liked the sound of jumping a train. It sounded wild and dangerous and in keeping with the wickedness I felt inside. I thought briefly of Jesus and how I'd pledged myself to him two years ago. Then I thought:

Where was Jesus when I was shelling the corn and scrubbing the floors and parboiling the hog, all of which I did before supper? And where was he when I prayed for him to save my mama? And where was he when I asked for this one thing—just to let Sweet Fern say yes to the National Singing Convention? I was as sick of Jesus as I was of Sweet Fern.

~

The next morning, while Sweet Fern was on the back porch, giving the children a bath, I packed up my hatbox with all my treasures, including the little wooden singing girl, the money I was saving for Nashville, the emerald Daddy had given me, my Motor Girls book, and the dress I'd worn to the fair. I figured I could mail the book back to Dr. Hamp once I finished reading it. I slipped the mandolin strap across my chest, and then Johnny Clay and I said good-bye to Hunter Firth and went down to Deal's and jumped a freight train.

Johnny Clay pulled himself up first, kicking open the door, and I ran beside him, on the ground, holding out my free hand. The train was going too fast, and I was scared to death of being left behind. "Johnny Clay!" I yelled and felt the train starting to outdistance me. The hatbox and the mandolin made it hard to run. Then I felt Johnny Clay's hand lock with mine. He pulled me in, and my feet swung above the moving ground, and then I was sitting next to him with my hatbox in my lap.

It took me a minute to realize that the car wasn't empty. There were three old men and seven or eight boys of various ages sitting back against the sides of the car, hands resting on knees or curled on their sides as they slept. Most of them looked dirty and tired, and I tried not to stare. I wondered if they were train robbers or bandits, just like the ones Granny had told me stories about, or if these were the kids Beach had spoke of to Johnny Clay, the ones riding the rails from one side of the country to the other.

"Someday we're really going to ride this train, Velva Jean," Johnny Clay shouted above the noise. "Not in the freight car with the hoboes but as real passengers with tickets and a destination and people knowing we're going and coming to tell us good-bye."

When the train picked up full steam, I forgot about whether the hoboes were outlaws and whether I would get sent to prison if the train detectives caught me. I even forgot about how much I was going to miss Daddy Hoyt and Granny and Ruby Poole and the rest. Instead I just concentrated on the landscape whizzing by. I hope Sweet Fern is happy, I thought. I hope they realize this is all her doing.

I held tight to the door and to my hatbox and sat cross-legged beside Johnny Clay, watching the trees and hills whir past. I closed my eyes and enjoyed the feel of rushing air on my face, and then opened them again so I wouldn't miss anything.

"Let's just keep going," I said. "Let's go as far as we can."

~

We got off seven or eight miles later in the next town over, a place called Civility, which looked a lot like Hamlet's Mill, only much bigger. It was the biggest city I'd ever seen. There were two diners, two cafés, a bank, a beauty shop, a grocery, a hardware store, three department stores, a doctor's office, a law office, a soda shop, a flower shop, a drugstore, a courthouse, three churches, and a movie theater.

Johnny Clay and I went to the theater and read the marquee: *Top Hat* starring Fred Astaire and Ginger Rogers. Johnny Clay emptied his pockets and found enough for two tickets, and as I lowered myself into the seat I thought: This is my new life. Picture shows every day and not a soul to tell me no.

After it was over, we stumbled out into the daylight, singing songs from the film. When we couldn't remember the words, we made them up. I danced along the street like Ginger Rogers. I swung my hatbox back and forth by its string and thought how happy I was that I would never have to see Sweet Fern again or have to listen to her ordering me around or telling me what I could and couldn't do. I thought how nice it was to be free from Sweet Fern and to have the whole world opened up to me so that anything was possible.

"Okay," Johnny Clay said as we walked. "Since we're starting a new life, I say we make some new rules."

"Rules? You have lost your mind. Why do you think we ran away?"

"But these are good ones. Like, we eat ice cream before dinner."

I thought for a moment. "And we don't wash our hands."

"And we always keep our elbows on the table."

"And chew with our mouths open."

"And stay up as late as we want."

"And go to the National Singing Convention," I said.

There were four or five automobiles parked on either side of the street. Johnny Clay paused at each one, shielding his eyes with his hand so he could see the dashboard. I covered my eyes and peered in the windows, too, but all I saw were dials and buttons that I didn't understand.

I said, "One day when I'm a famous singer, I'm going to have a shiny automobile, and I'm going to let anyone who wants to ride in it. When I drive past everyone'll say, 'There goes Velva Jean Hart. Just look how fancy.'"

We walked and danced down the street to the soda shop and sat on stools at the counter and ordered milk shakes and potato chips. I set my hatbox and my mandolin on the seat next to me and we propped our elbows up and made sure to chew with our mouths open. I felt very grown up.

"Get out of here now," we heard the man behind the counter say. He sounded angry. We looked up to see one of the hobo boys from the train standing at the counter.

"I'll work for it," he said.

"I don't have any work for you, kid," the man said. "Now get out of here."

The boy had that hungry look about him that dogs got when they came round after Granny's hens—the kind of dogs that were all bones and skin, not fat ones like Hunter Firth. The boy looked no older than fourteen, with ears that stuck out and arms he hadn't grown into yet. I stared down at his shoes and saw that they were full of holes.

"Give him what he wants," I heard Johnny Clay say. I looked at my brother and he was staring at the man behind the counter, the man who had been so nice to us when we ordered our food and paid him money up front for it.

"He with you?" The man said. His face was closed up like Sweet Fern's when she didn't believe you.

"That's right," Johnny Clay said.

The man eyed Johnny Clay and then the kid. He sighed. "What do you want?"

The boy barely even glanced at Johnny Clay. He looked like he wanted to die right there on the spot. "A hamburger," he said, just like a mouse.

"Make it a cheeseburger," said Johnny Clay. "And a vanilla milk shake."

The man turned without a word and began to fix the food.

"Thanks," the kid mumbled. He said it into his hat, which he still held in his hands.

Johnny Clay shrugged. "Where you from?"

"Ohio," the kid said.

"Where you headed?"

"California."

Johnny Clay nodded at me to move my things so the boy could sit down. I handed them to my brother and he set them on the stool next to him. The boy sat on the stool beside me.

"I'm Gary," he said.

"I'm Johnny Clay and this here's my sister, Velva Jean."

"Hey," Gary said.

"Hey," I said back.

"Why'd you leave?" Johnny Clay said to him.

Gary set his hat on the counter and rubbed his hands on the legs of his trousers. "My dad lost his job and told me they couldn't feed any more kids. He said I was old enough to look after my own self now."

I said, "What're you going to do in California?"

"Pick fruit. I heard there's jobs out there."

Johnny Clay and I had finished our drinks by the time the cheeseburger came. We sat there with Gary while he ate, and Johnny Clay paid the man behind the counter what he owed him and not a penny more because he said the man didn't deserve it.

I'd never seen someone eat so fast in my life. Gary ate like he hadn't eaten in months. After he was done, Johnny Clay told the man to make one more cheeseburger and to throw in a bag of chips and to put them in a paper bag.

"We don't have that kind of money, Johnny Clay," I whispered.

"Hush," he hissed back. "We got more than he does."

Gary took the paper sack and rolled it up tight and placed it inside his hat. The three of us walked outside. He said, "You all got a place to sleep tonight?"

Johnny Clay shook his head. "Not yet."

"There's a hobo jungle just up the track from here. You can't see it from the track, but it's about a quarter mile up from where we got off, on the left-hand side, hid in a grove of trees. You're welcome to stay there tonight if you want."

"Thanks," Johnny Clay said.

"If I ain't there, just tell them I said it was okay. But watch out for the buzzards." He kind of half smiled and then he turned around and headed back toward the tracks.

"What's a hobo jungle?" I whispered. It sounded like a terrible, dangerous place. I pictured a wilderness with buzzards circling overhead.

"It's where the hoboes camp," Johnny Clay said.

I watched after Gary. He was almost out of sight. "He kind of walks like a dog that's been kicked, don't he?" I said.

"Yeah." Johnny Clay sighed. "It makes you think."

"About what?"

"That things could be worse, Velva Jean." With a dead mama, a daddy who didn't want me, a Lord that betrayed me, and Sweet Fern for my new mother, I really didn't see how.

I thought how proud Daddy Hoyt would have been of Johnny Clay, to see him step up like that and help a friend in need, like Daddy Hoyt was always telling us to do. He liked to say it didn't matter how much money a person had, as long as they were willing to part with it to help someone who needed it more. He said that the richest people on earth weren't always the ones with money.

At the thought of Daddy Hoyt, I felt a hollowing in my stomach, as if it wasn't full of potato chips and milk shake. I wondered what Daddy Hoyt was doing up on Fair Mountain and if he'd missed us yet.

~

Hours later, when the sun dipped behind the mountains, Johnny Clay said, "We should get to the jungle before dark." A shiver ran up my spine at the word "jungle."

We stood outside the Bluebird Café, where we'd shared a plate of chicken and dumplings for supper, and studied the sky over Fair Mountain, our mountain. It was the first time I'd ever seen it from below. Down where we were, buildings, streets, cars, people were bathed in gold.

Together, we walked back toward the train tracks. A freight train had stopped and men were unloading. The engineer leaned against the side of the engine with his eyes closed, hands in pockets. A voice called out, "We got enough coal to last us to Dillsboro, but we'll need to take on more there." A face appeared, shaded with coal dust, the eyes rubbed white. Two long legs swung down from the train and two blackened hands reached in trouser pockets for a cigarette.

After the cigarette was lit, the boy looked up and saw us.

"What's he doing here?" I said.

"Who?" asked Johnny Clay.

"The moonshiner's boy."

Johnny Clay frowned at this.

The boy had caught sight of us and was smiling. He took a drag on the cigarette and nodded at us. "There a singing contest around that I don't know about?"

Johnny Clay and I stopped in front of him. Johnny Clay looked him in the eye. Johnny Clay was shorter by barely half an inch, which I could tell made him mad. "You work on the train?"

"Fireman."

"How long you been at it?"

"Since I was twelve. Almost four years now." The moonshiner's boy looked at me again and smiled. His teeth were white against the gray-black of his face. "There a singing contest here today?" he repeated.

"No," I said. "We left home." Johnny Clay punched my arm. "Ow! What?"

The boy nodded. "If I didn't work this job, I'd a left home a long time ago."

A crewman came running up the tracks. He didn't even look at us, just coughed in front of the engineer till the man opened his eyes. "Ready, boss," he said.

The engineer swung himself up into the engine.

"You all going back tonight?" the moonshiner's boy asked.

"No," Johnny Clay said. "We ain't going back." It sounded final, the way he said it.

The boy nodded. "If you change your mind, there's a midnight freight that's passing through on its way to Alluvial." He took one last drag on the cigarette, then pinched it out and wrapped it up. As he swung up into the engine, he looked right at me and grinned. "Prettiest face on Fair Mountain," he said. "Fair Mountain or anywhere else."

"What the hell does that mean?" Johnny Clay said as we watched the train roll out. He was staring after it as if he could still see the moonshiner's boy.

"Nothing," I said. *Prettiest face on Fair Mountain.*

~

The hobo jungle sat in a deep gorge several hundred yards from the tracks. The brush grew up high and the trees grew thick around it, so that we didn't see the jungle until we were almost in it. There were twenty or thirty boys of all ages—and three or four old men—cooking food in front of a campfire or sleeping on the ground or sitting in small groups and playing cards. A stream ran through the gorge and a few men were bent over it, scooping water into pots or flasks. Two girls sat on the edge of the group, smoking cigarettes and watching everyone with bored expressions. There was a smell to the camp—a tired, stale smell of rotten food and too many people.

Johnny Clay and me sat down by the fire, and I slipped my hatbox under my legs and bent my knees over it. I kept a firm hand on my mandolin and thought about how mean and dangerous I felt. And scared. "Are they all runaways?" I asked Johnny Clay. If Sweet Fern could see me now.

"Most of them," he said. "Or cast outs. Just stay close to me, Velva Jean."

I stared at the girls. They couldn't have been much more than nineteen or twenty, but they looked worn down. Their skirts were pulled up so their knees were showing. The girls were staring at me and at Johnny Clay and blowing smoke in our direction. There were two old men hanging around them. One wore overalls with no shirt and looked the same age as my daddy. The other was a lot older—at least as old as Daddy Hoyt.

Gary came up from the creek, his form just an outline in the darkening night. "Put that fire out," he said to someone. He carried a coffee can, which he set on the ground gently so that the water didn't spill. He sat down next to us. "Glad you made it," he said. "Are you thirsty?"

Johnny Clay shook his head. "A little," I said.

I thought Gary seemed different from when we'd seen him in town, more sure of himself. He pulled a cup from his pack, dipped it into the can, and handed it to me. It was a chipped yellow teacup with a blue handle and tiny daisies painted around the rim. I wondered where the cup came from. Was it from his mama? Did she miss it? Had she given it to him before he left? Were there others somewhere in Ohio—shelves lined with yellow teacups with blue handles and daisies around the rim? Was there an empty place where this one used to be?

Gary and Johnny Clay played a hand of cards with two other fellows. When I started yawning, Gary gave me his bed, which was no more than a blanket on the ground. I placed my hatbox under my head for a pillow and wrapped my arms around my mandolin.

I lay there for a few minutes and listened to the voices. Then the words began to blur together as I stared at the moon, which was white and glowing, casting a ghostly light over the sky. I tried to keep myself awake, telling myself I needed to come up with a song about a hobo jungle—a place where buzzards were grown men and the boys were old before they were young. As I was drifting off, I heard Johnny Clay and Gary agree to take shifts while I slept.

~

An hour or so later, I woke up and realized I had to go to the bathroom. Most everyone was asleep, including Johnny Clay and Gary. The new moon cast a cool glow on the camp and the people in it, so you couldn't see the dirty faces and the tattered clothes. I stood up and hopped around to get the life back into my limbs, and then I tiptoed to the other side of the creek where the grass grew high.

I squatted on the ground, trying not to jump at every sound. The night was still, but every now and then the breeze rustled the trees and I could hear the "hoot hoot hoot" of an owl. I tried to keep my eyes on my hatbox and mandolin and my brother who lay sleeping beside them. I was just finishing my business when I heard a twig snap behind me. I stiffened like I'd seen Hunter Firth do when he tracked a squirrel. "Johnny Clay?" I whispered.

I turned to see one of the girls standing behind me. She had hold of the buzzard with the overalls and no shirt, and he was grabbing her around the waist. "What're you doing here?" she said to me, and her voice was cold.

"She's a pretty one," the man said. "Worth more than fifty cents, that one." He laughed at this.

She slapped his arms and pushed him away. He only grabbed her tighter. She said, "Oh, but she ain't selling, are you, sister sunshine?"

They both looked at me, waiting, but I didn't know what to say.

She said, "She can't be selling because Sheryl and me has this place covered."

The man took his hands off her and started toward me. "I don't know. Seems there's plenty she could do around here."

I started to back up. I kept my eyes on them and tried to feel my way with my heels. When I reached the edge of the stream, I turned around and jumped across, landing on my right knee. I felt the rawness of a new scrape and the bruise that would be there by tomorrow, and then I picked myself up. I heard the man laugh again and lunge for me, and I scrambled away right into the arms of Johnny Clay. He pushed me aside and punched the man in the face, sending him flying backward into the stream, where he landed with a splash and a flood of curse words.

Johnny Clay grabbed my hand. He dragged me through the hobo jungle, scooping up my hatbox and mandolin, and didn't stop till we were at the train tracks. I looked back toward the camp, but all I could see were the trees and the grasses, grown up high and thick.

My heart was racing so fast I couldn't catch my breath. I looked behind us again, and no one was coming. I looked up and the trees were swaying gently back and forth against the sky. The moon had changed positions and the breeze was picking up. My scraped knee stung as the air hit it.

"Where're we going, Johnny Clay?" I asked.

"Home," he said.

TWELVE

The clock on the Baptist church said 12:40. A lone lightbulb burned bright over the door to Deal's General Store, but the school, the church, and the houses were completely black. The moon shone from a different angle in the sky, the same moon we saw in Civility. I had never seen Alluvial so dark and silent before. Somewhere I could hear the sound of an owl calling his mate, and then, seconds later, her answer.

As we started up the hill and into the trees toward home, the night closed in as the woods snuffed out the light of the moon. I had never been out so late in my life. Johnny Clay pulled out his flashlight, the one he always carried with him, and lit the way.

"You know Sweet Fern's gonna tan our hides," he said.

"I don't care I guess." I told myself I could still go home and be free of her. I would just ignore her when she talked to me and pretend like I couldn't hear her. I wouldn't do anything she said or even look at her until she finally got the idea that she and I were done.

I began to sing one of the songs from *Top Hat*. I hoped it would make me forget about Sweet Fern and about being scared of the woods and the dark. The closer we got to home, though, the less I sang and the less we said. We were both thinking about what kind of punishment would be waiting for us.

I tried not to jump at every sound. I was used to the noises of the animals and the bugs, but everything familiar seemed scary in the black of the woods. I kept my eyes focused on the beam of light that danced across the ground in front of us.

"What's that?" I said now and then, at the snap of a twig or the hoot of an owl.

"Nothing," Johnny Clay would say. "Nothing's going to hurt you, Velva Jean, not with me here."

I thought of the way he had punched the jungle buzzard, the way the man had fallen backward, feet over head, and the way he'd cursed a blue streak when he hit the stream. I told myself that Johnny Clay knew what he was talking about, so I left him alone.

There was a dark patch of woods in the center of the forest where the trees were especially thick and completely blacked out the sky. I knew home was on the other side of them, but I was always nervous walking through there, and until now I'd only been there in the daytime. This was where Spearfinger lived, the witch woman. Sometimes you could hear her shrieking in the distance, up above the wind and the treetops. She took on the shape of anything she liked—a bird or a fish or a person you loved—but underneath it she was made of stone. She roamed the woods looking for children, hoping to touch them with her bony finger and steal their souls.

As we stepped into the thick of the woods, I walked a little closer to Johnny Clay and tried not to look about me. I thought it would be just my luck, after all those years of wanting to see a haint, to finally see one now.

"What was that?" I asked again. Somewhere behind us, there was the snap of twigs, the crunch of leaves. I was terrified to look, sure I would see a ghost or maybe the Wood Carver roaming the woods on all fours. Would he remember me? Or would he even recognize me in his animal form?

"Nothing, Velva Jean. Jesus." Johnny Clay liked taking the Lord's name in vain. He thought it made him sound grown up. With my free hand, I held on to the back of his shirt, light enough so that he wouldn't feel it.

"Great Holy Moses!" he yelled, so suddenly I jumped straight into the air. He slapped at his face and chest. "They got me, Velva Jean! The cannibal spirits got me!" He danced up and down and laughed like a donkey.

I slugged him good and hard across the back. "Johnny Clay!" But it got me thinking about the Nunnehi, the moon-eyed people. Sometimes they played tricks, but more often than that—according to Granny—they protected wanderers lost in the mountains, guiding them home with their drums and their lanterns. I started to pray in my head for them to help us and guide us home safely.

And then we heard it—a kind of high-pitched scream that made us both jump. I knew what panthers sounded like—"painters," Granny called them. They sounded just like a woman being murdered. I'd heard them all my life, way up on the mountain, and Granny had always told us tales of the panthers that lived in the woods and hunted at night. Sometimes, she said, they waited in trees for people to pass by and then they would drop on them and carry them away. Sometimes they reached in the windows or doors of houses and stole human babies and dragged them off to their dens. Sometimes they would follow a person for miles until you didn't know where you were, and then you would turn around and there they would be, and they would drag you off and bury you in the leaves.

There came another howl, this one close by, somewhere to the left of us or the right of us, we couldn't be sure in the dark. We froze.

"Holy shit," Johnny Clay said, very low, and I knew now it was okay to be scared. I was trying to remember what it was we were supposed to do if we saw a panther. I couldn't remember if we were supposed to stand still like statues, like when you saw a mad dog, or if we were supposed to run. I knew Granny carried around a small ax whenever she went out midwifing, just in case she ran into one, but all we had was Johnny Clay's flashlight.

To the side of us, there was the sound of four legs, of pacing back and forth, first to the right of us, then to the left, suddenly in front, then behind. There was a flash of light red-brown—the color of the earth— the thud of leaves being crushed, of heavy breathing. There was a low growl, almost a hum. Then, it lunged, and I felt the hem of my dress tear right off and something cold and wet on my leg.

I screamed and we ran, crashing into trees and limbs. Johnny Clay was faster than me, but my legs were long and I ran hard behind him, keeping my eyes on his back and on the light bobbing in front of us. When it all of a sudden went completely dark, I smashed right into him so that we both almost fell over.

"Light's dead," he said. He clutched the flashlight with his hand like a weapon and grabbed my hand with his other one. There was a scrambling behind us, a scraping of nails, a pounding of feet. "Throw something at it," he shouted. "Hand me that mandolin."

And then I remembered something Granny had told us. "Take your clothes off, Johnny Clay! Granny said to take your clothes off and throw them at the panther cat so it'll attack the clothes instead!"

Johnny Clay tore off his shirt, throwing it backward over my head. I didn't look back at the sound of ripping cloth, just kept right on running. All I had on over my underclothes was the ugly green-brown dress Sweet Fern had made me last summer that was already too short in the arms and the hem. I tried to decide what was worse—being killed by Sweet Fern for coming home without that dress, or being killed right there in the woods by that panther.

"Throw something else, Velva Jean!" Johnny Clay yelled. We could hear the panther coming along again behind us, faster than it had before.

I decided that dress or no dress Sweet Fern was already going to kill me. I pulled that ugly green-brown dress over my head and let it drop behind me. Then I tore off my slip and threw that too. I ran, feeling terrified—but also light and free—in my undershirt and shorts.

Together, Johnny Clay and me ran as hard and fast as we could, my hatbox banging into my bare leg and my side. I ran blindly and by instinct, my free hand reaching out in front, trying to slap away the tree limbs that were hitting me in the face.

Because I couldn't see with my eyes, I tried to see with my ears, my nose, my memory. I could hear the running, the beating of four legs, of eight, if you counted Johnny Clay and me. And in the distance—very faint—I couldn't be sure, but it almost sounded like drumming.

"You hear that?" Johnny Clay said, his breath coming in gasps.

"Yes."

"Run toward it," he said.

We ran toward the drums. For one instant, I closed my eyes so that I could hear them more clearly. They seemed to grow louder, and we chased them. They faded and grew louder again, faded and grew louder. All the while, I could hear the panther beating down on us. Suddenly, the drums grew so loud that I wanted to cover my ears, and then they stopped altogether.

"There!" Johnny Clay shouted.

There were flickers of light up ahead, like lightning bugs or lanterns—here and there, lighting a path. A light would flash and then go out, and then, feet away, another light would flash. Somewhere I heard voices—from up high in the trees, from down low on the ground—close by, but too far away to make out the words. We ran for the lights and didn't stop until we passed the edge of the woods and Beachard's rock and reached the front porch of home.

We raced up the steps and fell into a heap, swearing (Johnny Clay) and crying (me). We were weary and frightened and hungry and half-naked and thankful to be back. I could feel the cold sting of blood running down my leg where the thing tore at me with its claws. I suddenly felt light-headed and swoony, and I lay back and tried to breathe.

"You're bleeding," Johnny Clay said, and I could hear the admiration in his voice. "It got you, Velva Jean!"

Sweet Fern was sitting there in the rocking chair waiting for us, a lantern on the floor beside her. I saw the whiteness of her face and the vexed look in her eye. There were lines around her eyes and her mouth that I'd never seen before, and I saw that she had been crying and that her cheeks were still wet. I knew at times like this she wanted to curse Mama and Daddy for leaving her with us children. I knew she nearly hated them for it. But I wanted to throw myself at her feet and wrap myself around her ankles. I wanted to tell her I was sorry, that I'd stay home without complaining, that I didn't need to go to the National Singing Convention, that I'd be good and obedient and I'd help her however she wanted me to—even if she had twenty babies—if only she wouldn't let me die.

"I been beside myself all day," she said, jumping up, "tramping around to neighbors' houses, having to ask about you two." She looked down at us and I knew we must have looked a sight, all tangled up and out of breath, and Johnny Clay lying there wearing only his union suit and me in my underthings. "And look at you. Just as naked as jaybirds, just as wild as mountain trash."

By this time, everyone had come running—Daddy Hoyt and Granny, Danny, Linc and Ruby Poole, Aunt Zona, the twins, Aunt Bird, who hobbled along as best she could, and even Uncle Turk, who had come up from the river to look for us. I knew Sweet Fern was mad enough to spit but she also looked like she might cry again. "I could kill you both," she shouted. Danny stepped forward and laid a hand on her shoulder. She brushed it off and stalked inside the house, and then, not even a minute later, she came right back out and bent down over Johnny Clay and me and hugged us so tight that we couldn't breathe.

I'm home, I kept thinking after we got done eating. Daddy Hoyt stitched up my leg where the panther got me, and I didn't even cry because I was so happy to be home and not dead in the woods somewhere. I didn't even cry at the burning when he rubbed spirit turpentine and brown sugar on it to help it heal. Afterward, while Granny helped me get ready for bed, Danny and Linc went out into the woods with their shotguns and their lanterns, hunting for the panther.

Sweet Fern said our punishment was to do extra chores for two months. I had to use every last cent of my Nashville money, including the five dollars I won singing at the Alluvial Fair, to buy some new material so she could replace that ugly old dress I'd thrown at the panther, and I wasn't allowed to work for Mrs. Dennis anymore, and now I would most certainly never be going to the National Singing Convention. Johnny Clay had to take an afternoon job down at Deal's until he earned enough to pay for the shirt and pants he threw away. This put

Johnny Clay in a bad mood, but not me. I was still so happy and grateful that I would have done anything Sweet Fern said.

Thank you, Jesus. The moment we started running through the forest, I began praying to help me make it back. *I promise you*, I'd told Jesus in my head, so that Johnny Clay couldn't hear, *I promise you that if I get home I will never turn my back on you again. And I promise that I will never leave home until it's time for me to go be a singing star at the Grand Ole Opry.*

At this point, I wasn't sure who had saved us—Jesus or the Nunnehi. I tried to conjure the sound of the drums Johnny Clay and I had heard in the woods, or what we thought were drums. For some reason, I couldn't hear them anymore, even in memory. Whoever had saved us, I was grateful.

I lay on my stomach in my own safe bed with my face turned toward the window. I heard a shout from the woods and a gunshot followed by another and another. There was a scream like a woman being murdered. I pulled the covers tight around me and buried my face in the pillow and started to cry. My leg throbbed where the panther had got me.

If it really is you listening, Jesus, I will do my chores without complaining and stop wishing for things I don't have, and, most of all, I will get along with my sister.

~

The next morning, I got up early to do the extra work Sweet Fern had laid out for me. My leg was sore and I limped a little, just like Red Terror. "You're going to have a pretty good scar," Johnny Clay told me, admiration in his voice.

I pulled the corner of the bandage away to examine it. "You think so?" I wasn't sure how I felt about that. Maybe one day I wouldn't mind wearing dresses. *Prettiest face on Fair Mountain. Fair Mountain or anywhere.*

Sweet Fern didn't say a word to us throughout breakfast, and afterward she disappeared into Mama's room and shut the door. "You children worried her to death," Aunt Zona said and clucked her tongue.

"And her, four months pregnant." Aunt Zona was over at our house helping out because she said Sweet Fern needed the extra set of hands. I looked at her, my mother's older sister who was not at all like Mama, and wondered when her hair had gone gray.

There were beds to be stripped and wash to be done, fruit to be canned, and green beans to be strung. And for Johnny Clay there were pigs to be slopped, cows to be herded and milked, and a list of things to be fetched from Deal's. But the two of us went outside and crawled under the porch to let our breakfast settle. I rested on my stomach, chin in hands, and Johnny Clay lay on his back and stretched out his legs, folding his arms under his head. I looked at my brother and he was long and tall and still growing. There was a layer of stubble across his jaw and upper lip that I had never noticed before. I thought of the place on my leg where the panther had gotten me, and I hoped—really hoped—that it wouldn't make a scar so I could wear stockings one day. I wondered if we were getting too grown to crawl under the porch and the thought made me lonesome, although I wasn't sure for what.

Linc came out of the woods then, frowning, his rifle over his shoulder. It hit me that he was a man now, tall and grown up and handsome, and that he looked a lot like our daddy, only more serious. Everyone looked new to me since we were home.

Linc walked up the porch steps and into the house. We heard him calling Danny. In a minute, they both came out onto the porch.

"I found the panther," Linc said.

I turned my head to look at Johnny Clay. His eyes were open and he was staring straight up through the cracks in the floor.

"Is it dead?" said Danny.

"Yeah. But we didn't kill it."

"How do you know?"

Linc didn't say anything for a good, long time.

"Linc?" Danny said.

"There weren't any bullet wounds," Linc said. "Its neck was broken."

"How . . ."

"Like someone twisted it till it snapped."

THIRTEEN

First the flags appeared on Seniard Mountain—green flags waving in the breeze. They were almost pretty. I could see them on a clear October day from Old Widow's Peak when I went up there to sing. The next time I climbed up there, I saw men standing around where the flags were. From where I stood, they were just dark figures without faces. Every now and then a man would pick up a flag and place it somewhere else.

Next, the flags continued down to Fork River Bald and, just to the east of us, to Silvermine Bald, one ridge over. After that there were flags as far as the eye could see, off in the distance as well as closer in, surrounding us. They stretched from Beech Gap, Mount Hardy, Buckeye Gap, Parker Knob, Bearpen Gap, and beyond, until they seemed to be closing in on us in a wide half circle. Finally, there were flags across the top of Devil's Courthouse, up where the giant kept his cave. This caused a sick feeling in my stomach that even Daddy Hoyt couldn't cure. I didn't say anything to anyone, but I knew what I needed to do. There was no getting away from Sweet Fern after what Johnny Clay and me had done, but I watched and waited for my chance.

While I waited, I worked on a song I was writing about a panther that lived in the woods. I was calling it "Old Red Ghost."

It calls, it roams, it haunts these woods, that old red ghost.
It knows the thing that I fear most, the old red ghost.

I hear its crying in the night when I'm in my bed.
I hear its crying and I know that it ain't really dead.

Finally, at the end of two weeks, Sweet Fern lay down in her bed with her stomach, and I was free. I ran up to Devil's Courthouse, up to the top, and there were the flags all around on the ground in a line. I picked up each and every one, and when I was done I dug a hole and buried them and said a Cherokee spell that was meant for keeping invaders away. Then I ran back down toward home, fast as I could.

I never told anyone what I did. I figured I had stopped that road from coming here. I lay in bed that night, too scared and relieved to sleep. I prayed the government men wouldn't find me and take me away. If they did, I hoped everyone would appreciate what I had done for them and always remember me for my bravery.

~

Sometime in late November, a truck rolled into Alluvial and eight men climbed out. Sweet Fern and I were down at Deal's buying some calico cloth and other supplies. One of the men came into the store and said, "Is there a place we can pitch our tent around here?" It was Beachard.

He was the only person I knew that had a way of appearing out of thin air and then disappearing just as sudden, and he could creep up on you because he walked so quiet. But right now he just marched into that store, big as day.

I threw myself at him. He said, "Velva Jean, you're strangling me," but I didn't care. I just kept my arms wrapped tight around his neck and squeezed and squeezed.

~

We tried to get Beach to come back home with us and stay, but he said his place was in camp with the rest of the men. They set up their tent—mounted on a wooden platform—in the field behind Deal's. Sweet Fern said, "It's too cold to stay in a tent."

Beach said, "Not with all of us packed in there. Not with our kerosene heater."

Beach and the men were here to measure the route chosen by the government. Beach came up to Sleepy Gap for supper that night, and we all gathered at Daddy Hoyt's. We built a fire in the stone fireplace and sat around the large wooden table, staring at Beach while he talked. We hardly touched our food even though Beach ate and ate. Between mouthfuls he said, "Our job is to obtain the necessary engineering data required for the preparation of the preliminary and final design and construction plans for the Scenic, to follow up the flag lines and measure the various levels, indicating the amount of fill or cut to be expected." And all of us just stared at him after he said it because we had no idea what it meant.

Each morning at daybreak, Beach and the other men carried their equipment and supplies up the mountains. They spread out across Devil's Courthouse, Silvermine Bald, Seniard Mountain, Beech Gap, and Mount Hardy. The mountains were so steep and rough that they had to climb over boulders and through thickets of wild trees and shrubs, and in some places they had to crawl and be pushed up by members of the group. Beach said they had to stop and rest sometimes because their knees got weak from the weight of all their equipment. They had to watch for bears and especially for snakes. And then, when winter hit, they worked even when it snowed, even when it turned bitter cold.

By dusk each day, they came back down to Alluvial. Johnny Clay hung around by their tent and tried to get Beach to hire him, but Beach said no. He'd heard all about the panther and our running away from Sweet Fern, and he said he wasn't going to get in the middle of that. He said if Johnny Clay wanted to join up with the Scenic, he would have to do it the right way and ask Sweet Fern's permission.

It took them a month to finish their work. They finished two days before Christmas. We begged Beachard to stay, and he said yes. On Christmas Eve, he and his friends from the Scenic came up to the house and we holed up and enjoyed the snow and the celebration because we knew he'd be leaving the next day and we didn't know when we'd see him again.

We hung stockings by the fireplace—one for everyone, including each of Beachard's friends—and we sang carols while Daddy Hoyt played the fiddle and Granny danced. Then Johnny Clay and I stayed up all night talking with Beach and the other men, drinking hot coffee with sugar and cream and eating the ginger snaps and caramel cookies we always baked special for Christmas.

From here Beach and the men were heading to Richland Balsam and the mountains west of that, where they would set up camp again down in a valley or a holler while they did their work. Beach said, "Maybe I'll be back. They're thinking of bringing the road up through Devil's Courthouse. We're measuring up there and plotting it on the maps. Although when we got there, all the marking flags were gone."

I didn't say anything to this. I drank my coffee and kind of whistled to myself and tried to look like I was bored by what he was saying and didn't care at all, like I was barely listening.

Beach said he didn't have any news about Daddy.

On Christmas day, Beachard left. We watched him walk down the hill, traveling sack bumping over his shoulder, talking and laughing with the rest of the men on the survey team. The rest of us sat down together to open our stockings—one orange each, a few sticks of candy, some nuts—but it wasn't the same with Beachard gone.

On December 31, we heard the news: Mr. Deal's brother-in-law, a man named Joe Hamilton, had seen a map posted in the county courthouse in Beaver Ruin, where he lived. It was a map of some land he owned, up near Wagon Road Gap, and he said as soon as that map was posted the land became property of the state and was transferred to the federal government. No one had ever come to see him or talk to him or ask him if he was interested in selling. No one had even come to let him know. Granny said it was just like what happened with the Indians.

Wagon Road Gap was south of Mount Pisgah, just over the mountains from us. For the first time, I worried about Sleepy Gap and our valley. I thought about what Daddy Hoyt had said about this being an outgoing road as well as in incoming one, but I didn't want either. There was no place I wanted to go anymore except Nashville, and that seemed far off. I didn't want anyone to come in or out except Beach. I was tired of people going. I was tired of going myself. I was ready for everyone to stay in one place for a while.

~ 1938 ~

At the glorious tho't how the saints rejoice!
For they know he is coming, don't you?
I love his appearing, I do . . .

—"I Love His Appearing"

FOURTEEN

The sign was handwritten and hanging in the window of Deal's, next to the advertising boards for Lucky Strike cigarettes, Coca-Cola, Pillsbury cake flour, and Remington Kleanbore Shells.

The Glory Pioneers present a revival
on the banks of Three Gum River
Alluvial, North Carolina
June 19–23, 1938. 7:00 p.m.
Come one, come all, and rejoice in His name!

I had never heard of the Glory Pioneers but for some reason I just stared and stared at that sign. Ever since I turned fifteen, I'd been waiting for something interesting or exciting to happen to me. Something more than being crowned Gold Queen again or being asked to a candy pull by Ez Ledford or Lou Pigeon or one of the Gordon boys.

Ever since I turned fifteen, Sweet Fern was saying things like "By the time I was your age, I was already married and having my first baby" and "You could have your pick of any boy on this mountain."

"I don't want a one of them," I told her. I was not about to settle down with Daryl or Lester Gordon or, worse, Hink Lowe. I wasn't about to settle down with any of the boys who ran around chewing tobacco and bragging about how many times they'd been to visit Lucinda Sink.

Now I stood in front of Deal's and stared at that sign, the Gold Queen crown tilted forward on my head. It was the last night of the Alluvial Fair and all around me everyone was dancing and music was playing.

"Would you like to dance, Velva Jean?" Hink Lowe didn't even bother to take the cigarette out of his mouth. He just talked right around it, so that it bobbed up and down when he spoke. He had grown up to look just like his daddy, all elbows and ears and knobby knees and pointy nose.

"No," I said.

It was the fifth time I had been asked and the fifth time I'd said no.

"Stuck up," he said and walked away.

Hink and the Gordon boys and Lou Pigeon and the others had been sniffing around the house now for months. They'd stopped asking for Johnny Clay and they'd started asking for me, but I couldn't stand any of them.

No, I thought. If I'm going to pick someone, it's going to be someone new and dangerous. Someone that makes the hairs stand up on my arms. Not one of these old mountain boys. I was holding out for Roy Acuff or Gary Cooper.

Come one, come all, and rejoice in his name!

The hairs on my neck bristled a little and a voice in my head said *Danger! Danger!* I was so caught off guard that when Daryl Gordon came up behind me and asked me for a dance, I said yes without thinking. That's how far away I was in my mind.

~

According to Johnny Clay, the Glory Pioneers were a God-fearing, devil-hating people who shunned music and dance and fun of any kind. He had heard one of them preach on the radio and said the man was so wild that just hearing the name Glory Pioneers gave me a case of the shivers. For a name so joyful, they sounded like wicked, frightening people. I pictured dangerous moonlight rituals, animal sacrifices, and the drinking of blood.

Glory Pioneers.

The night I saw the sign at Deal's, I lay in bed and said it again and again, enjoying the prickling sensation the words caused at the back of my neck.

Glory Pioneers.

It was too good to be true that these mysterious people were actually coming all the way to my very own valley. I heard the preacher was from somewhere else—"off somewhere," as Aunt Bird called it, which was what she called anyplace that wasn't on Fair Mountain—and he was supposed to be young and handsome and possessed by the spirit of God.

I didn't sleep at all. I got up before the rooster and slipped out before breakfast, before anyone else was up. I opened the door to Johnny Clay's room, but it was empty. I went downstairs and he wasn't in the kitchen or the front room or on the porch. I went outside and searched the barn, and then I went down to Cobber's Creek and found him panning for gold.

"I want to go to that revival," I said. "But I know Sweet Fern will say we're to stay away from it. She'll say we're forbidden." Sweet Fern didn't like strangers and she didn't trust people of other religions, even though her own husband was a Baptist.

Johnny Clay didn't say anything because he was concentrating. He had the pan under the water and his hands were working below the surface.

For three years, I had been on my best behavior, trying to get along with Sweet Fern and not upset her because of the way Johnny Clay and me had run away from home, and because of how sorry I was that her whole life had been disrupted by having to raise my brothers and me. On hard days—the days I felt sorriest for her—she got out the catalog plans for her future house and looked at them, her chin in her hand. "Someday," she would say, "I'm going to be here with all my babies— my own babies, not you and your brothers." She would point to each of the rooms one by one. Then she would fold up the plans and put them back in the cloth wrapper she had made just for them and walk around sighing and looking sad the rest of the day.

I had been on my best behavior because of those catalog plans all folded up in that cloth wrapper, but I had reached my limit. I said to Johnny Clay, "I really want to go."

Johnny Clay swished the pan back and forth. His arms were wet and shining in the sun. "Let's us go without telling her then," he said.

I could barely sleep the night before. I just lay in bed, wide awake, staring at the ceiling and scaring myself nearly to death, picturing the Glory Pioneers. Would they be dangerous? Would they be wicked? Would they be as fierce as Johnny Clay said? It was thrilling just imagining them. I wasn't sure what would happen to me at the revival, but I had a feeling, deep in the pit of my stomach where my good, true feelings come from, that it would be something *big*.

~

The mountains were dark except for the lanterns made out of brown root beer bottles hanging from the trees, the lightning bugs that dotted the blackness with twinkling pinpricks of light, and the moon reflected on the surface of nearby Three Gum River.

I stood in front of one of the benches lined up beneath the brush arbor, hymnal open in my hands, sawdust shavings covering the ground under my feet. The musty, bittersweet smell of the shavings burned my nose and helped keep me awake. It was warm, even for June. The air was still and sticky hot.

"We're going up there when the healing starts," Johnny Clay said.

"All right," I said.

"And you go up there with a limp and pretend to be lame. And I'll pretend to be blind. Then when he lays his hands on us to heal us, we switch and pretend he's made you blind and made me lame." He laughed at this and I couldn't help it, it made me laugh, too. Johnny Clay never did care about his mortal soul. "You promised," he said again.

"All right," I said. I wanted him to be quiet so I could concentrate. I was feeling nervous and excited, and his talking was getting on my nerves.

Johnny Clay had said the Glory Pioneers didn't believe in celebrating God with music, but here they were, songbooks in hand, singing loud as you please.

So far the Glory Pioneers were a big disappointment. They didn't at all live up to their name and the legend I'd created for them in my imagination. They looked like normal people, just as shabby and down home as me and Johnny Clay. I hadn't seen one bloodletting or even a hint of animal sacrifice.

After the hymn singing was over, we all took our seats and I lowered myself onto the hard wooden bench. I was starting to envy the people sitting on the ground. Because so many people had come to the revival and there wasn't enough room on the benches, some folks sat on quilts that were spread out over the sawdust shavings. Except for my own family, it looked like everyone from Sleepy Gap and Fair Mountain—and then some—had turned out. I didn't recognize half of them and figured they must have come down from Witch and Bone and Blood mountains and from Devil's Courthouse too.

"Fellow pioneers, please join me in welcoming the Reverend Harley Bright." I jumped at the sound of the man's voice. He was short, small as a boy, only with thick blond hair and stubble so you knew he was full grown. He was so short that I wondered if he might not be the shortest person in the world, shorter even than Iona, "the Human Baby Doll," who was only thirty-four inches tall. I'd seen her at the fair when I was thirteen and liked her almost as much as the armless fiddler who played the violin with his feet.

A tall man came forward and placed his hand on the short man's shoulder. He had to stoop a little to reach it. "Welcome, everyone." Suddenly, the congregation was standing again. I couldn't see his face, but I could tell the preacher was young and dark. He wore a pair of gray pants and a white shirt with the sleeves rolled up. He looked like he had just stepped right out of the audience. He opened his arms wide, the Bible clutched in one hand. "How wonderful to see so many pioneers of glory before me on this night, this beautiful night." He was quiet and calm. He motioned for us to sit.

"They call him the Hurricane Preacher," someone whispered behind me.

The Hurricane Preacher. This sent a chill up my spine. Maybe the revival wouldn't be a complete disappointment after all.

"'Thou shalt not tempt the Lord thy God.'" The preacher stood before us, one hand extended, the other holding the Bible to his chest. He emphasized each word and there was an undercurrent of something in his voice—anger, defiance.

As he stood facing me, I sat up straight on the bench. It was the moonshiner's boy. Or he used to be, last time I saw him three years ago. Only he was different. He was clean and confident. He was a grown man now—tall and broad with shadow on his chin. He looked like he'd stepped right out of a movie magazine, every bit as handsome as Gary Cooper. I wondered what he was playing at, with his face and hands washed, pretending to be a preacher, calling himself a Glory Pioneer.

"I'll be a son of a bitch," Johnny Clay said, and I knew he'd recognized him, too.

Even from where I sat, I could see that his eyes were a sharp, bright green. My own eyes were a mixture of green, brown, and gold like they couldn't decide what to be. Mama's eyes had looked just like a sunflower set against a soft blue sky. Johnny Clay's were as dark as coffee. But this man's eyes were like flashes of clear green fire.

I sat up perfectly straight because Granny said that made you seem majestic, like an Indian princess, and I carefully fingered my hair to make sure it hadn't curled too much in the humidity. The Reverend Harley Bright. *Reverend Harley Bright.* It sounded divine.

"'Get thee hence, Satan: for it is written, thou shalt worship the Lord thy God, and him only shalt thou serve.'" The moonshiner's boy skimmed the crowd. He seemed to be daring us to argue with him, daring us not to respond. "Who do you think you're worshipping when you partake of worldly things? The Lord thy God?" He laughed and shook his head. "Who do you think you're honoring when you drink or smoke tobacco or steal from your neighbor? Who do you think you're celebrating by dancing or shortening your hemline or painting your face?"

Even though I knew he was a no-good moonshiner's boy who smoked tobacco and had dirt under his fingernails and who had gone to jail and prison more than once, I could feel my cheeks turning pink. I tugged my skirt down over my knees and thought of the Magnet Red lipstick that was on its way to me, the one I'd ordered from an advertisement in one of Ruby Poole's movie magazines. I was afraid the Reverend Harley Bright would see the guilt on my face. If he knew about Magnet Red, he would probably never want anything to do with me. He would think I was a wicked, shameless woman like the women who lived in cities. I wondered if I could send the lipstick back.

"Who do you think you're gratifying by swearing or cheating or fighting? Jesus? *No!*" Several people jumped. "Satan!" He pointed at a lady in the front row. "Satan!" He pointed at an old man to his left. "You don't honor the Lord by dishonoring yourself, you only honor Satan." There were gasps. One lady fanned herself and another one dabbed at her upper lip with a handkerchief. "Get thee hence, Satan!" the Reverend Bright shouted, and waved the Bible up at the roof of the brush arbor.

There were mutterings and stirrings from the crowd.

Johnny Clay nudged me in the ribs but I ignored him. I was thinking that I hoped I was good enough for the Reverend Harley Bright and that he wouldn't find me common or sinful or shameful in any way. I thought I would write to the company that had sold me the lipstick just as soon as I got home that night. I wouldn't even wait for it to get there before telling them I didn't want it.

"What do you call a man who makes and sells whiskey in sight of his home—in sight of his own wife and child—and has done time in jail? Would you say he's worshipping the Lord or that he's courting the devil?"

"The devil, oh Jesus." An old woman in a blue dress began to cry, her shoulders shaking, her hands pressed to her face.

I wondered if there was any way the Reverend Harley Bright could find out I had ordered Magnet Red even if I was able to stop them from sending it to me. I was angry at myself now for doing something so vain, so reckless. Why hadn't I saved my money for something else—like a new Bible or a shape-note hymnal, something Jesus himself would have approved of?

" 'Watch therefore: for ye know not what hour your Lord doth come.' But the important thing is that he *doth* come! There is work to be done to ensure that you welcome him, not push him away."

A trickle of sweat made its way from my neck down the small of my back. My face was hot and damp and my hair was starting to curl, but the paper fan with the Bible scene lay still in my lap because I couldn't move. I felt rooted in place, like all my limbs had gone to sleep.

"But let us be careful of false fronts, of trickery, of those who misrepresent themselves as children of God. Like the men from the cities who are coming here to these mountains—our mountains—tearing down our houses and cutting down our trees and taking what belongs to us, even though they say they're building this road for us, to give us work and to help connect us to the rest of the world. Well, we didn't ask for work and we didn't ask to be connected. Jesus said, 'Take heed that no man deceive you. For many shall come in my name, saying, I am Christ; and shall deceive many.' Let us not be among the deceivers and let us not be deceived."

I wondered if it was deceitful to order a lipstick and then send it back before you even had a chance to try it on. I wondered if it was deceitful to do that and then pretend like nothing ever happened and like you hadn't even done it in the first place.

"Do we dare deceive? No! Do we dare be deceived? No!" The Reverend Harley Bright wiped his damp brow with a handkerchief and stared directly at me.

The palms of my hands started tingling and I felt my stomach jump like there were bugs inside it. My face started to burn so hot that I wanted to crawl under my seat. He looked at me like he recognized me, like he knew I was there all along, like he had every right to look at me, like he could see into my mind and into my heart. I thought I was going to faint right there on the pew. *Please God*, I thought, *don't let him know.*

"I am asking that you join me in banishing Satan, that you join me in worshipping and praising God, that you cast aside your sinfulness and realize your goodness, that you let me help you reach for that goodness, and that you reach deep inside yourselves and pull out the good and the true." Then he raised his Bible and pointed it so clearly and obviously at me that people turned around to stare. "I am asking that you hasten to God's side and get right with him and shun the devil."

He closed his eyes then and I slumped against the back of the bench. He had been talking right to me.

The preacher held up his hands, one palm open, the other embracing the Bible. He spoke loud and fast. "Jesus said, 'Go ye into all the world, and preach the gospel to every creature. He that shall believeth and is baptized shall be saved; but he that believeth not shall be damned.'" The word "damned" nearly rattled the rafters of the brush arbor and rang through the air like a small explosion.

We were all on our feet with the force of his words. I could see why he was called the Hurricane Preacher. I felt like he was reaching out from his pulpit and wrapping that voice of his—afire with damnation and the promise of salvation—around my neck like a glittering scarf. It was like he'd been speaking just to me—only to me—and for a moment, he had been.

He took up his guitar and started to sing "The Glory Song," only he changed the words of the verses, making up his own words to suit the day and the crowd and the sermon. He left the chorus the same. He closed his eyes and he banged the guitar and his voice was strong and rough.

Afterward he announced the altar call and those that wanted saving went forward to receive it. I got up and walked to the front with most everyone else. Johnny Clay got up and walked behind me.

The line was moving slow across the stage. The Reverend Harley Bright was shaking people's hands and touching their foreheads and saying prayers over every person. Each one went off crying and raising their hands, praising the preacher and Jesus. Johnny Clay poked me. He said, "You can be blind if you'd rather. I don't care."

I said, "I don't think he's healing people like that. I'm just going to shake his hand."

Johnny Clay didn't say anything for a minute. I didn't turn around or look at him. I could hear what he was thinking. I could hear him being mad. Then he said, real low, "Where's the fun in that?"

I stood there waiting my turn, waiting for the Reverend Harley Bright to lay his hands on me and make me whole again. When he finally touched me—his hand on my forehead—it was quick but electric. He pressed something into my hand. A handkerchief. It was folded into a square. It smelled like lilacs. On it was written: "Special Miracle."

Johnny Clay and I sat back down and watched as the rest of the people made their way across the stage. Johnny Clay slumped down low in his seat. He was sulking, but I didn't care because I knew then that I was in love. It would be forever, and it would be true, and it would be the most glorious, powerful thing on earth.

I had already been saved once, back in 1933. But now, on the banks of that very same river where I thought I had found salvation, I had just been saved for a second time.

~

Johnny Clay and I sneaked away every night that week to go to the revival, and Sweet Fern didn't find out. On the very last night, after the service, the short man walked up to us where we sat and said, "The Reverend Bright would like to see you." He looked right at me when he said it. Something about him was familiar. I thought of the day we followed the bad Barrow gang, of the moonshiner's boy and his skinny friend and his fat friend and his short friend, the one that was small as a child.

"What does he want?" Johnny Clay said.

"He likes to meet the members of his congregation," the man said. "Especially two such faithful attendants as you."

I looked at Johnny Clay and his eyebrows shot up. "He's already met her. You were there. You both met her that day I beat the tar out of him in Alluvial."

The short man didn't say anything to this, just started coughing. When he was done, he stood frowning up at us, waiting.

Johnny Clay turned to me. I gave him my sweetest look. He said, "Fine."

The Reverend Bright was sitting in a chair behind the altar, waving a fan back and forth, back and forth at his temple. His eyes were closed. I thought how smooth and white his skin was now that it was free of all that dirt, and how I wished I could reach out and touch it.

"Harley," said the short man.

The Reverend Bright opened his eyes and smiled. It was a smile that spread across his whole face. He stood and I tilted my head up to look at him. He was still taller than Johnny Clay by a half inch, something I knew would only make Johnny Clay madder. Harley Bright held out his hand to my brother, who almost didn't take it, and then he turned to me and did the funniest thing—he bowed.

"Prettiest face on Fair Mountain," he said right to me. I just looked at his own face, the way one side dimpled when he smiled, and the way he cocked his head to the side and kind of lifted one eyebrow in a way that made him seem real and human and more like the moonshiner's boy and less like the Hurricane Preacher.

Johnny Clay cleared his throat. He scratched the back of his neck where it was sunburned. "You preach a good sermon," he said loudly.

"You enjoyed yourselves, then?" the moonshiner's boy was staring right at me, just like he'd stared at me during his sermon on the first day of the revival.

"Oh yes," I heard myself say. "Yes."

"I like to make a difference where I can," he said. He looked at me like he was waiting for something.

"You did. It was . . ." I knew what I wanted to say but I wasn't sure whether I should say it, especially in front of Johnny Clay, who would never let me hear the end of it. I lifted my right foot and scratched the back of my left calf, where the panther scar was. It still itched sometimes. The reverend just looked at me, his mouth crooked up in a grin. He looked at me like he knew me and like he understood and like whatever I was going to say was fine with him. So finally I said, "It was like you were talking right to me."

~

When I opened my eyes the next morning, the first thing I saw was the framed picture Johnny Clay had given me for my last birthday. It was the first thing I saw every morning, propped up on the chest of drawers next to the bottle of perfume from Ruby Poole: Paris, by Coty ("a perfume that knows how to be tender and sparkling, witty and feminine, all in the same fragrant moment . . ."). It was a framed photograph of the Grand Ole Opry stage, empty except for a microphone.

"That's where you'll be one day, Velva Jean," Johnny Clay had said. "See there? That's where you'll stand."

It was the best present I'd ever got, and I loved to stare and stare at it until I could see myself on the stage, dressed up in my rhinestone outfit and holding my Hawaiian steel guitar.

For as long as I could remember, being on that stage had been my biggest dream, and after a while, my only one. But now I had two dreams. I was still going to be Velva Jean Hart, star of the Grand Ole Opry, but I was also going to be something else. I didn't know if I would ever see the Reverend Harley Bright again. But I'd made up my mind that if I ever did, I was going to be his wife.

FIFTEEN

Work on the Scenic had made its way south from Deep Gap all the way down to Bull Gap, right around Weaverville, just north of Asheville. Johnny Clay climbed up to Old Widow's Peak nearly every day with a set of binoculars that Daddy had brought him years ago, and then he came back down and gave us a report over supper. The binoculars barely worked anymore and you couldn't see far with them, but he swore he could see the construction men at work—boys as young as him and men as old as Daddy—cutting down trees and blasting through the mountain and making way for the road to come.

When I looked through the binoculars myself, I couldn't see a thing, but Johnny Clay said I was doing it wrong and didn't know how to use them. What I didn't tell him was that I wasn't trying to see Bull Gap. I was trying to look at Devil's Courthouse. I thought maybe those binoculars would pick up the moonshiner's house in Devil's Kitchen, and maybe I could see the Reverend Harley Bright. Now that the revival was over, I wondered if I would ever see him again.

Whether you could see it or not, the way that road was making its way down toward us had everyone on edge. The flags were back on Devil's Courthouse. I thought about going up there again and taking them down and burying them, but I knew somehow it wouldn't matter. They would only keep planting more.

Hink Lowe said the Scenic was a rich man's road. Root Caldwell said it was a sign of the devil. Old Buck Frey said he didn't care if there was a depression and they were giving people jobs, it just wasn't worth it—they were taking away more than they were giving. Even Uncle Turk said it would be the end of us. He said the government was trying to run that road right through the Indian nation to the gates of the Great Smoky Mountains National Park. The Cherokee were fighting it and he was joining them. On June 25, he packed up his gems and his polishing tools and all his earthly belongings and moved to the reservation.

On June 27, we got a postcard from Beach: "Am working on the Scenic near Altapass. Earning thirty cents per hour, six days a week. Digging stumps out of steep slopes, laying drainage tile in the mud, lifting five-hundred-pound rocks with hand cranes, planting trees and shrubs and flowers. Have been spreading my message up here where all can see. No sign of Daddy. Love, Beach."

~

One week after the revival, on Saturday, June 29, there was a rumble like far-off thunder, even though the sun was out and it didn't look like rain. The rumble grew louder and louder, like it was coming fast toward us, and I rushed out of the house, followed by Sweet Fern, Granny, and Johnny Clay. We stood there watching the cloud of dust that rolled toward us. Behind it came an automobile, a dark blue one.

Other than Danny Deal's truck and Dr. Keller's truck, we'd never seen an automobile this high up the mountain before. I couldn't imagine who it could belong to. The car came to a stop in front of the porch, and as the dust settled, the Reverend Harley Bright opened the door and swung his long legs out, the other half of him still leaning into the mirror.

"My goodness," Sweet Fern said. "Who on earth?" Her voice trailed off. I suddenly felt my face grow hot. My palms tingled, just like they had when I'd first seen the Reverend Bright, and I could feel my heart start to race. I'd never imagined he would come to call or that I would ever even see him again.

"It's the moonshiner's boy," Johnny Clay said. "From the revival."

"Revival?" said Sweet Fern. "Moonshiner's boy?"

"He's turned preacher," said Johnny Clay.

Sweet Fern fixed a look on Johnny Clay, on me, on Johnny Clay again, her eyebrows shooting up toward her hair. "What in the great blue yonder would a revival preacher want with you?"

"Oh, I don't think he wants me," Johnny Clay said.

Sweet Fern looked straight at me and only at me. Before she could say anything, Granny gave a low whistle. "All the way up here. And in an automobile."

Sweet Fern stared back at the car and at the man inside it and suddenly I could see exactly what she was thinking. Moonshiner's boy or no moonshiner's boy, revival preacher or no revival preacher, Harley Bright looked like a gentleman. Danny Deal's yellow pickup truck wasn't anywhere as nice as this blue automobile.

Johnny Clay muttered something and went back into the house. I stood there thinking that never in my life did I expect a man like Harley Bright to come calling on me, much less in a car.

Granny cleared her throat. "Don't think you're riding in it," she said.

"Certainly not," said Sweet Fern. "You'll stay right here and entertain him on the porch." But her eyes were bright like the gold found at the bottom of Johnny Clay's gold pans.

As the Reverend Harley Bright walked toward us, I thought that I was just like a girl in a movie. I suddenly felt glamorous and grown up, as if I was wearing a pretty new dress and had no freckles. Just look how fancy.

"Afternoon, Miss Hart," he said. *Miss Hart.* He pulled a spray of flowers from behind his back and held them out to me. He was wearing the same gray pants and white shirt from the revival, and on his head he was wearing a hat tipped down at an angle. He looked right at Granny and Sweet Fern. "I wondered if I could sit with her for a while."

Sweet Fern held his gaze for several seconds and then nodded. "That would be fine." She was putting on her best manners, the kind she reserved for company.

Harley Bright and I sat down on the porch, my bare legs swinging over the side. Granny and Sweet Fern watched and listened through the open door. I had never talked to a man before, not a grown-up man like this who looked at me in a way that made my stomach jump. I tried to remind myself that he was wicked and forward, that he was just a dirty moonshiner's boy who'd been to jail and who said things he shouldn't, who didn't care if his own mama lived or died and who was fresh to girls he barely knew. I sat there and tried to hate him.

He didn't say anything and I didn't say anything. He reached in his pocket for a cigarette. Then he took his hat off, setting it next to him on the porch. He ran his fingers through his hair. He lit the cigarette and took a drag.

I thought he couldn't possibly be interested in the things me and Johnny Clay talked about—spies and murderers and movie stars and the Grand Ole Opry and playing tricks on Sweet Fern—so for a long while I just sat and said nothing.

"Look," he said finally. "I hope you know that what my daddy does, that ain't me."

I thought about the old man with the still in the woods and the fat woman on the porch.

"Does he still make and sell moonshine?" I said.

"Yeah."

"Have you tried to save him?"

"Mama has, but he ain't interested." The cigarette hung on his lip as he rolled his shirtsleeves up to his elbows. He smoked for a minute. "You know, I done things in my life that I'm not proud of. I ran wild for a long time."

I said, "I remember."

He laughed.

I said, "Don't you preach against tobacco?"

He said, "Yeah. Nasty habit." He winked at me and took a long drag. Then he pinched the cigarette out and wrapped it up. Then he began to talk. He said he didn't usually like to talk about himself—as a rule, he didn't like anyone knowing his business—but for some reason he found himself talking to me more than he'd ever remembered talking to anyone, outside of giving a sermon. He told me about Devil's Kitchen, about the legends and myths of the place itself, and what it was like to grow up with a mama telling you the devil was close by, ready to come get you if you did something bad or wicked. He told me about working on the railroad, which he still did, and of his mama and his daddy—how he couldn't stand either one of them—and he told me about all the places he'd been to preach.

I was happy just to listen and to sit there beside him. He was even better looking close-up, and he smelled fresh and clean, like soap with a hint of tobacco. He sat with his palms flat against the porch, on either side of his legs, and his feet hanging down in front of him. His shoes were so shiny they caught the reflection of the sun. The veins in his arms tensed whenever he leaned forward or shifted. He had a way of gazing out into the horizon like he could see what lay past it.

He said, "How old were you when your mama died?"

This took me by surprise. "Ten." I was fifteen now, but I didn't miss my mama any less. If anything, I missed her more. I wondered if Harley Bright would think five years was too long to be sad about someone dying. I wished I could tell him I lost my mama last week or even last year so he would know how much it still hurt.

"Was it after you came up for the whiskey?"

"Not long after."

He nodded.

I turned my face away and stared out at the trees. I hadn't planned on talking about Mama. Even though I couldn't stand Sweet Fern, sometimes I liked to pretend that she or Granny was my real mother and that I'd never had one that died and went away.

Harley Bright was watching me. "I had three brothers that died before I was born." He looked down at his hands. "I miss them," he said to the trees. "That probably don't make sense. But I think about them all the time."

I didn't speak a word. I didn't move. I barely breathed. "It does make sense," I said finally. He looked at me and then he looked away again.

"It broke my mama's heart." His brow pinched up in the space above his eyes. "It nearly killed her. A baby born dead means a taint in the blood or a taint in the moral life of the parents. That's how Mama saw it. She blamed herself. She blamed Daddy more. The doctors said I wouldn't live."

"But here you are."

"Here I am." He smiled. I liked how white his teeth were and the way the little lines around his eyes crinkled.

"I didn't think I'd live after my mama died," I said. "I felt like I died, too." I had never told that to anyone, not even Johnny Clay.

"Ten years old is too young to lose a mama," Harley Bright said.

I nodded. I was afraid if I said anything I might start crying, and even though I didn't know much about how to act with a man, I knew that crying probably wasn't something you should do. At least not the first time he came to call on you.

"But here you are." He was smiling at me. I smiled back. I glanced at his hands, strong and rough and graceful, and wondered what it would be like to hold one of them. I couldn't believe I was sitting with the Hurricane Preacher, the moonshiner's boy, and that he was gentle and sweet. He hadn't said one fresh thing.

And then, for some reason, I opened my mouth and started talking. "When Mama died, everyone said things happen for a reason, that it was part of God's plan and that he needed her in heaven. It used to make me mad when they said that because I needed her here on earth, and what kind of plan takes a mama away from her children? What kind of plan takes three little babies away from their mama? What reason could there be for something like that?" What reason could there possibly be for leaving me with Sweet Fern?

He unwrapped the cigarette and lit it back up again. "Sometimes we don't know it right off." He took a long drag on the cigarette and then he blew the smoke out in circles. Without thinking, I stuck my finger through the middle, which made the circles break off into snakes that slithered away, and he laughed. "Do you still believe in the Lord?" he asked. "After all he's taken from you?"

"Of course I believe," I said. I didn't want the Reverend Harley

Bright to know that I ever questioned the Lord, even if Harley Bright, the moonshiner's boy, might understand. "God didn't take Mama from me." *My daddy did.* I looked down at my feet so that he couldn't read what I was thinking. They were stained red and brown with dirt. His shoes swung back and forth, shining bright in the sun. Please don't ask about my daddy, I thought. I didn't want him knowing my daddy had left when I was eleven and never come back, that I wasn't wanted by my own father. If Harley Bright knew that, he might think something was wrong with me and then leave and never talk to me again.

I said, "They say his voice is a trumpet that heralds great things. That it can open the doors to heaven, as long as you're willing to listen." It was something Mama had told me once.

We sat in silence. The flowers he gave me were making the air smell sweet. My head was spinning a little from the scent of them, from his cigarette, from him. The only sound was the click of Sweet Fern's knitting needles from inside the house.

"I can tell you something right now, Velva Jean Hart," he said. It thrilled me to hear him say my full name. The Reverend Harley Bright was looking into my eyes, so deep and intense that I had to think to breathe. In the sunlight, his green eyes were clear and sparkling, like Three Gum River in the shallows. His dark hair waved across his forehead in the heat. There were little dots of sweat along his brow and on his upper lip. His voice was steady and firm. "Reason or no reason, plan or no plan, nothing on earth would ever make me leave you."

~

The Reverend Bright came over every evening for the next three weeks, and we sat on my porch and talked. Once in a while, we walked—never drove—down to Deal's to get a soda, and Johnny Clay always came with us so that we wouldn't be alone.

Every night when we got home, Johnny Clay would start in. "What do you see in that slick-talking weasel?"

"Shut up, Johnny Clay," I told him before closing the door to my room and pulling the covers up over my head to let him know I wasn't speaking to him anymore. The only thing I didn't like about being courted by Harley Bright was that Johnny Clay couldn't seem to stand him.

"Be nice," I'd tell my brother just before Harley came to call. "I mean it. You better behave."

He would cross his arms and roll his eyes, and it got to where I had to ignore him when I was with Harley and just pretend that he wasn't there at all.

"Johnny Clay's just jealous," Sweet Fern told me. "He likes having you all to himself. All his life, it's been just you and him, and now he can't stand someone getting in the middle."

Harley wanted to take me to a restaurant in Hamlet's Mill, but Granny and Sweet Fern said absolutely not—they wouldn't let him drive me anywhere. "A car's no place for a lady," Granny said. She herself had never set foot in a car and, at seventy-two years old, she didn't plan to. She went everywhere on the back of Mad Maggie, her mule.

Because we couldn't go to all the places he wanted to take me, Harley would tell me about them in detail so that I could picture them. My very favorite was an inn in Balsam, twenty-five miles down the track, where he said they served the finest steak in Carolina, large and lean and smothered in a lime-pepper sauce. My mouth watered every time he told me about it, and I said, "One day I'm going to go there and eat one for myself."

Harley smiled at me then, so sweet I almost cried. "And I'm going to take you."

One night we took an old blanket and sat out under the stars a few feet from the house. Johnny Clay sat down in the rocking chair up on the porch, watching us. We talked low so he couldn't hear.

I pointed to the sky. It was nearly black except for the moon and the stars that were sprinkled across it like jewels. Mrs. Dennis had taught us about the stars, and one time, back when I was in seventh grade, we'd all met down at school at night and climbed onto the roof and she showed us where they were, one by one. "That right there," I said to Harley now, "is the North Star. It's the only star in the sky that never moves." I lowered my arm and we stared upward.

"Mama always said that things are written up there in the stars for each of us, that everyone has a story and it's all right there waiting," I whispered. I'd always wanted to believe it, but I'd never been sure. I knew it was written in the stars for me to be a singer, but had it been written somewhere that Mama should die when she did and leave us orphans? We leaned back on our elbows. I could feel Harley's arm pressed against mine, feel the material of his shirt against my skin.

After a long moment, Harley said, "My mama said I was chosen by the Lord to be a preacher. She said I was destined." He sounded matter-of-fact, even a little cold. He rarely talked about his mama.

I stared at his profile, the way it was lit up by the glow of the stars and the moon.

"I nearly died when I was born," he said, "just like my brothers. I guess I told you that already. I was puny and weak and the doctor said I wouldn't live. Mama prayed over me and made a promise to the Lord that if he would spare my life she would make sure I entered God's service. All the other preachers I know were called by Jesus. But I was called by Mama." He shifted, brushing closer against me so I felt warm and weak all over. His voice got big and loud and irritated. "'Your brothers died so that you could lead,' she said. 'You cannot let them down.'"

"How old were you when she called you?" I asked.

"Five. Maybe six. But I didn't start listening till I was sixteen." He said, "I always wondered why I lived when my brothers didn't. Mama said I lived for a purpose, but I always thought that was her way of making herself feel better because they died."

I thought about living for a purpose and how mine was to sing at the Grand Ole Opry. Daddy Hoyt's was to heal, Granny's was to deliver babies, Linc's was to farm, and Beachard's was to spread the word of God as far and wide as he could, writing messages like "Find Jesus" and "Search for the Lord" on rocks, trees, railroad trestles, and old rundown buildings. Johnny Clay's purpose changed all the time, but he always had one. Like being a pilot or a cowboy or a gold-panning champion. I guessed Sweet Fern's purpose was to have babies and make my life miserable. My mama's purpose had been to love and be loved.

Harley went on: "I got so sick of living for a purpose. I did every wicked thing I knew to do because it made Mama mad. Mama said parties and dancing would only lead you to the devil. So I danced and I drank. She said Daddy was going straight to hell for making whiskey, but he's always been nicer than her so I helped him make moonshine. She said stealing was wrong and sinful, so I stole. She said music went against God, that it was a sin to sing. So I took up guitar and sang as loud as I could. She said don't smoke tobacco, so I smoke. She said home is where the heart is, that my duty is to my mama and daddy who only got but one child, and that I got to stay close and look after them. So I took a job on the railroad when I was twelve. I lied about my age, told them I was older than I was, so they would hire me. I took the most dangerous job I could think of—fireman—just to make my mama worry. If there's a wreck on the line, it's the engineer and me that are the ones most likely to get hurt or killed. I knew that would keep her up at night."

He laughed, but I could tell he felt uncomfortable. "I'm telling you every bad thing. If Sweet Fern could hear me. Or your brother up there, trying so hard to listen."

"I don't care," I said. And I didn't. Sitting next to him was more exciting than sitting with the Wood Carver who was an actual murderer. I felt a thrill right down to my bare red-brown toes.

"Well," he said. "When I was sixteen, the freight stopped in Clearwater. There was a Baptist preacher holding a revival right there by the tracks. He shouted and the people screamed and fell to the ground. Every word was bullshit, pulled out of his ass to make those people love him. But they needed it. They were lost souls, all of them, poor and miserable and hungry. I knew just how they felt. I was one of them. That preacher gave them what they needed to hear and when he left, you should have seen them—they looked like the richest folks in the world. And so did he, and not just because of the money he collected. That was when I knew I'd found my calling. I wanted to do that, to reach people that needed it, even if I had no idea what I was talking about. I wish I could tell you I was called by some higher power, but I wasn't. I just wanted to do what that preacher did. Make money and make people feel good."

"Did you ever want to have a church of your own?" I knew he traveled from town to town, up and down the mountains, and sometimes over into Tennessee. I knew he went on his own and sometimes he went with the Glory Pioneers.

He just shook his head. He stared up at the North Star again. "I want to reach as many people as I can, not just the same old souls every week. I just want to preach the word of God, as best I can, anywhere people will listen. The fellas on the railroad call me Preacher of the Rails. Each town we stop in, I blow the engine whistle as a call to prayer and then I preach to whoever answers."

Something came over me then. I couldn't help it. I suddenly wondered if he had a girl in every town, on every mountain, a girl just like me he sat with under the stars and told things to. A girl who thrilled at the touch of his shirt sleeve against her bare skin or the shine of his shoes in the moonlight. A girl who loved the smell of his soap and tobacco and the way he swore and sometimes fell silent when he felt like he was talking too much. I wondered if he called on these girls in his blue car, if he brought them flowers he picked or a cold Cheerwine because he knew it was their favorite.

I sat there and thought this, and the more I thought it, the more upset I felt. How dare he come up here and make me care about him. How dare he make me think I was special when there were hundreds of other girls just like me sprinkled all over these mountains. Girls without freckles. Girls who weren't orphans. Girls with daddies who stayed home and didn't wander off. Girls with pretty dresses and clean feet. Girls with nice sisters and brothers who were polite and cordial and made him feel welcome. Girls who didn't order lipsticks from catalogs. While I was sitting there, frowning down toward the ground, he sat up and took my hand.

"I almost didn't preach here in Alluvial," he said. "My mama says, 'There's nothing up there in those mountains—all the ones but Devil's Courthouse, of course—but a bunch of holy rollers and heathens, no better than a flock of geese.'" He said it in such a funny voice that we both laughed. Then he looked right into my eyes and I felt a chill run through me. "But maybe the Spirit actually called me."

No, I thought, *it was written*. And then I looked down at our hands, the fingers laced and intertwined. The sight of them was almost more wonderful than the feel of his flesh on mine. You almost couldn't tell whose hands were whose by looking at them.

SIXTEEN

On a clear blue morning one month later, Daddy Hoyt found me sweeping the front porch. After that it was help Linc round up the cattle and bring them home. And then, if there was time, help Sweet Fern with the sewing. Today, though, I didn't mind the work because later I would see Harley and the world was bright, just like it had been ever since he'd first come calling. Today I didn't even mind Sweet Fern.

Daddy Hoyt had on his herb-gathering pants, overalls with what seemed like a hundred pockets, which meant he would spend the day in the woods, collecting the plants he needed, and not reappear till sundown. He cleared his throat and I stopped sweeping. "That boy came to me at dawn, Velva Jean, and asked me for your hand."

I felt my stomach leap, but I didn't say anything because Daddy Hoyt looked serious and he wasn't smiling. My heart started beating so fast I thought I was going to have to sit down.

"I told him you were too young, that he'd have to wait till you were sixteen, but he's got his heart set on marrying you. He said he'll wait forever, as long as it takes." He walked up onto the porch, kicking one boot and then the other against the steps, careful not to track dirt where I'd swept. He lifted my chin in his hand and looked right into my eyes. "Your daddy may have left Sweet Fern in charge of you all, but your mama asked me to look after you. She laid in there in that bed and took my hand and said, 'Daddy, you watch over them after I go to heaven.'"

The tears came and I tried to blink them away. "Mama told me she'd be here to see the big things happen."

"And she is. She's still around you, Velva Jean. But she can't give her blessing to this young man. That's for me to do."

Daddy Hoyt pulled out his handkerchief and dabbed at my eyes. His hands were big but gentle. "You hardly ever ask me for a thing, Velva Jean, so if you ask me for this I know it's important. I can't say no to you. I want you to think good and hard about this. I got my reservations, but I'm not marrying him. I'm not living with him. I'm not the one that's got to be with him for the rest of my life. All I ask is that you're sure."

I wanted to say, I'm sure! I'm sure! I was surer than I'd ever been about anything. But I kept silent.

"When I married your grandmother, I knew I could have done without everything but her if I'd had to." I thought of something Ruby Poole had said once, when I asked her how on earth she could live in Sleepy Gap after coming from such a big city. She said that she would live in a tree as long as she could be with Linc. I finally knew just what she meant. I thought I would love to live in a tree with Harley. I thought I would live with him anywhere.

Then I remembered Mama telling me to "live out there," and I wondered if this was what she meant. I couldn't imagine anything more exciting or wide open or big than loving Harley Bright. I thought about my daddy and how I hoped he was safe somewhere even after all he'd done to Mama and to us, and I thought about how I used to think I'd never feel this happy ever again.

"You're choosing for life," Daddy Hoyt said.

"I know," I said.

We stood there not talking. *I'm sure. I'm sure.*

He sighed and stretched his head back so he was looking at the ceiling of the porch. I looked up, too. There were still little bright blue aster flecks where Mama had painted it once, long ago—"to keep the bad spirits away." The paint clung to the ceiling and the front door in patches, but it seemed, at last, like the bad spirits were leaving.

~

Harley asked me that night after supper. We were sitting on the front porch and he took my hand and he said, "Velva Jean Hart, I want to spend my life with you. Don't think for a minute I think I deserve you. But I love you, and if you'll have me, I'll spend the rest of my days trying to earn your love in return."

"Don't be silly," I said. "I love you. What do you mean you don't deserve me?"

And just like that, we were engaged.

After Harley left, I sat up waiting for Johnny Clay, who had gone down to Alluvial with the Gordons. Finally, Sweet Fern came out onto the porch.

"You coming to bed, Velva Jean?"

"I'm going to wait up for Johnny Clay."

She leaned against the doorframe. I could tell she wanted to say something—she was the only one of the family who hadn't congratulated me, the only one who hadn't hugged me or said how happy she was over my news. But I knew she had to be happy because now, sooner than later, she and Danny and the children could move down to Deal's to the catalog house Danny would build, and she could just think about herself and her husband and her babies for a change. We'd taken up so much of her life.

For the first time that I could remember, I felt bad for Sweet Fern, for all she had gone through being left with us, a responsibility she didn't want when she already had so much of her own. So I said, "You're such a good wife to Danny. Tell me how to do it. I want more than anything to be a good wife to Harley."

For a moment, I was afraid she was going to cry. Her face started to crumple and her eyes got wet, but then something passed behind them and I could see her draw herself in.

"There's a passage from the Bible that you need to remember," she said, and her voice was soft. "'Who can find a virtuous woman? For her price is far above rubies. The heart of her husband doth safely trust in her, so that he shall have no need of spoil. She will do him good and not evil all the days of her life.' You remember those words, Velva Jean, and you'll do just fine."

~

By midnight, Johnny Clay still wasn't home. I had already added the entry to the family record book: "August 30: Harley Bright proposes to Velva Jean Hart." Now I sat on the front porch steps and counted the stars and tried to remember the constellations. I sang songs, low enough so that I wouldn't wake anyone, and I thought about the kind of wedding I would have.

"I'm going to wear Mama's dress and have Ruby Poole do up my hair," I said to Hunter Firth. "And we'll decorate Sleepy Gap Church with flower garlands, and afterward we'll have singing and dancing till the sun comes up." I scratched him behind the ears and his back leg made a dull thumping on the wood.

By twelve thirty, I thought I would just go inside even though I wasn't sleepy one bit. I was so happy and excited that I doubted I'd ever sleep again. "Good night, brown dog," I said, and kissed him on top of the head. I walked to the door and it was then that I heard a crashing in the trees, up the hill from the house, on the edge of the woods near Mama's grave. It sounded like something had come down from the sky and hit the leaves hard. I froze and listened and there was silence.

"Johnny Clay?" I said, but too soft for anyone to hear but me. Hunter Firth pointed his brown nose at the woods, and I watched as the bristly hairs on his back stood up. "Just a rabbit or a coon," I told him, but I still stood there listening.

Suddenly, there was a scrambling and scraping of leaves, and the sound of something or someone running away. I turned cold down to the bone. Hunter Firth took off after whatever it was, barking and growling.

I watched until he disappeared into the black of the trees. I could still hear him howling, but the sound got further and further away. "Hunter Firth?" I called out. I walked down the porch steps and stood in the yard. I couldn't see that dog anywhere.

Then I saw a shadow come moving up the hill from the direction of

Alluvial. As I watched, it grew larger and larger, and out of it there suddenly came the dark figure of a man. Before I could scream or run back to the house, I recognized the broad shoulders and the gold-brown hair in the moonlight.

"What're you doing, Velva Jean?" Johnny Clay called.

"Waiting for you."

"Something wrong?"

"Just a noise in the woods. Probably an animal. Hunter Firth took off after it." I rubbed my arms where the chill bumps were and told myself it was fine now that Johnny Clay was here and whatever it was had gone away.

"That old dog. He'll go after anything."

We sat down on the steps and watched the woods.

"Why are you waiting up?" Johnny Clay said. He wiped at a dirt spot on his pants.

"Just wanted to see how your night was."

He shrugged. "It was okay."

"Was Alice Nix there?"

"Yeah."

"She's sweet on you."

"She's sweet on everyone."

We sat there. Johnny Clay yawned. I tried to think of a way to tell him what I had to tell him. "Harley Bright asked me to marry him," I said at last.

He stared at me like I had a possum on my head. "You're only fifteen."

"We'll wait till I'm sixteen."

"You said yes?"

"Of course."

"Daddy Hoyt said yes?"

"He asked me if I was sure and I said I was, so he gave us his blessing."

He shook his head. "He just did it because he can't say no to you."

I didn't say anything. But he could probably tell I was getting mad because I squared up my shoulders and narrowed my eyes. Daddy always said I looked like Mama when I was mad—that my eyes and lips disappeared just like hers did.

"Look, Velva Jean, you know how I feel about the Reverend Harley Bright." He said "the Reverend Harley Bright" like he was saying *collards* or *pig innards* or *head lice*, or something else disgusting.

"You'd feel that way about anyone I wanted to marry. Because you're jealous. You want me all to yourself."

"Maybe so. And maybe there's no one good enough for my sister. Maybe if Charles 'Buddy' Rogers came up here himself in that airplane of his from *Wings*, he wouldn't even be good enough. Or Fred Astaire in his dancing shoes. But it ain't just that. It's him, Velva Jean. I don't trust him."

"You said yourself he preaches a good sermon."

"I think he tells people what he thinks they want to hear." I could feel my lips disappearing. "What about the Opry?"

I hadn't even thought about the Opry, but I wasn't about to tell him that. "I'm still going."

"How? You really think he'll let you once you become his wife?"

I shot him my fiercest look, the one I secretly practiced on Sweet Fern when her back was turned. "No one's got to 'let' me do anything, Johnny Clay. I'm still going when I turn eighteen. Now Harley'll just go with me." I thought about what the Wood Carver had said: "There are no straight lines anywhere, and that goes for pathways too."

Johnny Clay laughed. "The Reverend Harley Bright, moonshiner's boy and railroad fireman, in Nashville."

"I'm serious, Johnny Clay."

"Okay, Velva Jean. But I don't see it."

I didn't say anything, just sucked in my lips, narrowed my eyes, and pulled my shoulders back so far that it felt like my shoulder blades were touching.

Johnny Clay sighed. He said, "Does he really make you happy?"

I looked at him then. "Yes."

"And there's nothing I can say?"

"No."

He blinked, looked down at his hands, looked back up at me, up at the stars, and then back at his hands. "Well. I guess what's done is done and I got to live with that."

Hunter Firth came running out of the woods then, his tongue hanging out. He ran right up the steps and jumped into Johnny Clay's lap. We watched that old brown dog as Johnny Clay rubbed him behind the ears. It was easier to watch him than it was to talk to each other right then, so we just looked at him till he closed his eyes and went to sleep.

"It's funny," Johnny Clay said finally.

"What?"

In the moonlight, Johnny Clay looked like both Mama and Daddy. He had Mama's high cheekbones, which was the Cherokee in her, and he had Daddy's strong jaw and straight nose. "When Mama died I promised never to leave you, but now you're getting ready to leave me."

"No I ain't, Johnny Clay." I took his hand and laid my head on his shoulder. "I'm always going to be right here."

"Promise?" he said. His voice sounded sad and distant.

"Promise."

SEVENTEEN

I leaned in close to the bathroom mirror and studied my face. I didn't look any different. "Now I am a woman," I said out loud. But I didn't feel any different either. I wondered if it took a while to sink in. I paused as I was buttoning my dress and pinched at the skin on my chest. Thank God I had grown bosoms after all—not big ones like Sweet Fern's, thank goodness, but not flat ones like Rachel Gordon's either. Now that I was married, I hoped Harley wouldn't expect me to start rouging them like Lucinda Sink. I pinched over and over until my skin was a faint pink and then turned this way and that to see how it looked. I didn't think it did a thing for me.

On November 5, I turned sixteen. On the sixth we were married, and on the seventh we were on our honeymoon, a word I thought every bit as pretty as *ambrosia* or *glory* or *heaven*. *Honeymoon*. I liked to say it to myself over and over again.

The Balsam Mountain Springs Hotel was a three-story Victorian inn. It had been built in 1905 and opened in 1908 as a tourist attraction at the highest railroad depot this side of the Rockies. It sat on twenty-three acres, at 3,500 feet, looking out over the hills and hollers—proud, sprawling, beautiful, so large and lovely and grand that it didn't look real. It was like something from a fairy story.

There was an iron four-poster bed that filled most of the room and a modern bathroom just down the hall that you didn't have to go outside for and that we shared with other guests. On our first night there, we sat in the restaurant and ordered a steak with lime-pepper sauce, one for each of us. It was the best thing I ever tasted and I ate every last bite. Afterward I purchased some picture postcards in the lobby and we went up to one of the long porches that ran the whole length of the inn on the first and second floors, and sat down in rocking chairs. Harley watched me while I wrote a card to every single member of my family—even Celia Faye and Clover, who could barely read—telling them about the bathroom, the inn, the steak, and the train ride there. When I was done with each one, I passed it to him and he signed his name at the bottom right beside mine.

Then we sat there and looked down the hill and across the railroad tracks and out across the holler at the mountains beyond, at the little houses that dotted the hillside—chickens running in the yard, smoke winding from chimneys, figures moving in and out of barns and smokehouses and homes. In front of one of them, there was a woman pulling wash off a line. I was too far away to see her face, but her hair was falling down and her back was bent. She didn't look old, but she walked old. I wondered how many fancy people had sat here in this same chair and watched that woman and thought how poor she looked and how poor her house looked with chickens running wild in the yard and wash hanging out on the line for everyone to see. *These primitive mountain folk, these rural mountain poor . . .*

"The inn sits on twenty-three acres," Harley was saying, "and is known for its healing springs. There are seven springs, and people come from all over the country to bathe in them and feel their powers."

I couldn't look away from the woman. I watched as she walked up the steps to her house, laundry in her arms, and disappeared. Over the mountains, the sun was setting. The sky was turning pink and gold and orange. Down in the valley, it was getting dark. It seemed strange that the sky could still be so light and bright when the valley was already turning black. The air was chilly. Winter always came faster to the mountains than it did down below. Harley stood up and held out his hand. He said, "You're cold. Let's go back to our room, honey. We can find the springs tomorrow."

Then it hit me that this was the first time I was completely alone with Harley—no Johnny Clay, no family, no Glory Pioneers, no fellow travelers. It was just us, husband and wife. We went back into our room and sat on the bed and held hands and then he leaned in and kissed me. Before I knew what I was doing, I put my arms around him and kissed him back.

The hairs up and down my arms—the little ones that were still gold from summer—were standing straight up. I felt like my entire body was on alert, like Hunter Firth when he was tracking something. Harley pulled me in tighter and we fell back on the bed so I was lying on top of him. Even as I felt myself spinning, floating, I thought, there we are like two wild animals, as if I was watching us from up above or from across the room.

No one had ever talked to me about sex—not even Granny—but I knew it was something men and women did when they got married, and something men sometimes did with Lucinda Sink before they had a wife to do it with. When Harley rolled on top of me, for just a second I wondered what on earth I was supposed to do, so I just lay there and tried to breathe with all that weight on my lungs. He certainly don't look like he weighs this much, I kept thinking. I wondered what was so good about this that made Sweet Fern want to keep having all those children.

But then he kissed me again and he shifted his weight and suddenly he wasn't suffocating at all, but strong and manly and I wanted to be covered by him, by my husband, by this big, dark, sturdy man. I felt a strange tingling in my toes that was working its way up my body—just like when I was saved—only it was more like a lightning bolt because it was happening everywhere all at once.

And then we were rolling and rolling and the bed seemed to have grown, and I lost my breath, and all I could think was, Harley, Harley, Harley. The moonshiner's boy. The Hurricane Preacher. Harley Bright. And then it became a kind of rhythm, and we moved to it, and it wasn't really beautiful, but more like two animals rooting around in the woods after something. I was surprised at myself. I am worse than Lucinda Sink, I thought.

Afterward we lay side by side in the dark and I stared at his profile and fit my fingers into his dimples, the twin ones right by the corner of his mouth. My dimples, I thought. My face. My husband. I thought I would be embarrassed to look at him, after what we had done, but I wasn't.

"Harley?" I was too awake to sleep. "Do you think we just made a baby?" I knew enough to know that this was how you made one.

"No."

"How do you know?"

"Because it's too soon. We're barely married, Velva Jean. You don't mean you want a baby right away."

"No." And I didn't. I'd never thought of babies except to pray that I myself wouldn't have any. I saw what they did to a person. And what would I do with one once I went to Nashville?

"Because now is not the time," he said. "We need to be married for a while first."

"But how do you know we didn't just make one?" I was suddenly worried. Suddenly the last thing I ever wanted was a baby.

"Because I made sure of it." He pulled me close, my head on his chest. "Get some sleep, Velva Jean." His voice was blurred, drifting.

"Harley?" I laid a hand on his chest. His heart was still beating fast, but I could feel it slowing. "Harley?" I said again.

He was already asleep.

~

There was billiards, Ping-Pong, lawn tennis, card parties, and a box social on the front lawn. During the day, we took long walks over the grounds and splashed in the springs up to our ankles. We held hands and talked about the house we would build, up behind Mama's—a pretty house with a wraparound porch and dormer windows and blue shutters the color of asters. There would be flower boxes at each window and yellow gingham curtains blowing in the breeze and sunshine spilling in and out of every room. We talked about it so much that I could see every detail in my mind, just like the house was already put together and waiting for us.

In the evenings, an orchestra played in the grand ballroom on the first floor. I tied back my hair and put on my nicest dress—one that Harley had bought me for the trip: swirling navy skirt, red plaid Celanese taffeta blouse, short-sleeved navy bolero jacket. It had cost $2.98 and was as cute as anything Ruby Poole owned. Then Harley and I went downstairs to join the other guests. Mostly we just held on to each other and rocked back and forth to the music—"Pennies from Heaven," "Stardust," and "Moonlight Serenade."

The third night we were there, we stood out on the balcony and listened to the music coming up from downstairs—soft and sweet in the early November air—and I watched for the woman to appear out of her house. I wondered if she could see the dancers and hear the music and if so what she thought of them. I wondered if she hated looking up here at such a beautiful, grand place, if it reminded her of how poor she was and of all she didn't have, or if the sight of it made her glad. I thought that if I lived across from the Balsam Mountain Springs Hotel I would both hate it and love it, that it would make me both angry and happy at once.

"Isn't the music beautiful?" I said. I was full from the lime-pepper steak, but I still felt like dancing. "Let's go down there right now," I said. I thought that while I was here in this world I might as well enjoy it. I would be back in the other soon enough.

"Mr. Bright?" A man from the inn came running down the porch. He waved something in his hand. "Harley Bright?"

"That's me," said Harley.

"Telegram for you."

The man handed him a square of paper. It said: "Son—Come home. Your mama's dead. Levi Bright."

I looked at the lights on the porch, at the warm lights of the inn. I looked at the stars in the sky—at the North Star, which never moved and always stayed the same—and at the black outline of the mountain across the holler. Inside we could hear music and laughter. It sounded like a celebration.

~

On Friday, November 11, I woke up in Mama's old house and went to the window. The sky was dark with clouds and the ground was wet. There were red-brown puddles all across the yard, and whenever the wind blew, water showered down from the trees. The air had turned bitter cold overnight. Harley would be over at his house, arranging for the casket and writing the eulogy and comforting his daddy while Mr. Cabe, the undertaker, got Li'l Dean ready for the funeral.

She had died of a heart attack. Li'l Dean Eufasia Milner Bright dropped dead on the steps of her own front porch, her arms weighed down with buckets of muscadine grapes she'd been picking. Harley said she made what she called her "muskydine wine" for medicinal purposes, but I wondered. Levi found her in a pool of muscadine juice, and wiped the grapes off his wife's face before even checking her pulse, because he knew she would far rather be dead than untidy. As soon as he heard the news, Harley was sure his mama had done it on purpose so that we would have to cut our honeymoon short.

Instead of putting on my navy and red dress with the bolero jacket and eating a lime-pepper steak, I pulled on my old work clothes and spent the day helping Sweet Fern and Danny pack up their things so they could move back to the apartment over Deal's.

"We can wait till after the funeral," Sweet Fern said. "We don't have to go yet, Velva Jean."

"No," I told her. I knew how excited she was about going home after all these years. I knew the sooner she got there, the sooner Danny could begin building her house and the sooner she could get on with her life. "There's no reason you need to stay."

Danny drove his yellow truck up to the house and Johnny Clay and Linc and me helped load their things into the back of it. When it was time for them to go, Danny picked up Corrina and then Justice and put them in the cab of the truck, and Dan Presley climbed in after. Danny said, "Sweet Fern, get on in this truck."

She said, "Absolutely not. The baby and me are walking."

Sweet Fern was holding baby Hoyt as she hugged Linc and then Johnny Clay. When she got to me, there were tears in her eyes. She didn't say anything, just pulled me in tight with her free arm, and then pulled away just as quick. Then she turned and followed the truck as it started off. We stood and waved as they headed down the hill.

Johnny Clay said, "I guess that just leaves me."

"And Beachard," said Linc, although we knew this didn't count for much. Beach was still gone. And even when he was there, we always knew it wouldn't be for very long. He was gone more than he was home, just like Daddy always had been.

The three of us, Linc and Johnny Clay and me, walked back into the house. It looked empty, like the life had suddenly gone out of it. The newspapers were yellowed and curling on the walls; the cushions on the settee were faded and worn; the curtains Sweet Fern had made when she and Danny moved back in were frayed at the ends.

My honeymoon things sat, still packed and waiting, in the middle of the front room. I hadn't known what to pack so I had taken everything—all of my dresses and undergarments, which were inside the little brown suitcase Daddy had once bought for Mama but that she never used because he was the one to go places, not her. And all the treasures from my hatbox, including the little singing girl the Wood Carver had given me, the emerald from Daddy, my Magnet Red lipstick—which I'd never returned—and my Nashville money, which wasn't much but which I'd started to save up again whenever and however I could over the years.

"It looks different," Linc said. "Smaller somehow."

"Think of all the people that used to live in here," said Johnny Clay. "Us, Mama, Daddy, Sweet Fern, Beachard."

"It felt bigger then," I said. "I don't know how, with all those people, but it did."

That night, I took down the family record book and, below my wedding date and "Velva Jean leaves for her honeymoon," I wrote: "Sweet Fern moves back to Alluvial."

~

The next morning, the rain had gone away, taking the clouds with it, and leaving only bright blue skies behind. I woke up to the sun in my old room where I slept with Harley because I couldn't bring myself to sleep in Mama's. We had somehow fit ourselves into the two narrow beds, pushed together to make one, Harley's feet hanging off the ends. I slipped out, careful not to wake him. Johnny Clay had gone off somewhere early, gold pan in hand. He had been avoiding Harley ever since we came back.

I stood on the porch in my bare feet and stared up toward the trees and toward Mama's grave. I used to think about Mama all the time and wish for her. I thought of her saying that she would be there for all the big things that happened to me. But I wasn't sure I believed it. Mama still felt gone. Was she there with me when I walked down the aisle of Sleepy Gap Church holding on to Daddy Hoyt's arm? Was she there when Reverend Nix shouted out to everyone that Harley and me were husband and wife? If she was there, was she happy? Did she like my Harley Bright?

I heard a humming sound—a sound like bees—and knew the mountain was making music. As I stepped off the porch into the clear white light of day, I covered my eyes to block the sun. It was so bright that I couldn't see, and I stood there for a moment, blinded.

EIGHTEEN

One week later, on November 20, we moved to Devil's Kitchen. The day before we left, I went up to Old Widow's Peak by myself, where no one could see me, and cried like a baby. I didn't want to leave my home, this place I loved more than any other place on earth, and I didn't want to give up my dream of the house with blue shutters and dormer windows. But we had to go and I knew we had to go. We couldn't leave Harley's daddy on his own, much as Harley wanted to. Besides, Mama's house belonged to Johnny Clay now, and to Daddy, if he ever came back. And the house with the blue shutters didn't even exist, except in my own mind. I guessed now it never would. Meanwhile, over in Devil's Kitchen, there was a sad old man who had just lost his wife and who needed looking after. Moving was the right thing to do. Harley and I would just have to be men about it, as Johnny Clay liked to say.

The next morning, I went from house to house and told everyone good-bye, and then Harley and me loaded up our belongings and drove three miles in his automobile to Devil's Kitchen. I stared out the window of the dark blue DeSoto all the way and did not cry once.

When we got there, Levi was sitting on the front porch steps, talking to himself or to Jesus, it was hard to know. Harley saw his daddy and swore under his breath. "Daddy, we're home," he shouted out the car window.

Home. I couldn't believe it. This was going to be my home from now on. I took in the house and the barn, the chicken house, spring-house, cornfield, and meadow. Levi's house was big, bigger than Sweet Fern's that Danny was going to build for her. Wisteria and roses grew all the way around the front of the porch. The vines twined around the railings and posts. Even in winter, it was pretty. But it wasn't home. I climbed out of the car and shut the door.

Levi stood up and waited on the edge of the porch, hands on hips, his bony elbows pointed heavenward. "I can live on my own," he hollered. "I don't need babysitters."

"We're here to stay, Daddy," Harley said, lifting two suitcases out of the backseat—one packed with his clothes, the other, my Mama's, filled with all my earthly belongings. "You'd best get that straight." He set the suitcases on the ground and untied the rocking chair that was strapped to the top of the car. It was the one piece of furniture I wanted from Mama's house. Daddy Hoyt had made it himself out of the left-over wood from his fiddles.

Levi walked down the steps, hands still planted on his hips. "God-dammit, boy, I don't need you here."

My legs felt shaky from the ride. I focused on smiling, but the old man terrified me. He'd never said more than two words to me, and he always seemed to be barking at Harley or cursing or muttering to him-self. I was scared he was going to think of me as a whiskey thief, scared he might shoot me or turn me over to the sheriff. For the first time that day I felt a tickling in my nose and behind my eyes that meant I hadn't cried myself completely dry.

"Behave yourself, Daddy." Harley looked over his shoulder at me, nodding for me to join him. "Come on up here, Velva Jean."

Levi peered past his son and looked me up and down. "What she ever sees in you, I don't know."

Harley set the suitcases on the ground. I reached the porch and stood next to him, clutching my hatbox and mandolin. I had almost left the mandolin at home, but I thought better of it at the last minute. Even an unwanted instrument was better than no instrument at all.

"How do," I said to my father-in-law, wondering what to call him.

Levi grunted and stumped off into the house, where we could hear him slamming things around. The muscles in Harley's jaw twitched and then he smiled. "Allow me." He swooped down and picked me up and carried me up the porch steps, over the muscadine stains that were still there in the wood, and toward the front door.

I wrapped one arm around his neck while the other held on to my hatbox and mandolin. "What are you doing?"

"I'm carrying my bride over the threshold," he said, kicking the door all the way open. "Welcome home, Mrs. Bright."

~

The next day, I woke up in a strange bed in a strange room in a strange house. The walls and ceilings were made of hand-planed yellow poplar, aged to a deep gold. For a moment, I couldn't remember where I was. Then I saw the family photographs on the walls—Harley as a boy; Li'l Dean and Levi on their wedding day; a set of baby pictures. Harley was already up and I could hear him moving around downstairs.

Li'l Dean's daddy and his brothers had built the house. I thought about the woman who used to sleep in this same bed in this same room, Harley's mama. I tried to picture her lying here on this cherry four-poster, atop this mountainous feather bed, underneath this quilt and woven coverlet. I tried to picture her with Levi, talking about all the things they would do and all the places they would go, the way Harley and me did before falling asleep. I tried to picture Levi lying on top of Li'l Dean the way Harley liked to lie on top of me. And I tried to picture the young Harley living across the hall from them in the great big room—the one where Li'l Dean and all her brothers and sisters had slept when they were kids, the one that was Levi's room now.

I swung my feet over the side of the bed. On one wall, there was a cherry chest of drawers and a cherry chifforobe, Li'l Dean's pride and joy. On the wall closest to the bed hung three baby pictures, which looked like they were of the same baby in different poses. Harley, I guessed, lying in his crib. But when I looked closer I could see it wasn't a crib at all, but a coffin—three coffins, three babies. Of course: *I had three brothers that died before I was born.*

I pulled back and looked close at the photograph of Harley, age ten or eleven. His tie was crooked, and his wild hair was slicked into place. A young-old boy. He looked itching to burst out of the frame, to come to life.

I stared hard at the picture of Li'l Dean. She was young in the picture but she looked just the same as when I'd seen her sitting on the porch in her rocking chair. She peered out of the photograph with eyes the size of dimes. Her lips were pursed up so tight it looked like she'd swallowed lemons. I leaned in close and said, "I am not afraid of you."

Then I unpacked the record book from my suitcase and wrote down: "November 20: Velva Jean moves to Devil's Kitchen." After a minute I added, "Heart breaks."

~

The trees and the sky were starting to close up for winter, and this felt right because just as soon as my life had opened wide, it felt like it was closing. The first day in Devil's Kitchen was long and lonely. Harley worked a short train down to Sylva while I milked the cows, separated and stored the cream, gathered eggs, fed and watered the hogs, and swept and straightened the house. As I worked, I sang, just so I could hear the sound of someone's voice, even if it was my own.

> *Outlaw Joe, don't you forget me,*
> *After all that we been through,*
> *After the train I robbed, the loot I stole,*
> *The folks I killed for you . . .*

It was a song Johnny Clay and me wrote years ago to pass the time while we worked. When we were little, we used to sing it on purpose as loud as we could because it made Sweet Fern mad to hear it. I thought about Johnny Clay over there in Mama's house now, all alone. It made me sad to think of him, and I wondered what he was doing.

I was used to my big family and all their noise. It was too quiet at Harley's house—no radio, no laughing, no singing, no shouting or talking over each other, no babies crying. I almost missed Sweet Fern.

I didn't see hide nor hair of Levi. He had disappeared into the woods after breakfast. I thought that I didn't need to find a mountaintop or a hill to sing on like I used to do back on Fair Mountain, because I could hear myself just fine right here.

When it got on toward supper, I went into the kitchen and rolled up my sleeves and started cutting up vegetables for soup. For some reason, it was the only thing I could think to make.

There was an actual icebox, not just a springhouse, but the stove was the same—an old comfort stove just like Mama had and just like Ruby Poole had. Granny still used a Dutch oven. I tried not to think of what Granny would be fixing over at home. Here there were sauce stains on the stovetop and biscuit crumbs on the counter. Levi had been living on his own for almost two weeks and, by the looks of things, not cleaning up after himself. I walked into the front room and looked at the matching green and ivory settee and chairs, the rocking chair, the bookcase, the side table, the framed pictures of Jesus on the wall.

Above the fireplace, there hung a portrait of Li'l Dean that Harley said she had ordered herself from a traveling artist. Her fat, disapproving face stared out of it like she could see and hear everything and didn't appreciate any of it. That picture gave me the spooks.

Levi's house was bigger than anything I was used to. Besides the bedrooms and kitchen and front room, there was Harley's office (an old mudroom off the back porch), a dining room off the center hall with a long table, and a screened porch in the back, where Harley kept his shaving table and mirror. The dining room was dark as a cave because it faced out onto the wraparound porch. That room was so dark, it made me mad. It made me feel like I was being buried alive.

I'm hiding out,
I'm heading south,
I'm coming now to fetch you, Outlaw Joe

"Soup for supper?" Harley said when he walked in the door. I jumped and nearly dropped the carrots, and then he picked me up and twirled me around and kissed me for a good five minutes. "How did you know that's what I wanted?" I knew he was lying, but I loved him for it. He put me down. "What was that you were singing?"

" 'Outlaw Joe,' " I said. "Something Johnny Clay and I wrote a long time ago. I've been singing it all day so I wouldn't go crazy. It's so quiet up here without anyone to talk to and no radio to listen to. Your daddy's been up in the woods all day and I got no one but your mama's picture for company. I had to sing to myself just so I could hear the sound of a voice."

Harley didn't say anything, just went into his study and sat at his desk and stared at the wall. All during supper he didn't say more than five words, and after the meal was over he walked onto the porch and smoked cigarette after cigarette. When I went out to check on him and call him to bed, he said, "I'll be along in a while, Velva Jean."

~

Harley was gone the next morning when I got up. When I walked downstairs, Li'l Dean's picture was missing and nowhere to be seen. When I walked outside, the car was also missing and there was no note to say where Harley had gone off to or when he'd be back.

I worked all day just like the day before, and I sang every song I could think of. In the afternoon, I wandered outside, across the stream and through the woods and up and down, until I found a hill where I stood and sang for a while in a bright patch of sunlight, just to hear myself. Then I walked back to the house and sat out on the porch in Daddy Hoyt's rocking chair because it felt like home. Harley had said, "We'll put it here on the porch so you can sit and watch the sun rise or set," but I knew he didn't want the chair in the house because he thought it was ugly.

Late that evening, supper was already on the table when I heard Harley's car pull up outside. I was trying not to be mad, trying not to wonder where he'd gone to all day. I promised myself I wouldn't fly off the handle and get angry at him as soon as he walked in the door. Especially not in front of his daddy, who sat spreading butter on the gingerbread even though it didn't need it.

The door flew open and all I could see was a large brown box standing on one end. Levi didn't even turn around, just kept on eating, but I set my napkin down and walked into the living room. The box was actually a kind of cabinet. It stood as high as my waist and was made of a rich brown wood. It was the largest, most beautiful radio I had ever seen. Harley was pushing it into the room. I just stood and watched him, my mouth hanging open.

When the radio was all the way in, he said, "Where do you want it, Velva Jean?"

I tried to say something, but nothing came out.

"It's a radio and a phonograph," he said. "I didn't know which you'd rather have, so I got one with both. Had to go all the way to Hamlet's Mill for it." He squatted down and wiped it off with his handkerchief, rubbing at the wood, making it shine. "How about over here?" He waved to the wall by the door and pushed the radio up against it. He turned a knob and there was the scratchy sound of static. "It runs on battery." He kept turning the little knob till there was the faint sound of music. He turned the volume up loud so that the music filled the house and went out into the night.

He wiped his forehead with the handkerchief and then wiped his hands. "I don't ever want you to be lonely." And then he took me in his arms and we danced right out onto the porch.

NINETEEN

At the end of the large upstairs room where Levi slept was a little room, directly over the kitchen, that could fit exactly five hundred canned-food jars. There were shelves all the way around and the flue came up through the room to keep the food from freezing. There was a window in there that faced due west and got all the afternoon sun.

Sometimes when Levi was up in the woods, I went into the canning room and stood at this window and looked out. Standing there felt like being at the top of the world, far away from everyone and everything else.

A week after I moved in, I was in there looking out when I saw Johnny Clay come walking toward the house. From where I stood, he looked like Huck Finn or Heathcliff, someone brave and bigger than life, come to rescue me.

Just then he looked up and saw me. He raised one hand and waved. "This is the goddamnedest place I ever saw," he shouted. "Goddamn briars and brambles and shit. Miles away from anywhere. I don't know how you live here, Velva Jean."

~

Johnny Clay stayed for supper, which gave Harley a chance to ask him what he knew about the Scenic. Johnny Clay didn't like Harley and Harley didn't like Johnny Clay, but Johnny Clay always knew everything about everything, and there were things Harley wanted to know and things Johnny Clay wanted to tell.

Harley started right in. "Are they cutting through Silvermine Bald?" He had strong opinions about the Scenic, which he didn't believe in.

"Not yet, but they're setting up camp there," Johnny Clay said. "They're starting construction soon between Seniard Mountain and Reinhart Gap." I set down my fork. Seniard Mountain was just to the east of us, Reinhart Gap to the west. Our mountains and the Alluvial Valley were right in between. It was one thing to see little green flags along those mountains. It was another to hear that construction was starting.

Johnny Clay laughed. "It's going to be the worst section of the road to cut. Good luck, I say."

Harley said, "They'll need it." Then he swore to himself. "What did they expect, coming here?"

I said, "If they're running that road from Seniard Mountain through to Reinhart Gap, that road must be coming right through our mountains." Even after the flags on Devil's Courthouse and Beachard coming to measure and make his maps, I hadn't wanted to believe it. I had told myself it wouldn't happen, that—in the end—Stanley Abbott and his road would stay away.

Johnny Clay said, "They're going just south of us. Kind of winding around past us in a half circle." Then he asked Levi to pass him the biscuits, like nothing else was happening in this world. He soaked one in gravy and took a bite. "They're bringing men in from all over. Stone masons from Italy and Spain. Men from up north and from the Midwest and from other parts of the South. Everyone wants to work on this road."

Harley said, "Idiots." He swore again.

Johnny Clay said, "I don't know. Some of the work they're doing is exciting." I couldn't tell if he was baiting Harley or if he meant it. I suddenly wished I hadn't invited him to supper.

Harley glared at him. Before he could say anything, I leaned over the table and said, "Don't you think for a minute you're going to be one of them."

Johnny Clay didn't say anything to this because he was leaning over his plate to study the table. He was looking at the sweet potatoes. He said, "Could you pass me those? Whatever they are, they sure look good."

This made me mad. That road coming through my mountains. My brother so full of himself. And a room so dark you couldn't tell what you were eating. I looked right at Harley and said, "Please excuse how dark it is in here. It's just the worst kind of dark."

~

The next day, I awoke to a horrible banging and hammering. When I came downstairs, Harley was standing in the dining room, which was flooded with light. Squares of all sizes were cut into the wall and he was fitting panes of glass into the squares. He said, "I don't want you to have any more darkness, Velva Jean. You've had enough already. I don't want you to have anything but light."

When he was finished, none of the windows matched in size, but the light just poured right in. The dining room was the brightest room in the house. We didn't even have to use the oil lamps at supper.

~

Harley preached all through December, working the freight as fireman, and we rode with him—Clydie, Marlon, Floyd, Floyd's wife Lally, and me. We rode from nearby town to town and holler to holler. Long Swamp Creek, Nacoochee, Bethel, Retreat, Cruso, Center Pigeon, Spring Hill, Owl's Roost, and Hesterville. I thought about what the Indian fortune teller had said about traveling. I figured my fortune was finally starting to come true.

No matter where we went, people were hurting from the Depression. I noticed it now that I was out of the Alluvial Valley and away from home—there was a look these strangers had, these people I didn't know, a look about their faces that seemed haunted, like they had, just barely, lived through something horrible.

It was Clydie's job to drum up the crowds. He went up and down the streets or worked his way in and out of the hills and hollers, starting at the general store or train depot and moving outward from there.

He had the charisma and color of a circus barker and knew how to fill seats. He would promise people anything he thought they wanted to see or hear.

The week before Christmas, Harley found an actual circus tent to buy for the Glory Pioneers. It was torn at the corners, with holes in the roof. He and Clydie haggled with the circus owner until they got it for cheap, and then Lally and I patched up the holes with old feed bags. Even with the patches, it was a beautiful tent—brightly colored in orange and red and blue. Harley said that once we put it up people would be able to see it for a good mile. And it was true. People saw that tent and couldn't stay away.

Harley was just like my daddy—he couldn't sit still in one place. As soon as we got home, he wanted to leave. We weren't back a day, and he was pacing the floor, walking the porch, staring out across the mountains, holding that cigarette, off somewhere in his head. Much as I hated to admit it, I yearned to be gone, too. Devil's Kitchen was quiet—too quiet. I found myself standing on the porch with Harley, gazing out over the trees and the valley and way out above the mountains and wondering where and when we were going next. I guessed it was my daddy in me that made me want to roam.

~

The last week in December, the snow settled over the mountain like a great white blanket. It bent the trees and buried the mounds of Cemetery Fields and froze the water that slid down the face of Falling Rock. It covered the bald at the very top of Fair Mountain, and it turned the dark peak of Devil's Courthouse white, up where the Wood Carver lived all alone. It worked its way into the crevices of the rock face and, we imagined, probably chilled Old Scratch himself, deep in his cave.

With the snow came a great, overwhelming quiet. The world seemed dead and still. Up on the mountains, work on the Scenic stopped. We stayed in our houses and watched the world from the inside and the snow kept coming, and when it was finally done falling, it covered us and smothered us and the weight of it left us barely breathing.

It was in the midst of this that revenuer Burn McKinney's house burned to the ground—fierce red in the midst of all that blinding white. No one would say who did it, but everyone knew Swill Tenor was involved. Afterward Swill said, "Just you wait, he won't stay here now." But Burn McKinney stayed. And there were those—Hink Lowe and the Gordons, who were bored and angry at the snow and trying to stir up trouble—who claimed they had seen a giant, long-haired man in the woods, crawling away from the fire on all fours. There was always someone itching to blame the Wood Carver for anything bad that happened on the mountain.

Harley and I were pent up at home, unable to go anywhere. We stood on the porch and stared out at the mountains, covered in snow, and went places in our heads. He snapped at me and I snapped back, and Levi stalked off into the woods in the bone-chilling cold so that he didn't have to listen to it. Something I learned about my husband was that he didn't like to feel pent up. The minute he felt boxed in by anything, he got restless and edgy, like an animal in a cage.

At the end of the week, just before New Year's, I was out in the chicken house, hands freezing, breath blowing out like smoke. I heard the crunch of footsteps in the snow and went out to see who it was. Floyd Hatch and Clydie Williams came walking up over the hill.

"Harley around?" Floyd said.

"He's in his office." I followed them to the house, praying they had somewhere for us to go that would get us out of Devil's Kitchen, away from the snow and the sameness.

The four of us sat down in the front room, Harley and me on the settee, and Floyd and Clydie across from us in the matching chairs.

Floyd said he wondered if we should bring our message up to the CCC camp, where the Scenic workers were living. The Civilian Conservation Corps had set up a camp on Silvermine Bald as part of their work-relief program, the one President Roosevelt had started for the young men of families that didn't have jobs. The CCC camp was one of thousands around the country, each one made up of around two hundred men paid to do outdoor construction.

"The men up there could use some inspiration," Floyd said. "They're far from home. They're missing their families, especially right about now, what with the holidays. Tempers are running high because they are all types of men from so many places. Boys up from the South, down from the North. Whites, Jews, Italians, Germans, Indians—"

"Nigras," Clydie said. "But they got them living at another camp."

Floyd said, "The work they're doing is the worst type of work I ever seen. Breaking through the mountainside with sledge hammers and drills—shit I wouldn't do for a gold nickel." Floyd had this skinny face with great big eyes. He was so serious now, he looked like a haint.

Harley listened to him talk. He didn't say anything about the Scenic, about how much he was against it, although I knew him well enough to know he wanted to. He just sat there, tipped back in his chair, smoking a cigarette, and afterward he said, "I don't believe in this road; you know I don't. I think it's a piece-of-shit idea. Those assholes coming in here to give us their charity like we can't take care of ourselves. I'd like to blow their heads off." He took a long drag on his cigarette before crushing it out in the old jar lid he used as an ashtray. "But if it'll get us the hell out of here, then let's go."

~

The CCC camp was on the north face of Silvermine Bald, protected by high, dark trees. No railroad ran up that way, and there weren't any roads except for the one they were building. This time Floyd, Clydie, Marlon, Harley, and I traveled on horseback.

The camp was managed like an army base, with barracks that housed not only the men but the camp store, lobby, commissary, office, kitchen, supply room, and dining rooms. Men got up at 6:00 a.m. and went to work by 7:45. They worked until 4:00 p.m., with a break for lunch. Peace officers tried to keep order in the camp by threatening workers with dishonorable discharge, but lately tensions were running high and mean between the men. One of the leaders was a boy from Texas, a fellow named Blackeye. He had a redheaded half brother, Slim, who was almost as bad as he was.

Harley preached in the lobby, which was a barracks with a large heating stove in the middle of the room and benches along the wall. The men marched into the room in lines, just like soldiers, and took their seats. They even wore uniforms like soldiers. While Harley preached, the men sat on those benches and watched him, some of them smoking and chewing tobacco. Sometimes Harley prepared sermons and other times he just made things up as he went along. I knew he had prepared a sermon for today, but when he started talking I could tell he'd laid it aside.

He said, "As I was traveling here, I looked at the smoke coming down over the mountains. Those mountains were smoking. They looked like they were on fire. It looked like the fire might be coming up from the earth itself, or from down below the earth. Up we went, up the mountain, and the further up we came, the more it seemed like we might be going to see the Lord himself. But all that smoke called to mind a warmer place. Maybe we were going to see Old Scratch instead."

Blackeye and his brother Slim and the rest of their gang stood along one wall and chewed tobacco and glared at Harley. They glared at him even when he talked about how he was an ex-convict and how if it wasn't for the Lord he might never have been a free man, free to make his own choices out in the world, to work with his hands, to hold down a job, to do honest work like they were doing here on the Scenic. Then he told the story of the prodigal son, who wasted his life with riotous living and when he had lost everything returned home to seek his father's forgiveness.

Then Harley sang a song he'd made up to the tune of "Give Me That Old Time Religion." It said the same kinds of things his sermon had, all about doing honest work and seeking God's forgiveness and trying to get along with one another in a CCC camp.

When the others came forward afterward to shake Harley's hand and thank him for being there, Blackeye and his boys still stood against the wall. I thought, Lord, just let us get out of here without any trouble. And then the men walked out in a line, one by one, and Blackeye and the others fell in and I watched them go.

As I did, I noticed a man walking one line over. I could only see him from the back. He had brown hair, dusted with gray, and long legs that looked like they wanted to dance instead of walk. There was something about the way he moved that made my heart clutch up in my chest.

We hadn't seen Daddy since I was eleven, that time he came back and I sent him away. Two more months had passed, and then three, and then four, and before I knew it, he'd been gone a year, then two years, then three years, then five. On every birthday, my stomach jumped a little and I waited for him to come walking in, traveling sack slung over his shoulder, grinning that big old grin. I didn't really think he would, but I still watched for him. I wondered if he was dead or alive, if he was off somewhere with another wife and family, maybe even a daughter he liked better than me, and if I would know him if I saw him again.

I pushed forward now toward the man. He was almost to the door. I was trying to find my voice but it was stuck down in my chest, down around my heart. There were men in between us and I lost sight of him over their heads. Finally, I shouted, "Daddy!"

The man turned just a little, enough for me to see one ear and part of his cheek.

I shouted, "Lincoln Hart!" A couple of the other men turned around now and stared at me. But the man with the brown-gray hair looked straight ahead. He picked up those long legs and walked right out of the room.

~

On the way home, Harley closed his eyes and gave his horse his head. I said, "Thank you for doing that. That was good what you done."

He said, "I still don't believe in that road. They got no business coming in here like this. But I don't want anyone killing anyone neither. Besides, it was good to get out for a while, wasn't it?"

"It was."

He took my hand. He wasn't feeling caged or pent up anymore. He sang a song, very low.

Come take a trip in my airship
Come take a sail among the stars . . .

I watched the trees and valleys go by, blanketed with snow. I thought: This is one of the great beauty spots in all the mountains. I am lucky to get to live here.

Harley swung my hand back and forth as he sang.

Come have a ride around Venus
Come have a spin around Mars . . .

I thought of all my husband's moods and selves—so many I already knew in such a short time. This was happy, contented Harley. There was the restless one, the caged one. And there was the wicked one—Clyde Barrow. There was also the Hurricane Preacher; the wounded, resentful son; romantic and passionate Harley; the thoughtful and kind friend who knew everything about me; the charmer; the Harley who could turn on a dime with a quick, quick temper; the Harley who got on his soapbox. I learned a new one every day. I wondered if I would ever know them all.

Then I thought about the man with the long, dancing legs and wondered if he was my daddy, and if he was, why he had turned away like that.

~ 1940 ~

Soon he will call me to his side,
My burdens I'll lay down,
Until then I wait faithfully,
Remaining homeward bound.

—"Homeward Bound"

TWENTY

On the night of February 24, 1940, I was down in Alluvial, sitting with Sweet Fern and Danny in their catalog house next to Deal's. Harley had left that morning on the Terrible Creek passenger line, even though you didn't get paid as much to work the passenger line as you did to work freight. I didn't go with him because it was a short trip, and he didn't plan to do any preaching. He was supposed to be back in time for dessert.

The house was pretty and clean—a tidy white box with a broad front porch, three bedrooms, a living room, a kitchen, and a sewing room, which was Sweet Fern's pride and joy. Sweet Fern loved to show off her house. She walked around beaming and patting her hair in a self-satisfied way, and she was almost civil to everyone, including me.

She was twenty-seven years old now and she had four babies. Danny was working at Deal's, with his daddy and brothers, and on weekends he got into his yellow truck and drove down to G. P. Reynolds Grocery in Hamlet's Mill, where he was learning to be a butcher. Mr. Deal said the wave of the future was to sell meat.

We were eating Sweet Fern's honey fried chicken and three-week slaw. She was fussing at Dan Presley and Corrina for pulling each other's hair, and Johnny Clay and I were arguing over the war in Europe.

"This is going to change the world," he said. "The entire world, including here. It's only a matter of time before we get involved. I'm going to be the first to sign up just as soon as we do."

"I want you to listen to me good," I said. "If you sign up, so help me God, I will never speak to you again."

He just laughed at this and stuffed his mouth full of slaw. "You'll change your tune when I'm a hero," he said.

"Don't talk with your mouth full," Sweet Fern said. "You look like mountain trash."

Sitting there with them felt familiar and comfortable. I'd never said a word about the man at the CCC camp who might have been our daddy. I told myself it wasn't Daddy, it was someone else, because it was worse to think about Daddy being close by and not wanting us than it was to think about him being far away and not wanting us. I had put it out of my mind and I tried not to think about it again.

After supper, we sat outside on the porch, drinking coffee and eating Scotch cake with chocolate icing. As I finished my cake, I stared into the night, over toward the railroad tracks, and thought how much I didn't want to walk home by myself. I thought: Harley Bright. Just this once I'd like you to be on time.

"I can walk you home," Johnny Clay said. His eyes had a smirk in them.

"No," I said. I did not want him thinking I needed him to fix this, that there was anything to fix. "I'm comfortable here." I rocked back and forth a little. "It's such a nice night. I think I'm just going to sit here a while longer." It was actually chilly and raining a little, had been raining off and on the entire day. Weather like this made me blue and angry. Johnny Clay knew this, but it was too late—I'd already said it.

"It's getting on toward ten o'clock," Johnny Clay said.

"Ten o'clock?" Sweet Fern stood and shooed Dan Presley into the house. He complained and rubbed his eyes. The other children were already asleep.

"I know what time it is," I said. Rock, rock, rock. I looked out into the rain like it was the most fascinating thing, like it didn't make me feel desperate and sad. Dammit, Harley. I hated him being late and I hated being left behind, just like when I was little and Johnny Clay used to leave me at home when he would go off with the Gordons and Hink Lowe. Even on a short trip, I hated being left all alone.

Danny Deal was smiling as he ate his second helping of cake. I sat there rocking and watching the rain and ignoring Johnny Clay. "What?" I said to Danny.

"Nothing," he said.

Johnny Clay laughed.

Then—out of nowhere—the night exploded. There was a blast louder than thunder. Johnny Clay was standing and he lost his balance for a minute, like the earth knocked him sideways. I covered my ears. I thought: That's it—the Germans have got us. They're here and we are at war and we are all going to die. Then there was the scraping of metal against metal. No matter how I pressed on my ears, I could hear it—like nails on a blackboard, like a woman's scream, like the panther cat, only worse. It was a sound that you felt more than heard, right down to your fingertips, right down to the soles of your feet. It vibrated through your bones.

Then the sky lit up over toward Bone Mountain. It was like a glowing red ball that grew bigger and brighter, like the sun had fallen from the sky and crash-landed on earth.

We were all on our feet, Danny, Johnny Clay, and me. Sweet Fern was back outside, holding Dan Presley by the hand. Coyle Deal raced down from Danny and Sweet Fern's old apartment. Dr. Hamp and Mrs. Dennis—her hair up in pin curls—appeared. Just after them came Reverend Broomfield and his wife, who wore coats over their nightclothes. Elderly Jones, the only Negro on the mountain, stood on his front porch. Next door to him, at the Alluvial Hotel, a woman with red hair ran outside. Her hair spilled around her shoulders and she was dressed in pink silk. When Sweet Fern saw her starting toward us, she took Dan Presley into the house.

No one spoke, and then we all talked at once.

"What was it?"

"Where was it?"

"Bone Mountain?"

"The Germans?"

"Are we at war?"

Lucinda Sink hovered in the yard, behind the Broomfields and Mrs. Dennis. I could tell she was cold and maybe embarrassed. She had a little pink shawl over her pink silk robe. She wrapped it around her and stood there, listening. I glanced at Johnny Clay. He was watching her, but not so anyone could see. He would look at the floor and then up at one of us and then out at the yard real fast. Over and over again.

All of a sudden, Daddy Hoyt was there, down from Sleepy Gap, Granny right behind him, her face white as a sheet, and then Linc and Ruby Poole after them. Ruby Poole was holding their baby. Lucinda Sink backed away into the shadows. I thought: What on earth is everyone doing here? Why did Ruby Poole bring baby Russell out into the night air? What is happening to us? Are we going to die?

Then there came the Gordons and the Lowes, the whole mess of them, and the True sisters. Reverend Nix and Alice and Dell Haywood and Hiram Lee and the Messengills and the Freys and the Toomeys and Shorty Rogers and his daddy. Then Mr. Deal came running out of his house, in back of the store, his overcoat pulled over his pajamas. Jessup followed after him.

"It's a train wreck," Mr. Deal said. I looked down at his feet. He was barefooted in the wet grass. The rain was coming down. "A passenger train jumped the track over on Bone Mountain. I got a call from the depot in Waynesville."

"Any dead?" said Daddy Hoyt.

"I don't know."

"Where on Bone Mountain?" asked Danny. He was still holding his cake plate in one hand and his fork in the other. His arms just sat up in the air like they weren't even part of him.

"Just past Terrible Creek."

Harley. It could be Harley trapped or even killed up there.

"We need to call the Terrible Creek Depot," Mr. Deal said, and he and Daddy Hoyt went hurrying through the wet grass to Deal's to use the telephone. The rain fell harder. Reverend and Mrs. Broomfield moved up onto the porch. From the shadows, Lucinda Sink looked at Johnny Clay and he looked at her so long and obvious that anyone could have seen it. I stared at both of them and thought, what is going on here? Then she turned around and went home.

The front door of the Alluvial Hotel swung closed. Johnny Clay flinched. In the distance, the sky glowed red.

We all stood or sat and waited for Daddy Hoyt and Mr. Deal to come back; Sweet Fern fluttering around, tidying up, taking away the cake plates. She passed behind me once and placed a hand on my shoulder, just for a moment, letting it hover there.

Finally, we saw Daddy Hoyt and Mr. Deal coming toward us. I got up and ran to meet them. Daddy Hoyt took my hand and together we walked up onto the porch. He was stooping a little from the rain—it always gave him rheumatism. "No one answered," he said. "We had the operator dial it over and over again, but no one picked up." He gave my hand a squeeze.

"Lines must be down," said Coyle.

"We'll just go there, to Terrible Creek," said Linc. He looked at Danny. "You coming?"

"Yes."

"I'm going, too," said Johnny Clay.

"Me too," I said.

"No," said Sweet Fern. "You stay here, Velva Jean. I don't want you going over there." She looked at Danny, at Daddy Hoyt, at Granny. "We don't know—we don't know what it's like there."

"I'm going," I said, letting go of Daddy Hoyt's hand and moving past her. I went inside and took my coat from the peg by the door and came back out, slamming the screen door behind me. I walked right over to Danny's yellow truck and climbed into the cab. A minute later, my granddaddy and my brothers and Danny appeared. One by one, they climbed into the truck bed. None of them said a word.

~

The train zigzagged, an angry red blaze, across a deep cut of Bone Mountain, just past the mouth of the Miry Branch Tunnel where, sixty years earlier, nineteen convicts hired to build the tunnel drowned in the creek. Now they lay buried on top of the tunnel in unmarked graves. From the start it had been a place marked with sadness and death.

On one side of the tracks there was a wall of rock three hundred feet high. On the other side, the black nothingness of Terrible Creek. This was one of the steepest grades, the sharpest curves. The engine had jumped the track, shot across the other tracks at the right-of-way, and smashed into the wall of rock. When the engine hit, the boiler exploded. The baggage car, just behind it, had got free somehow, rolling on down the rails until it stopped, easy as you please, two hundred yards away. But the mail car, just behind that, had slammed into the locomotive so hard that it flattened itself, and then the cars right after smashed one on top of the other—one, two, three—until they piled up into a mountain of twisted steel and glass. The roof of the third car was torn completely off, just like it was made of paper. The next eight cars were turned on their sides, windows broken. Here and there, feet poked out of them, or legs or arms. The last four cars stood upright.

The smoke was so thick you could barely see, and I was coughing so bad that Daddy Hoyt handed me his handkerchief and shouted at me to get back in the truck. "No!" I hollered.

You couldn't hear yourself think. It seemed like hundreds of people were climbing through the wreck, looking for survivors. They came from the hollers and the mountains, from the CCC camp, the band mill, the logging camp, and from town. A rescue crew was already working with searchlights and acetylene torches, but we moved in darkness. On the ground, train cars were mixed up and jumbled, smoke rising, people screaming, bumping in the blackness. Women moved in nightgowns, like ghosts, some of them bleeding, crying. Men in pajamas sat on the ground, on an upturned boxcar or on some part of the rubble, and waited to be helped. I started for the locomotive. "Harley!"

Daddy Hoyt picked me up and pulled me back. He shouted something over his shoulder, and Johnny Clay grabbed hold of me. I fought him, kicking him and punching him and slapping him hard. "Harley!" I shouted.

"Stop it, Velva Jean," Johnny Clay yelled.

Linc and Danny were making their way toward the engine. Daddy Hoyt was talking to a man in a black hat. Men and women were wandering through the wreckage, crying—some dressed normal, some dressed in nightclothes. The people on the train had been sleeping when it happened. They hadn't had any warning. They picked their way over great beams of wood, piled high like kindling, and rocks and water to the cars that lay half-buried, half-crushed on their sides, smoke rising up and covering everything.

Linc and Danny disappeared into the crowd of men who were pushing aside pieces of glass. I could see Jessup nearby, his arms around a little boy. I saw men I recognized from the Scenic. I didn't see Mr. Deal or Coyle or Reverend Broomfield anywhere. The crowd had swallowed them whole. But Uncle Turk was there with his Cherokee wife, carrying people out of the ruins. He looked like a full-blooded Indian himself, his long braid hanging down his back.

A man sat nearby on a hill of fallen beams crossed like charred pick-up-sticks. He held his hat in his hands and he was weeping. He wore a jacket that had a patch on it. "Assistant Foreman" the patch said.

"The train came too fast," he said when he saw us looking at him. "All trains are under orders to reduce speed when approaching this curve. There's a maximum speed of forty-five miles per hour. I went to the north end of the bridge to give the engineer a signal, but he was going fifty-five, maybe sixty." He wiped his eyes. "The engine skipped the track then went down, and then came the mail car, and then the boiler burst. It was like it was happening under water, like time slowed down. I could see the engineer's face. Straight Willy Cannon, on account of he's straight as an arrow. A straighter guy you couldn't hope to find. And now he's dead."

"Dead?" My voice sounded like it was coming all the way from Alluvial. All I could hear were Harley's own words: "If there's a wreck on the line, it's the engineer and me that are the ones most likely to get hurt or killed."

Please God, don't let Harley be dead. I had been thinking it over and over. *Please don't let him be dead. I will do anything you want. I will give up anything. I will stay at home forever and never leave and never even dream about going to Nashville. I will do nothing but good all my life. Just please, please, please don't let Harley be dead.*

All around me were people with loved ones and families like mine who were praying for them to be saved. I thought about all the bargains that were being made with God right that very minute and wondered if mine would be heard among all those others.

~

One of the rescue workers found Harley lying on the banks of Terrible Creek, pinned there by an upper berth. At first, he said later, he thought Harley was dead—he was lying so still, just like a corpse, his chest and stomach burned from the fire, his right leg bent like a pretzel, his shirt melted away from the heat—but then he blinked his eyes open and stared up at the man and said, "My leg is gone, ain't it?"

The rescue worker—whose name was Scott Benjamin Jefferson Davis Redbone III, but who everybody called Big Ben—ran away from the creek and grabbed two men, the nearest men he could find, and they went back to the creek bed and pulled the berth off Harley and put their arms around him as careful as they could and picked him up and carried him out of the smoking, burning wetness to dry land. I couldn't tell at first what they had when they came out of the darkness, three grown men bent over the weight of another. Then I saw two boots and two hands hanging down, fingers dragging the ground, and a mess of dark hair.

I picked up my skirt and I started climbing through the steel and glass and downed wires to get to him. I couldn't tell if he was dead or alive. My throat had gone so dry that I couldn't swallow. Someone was shouting my name, but I couldn't tell from where. I just wanted to get to Harley.

"Back away, Velva Jean," Linc said when he saw me coming. He had come up from nowhere, out of the smoke and the steel. His face was red from the heat. Trickles of black ran down his forehead and cheeks. "Some of those may be live wires." Big Ben and his men carried Harley to a flat patch of ground, covered in scrubby grass, and laid him down on top of it.

"We need a doctor over here!" Big Ben yelled. Then he got to his feet and ran for one himself.

When I moved in toward Harley, Linc grabbed my arm. "You let the doctors do their work. He's bad off, Velva Jean. He was near that boiler when it burst, standing right there beside it. That explosion knocked him clean out of the engine and into Terrible Creek. It's a miracle he survived."

"Go get Daddy Hoyt," I said. "Daddy Hoyt can fix him."

"He can't fix everybody," Linc said. I thought it was mean of him to say so at a time like this.

"Find him," I said.

He ran off into the night.

I sat down by Harley. His eyes were closed. His arms and face were black with coal dust. His chest and neck and stomach were burned raw, scraped pink and red practically down to the muscle. He looked like an animal that had been skinned. I made a move to touch him, then pulled my hand away, letting it hang there in the air over him. His shirt was burned away so that here and there only tiny spots of blue held on to him. The rest was flesh, angry and blistered. His left leg lay like a normal leg, thrown out straight and long, the boot tilted out to one side, pointing up toward the trees. But the right leg was twisted weirdly, meanly, in a way I'd never seen a human leg do. There was blood at the knee and at the ankle. One of the men saw me staring at it. "Best not look," he said, and I turned away.

I took Harley's hand and watched his face to see if he would notice. Nothing. "Harley," I whispered. Nothing. "Harley," I said a little louder. Nothing.

"You his wife?" Big Ben was back. There was a short man with him. The short man had gray hair and glasses and a red medic symbol on the sleeve of his coat. He carried a bag.

"Yes," I said.

"He's lucky to be alive," Big Ben said. "He's lucky he can breathe."

I nodded. The doctor unrolled bandages from his bag. He kneeled down beside Harley. "Christ," he said. "He was in the engine?" He looked at me. I nodded again. He looked away, busy working.

I sat back, still holding Harley's hand, watching, and waited for Daddy Hoyt to come fix him.

~

There were voices everywhere, and the sounds of people in pain. I heard someone say there had been convicts in the very last car, separated from everyone else. They could find all the prisoners but one. There were seven of them being taken to Butcher Gap Prison. But now three of the guards were dead and one of the convicts was gone missing. No one was sure if he was with the dead or if he'd run off in the confusion.

Daddy Hoyt and the doctor were in discussion over Harley. I had stopped listening and now their voices joined the background hum. I was tired of listening. There was too much to listen to.

One of the lawmen was saying, "He could be anywhere by now. Impossible to tell until daybreak or till we get more goddamn light in here."

The rain had stopped. The clouds shifted. The sky was clearing. It was still dark, but the moon was breaking through. It was probably past midnight now. In the new light I saw a man standing in the wreck, just one of many men. But he was taller than most of them, black hair flowing, long beard, hat pulled over his eyes. Shirtsleeves rolled up, long muscles, and favoring his left leg. He was stronger than three men. He was pulling bodies from the cars that were stacked one on top of the other. He could carry two bodies at a time. His face was wet, but not from rain or sweat. He was doing something that the other men didn't seem to want to do—he was taking out the dead.

When he pulled them out, he would lay them on the ground, not throwing them down like some of the other men did, but gently, like he was afraid he might break them. He was folding their hands over their chests and closing their eyes. Then he would go back for someone else. I was watching him so hard that when he came out by himself, looking around him like he needed help but didn't want to ask for it, I got up and went to him.

The Wood Carver didn't say a word to me about what I was doing there or what he was doing there, down out of his little cabin on top of the mountain. Instead he said, "There's a woman in there with her husband in her arms. She won't let him go. He's dying or dead, I can't tell. But she has a chance. I need your help."

He ducked back into the train car. I waited. I looked over my shoulder toward where Daddy Hoyt and the doctor were bent over Harley. Daddy Hoyt was doing something I couldn't see while the doctor stood back a little. I hunched down and went in after the Wood Carver.

Inside the car was only blackness. I reached my hands in front of me, feeling. "Here, Velva Jean," the Wood Carver said. His voice was deep, calm. I followed it. I felt his hand, large and rough, taking mine and guiding me.

The smell was stale and sour and rotten. It made me wretch.

"Breathe through your mouth," the Wood Carver said.

There were bodies here and there. The steel of the cars was wrapped around some of them. There was blood everywhere. And the sound of crying. The woman was lying underneath an upper berth, her arms around her husband.

"I need you to pull her out when I lift this off of her," the Wood Carver said.

"I'm not leaving him," the woman said.

I looked at the woman. Her husband lay against her. It was hard to tell if he was dead or alive.

"Velva Jean," the Wood Carver said. "I need you to pull her out when I lift this up."

"Yessir," I said.

I crouched down beside the woman. She was bleeding from her head right down into her eyes. She didn't even blink it away. She just looked right at me through the blood. "I'm not leaving him." I thought about Harley and him lying out there, unconscious, fighting to breathe. I thought about all the deals I'd been making with Jesus. I looked at this woman's husband close-up, and I reached over and I felt his skin and it was cold and dead, just like Mama's when I felt it in the coffin.

"Ma'am," I said. "We need to get you out of here. You need to come with us and then we'll do what we can for your husband." I didn't know what else to say to her. Then I said, "He wouldn't want you sitting here like this when there are people here to help you."

She started crying harder. I put my arms around her and I worked my hands up under hers so that she had no choice but to loosen her grip on her husband. *Lord, forgive me.*

The Wood Carver leaned all his weight into the upper berth and flipped it like it was no heavier than a pancake. I pulled the woman out and we tumbled together, and then the Wood Carver picked her up and carried her out of the train.

~

I ran for help. Because I couldn't find a doctor or a nurse, I ran to one of the lawmen, the one who had cursed the lack of lights, and told him we'd found a woman alive in one of the first four cars.

He came quickly after me, talking into his radio, to where the Wood Carver waited in shadow, holding the woman in his arms. I thought how brave the Wood Carver looked, so tall and strong and larger-than-life. He stood with his head bowed down over the woman, his hat covering his face. The woman was crying now, her head against his chest. Her eyes were closed.

The lawman said, "You're a hero."

The Wood Carver said, "No more than anyone else."

The lawman was looking at him, trying to see his face. The Wood Carver set the woman on the ground, soft as a feather. She opened her eyes and said, "My husband."

"Her husband is still inside," I said.

The lawman said something into his radio about needing a doctor. Then there was static and he shook it. "Goddamn radio," he said. "Never works. Have to go find one myself."

The Wood Carver watched him go. And then he walked toward the train. I looked toward Harley. Daddy Hoyt was still with him, but I didn't see the doctor. I wanted to be there, but I didn't want to leave the woman alone. I sat down next to her. "My husband is in there," she said.

A few minutes later, the Wood Carver returned. He was carrying a body. He laid the body down on the ground near the woman. He crossed the man's arms over his chest. He closed the man's eyes. The woman started crying again. "Thank you," she said.

"Go back to your husband, Velva Jean," he said.

When I got back to Harley, I looked over toward where the woman sat, on the small rise of a hill, her husband laid out beside her. Somebody was tending to her. The lawman was there, too. But the Wood Carver was nowhere to be seen.

~

Danny Deal handed the truck keys to Johnny Clay. Danny had lost his hat somewhere in the confusion, the blue hat that Sweet Fern had given him two Christmases ago. He had wrapped his coat around a boy whose shirt was blown right off him in the blast. Danny told him to keep it. Now Danny had his sleeves rolled up over his elbows. Like Linc, his face was red and wet. He didn't seem to feel the cold. "You take Velva Jean and Harley home in the truck. I can ride home with Daddy and the rest."

Danny and Johnny Clay carried Harley to the yellow truck and laid him down in the back. I took off my coat and rolled it up and made a pillow for his head. His eyes fluttered open for a minute and he looked up at me. "Velva Jean?"

"I'm here," I said.

"Straight Willy's dead."

"Yes."

"They're all dead but me." He closed his eyes again. He'd been going in and out of consciousness since they found him. His breathing was short and raggedy. I brushed the hair away from his face, careful not to touch his burns, careful not to bump his bad leg, which the doctor had set with a piece of wood and some strips of cloth. "You give him a poultice of comfrey leaves or paper soaked in vinegar to help take down that swelling," Daddy Hoyt had told me. "And as soon as you get home, you send Johnny Clay for Aunt Junie. You hear me? As soon as you get home, Velva Jean."

"I'll take good care of your truck," Johnny Clay said to Danny now. My brother took my hand and helped me down.

"You'd better," Danny said, but he was smiling.

He said, "How's our patient?"

"He's sleeping," I said. "Aunt Junie talked the fire right out of him."

"Good," he said. He turned his face just slightly so it caught the moonlight. The lines on his face were little hollows around his mouth and eyes. "Velva Jean. Johnny Clay. You need to come with me."

~

Danny Deal was lying upstairs over his daddy's store, covered in an old gray blanket. He had crawled underneath the mail car, trying to reach a man trapped there, when the car shifted, crushing both of them. Danny had died instantly, as far as they could tell. He was cold when Daddy Hoyt found him. My granddaddy had wrapped him up and brought him home.

Mr. Deal thanked us for coming. He was always polite, even at the worst moments in his life. Jessup sat by the window, smoking cigarette after cigarette, his one blue eye leaking single tear after single tear, and I heard Coyle tell Linc he planned to sue the railroad line *and* the family of Straight Willy Cannon. The children were nowhere to be seen. "Granny and Ruby Poole are looking after them at the house," Linc said.

Sweet Fern sat beside the body in a straight-backed chair, her face gone white. She wore a soft brown shawl—the exact color of her hair—pulled around her shoulders. Her hands were folded in her lap. Her ankles were crossed neatly, one over the other. She looked like a lady, proper and prim. Except for her white, white face, she looked like she might be expecting teacakes and coffee and the latest conversation.

She wouldn't speak to anyone. I went right to her and threw my arms around her and cried and cried. I said, "Sweet Fern, I'm so sorry. I can't believe it. I'm so sorry. Oh, Sweet Fern." I smoothed her hair and held her and rocked her.

She said, "We can't have an open casket. He's not fit to be seen."

I said, "Oh, honey." I put my cheek against hers. It was cold and so dry, like paper.

She said, "I don't know what people will think. He can wear his

TWENTY-ONE

Aunt Junie sat on the edge of the bed beside Harley. Her little hands worked and her glasses slid down her nose and she talked the fire right out of him. "God sent three angels coming from the east and west. One brought fire, another salt. Go out fire; go in salt. In the name of the Father, the Son, and the Holy Ghost." She chanted it three times softly, moving her hands above and across Harley's chest, pushing her hands away from him, and then blowing on the burn.

Afterward she stood up and pointed at Johnny Clay. "You," she said. "Repeat it three times and do just what I did."

"I'll do it," I said.

"Has to be him for it to work," Aunt Junie said. "I can't teach a person of the same sex. It has to be a man."

Johnny Clay looked at Harley lying there, and then he looked at me. He frowned and for a minute I didn't think he would do it, but then he rolled up his sleeves and leaned over the bed. "God sent three angels coming from the east and west," he said. He moved his hands above Harley's chest, as if pushing the burn away toward the door. "One brought fire, another salt . . ."

"Good," Aunt Junie said when he had repeated it three times. "Get the daddy in here."

"The daddy's crazy," Johnny Clay said.

"I don't care if the daddy's a wild rabbit. Get him in here," she said.

Johnny Clay disappeared and returned a minute later with Levi. The old man was wild-eyed and sad. His cheeks were damp and he smelled of whiskey.

"You," Aunt Junie said. "Repeat this and do what I do."

Levi stared down at her in alarm. I patted him on his back and rubbed in little circles between his shoulder blades where they knocked together like chicken wings.

Aunt Junie began waving her hands over Harley. "God sent three angels coming from the east and west," she said.

"God sent three angels coming from the east and west," Levi croaked. His old fingers waved back and forth, the knuckles swollen like the knots of a tree.

Junie said each line and Levi repeated it, and at the end of the last one he added, "Amen."

"I need a third," she said. "I need another man."

"There ain't no other men," Johnny Clay said. "All the men are over at Bone Mountain, helping with the accident."

"I need three for this to work, not counting me," she said.

"You'll have to use Velva Jean," said Johnny Clay.

She stared at me over her glasses, her blue eyes searching.

"She's the luckiest person I know. Our mama said she was born under a lucky star. Granny says she's charmed. She's got a voice that could soothe a wild bear and make grown men cry. If Velva Jean can't heal someone, I don't know who can."

Junie's hands were working—one hand kneading the knuckles of the other. Worry hands, Granny called them.

"It's either that or Elderly Jones, the Negro. He's all the way down in Alluvial, and there ain't no way he's coming up here to do witchcraft."

Junie sighed. "Repeat after me," she said in my direction.

"I don't have to repeat it," I said. "I know it by heart." I held my hands over Harley's chest. I lowered my voice so that it was barely a whisper. "God sent three angels coming from the east and west. One brought fire, another salt. Go out fire; go in salt. In the name of the Fa-

ther, the Son, and the Holy Ghost." I said it three times in all while I waved my hands and blew on the burn.

"Now what?" I said.

"Now," she said, "we wait."

One hour later, Harley's breathing was easy and clear. The blisters were gone and his skin was white and smooth and new, like a baby, like the marble of a statue. Aunt Junie laid her hand over his heart and cocked her head, as if listening. "Yes," she said. "Good." She fixed her eyes on me. "It shouldn't have worked but it did. You are charmed like your brother says. That can be good and bad. I hope for you it's always good."

Then she shuffled out of the bedroom, down the stairs, and outside into the night.

~

At four o'clock that morning, there was a knock on the door. "I'll get it," I told Johnny Clay. Harley was asleep upstairs, and Johnny Clay and I were sitting up talking. I'd made us coffee, which we mixed with sugar and milk, just the way Mama used to make it for us on our birthdays or Christmas. We were eating jam cake and divinity, left over from two days ago, and trying to pretend like everything was okay, like so many people hadn't died over at Terrible Creek, like I hadn't seen a woman become a widow. The truth of it was, I was sad for everyone, but I was grateful for myself. *Thank you, Jesus*, I was saying over and over in my head. It was all I could think of. I was too full and tired to think of anything else. *Thank you for taking care of Harley.*

Daddy Hoyt stood on the front porch, hat in hands. Beyond him was Linc in some car I didn't recognize and a strange man behind the wheel. The man had brown hair on his head and a long beard that was silver in the moonlight.

Daddy Hoyt had always seemed so tall to me, like the tallest man I'd ever known. But every now and then I saw him as he really was instead of how he'd always been, the way he looked to me in my mind. It was like sometimes—every once in a while—he moved into focus and I saw that the years had stooped and bent him some, and I noticed the way he touched his hand to his back where I knew he felt the rheumatism.

blue suit, the navy one he wears to church." She glanced down at the body. "Wore," she said. She blinked and looked away. I picked up her hand. It was shaking.

~

Downstairs, the store was dark and cozy and crowded wall to wall with goods. The counter ran the length of it and was covered in displays, large scales for measuring, and an old-fashioned cash register bought long ago by Mr. Deal's daddy. Shelves ran floor to ceiling behind the counter, stuffed full of shoes, hats, and yard goods; headache and tooth powders; ammunition; seeds and tools; cigarettes; bottled and canned foods and drinks; weed killer; paint and candy.

A group of men was sitting around the radio, listening to the news and talking over the announcer. Reports kept coming in from Terrible Creek. Thirty-three people dead. Thirty-four now.

"The railroad should have done something about that curve by the creek," a man said.

"It was God's will," somebody else said. "Something this awful happens for a reason our eyes aren't meant to see."

"Well, if you ask me," Mr. Gordon said, "the Wood Carver had a hand in this. Mark my words."

Root Caldwell said, "Oh, it's his conjuring, to be sure."

I stopped right then and almost said something. I thought of the Wood Carver carrying out the dead and laying them on the ground, of the way he shut their eyes for them and crossed their arms over their chests and laid them to rest.

Instead I went outside and sat down on the wood of the porch and wrapped my arms around my knees. I closed my eyes and rocked back and forth, trying to breathe.

In a few minutes, Johnny Clay came out after me. He sat down beside me and didn't say a word. Just sat next to me so that I knew he was there.

~

I walked home to Devil's Kitchen later that morning, long after the sun had come up. I was so tired I could barely make it up the hill. I talked to myself the whole way: Just one more step. You can do it. Just one more. You're almost there. I didn't remember ever feeling so worn out.

When I finally reached our yard, there was someone sitting on the porch steps. As soon as I got close, the figure stood up and started toward me. It was a man, lean and taut, like he was made of wire. His skin was dark like an Indian's, but the sun caught his hair and it shone like a copper penny. His long legs worked like he was walking through water, not twigs and grass. I'd forgotten how he moved—graceful, like a dancer, like a branch in the breeze, like something of the earth. Beachard.

I was trying to think of when I'd last seen him and how much had changed since then. Danny was dead and Sweet Fern had all those children, and Linc and Ruby Poole had Russell, who was almost two years old. Granny still rode up and down the mountains on Mad Maggie the mule, bringing babies into the world, and Daddy Hoyt was still healing everyone who needed it and making fiddles. Johnny Clay was a gold miner, the best one in the state; the best they'd ever had at Blood Mountain Mining Company. Mr. Doolen, Johnny Clay's boss, said Johnny Clay could even be world champion if he wanted to. And I was a married woman.

Now Beach was back, having ridden and walked through the night, hitching rides like Johnny Clay and I had when we were kids, riding in the freight cars with the hoboes. He said he came just as soon as he heard about the Terrible Creek wreck.

He stayed with Harley and me the rest of that day and night, and I fed him breakfast and lunch and supper and fussed over him and made him all his favorites. That night after the wreck, the two of us stayed up talking. We sat on the porch and rocked and I stared at him, trying to memorize his face—this new face, the one I didn't recognize because it looked so grown up to me.

"Did you ever sleep in hobo jungles?" I asked him.

"Sometimes," he said. "And sometimes I took my pack and went on my way."

Beach told me about his travels. When he was done surveying the route for the Scenic and had helped them finish their maps and measure their levels, he took off on his own and went as far southwest as Alabama and as far north as Kentucky. He had been to Georgia and South Carolina and Tennessee, mostly by foot and sometimes by train. He had written his messages on trees and rocks and barns. To earn money, he picked up work here and there on railroad crews, and then he came back and took more work on the Scenic. They had just finished a section up near Gooch Gap, and he told us how the tourists were already turning out to drive on it.

"What was it like," I said, "the world out there?"

"It's just like it is here, Velva Jean," he said. "For the most part, the people are the same. Everyone wants something to believe in. Everyone wants someone to love."

"So you're back now," I said. I was thinking that it was amazing what could happen in twenty-four hours. Danny was gone. Harley had nearly died. At least there was one good thing to put in the record book for February 25: "Beachard came home."

"For now. For a while." Beach scratched his head. His hair had grown long, brushing his shoulders. He pulled it back in a ponytail at the base of his neck. His face was thin and lined from the sun. He looked older than nineteen. His eyes were dark, flecked with gray and blue. They were Mama's eyes except for the color. "That's a good road they're building. A road of unlimited horizons. That road is a miracle in the making."

I looked at Beach and I said, "You can't leave," and even as I said it I realized how silly it sounded, like telling the wind it couldn't blow or telling the sun it couldn't shine.

Beach just looked at me and smiled. "I can't believe you're married," he said. "Look how much I missed while I was gone."

~

On February 28, Danny was buried in the little Baptist cemetery next to his mama, back beyond Deal's in a heart-shaped grove under a ring of beech trees. Linc and Beachard and Johnny Clay and me stood around Sweet Fern, who held hands with the children, her back straight and fixed against her grief. The children cried and she didn't, although her eyes were so red and swollen that I knew she was crying when no one else was around. Around us, she pretended she was fine, that everything was fine, refusing to talk about Danny or the accident.

After the funeral, Mr. Deal took me aside and said, "I just want you to know that I'm going to do everything I can to look after her."

I walked Sweet Fern and the children home, trying to think of the magic thing to say to get through to her, to reach her, to make her reach out to me. But all I could think to say was, "It was a lovely service." I knew anything more than that wouldn't have been welcome.

"Yes," she said.

When we got to the catalog house, there was something on the steps that led up to the front porch, something blue. Dan Presley ran the rest of the way to see what it was. "Don't run," Sweet Fern called. She shifted baby Hoyt on her hip.

Dan Presley picked it up and waved it, and then he put it on his head. It was Danny Deal's Christmas hat.

"Where did that come from?" Sweet Fern said. Her face had gone white. Her lower lip was trembling.

"I don't know," I said. "Danny lost it that night. Someone must have found it and brought it back."

"Of course someone brought it back," Sweet Fern said. "But who?" She looked around us at the train tracks, at the woods, at the old overgrown cattle road down the mountain, at the hill leading up to Sleepy Gap. She walked past Dan Presley, grinning in his hat, at Corrina and Justice, lined up to take their turns. And then she walked into the house that Danny had built her and shut the door.

~

That night I dreamed about Johnny Clay, about the time when we were children and Daddy Hoyt sent us to Harley's for whiskey. Only in the dream, Daddy was there and he was the one who sent us instead.

"Ain't Daddy brave?" I said to no one in particular as I watched him go off into the woods. His shoulders were straighter and broader than in real life. He seemed taller too. "Ain't it good that he never left us? Ain't it wonderful the way he takes care of Mama?" Daddy turned around and waved at me, shouting something that I couldn't understand. There was sound but no words, and before I could ask him to repeat it, to say it slower, louder, so I could understand, he disappeared.

When I woke up the next morning, Harley was still asleep. I tried not to think of Mama, her face fading into the pillow. I sat with him a while and held his hand and sang to him.

> *Come take a trip in my airship*
> *Come take a sail among the stars . . .*

Get better, get better, get better, I thought. Get up, get up, get up. I went downstairs. I was restless, all cooped up. I wondered when Harley would be able to get out of bed, when things could get back to normal. I wanted everything to be like it always was. I wanted to know he would be well and strong again like he was supposed to be. I wondered when we could get on the road to go preaching. I missed the singing. I missed him. Then I thought of Sweet Fern, down in Alluvial, whose normal days were over.

I wrapped myself in Mama's shawl and walked outside and stood on the porch, and it was then I saw the tree—a large oak standing directly across from the house. There on the trunk, scratched into the wood, it said: "You are loved." And I knew Beachard was gone again.

~

One week later, Harley was propped up in bed, still weak but beginning to get his appetite back. I stood in the kitchen, pouring coffee and stirring oatmeal in a bowl. I got out some bread from the bread box and some butter from the icebox and added them to the tray. I was just wondering if I should slip out back and pick a few wildflowers, maybe put them in a little vase to give the tray some color, when I heard a rumbling from outside.

By the time I got to the front door, the rumbling stopped. I opened the door, and there sat Johnny Clay, looking like the cock of the henhouse, behind the wheel of Danny Deal's truck.

I walked onto the porch. The window on the driver's side was rolled down and Johnny Clay's elbow was hanging out. There was someone with him. It was a long-haired boy who wasn't one of the Gordons or Hink Lowe. He sat beside Johnny Clay, loose-limbed and easy. He was Indian, maybe Cherokee. He was saying something to my brother and my brother was laughing. I felt a sharp stab of jealousy.

Then Johnny Clay leaned his head out and grinned at me.

I climbed up on the running board and held on to the side. I said, "What are you doing with Danny's truck?"

"It ain't Danny's truck. It's mine. Sweet Fern gave it to me."

"Why would she do that?"

"Said she didn't want to look at it anymore. Couldn't stand the sight of it. She told me to take it away and never let her see it again."

The long-haired boy leaned forward a little and looked at me. He had sleepy dark eyes; wide, high cheekbones; and an unshaved face. I didn't know what to make of him at first because he sat there staring, like he was taking everything in, running his eyes up and down our house, our yard, me. He wore beads around his neck—burned red beads like the ones Daddy Hoyt offered to the earth when he took his plants. His hair was brown-black, the color of chestnuts, and almost reached his shoulders.

Johnny Clay said, "This is Butch Dawkins. He's from Louisiana. He's working up on the Scenic. He's a blues singer."

I looked at Johnny Clay, thinking he was pulling my leg. Who ever heard of an Indian singing the blues?

I said, "Hey."

Butch said, "Hey." He didn't say, "How do you do," or "Nice to meet you, ma'am," like the other southern boys I knew.

I said, "Are you Cherokee?" He didn't look like any Indian I'd ever seen.

Johnny Clay laughed. He said, "Jesus, Velva Jean."

Butch said, "I'm half-Choctaw, half-Creole." He sounded lazy when he talked, like he'd just woken up.

I said, "Why did you come out here, all this way?"

He said, "I'm on a journey. This is part of it."

I said, "Where're you headed?"

He said, "I figure I'll know when I get there."

Johnny Clay said, "He's going to Chicago, home of the blues. Or maybe New York City." Butch didn't say anything to this. He took something out of his pocket—a dark brown paper the size of a small square—and began rolling a cigarette right there on his leg.

I wanted to ask him other things, like did his family know where he was and how long had he been on this journey and did he play guitar or harmonica or both.

Johnny Clay said, "Velva Jean has the prettiest voice in the valley."

Butch looked at me for a long moment. Then he nodded like he'd been thinking this over and decided Johnny Clay was telling the truth. He stuck the cigarette in his mouth and lit it. He took a drag. Then he flashed me a smile. A slow and lazy grin that brightened up his whole face. It was like he'd been saving up for it all this time. His teeth were a little crooked, which made his smile look crooked, too. He had a gap between the two front ones. He said, "You'll have to sing me a song sometime."

Johnny Clay let go of the brake and rolled the truck forward a little. I held on tight. I forgot about Butch Dawkins right then and started thinking that even though I didn't know how to drive and even though Harley and I already had a car, I wished I could have this bright yellow truck. I thought of Cora Kimball and the Motor Girls and all their motoring adventures. But then I thought about poor Danny, and I felt horrible.

"Don't it make you feel bad to drive it?" I said to Johnny Clay.

"No," he said. "Because Danny loved this truck and it was meant to be driven. He wouldn't want it just sitting there, and Sweet Fern will only let it rust."

"Where are you off to?"

"I wanted to see if you want to go for a drive."

I wanted to more than anything. "I can't," I said. "I have to take Harley his breakfast."

"How's he doing?"

"Better. I wish I could go for a ride." If I had a truck, I thought, I wouldn't walk anywhere ever again. I would drive everywhere, even if it was only from the house to the barn.

"Some other time," he said. He turned the engine back on and it sputtered and shook.

"It sure is loud," I said. I thought it sounded wonderful. I wanted to write a song about it right then and there, all about a man with the blues who paints his truck yellow and then gives it to a brave and lovely boy who dies. Something about how you could see it coming and going, and how that truck was still here to cheer us, even after Danny was gone. I stepped off onto the ground.

Johnny Clay backed up the truck and turned it around. He waved his hand out the window to me—just like the queen of England—and drove on down the hill. I stood there with the tears running down my face till I couldn't see the truck any longer, and then I picked some daffodils—not quite as bright as the truck but almost, nearly—and took them inside to put them in a vase for Harley.

TWENTY-TWO

Harley didn't heal quick enough to suit him. By March he was strong enough to come downstairs. He would hop down on his one good leg and lie on the settee and try to write in his notebooks, the ones he used for his sermons. I would walk through the room to bring him some coffee or tea, and he would usually be staring into space or sleeping or listening to the radio, the pages blank, the wastepaper can filled with others he'd thrown out. He tore whole pages out of his notebooks, and then ripped the notebooks in half and threw them in the garbage. He said he wasn't inspired.

By April he didn't even bother picking up his notebooks. He just sat in the living room, listening to radio shows—*Hour of Charm, Life Can Be Beautiful, Burns and Allen, The Jack Benny Program*. His favorite was *The Lone Ranger*. He would lie there and talk to the radio, just like the people inside could hear him, just like they were real. He loved the story of the Lone Ranger—that he was the only one of six Texas Rangers who had survived a deadly ambush. That nearly dead, the Lone Ranger was nursed back to health by the Indian who found him. That, when the ranger woke up, he asked Tonto what happened and Tonto said, "You only ranger left . . . You lone ranger." This got to Harley because that's how he felt. As far as he could see, he and the Lone Ranger had a lot in common.

The railroad made it clear that his job was waiting for him anytime he wanted to come back. He told them he'd be back as soon as he was strong enough, as soon as he could move around on both feet. He needed all his strength to be a fireman. But I could look at him and see he didn't have it in him. He didn't have much of anything in him anymore.

Clydie and Marlon and Floyd came to check on him one day, bringing along the map they'd marked up with places to preach. I could tell they were worried about Harley, too, just lying there, not even thinking about the Glory Pioneers. He told them not to spread out that map in front of him, that he wasn't up to looking at it.

"If it's the distance you're worried about," Clydie said, "we can just stick you in the back of Floyd's truck. Hell, you can preach from there, sitting on your ass, for all I care."

"I ain't worried about the distance," said Harley. But I thought that was part of it. He didn't seem to want to be far from home. He didn't even want to go outside much, not even to sit on the porch or to check on the DeSoto. More and more, he just lay there on that settee and listened to the radio until, one by one, the stations signed off for the night.

Harley had given up, but I didn't know why. Right before my eyes, he had just given up. It was a side of him I hadn't seen before, a whole new self. It was as if the burns from that train wreck had burned some of his old selves away and left others behind—wounded Harley, hurt and resentful Harley, angry Harley, and new versions of him I didn't recognize: weak Harley, scared Harley, mean Harley.

For the very first time in my life, I wished I was a boy—a man. If I was a man, I would teach myself to drive, and then I would go out preaching and singing and spreading the word of God for all to hear. You wouldn't catch me lying around on some settee listening to the radio. You wouldn't catch me with the blankets pulled up over my legs, thinking I was the Lone Ranger.

~

On Sunday morning, April 7, I got up early and walked down to Alluvial to meet Sweet Fern and the children at the catalog house. Sweet Fern said she was too tired to go all the way up to Sleepy Gap Church, so instead we were going to Free Will Baptist. There was a knock on the door as we were getting the children ready, and it was Coyle Deal, come to walk us there.

After the service, Sweet Fern had us back to the house for coffee and sweet bread. We walked up the steps and wiped our feet on the mat, and then we went inside and the rooms seemed empty, even when the children began running through them.

"Please," Sweet Fern said. "Mama can't hear herself think."

Coyle and Sweet Fern and I sat at the kitchen table, which was neat and tidy with a pretty blue cloth, pale like a robin's egg. The children went outside to play and suddenly it was quiet.

Coyle cleared his throat. "That was a nice service," he said.

It was a lovely service.

The house was too quiet. I kept expecting Danny to walk in, smiling his easy smile, shaking the sandy blond hair out of his eyes, coaxing a laugh out of Sweet Fern. She was always softer around him. Now she was closed up, so far away from all of us that I didn't know how to talk to her.

"The sweet bread is delicious," I said.

"This coffee is good," Coyle said.

"Thank you," said Sweet Fern. Her eyes were tired. There was gray in her hair. The color of it—just a dusting of gray on brown—reminded me of the man at the CCC camp. There were lines around her eyes, underneath and in the corners. She looked thinner. She wasn't even eating, just watching Coyle and me, and every now and then sipping at her coffee. She looked too thin.

"Are you eating?" I said. "Do you eat anymore?"

She looked surprised. Then her face gave a little and she cleared her throat. "When I remember to," she said.

~

All the way home, I told myself that Harley would be up and dressed when I got there. He would be sitting at the table, eating the breakfast I left on the stove for him and reading the newspaper or talking to his daddy. He might be out for a walk or sitting on the porch or taking the car down to town. Or, even better, he might be in his office, drinking coffee and making notes on a sermon, planning our next preaching trip to Hazel Bald or Center Pigeon or Long Swamp Creek. I started walking faster.

When I got home, I didn't see him outside. The DeSoto was parked out front, just where it was when I'd left, just where it had been for weeks. I walked toward the house and I could hear the radio before I got there. I opened the door and saw Harley lying on the settee, the blanket over his legs.

Levi was in the kitchen, helping himself to the sugar. He didn't think I noticed that every time I came back from Deal's he walked away with half the sugar supply, taking it up to the woods to his still.

I sat down next to Harley, and I said, "I could learn to drive. That way you can still preach wherever you want to."

Harley stared at me. It was like he had never seen me before. He said, "What the hell are you talking about, Velva Jean?"

I said, "I thought if you were worried about getting back on the train, I could drive you. I know you can't drive yourself yet because of your leg."

He said, "I ain't going anywhere, Velva Jean."

"But you will," I said. "You'll get back up and preach again, and I can drive you. I'll teach myself." I couldn't get it out of my mind. Ever since Danny had brought that yellow truck home, and then ever since Johnny Clay drove it up here, it was an idea I had been working on. Just like Bertha Benz and Genevra Mudge. Just like Hypatia driving her chariot through the streets of Alexandria.

"No wife of mine is going to drive," said Harley. He leaned around to look at his daddy. "Can you just imagine the shit I'd get?"

I stared at him like he'd gone mad. Ever since the accident, he came out with the oddest things. This is Mean Harley, I thought. I was learning to identify the new selves.

Harley started laughing. "Velva Jean, you should see your face."

Levi said, "If the good Lord had meant for women to drive, he would have given 'em sense."

They both howled at this. I raised one eyebrow at Harley, Johnny Clay–style. This was my way of letting him know I was unhappy with him without having to say so in front of Levi.

"What?" Harley said. "It was funny."

~

The next evening, I sat down and waited for *The Lone Ranger* to be over. As soon as it ended, I stood up and turned off the radio. I said, "Harley Bright, God didn't call you to work as a fireman and he didn't call you to work as a farmer. He didn't call you to work moonshine like your daddy and he didn't call you to sit on that settee. He called for you to preach."

Harley didn't say anything for at least a minute. He smoothed the shirt over his chest and then patted the area over his heart with his fingers—kind of thumped it—where he had been burned the worst. It was something he did now, ever since the accident, like he was reassuring himself that he was still here.

Then he said, "I ain't up for a lecture."

"Seems to me you ain't up for much these days."

He stopped patting himself and his eyes flashed at me, angry. "Seems to me I've earned the right to sit here on this settee all day if I want to, after all that's happened. Besides, we ain't hurting for money. The railroad paid me off pretty good."

"Yes. You're right. A lot has happened. And it was all very bad and very terrible. But you got to stop feeling sorry for yourself, Harley Bright. You got to start realizing how lucky you are to be here. What if the Lone Ranger had just sat at home on his settee instead of leading the fight for law and order? You think the Lone Ranger would have just given up?"

Harley didn't say anything, just sat there and fumed.

"I just wondered how long you were planning to sit there. I don't mind if it's another week or even another three weeks, so long as you're planning to get up eventually. But if you're just sitting there with no idea of when you're going to move again, then I mind."

"And what do you expect me to do? Go back out there and talk to people? Get them all fired up about the Lord? Save their souls?"

"Yes," I said. "I do."

"Then you believe in me more than I believe in myself, Velva Jean."

I said, "Maybe that's what you need. Maybe you need someone to believe in you just like Tonto believed in the Lone Ranger."

Harley looked at me long and hard. He said, "I'd like to listen to some music."

I stood up and walked over to the radio. I remembered how happy I was, once upon a time, back when he first brought it up here for me. I thought how much I hated it now. I turned it on.

The Carter Family was singing. I tried to think where my mandolin was or when was the last time I had picked it up and played. I almost never thought about the Opry anymore. I had stopped saving my money for Nashville.

He settled himself back and closed his eyes, which meant he was done talking and done with me.

I thought I would go upstairs and find my mandolin and maybe play a song or two, but instead I went into the kitchen and finished washing the dishes that were stacked up from supper.

~

The next day, Harley got up early and got himself dressed and limped to the car and drove down to the railroad office to officially quit his job as fireman. And then he announced that he was dedicating himself full time to the Lord. He opened the mudroom and dusted off the desk. He shuffled through his papers and hopped around, filing things in his cabinet, emptying his wastepaper can, and then he sat down and began to write. He wrote all the way up until supper. The radio stayed off the entire day.

I was so glad to see him working—to see him up and off that settee—that I didn't say anything like, "Where do you expect to earn the money to live on?" I didn't know any preachers, other than the famous evangelist Damascus King, who preached full time without doing other work. There just wasn't any money in preaching. Of course there sure wasn't any money in sitting on the sofa and pretending you were the Lone Ranger.

TWENTY-THREE

By May, Harley took to walking to build up his strength. He set out in the mornings, at first with his cane, hobbling up through the field in back of the house, toward the tree line, up toward Aunt Junie's. Or he would head over toward Blood Mountain or Bone Mountain or over toward Cemetery Fields or Falling Rock, up toward the forest and the ridges and the sky. Or he would go down the hill toward Alluvial, skipping a little so as not to fall, putting most of his weight on his one good leg, going sideways down the slope.

He would come back around lunchtime, his sleeves rolled up, his arms turning brown from the sun, his face and shirt wet from the effort of it all. He pretended like his leg didn't hurt him still and like it didn't frustrate him to have to depend on a cane. But I knew better. One morning I watched him go and he had left the cane behind. He was limping, but barely. His jaw was set. I knew his limping days were numbered.

He started preaching to himself while he was out. I would hear him coming back. His voice had taken on a booming quality that it never had before. He would come roaring up the hill or down the hill or over the hill, shouting to the heavens. It was like he was trying hard to be heard and like he thought shouting was the only way to do it. He was shouting at Jesus like he was angry at him. I could tell Harley had some things he and Jesus needed to work out.

One day he didn't come in to lunch but stayed outside in the yard, pacing. His limp was almost gone. He stood strong on that bad leg. He was raising up his fists to the sky and saying, "Get the fire burning, Lord! Get the fire burning!" Something about the way he said it, over and over and over again, made me get chill bumps.

The next morning he left after breakfast, just as he always did, but when lunchtime arrived, he hadn't come back. I walked out onto the porch and looked and listened. I walked around the house and up the hill toward Junie's. I walked over to the forest, over toward Blood Mountain and Butcher Gap. I walked the old dirt path the DeSoto had worn that went on down to Alluvial. I waited and listened, but I didn't hear anything but birds chirping and a hawk somewhere close and a rustling in the ground cover, which I knew was a squirrel or a snake.

Harley didn't come back till suppertime. I was upstairs, folding the laundry, when I heard his voice. "Velva Jean!" He was yelling my name down below. "Velva Jean Bright!"

I poked my head out the window and said, "What are you yelling for? Where have you been?"

He was standing in the yard, hands on his hips, head thrown back, shirt sleeves rolled up, skin tanned and glowing. He was beautiful, all lit up in the fading pink-gold sun. He said, "Get down here right now. I got something to show you."

~

I followed him into the woods, and soon the light was dying away. I said, "Harley, it's dark. I can't see. The chiggers are out." I hated chiggers. The bites were hard and mean and itched worse than mosquito bites. But Harley wasn't listening. He was leading me over and down the hill, somewhere above Alluvial. He had found a lantern in the barn, and we were picking our way through the brush and the trees, here and there over an old Indian trail that you could barely follow. It was a black night. There was no moon. The stars were faint and far away.

Harley was pulling me by the hand. He wouldn't tell me where we were going. He hadn't wanted any supper, had just told me to come on, hurry, that he had to show me something and it couldn't wait.

I gave up and let him lead me. The woods were thick around us. I didn't think of panthers or convicts or bears or haints because I never thought of those things with Harley. I knew he would protect me. I knew he wasn't afraid. Weak and scared Harley had gone away.

We must have walked a mile, maybe two, through the dark and the woods, over the hills and hollers up above Alluvial. Finally, Harley slowed down, holding the lantern in front of him, up over his head. He said, "We're here."

He pointed and I saw the sign. It was painted white and there were letters written on it: "The Little White Church." Harley pulled me forward, and we walked past the sign, down an overgrown dirt road now covered with grass and wildflowers. The earth's floor was soft like a carpet. Our feet didn't make any sound. We walked a few yards under a canopy of trees and then came out of the trees, and the ground leveled off and we were in a clearing. It was a sweet little slip of a holler, just a small, round space of land, and in the middle of it sat a one-room building painted white. "Pathways" it said over the door.

There was only the flickering light from the lantern that night, but sitting in the middle of that clearing, the little white church seemed to glow. It was like Jesus himself was there, lighting it up from the inside. Harley and I walked to it together, hand in hand. I thought: The Holy Ghost is with us. He is here with us right now. He is in this church. I suddenly felt like crying.

Harley opened the door to the church and I stepped inside. I had been in old churches before, abandoned ones without a congregation or a preacher. I knew the smell of them—musty, dusty, mildewed, forgotten. This church smelled clean. It smelled like life. The pews were solid and the floor was wood, freshly swept, and there was one stained-glass window, under the steeple, of the Virgin Mary, her head bowed in prayer. That window was lit up like it was on fire, even though there was no moon or sun, nothing to make it shine like that. It was the most beautiful thing I had ever seen. The minute I saw it, I couldn't take my eyes off it. I stood there in the aisle and stared at it and I started to cry.

~

Harley sat down on the front steps of the church and said, "I want to tell you a story." I sat down beside him.

He said, "I went walking this morning, up toward Junie's, when I felt the call to come over this way. In all my years of living in Devil's Kitchen, I've never been down this trail. But I felt something come over me and it was so powerful that I couldn't resist it. I didn't know what I was looking for, so I asked Jesus to show me what it was he wanted me to see. I said, 'If you don't show me now, Lord, I'm going to turn back, because this leg of mine is starting to ache and I don't know how much longer I can walk on it.'"

Harley rubbed at his sore leg while he talked. "Now you know the Lord and me ain't always been on good terms. I never really felt the calling—not a true one, not the kind of calling a preacher should feel. So I thought I'd test him. I said, 'Okay, Lord, let's just see what you're made of. Let's just see if you're real. You want me to believe? I'm listening. Something pulled me from that wreck. Something made me survive. You got my attention. You want to convince me once and for all? Now's your chance.'" His eyes were shining.

"So I kept walking, and not ten yards later I saw it." He patted the step. "And sitting right here was a woman and a man holding service. Just the two of them. Brother Jim Harriday and his wife, Sister Gladdy. They said this church belonged to Sister Gladdy's granddaddy, and that he built it himself with his own two hands. She's the only one left of the family now and she and Brother Jim come all the way over from Blood Mountain to take care of the church. They come every Saturday and they hold service. I offered to preach them a sermon, so we went inside the church and I preached. I never in my life held service for only two people, but I tell you, I never felt so moved."

He looked up at the sky. The stars seemed to be growing brighter. He said, "They asked me to come back next Saturday and I said yes. I told them I'd come to preach as long as they wanted me to."

I didn't speak because I couldn't—I was afraid of disturbing this beautiful thing, afraid it would go away.

Harley said, "And I know I can fill those seats. It may take time.

But me and Jesus can fill those benches. It's God's will, just like it was his will that I find this church. And if it's not—well, I guess I'll just keep preaching to the Harridays. But if it is—well, this little white church won't know what hit it."

~

The next Saturday, I walked over to the Little White Church with Harley. Back through the woods, over hills, across Panther Creek, down, down, down, up again, through trees and bramble and brush, over the old Indian trail. In the light of day, I thought it was even more of a miracle that he had found the church at all or that he could find his way back to it a third time.

The door to the church was thrown open. A short, round woman stood on the steps, sweeping. Her gray hair was pulled into a bun at the base of her neck. She wore sturdy black shoes, which her feet swelled out of, and a long dress that reached nearly to her ankles. She turned at the sound of us and squinted and then her face lit up in a smile. She said something into the church and then she came to meet us.

A man appeared in the doorway. His white hair was thick on the sides but thin on top. He wore black glasses that sat on a nose so round and bumpy that it looked like it was shaped out of clay. He was tall and skinny, but his stomach stuck out and hung over his pants.

Mrs. Harriday took my hand in hers. Her hands were warm and fat. When she smiled, most of her front teeth were missing. She said, "For years I been sitting on this doorstep and praying to Jesus and asking him to make my granddaddy's church a living church again. I almost gave up, then one day, just last week, there come preacher, just as tall and handsome as could be, walking down the lane, like something sent from heaven."

Over her shoulder, the light from the stained-glass window was blinding. The Virgin Mary shone like an angel. Sunshine poured into the church. The wood on the benches and the floors gleamed.

Harley went inside and preached that day, just for the Harridays and me. His voice echoed as he spoke about signs and faith and God's goodwill. There was a painting of the Last Supper on one wall and one of Jesus wearing a crown of thorns on another. A simple wooden cross was nailed to the pulpit. Harley stood behind it in his shirtsleeves. He wasn't wearing a suit. It would have seemed out of place. He didn't pace or jump and he didn't shout or gasp. Instead his hands rested easy on the wood of the pulpit, his voice strong and clear. He looked at home.

I gazed up at the Virgin Mary. Her hands were folded. Her head was bowed. She looked so peaceful, framed in bright gold light, like nothing could ever harm her. I thought that not since Mama died had I felt so good and happy.

After Harley was finished, I sang "Sweet Heaven in My View." It was an old mountain song about a girl who finds her way in the world after her mama dies and her daddy goes away.

Mrs. Harriday stood up and rocked back and forth and waved her hands, eyes closed. She said, "Lord, I thank you for bringing us preacher and dear, sweet Sister Velva Jean. Lord, I thank you for answering my prayer." She jerked and swayed and then she spoke in tongues.

Afterward Harley and I helped the Harridays close up the church. I asked about the stained-glass window, and Mrs. Harriday said, "My granddaddy was a glassblower. That was the only stained-glass window he ever made. Said it was the hardest thing he ever done. After he done it, he swore never to make another. He just wasn't happy with the way it turned out." We all stood looking up at it for a long time. The sun caught the colors and sent blues and reds and greens and golds shining down onto the floor and the pews and the white walls of the church. The light danced so that the church seemed alive.

~

Harley and I went back every Saturday after that and held service with the Harridays. Each Saturday it was just the four of us. When Harley and I would leave, as we would walk home, he would talk about his plans for the little church. He said, "If it's God's will, I'll keep preaching to those empty benches. But I pray that he'll see fit to fill those benches with people."

It was strange to hear him talk about God all of a sudden, to know that he believed and wasn't just pretending or half-believing or trying to believe because he was supposed to.

"The benches aren't empty," I would remind him.

"Of course not," he'd say, but I knew it bothered him, all those empty seats. He was itching to fill them. His mind was busy trying to think of ways to get people in there.

"I thought you didn't want to be tied down to one church," I said. "What happened to reaching as many people as you can, not just the same old souls every week?" I was happy Harley had found the Lord and I was happy he'd found the church, but I missed being out on the road. I wanted to go from town to town, from holler to holler, just like we used to before Harley's accident. I'd been waiting for him to get stronger, for him to be ready to travel again, and now I was suddenly feeling a panic, deep in my chest. I could see my life in Devil's Kitchen and each day looked the same as every other day—the cooking and the cleaning and the farm work, picking up after Harley and Levi, and every weekend coming over to have service with Harley and the Harridays.

"That's how I used to feel," he said. "But I'm supposed to be here. I've been called here for a reason, Velva Jean."

The very next Saturday, when we got to the church, there were a man and two women waiting with the Harridays. The man was gnarled up and ancient. The women looked exactly alike, only one was old and one was young. Both were pale and soft, like they weren't used to the sun.

Sister Gladdy was beaming. When she saw us coming, she stood up and walked forward to meet us. "We have brought you some new members, preacher," she said.

The old man was named Mr. Finch. The women were Oderay Swan, a widow, and her daughter Pernilla, who lived with her mama and took care of her.

Harley didn't exactly show off when he was preaching, but you could tell he liked having the extra people. He lit up a little. His voice grew louder. He paced back and forth behind the pulpit. Something in him had caught fire.

Harley and I sang a song called "Just Over in the Gloryland." We kept our eyes on each other while we sang, and I forgot all about everyone else. After service that day—after Mr. Finch and the Swans promised to return the next Saturday—Harley and I told the Harridays we would close up the church ourselves. When they were gone, Harley prayed over each bench that more people would come and that the little church would be filled.

That night, he woke me deep in sleep to tell me he'd had a dream. He sat up in the bed and the light from the moon came in at such an angle that it outlined his arms and his shoulders. I suddenly had the urge to kiss him and pull him down on top of me. His lips were full and his eyes were spinning away, across the room and beyond. He was working on being somewhere else.

He said, "I dreamed that the church was filled with people, so many that they couldn't all fit inside. They were spilling outside onto the grass, and we opened the windows and they lined up beneath them and listened to my sermon." His voice was full. His eyes were full. He picked up my hand and held it. "They came from all over the mountain, just like they were going to the healing springs. And I healed them, Velva Jean. I healed their souls." And then tears slipped down his cheeks, first one lone tear and then more, coming quickly, so many that I couldn't count. I gathered him close because he was with me in the bed and not gone. He was right there with me, and I held him as tight as I could and told him everything was going to be okay.

~

To prepare for all the people that would come, Harley moved services to Sunday mornings and added services on Monday and Wednesday nights. On Sunday, Harley preached to the Harridays and the Swans and Mr. Finch and me, and on Monday and Wednesday Harley and the Harridays and I waited in the little church, oil lamps burning, mosquitoes and moths fluttering in and out. When no one came, we held service anyway.

Afterward I said, "Maybe we should cut back and just stick to Sunday. That would leave us time to travel during the week."

But Harley was stubborn. He said, "They'll come. Just give them time."

He and Mr. Harriday cleared a wide trail leading to the church so that people could find it easier. Sister Gladdy and I planted flowers, making a path right up to the church steps. While I planted, I prayed in my head. *Thank you, Jesus, for showing Harley this church. He's always needed to believe, and now he does, and that's a wonderful thing. Please let people come and fill these seats. But if they could just come only on Sundays so that we could travel during the week, I surely would appreciate it.*

One Sunday morning, Janette Lowe walked down that path and climbed up the steps to the church. I could not have been more surprised if Jesus himself had walked in because, as far as I knew, no Lowe had ever set foot in church except for Janette's mama, who used to dance with the Spirit for hours back in the day before she met Frank Lowe and had fourteen children and was forced to take to her bed.

Janette appeared in the doorway of the Little White Church, looking lost and nervous. Her feet were bare and dirty, and her dress was the same one she always wore, an old one handed down from her sisters Marvel, Praise Elizabeth, and Jewelette. But she had made an effort. Her hands and arms looked like they'd been spit washed, and her yellow hair was combed back and tied with a ribbon at her neck.

The next Sunday, Buck Frey and his family appeared, all the way down from the top of Devil's Courthouse. The following Sunday, two more families came, making their way from Bearpen Creek. Somehow word was spreading throughout the valley—Harley Bright was an inspiring preacher. Jesus himself had called him to reawaken the Little White Church, which had sat empty for so long.

Harley was beside himself. At home he was nicer to his daddy and sometimes he walked around singing. He'd sing right out—when he was washing the car or working in the field—like he couldn't help himself. As guilty as it made me feel, I kept up my prayers. *Jesus, thank you for bringing us all these people. Can you please, though, if it's not too much trouble, make sure they come only on Sundays so that Harley and me can go on the road again during the week?*

But together Jesus and Harley couldn't be stopped. Within a month, the benches of the Little White Church were filled with men, women, and children—some I knew and some I didn't—dressed in their very best clothes. They came from Hogpen Gap and Panther Hole, from Laughing Holler and Snake Hook Den, Sleepy Gap, Alluvial, and Devil's Kitchen. They showed up for service on Sunday, on Monday, and on Wednesday.

When there were too many people to fit inside the church, we opened the windows and they stood outside or sat on the grass. Standing up at the pulpit, Harley looked like a movie idol. They hung on his words, and they sang along with us while he played guitar and I played mandolin. During services they stood up to testify. Sometimes they wanted to be prayed for, sometimes they wanted to give thanks, and sometimes they wanted to say something about the world we lived in, like Mr. Harriday, who feared for the spiritual welfare of young people, especially now with the new road coming through, making it possible for them to go anywhere.

All the while the Virgin Mary looked down on us from her stained-glass window—the one Gladdy Harriday's granddaddy never could get right to suit him—and seemed peaceful and pleased that we were there. The little church was, at last, alive.

~

On the last Monday night in June—four months to the day since the train wreck—Harley stood at the front of the church, skin tan from working in the sun, handsome in his white shirt, dark hair waving, green eyes shining, white teeth flashing. He said, "I want to talk to you about choice." He laid his hands, broad and calm, on the pulpit. "That night in Terrible Creek, I didn't have a choice about what happened to me. Neither did the thirty-four people that died in that accident. Some would say Straight Willy Cannon was the only one with a choice that night, and he made it when he took that curve at sixty miles per hour instead of forty-five. I guess you could say he chose for all of us.

"But now it's my turn to choose what I do with the rest of my time. I could sit at home and give up. Or I could get up and say that maybe I lived for a reason; maybe Jesus spared my life so I could do some good and come here today and talk to folks like you and help you just like the Lord helped me."

Harley's voice was growing stronger. I could hear the fire starting to burn beneath the surface of it. "There's a woman from Hamlet's Mill that lost her husband and her mother in the train wreck. And now she's turning tricks over in Civility, a scarlet lady." Harley thumped the pulpit with his hand. "That's her choice.

"There's a man from right here on Fair Mountain that broke some ribs and lost a finger in the Terrible Creek wreck. Now he's serving time down there in Butcher Gap." He thumped the pulpit. "That's his choice.

"Well I was in that wreck, too, but you know what my choice is? I'm choosing to go toward life." He banged the pulpit and several people jumped. "That's my choice."

I suddenly forgot to look at the Virgin Mary and I forgot to look at the women looking at Harley. Instead I looked right at my husband. He was pacing back and forth. He looked angry and happy all at once, like he could barely contain himself. The Hurricane Preacher.

"You've made choices, too, and that's why you're here, not down in Butcher Gap Prison. But maybe you need to hear that someone believes in *you* for a change. After my accident, I just laid up on my settee and felt sorry for myself. I kept thinking, why did this happen to me? Why me? Well, you know what? The Terrible Creek train wreck didn't happen to me. It happened to all of us, especially to the thirty-four people who died. But it took my wife—that woman right there," Harley pointed to me and I sat up straight, "to believe in me before I would get up off that settee and believe in myself." People craned their necks around and stared at me. "Maybe what all of us need is for someone to believe in us like Tonto believed in the Lone Ranger."

Harley held up his Bible and closed his eyes. " 'I have fought a good fight, I have finished my course, I have kept the faith: Henceforth there is laid up for me a crown of righteousness, which the Lord, the righteous judge, shall give me at that day: and not to me only, but unto all them also that love his appearing . . .' Amen."

Sweat was beading down his face, dripping onto his white shirt. His hair was curling and his eyes were blazing and his cheeks were flushed pink. He looked like a hellcat, all taut and pent up and ready to dance.

I wiped my eyes and thought: The Lone Ranger rides again.

TWENTY-FOUR

arley and I were the perfect family, running the perfect church. Our world, the new one Harley was building for us, stayed in perfect order until the fourth of July. But on the afternoon of the fourth, Levi was arrested for carrying whiskey down the mountain on a wagon bed covered with a load of fruit. He was taking it to the train so he could send it to Civility, to a man there who shipped it for him to New York City, when Deputy Meeks caught him and locked him up.

Sheriff Story arrived at our door, looking worn out. He said, "Harley Bright, I should really take your daddy down to Hamlet's Mill this time and lock him up. We should put him on trial and send him over to Butcher Gap for a while."

Harley said, "What if I promise to look after him, Sheriff? Keep him out of trouble? I know I can keep him on the straight and narrow." Harley looked as fierce as a wild dog.

The sheriff sighed and scratched his head. He said, "It's late and he's an old man. You can come down and get him, take him home. But don't let me see him back there again."

The sheriff got into his car, and Harley and I got into the DeSoto and we rode down to Alluvial and found the old man sitting in the same cell Harley had once sat in himself, back when he was Clyde Barrow, leader of the bad Barrow gang. There was the same bench Johnny Clay and me had sat on while we waited for Sweet Fern to come and fetch us home.

Then Harley sent me over to Deal's to get him some cigarettes because he wanted to have a word with his daddy in private. The night was warm and alive—the sounds of tree frogs, firecrackers, shouting, music. As I walked up onto the wide wooden porch of Deal's, the music got louder.

From inside there was a sound like a dog howling, like a panther wailing. Folks were scattered everywhere—on chairs, across the floor, in windowsills, on the counters. They were all staring at Johnny Clay's friend Butch Dawkins—half–Choctaw Indian, half-Creole—who leaned against the cold potbellied stove, guitar in hand, playing the meanest blues I'd ever heard. Mean, low-down, roll-around-in-the-street, get-down-in-the-gutter blues. Boys from the Scenic were gathered all around, stomping their feet, clapping their hands. Some of the local boys were there, including Johnny Clay. Some of the old men were there, too, people like Mr. Gordon and Hink Lowe's daddy. There were a few women, but I didn't recognize any of them.

I'd never heard music like that. It was raw and angry and sweet all at once. It made me think of a thunderstorm and lightning and the way I felt after a good cry. It made me think of the bad women who lived in cities—women who rouged their bosoms—of hobo jungles, of riding the rails. It made me think of mean corn liquor that didn't leave a hangover. It made me think of running from a panther, of blood streaming down my leg, of a train wreck in the dark, dark night. I saw Danny Deal's body lying cold under a blanket. I saw his bright yellow truck and me behind the wheel.

That music stirred me up inside, all the way down to my feet. It made me want to shout and run and sit down and listen and sing along—if there had been any words. It made me want to make up words. I wanted to find Harley and kiss him hard and long and do other things with him, out in the night, in the open, not just in our bedroom. I wanted to dance and dance and dance. That music just stirred me up, both good and bad.

The whole time he played, Butch never once looked up. He closed his eyes or he looked right at that guitar, his hair hanging down around his face. It was a steel guitar, the most gorgeous one I'd ever seen—nickel-plated brass as shiny as Three Gum River on a sunny day. He was playing it like a slide guitar, holding it up against him and not horizontal, and he worked the fingerboard with a slide made from a broken bottle neck. His work shirt lay on a nearby chair. He had stripped down to a white undershirt, and I stared at the tattoo on his arm—a guitar with writing on the neck and flames shooting out of the pegbox. "The Bluesman," it said.

Then he started to sing—it was soft and low, like a growl; then it got louder, stronger, still a growl; then a moan, then a howl, like it came from somewhere private, where all his feelings were stored up. I felt strange and unsettled, like we shouldn't be listening to him, like we were all of us witnessing something too personal. All the time, his eyes were closed or he sang to that guitar. The hairs on my body stood up. I wanted to yell at him to stop it, to stop it right then and there. I wanted to take that guitar and smash it.

I felt a hand on my arm. I turned to find Harley standing there. I blinked at him, trying to focus. He said, "Let's go home, Velva Jean." Levi was standing just beyond, sleepy, rubbing his eyes. I followed Harley to the car and helped him put his daddy into the backseat. We drove home, the three of us, not talking the whole way.

~

Harley was madder than I'd ever seen him. When Levi went up to bed, joints cracking, Harley yelled after him, "We'll deal with this in the morning, old man." He walked into our room, and I followed him and he slammed the door behind me. Then he opened it and slammed it again.

I sat down on the bed and said, "On the bright side, your daddy is a genuine businessman." I just couldn't get over it. You could say what you would about him, but Levi Bright was not lazy. "What's more," I said, "as a person whose own daddy has been thrown in jail a time or two, I am here to let you know that you will survive this."

Then I thought of the music that I'd heard down at Deal's—full of pain and anger and feeling, so much feeling that it hurt to hear it. I reached for Harley. I said, "Let's forget about your daddy. Let's not think about him. Let's think about us."

Harley said, "What's got into you, Velva Jean?"

I pulled him down and kissed him and conjured up the rhythm of the song in my mind. I said, "I just don't want you to be upset. I just love you." I just want you to look at me like Butch Dawkins looked at that steel guitar, I thought. Like I'm the only thing to be loved in this whole wide world and you can't bear to look away from me.

I wanted to get the music out of my head. I wanted to remember it forever. I kissed Harley and he kissed me back. We moved to the rhythm of the song in my head, the song that wouldn't get out now even if I wanted it to.

~

We ate breakfast in the morning at the dining room table, the light coming in from every window, and Harley sat with his arms folded, not touching his food. He looked right at his daddy and said, "Your bootlegging days are over."

Levi reached for the grits and helped himself to more.

Harley said, "I mean it."

Levi chewed and swallowed and wiped his mouth. He leaned in, his elbows on the table, and he said, "You touch my still and I'll shoot you." He went right on eating.

Harley said, "You wouldn't shoot your own son."

Levi said, "I would if he tried to take what's mine. 'For God commanded, saying, Honor thy father and mother: and, he that curseth father or mother, let him die the death.'" Harley sat there in shock at his daddy knowing any of the Bible by heart. Levi said, "I wouldn't be casting stones if I was you. I'd be keeping quiet and honoring your father."

Harley wouldn't speak to his daddy for days afterward. Then he started worrying about how we acted—not just Levi, but all of us. Harley stopped swearing, stopped drinking whiskey, and tried to stop smoking. He said we had to be an example to the folks at the Little White Church. "They're looking to us to lead them," he said one morning. "We got to put our best foot forward. How would it look if I'm up here swearing and smoking, with a bootlegging convict for a father?" He picked up a pack of his cigarettes—Lucky Strikes—and tossed them into the wastepaper can across the room. "No more smoking for me. I got to set an example."

I knew he meant it and that he was trying because this was important to him, because Jesus himself had finally spoken to him and had shown him the Little White Church and had probably saved him from the Terrible Creek wreck besides. Harley felt he owed a lot to Jesus and he didn't want to let him down. He wanted to do right by the Lord and that church and its people.

But later that night, Harley dug the cigarettes out of the trash and stood on the porch, the lit end of his cigarette glowing in the dark. He stood with his hands on his hips, staring out at the mountains, then took a long, deep drag and blew smoke rings into the night. His eyes were closed. He crossed one arm over his stomach and held the elbow of the other arm. That other arm hung out in the air, cigarette dangling. He was still mad about his daddy and it showed on his face.

The next morning, the cigarettes were back in his pocket. He didn't mention quitting again.

That afternoon we worked together outside, side by side in the barn, in the chicken house. We were gathering eggs when, all of a sudden, out of nowhere, Harley said, "Velva Jean, I don't want you running wild around the mountain, especially with your wild brother."

I thought: Don't you take this out on me.

I said, "What do you mean, 'running wild'? What do you mean, 'wild brother'? I'm not the one that got arrested."

He said, "No one faults you for it, Velva Jean, what with your mama dead and your daddy gone at such a young age, but everyone knows you Hart kids grew up running loose with no one but Sweet Fern to watch you." He was trying to say it funny, like a joke, like he was on my side, like we were in it together.

He might as well have slapped me in the face, talking about my brothers and me like we were nothing more than a bunch of chickens. I said, "Is that what you think of me?"

He said, "Lord no, Velva Jean. You know better than that."

I said, "And I suppose you're nothing but a moonshiner's son and an ex-convict."

He stared at me and then he colored. He looked like he would blow his top, and then he laughed. "I guess I ain't. A moonshiner's son with the devil for a mother. And a prison record to boot."

"Well, we're a pair," I said.

"And now we got to lead this church," he said.

Neither of us said anything. I was still smarting. I gathered eggs one by one. I hated chickens—the smell, the noise, their beaks, their beady eyes, their feathers. They made me nervous. I hated taking the eggs from them. Granny always said if you heard a hen crow instead of cackle it meant someone in the household would die. This was reason alone to hate chickens. I moved down the line, gathering one egg after another, adding them to my basket.

Harley came along behind me. He was tossing in some feed. He wasn't even looking to see that it got into the cages. Finally, he said, "You are going to have to do something about your brother, though. About these rumors I been hearing."

I didn't ask what rumors he meant. I didn't want to know. I said, "Harley, don't worry so much about your daddy or me or my brother or us or about that church. Just worry about yourself. Those people like you fine just the way you are. You opened up that little church and gave it life again. Just be as good and true as you can. That's all anyone can expect."

~

The very next day, Johnny Clay came rattling up to my house in the yellow truck. He told me he was chasing a gold vein he'd heard about, down near Toxaway Mountain. He didn't even turn the truck off, just leaned out the window and yelled to me. He seemed to be in a hurry.

I said, "Why don't you come in for a minute. Or why don't we go for a ride somewhere first and talk about it?" I was itching to get out of there for a while and take a ride in that truck.

He said, "There's nothing to talk about, Velva Jean. I got to hit that vein before someone else does. I got to make me a fortune."

"Why?" I was leaning in the truck window, feeling the rumble against my skin like it was a part of me. I wanted to hang on and climb in and tell Johnny Clay to hit the gas and just start driving.

"Because I got to make something of myself." He had a mad look about him. He looked like he was ready to fight.

"You're good the way you are," I said. "You're perfect. You're the best there is."

"I can be better," he said. And there was that mad look again.

"Who's telling you that?" I said.

"I'm telling me that. Now get down. I got to go." He kissed the flat of his fingers and then laid them against my forehead and pushed me out of the window. "Git."

"You better come back soon," I said.

"I will. As soon as I drain that vein dry." He winked at me and then shifted gears and drove like wildfire down the hill. I stood there waving after him, just like the queen of England, but he was already gone.

~

The Sunday after Johnny Clay left, Butch Dawkins showed up at the Little White Church. The minute I saw him, I could hear his music in my head. I could see him, guitar in hand, tattoo flexing, leaning up against the stove at Deal's. I watched him during the service, looking for signs of the song I'd heard—the raw emotion, the way-down-in-the-gutter blues. To look at him, you couldn't see a lick of it. He was loose-jointed, unhurried, easy in the way he moved.

After the service, while Harley was shaking hands all around, Butch walked up to me and said, "We're going to have a sing down in Alluvial. A group of us are playing. I thought you might want to come."

"I don't think so," I said.

"Okay," he said. "I just thought you'd like the music. Give you a chance to hear some things you maybe don't get to hear too often. Some of the boys play original tunes. Like the one I played the other night when you were there."

My face grew hot. "I just stopped in to buy cigarettes for Harley."

He said, "You should have stayed. Next time bring your mandolin. Johnny Clay says you play. He says you write songs and sing them, too. You should bring one along."

I thought I would rather die than sing and play my mandolin in front of Butch Dawkins with his steel guitar and his tattoo and his howling and his mean down-in-the-gutter blues. I thought how silly my mandolin would sound and my songs about panthers and moon-eyed people and orphan girls. Suddenly all my songs seemed silly. I said, "Maybe. We'll see."

The next Sunday, Butch came back with some of the boys from the Scenic—a colored boy and an Italian boy and two boys from up north somewhere. Some folks stared, but Sister Gladdy took their hands and squeezed them, and I invited them to sit up front near me.

Before Harley started his sermon, Butch leaned over to me and whispered, "You missed a real good sing." He didn't take his eyes off Harley. "Some of the best blues I ever heard. Was a man there all the way from Reedsville who picked the guitar with his teeth. And another fellow who could play the harmonica without using his hands." I looked at Butch to see if he was teasing me. He was staring straight ahead. "Yessir," he said. "It sure was something to see."

I sat there, the rest of the service, trying to imagine such things.

Afterward Harley shook hands with Butch and his friends, but when we were alone walking home—just us—he said, "What did that boy say to you before service?"

I said, "Nothing."

He said, "Was he talking about that road?"

I said, "No. He was just talking about music."

"Music?" Harley shook his head. "I don't know why they want to come down here. They got a church up there at their camp. I hope that's the last time I see them."

Sometimes Butch came to church, and sometimes he didn't. Sometimes he brought friends with him, and sometimes he came alone. Each time, he told me things about music, the sings they had and about the men who came to them—a blind man who played the banjo and the fiddle, a one-armed guitar player, a man who could play harmonica and stand-up bass and tambourine at the same time. Harley never asked again what Butch said to me, but I would catch him watching us after the service if Butch and I were talking, and every now and then he would preach against outlanders and interlopers and roads coming in where they had no business being.

It got to where I looked forward to going to church, just in case Butch might be there, because he knew about things that no one else did. He knew about music that was raw and real, that stirred you up in good and bad ways, and people who played guitars with their teeth. Each time he was there, I heard his song in my head and the goose bumps rose up on my skin. Each time he wasn't, I sat through the service distracted, wondering what he was doing, when he might be back. I hoped he would invite me to another sing. Maybe, just maybe, I would go. I wouldn't have to take my mandolin or any of my songs. I could just go and watch.

Every Sunday I sat in the front row at each church service, and afterward I stood with Harley and greeted people. I prayed for their loved ones who were sick and I prayed for the souls of those who were lost on the wayward path, those that had backslid and those that were down in Butcher Gap Prison. I visited the sick and I went to the funerals of those who died. When someone's cow went dry, I took them milk from ours. Harley and I helped Mr. Finch get up his hay before a storm came in and ruined it. For a week every night before supper, I walked a mile through the holler to treat the Swans' injured cow. When Jerlivee Betts took sick, I fetched Granny to tend to her so that Jerlivee wouldn't lose her baby.

I hosted weekly circle meetings at our house for the ladies of the church. We would sew or knit things for the needy—quilts or blankets or gloves or socks—and then we would send them to the poor or to lost souls in danger of going to hell. These people usually lived in New Guinea or some other foreign place that we had heard of from Brother Jim. Every few weeks, I would take a mission box down to Deal's and Mr. Deal would mail it for me.

I learned to make extra at mealtimes because you never knew who might stop in. As hungry as we were sometimes, there were always folks hungrier. While I did all this, Harley helped fix barns that were falling down and roofs that were leaking. If someone needed a ride somewhere, he drove them. If someone needed praying over, he went to them and prayed all night if he had to.

The whole time I was looking after injured cows and leading circle meetings and praying for those less fortunate, I tried not to have resentment in my heart—at the Little White Church, at Harley, at Jesus himself for keeping us here in this place, rooted like a tree or a shrub. The outside world seemed far away—all those towns and hollers we used to visit. And, more and more, Harley seemed far away. I missed him—the Harley who had time for me, for us; wicked Harley; fun Harley; wild Harley; bad Barrow gang Harley. This new Harley was more serious. He cared too much what people thought. He didn't want to do wrong. He wanted to do good. He wanted me to do good and his daddy to do good. He wanted to live up to Jesus, who he thought was watching over him, making sure he had earned that church.

~

By the end of July, we were out of money. I hated to bother Harley because he was in such a good mood, but I had to go to him in his mudroom and tell him we didn't have any more. Harley sat at his desk, a notebook open in front of him, tapping his chin with his pencil. Levi was out on the back porch, shaving and talking to himself, and Harley said, "Daddy, will you hold it down? I can't think with you making all that noise."

Then he looked at me and frowned a little and I knew he was in danger of losing his good mood. He said, "Can it wait till tomorrow, Velva Jean? I'm right in the middle of my sermon."

I thought of the groceries that were needed, the things Harley would want and expect—his coffee, his cigarettes. We owed the Rayford boys two weeks pay for helping out around the farm. I thought of my Nashville money, upstairs in my hatbox. I guess it's just sitting there, not being of much use to anyone. I guess I can just use that. I said, "It can wait."

~

Every summer, on the last Saturday afternoon in July, everyone on Fair Mountain and Devil's Courthouse and even some folks from Blood Mountain and Bone and Witch gathered for the summer social on the grounds of the Alluvial School. People arrived on foot or on horseback, whole families, bringing cakes and cookies and sweet breads and guitars, if they had them, coming to eat and talk and sing and dance. Linc, Ruby Poole, and baby Russell walked over from Sleepy Gap with Aunt Zona and Daddy Hoyt. Granny followed behind on Mad Maggie, carrying a box of fried pies from Aunt Bird. Boys came down from the Scenic—colored boys and Italians with dark hair and dark eyes and Yankee boys with funny accents and local boys from other counties. Men came up from the band mill and over from the Indian nation. Butch Dawkins was there with his guitar.

Uncle Turk came just to celebrate because the Cherokee had won their five-year battle with the government over the route of the new road. He found Granny and Aunt Zona and me in the crowd and said, "They wanted to bring that road through the heart of Cherokee lands, but we won. They have to stop at the front door of the reservation. They can't come in. This time, they won't be taking our land from us."

Other news wasn't as good. The road they were cutting from Seniard Mountain, near Yellowstone Falls, over to Silvermine Bald was almost finished, and Aunt Junie had gotten notice. Buck Frey carried the news to the social, along with a banana pudding his wife had made. He stood under a shade tree, next to Harley and me, and said, "Did you hear about Junie? The government offered her forty dollars per acre for her land."

The smile dropped off Harley's face. He said, "Aunt Junie?"

Buck Frey was an old man. He was missing all his teeth and because of this his face looked like a fist, the way it folded in on itself in the middle. He said, "She ain't the only one. A government man named Sam Weems was up to see me about taking my land, all thirty acres, and then he went over to see the Toomeys. No one said nothing about forty dollars per acre, though. He said my land was only worth six."

At that Buck Frey spat right on the ground.

I was thinking about the Wood Carver. He lived up there on top of the mountain, near the Freys and the Toomeys.

No one expected Aunt Junie to come to the summer social. She hardly ever came down the mountain for anything other than the rare trip to Deal's, but this hot afternoon she appeared out of the woods, long after everyone else had gathered, carrying a spice layer cake. She marched up to Harley and me, and he leaned down to talk to her. His face was still cloudy. His eyes were flashing. He said, "I heard about your notice. I could kill those government men. What can I do?"

"Nothing," she said. Then she laid her hand on his chest, where she had healed him. She closed her eyes and grew still. After a minute, she opened her eyes and smiled. She said, "You're good and strong, Harley Bright."

"I wouldn't be here if it wasn't for you," he said. He took her hand and held it. She looked up at him with her bright blue eyes, and then she walked away.

Pretty soon the music started. Harley brought out his guitar and Daddy Hoyt pulled out the fiddle and everyone else took out whatever he or she had brought, and we sang and played and people danced, everybody from little children on up.

When Butch Dawkins leaned up in the doorway of the school and started to sing and play a song he wrote himself, folks got quiet and stood still to listen. It was a different kind of song from the one he'd sung at Deal's—fast and quick. His fingers flew over that guitar with a speed you never would have expected from him. His voice was rich and deep. I can't remember the words of the song—something about coming home to the place where you'd been all along. All I remember is the way his hands flew over the strings and the way he stared at the guitar as he played. The guitar shone in the sun and I wanted to take it from him and play it myself, but mostly I wanted to be that guitar, to be able to make music that was wild and free and thrilling.

When the song was over, Harley said, "Sing with me, Velva Jean."

The last thing I wanted to do was sing in front of Butch Dawkins. He might laugh at me or think my songs were silly. I said, "I don't feel like it just now."

Harley said, "Suit yourself," and started playing without me. And then everyone was singing and dancing again.

At some point, I looked up, up toward the sky and the sun. Near the peak of Devil's Courthouse, I could have sworn I saw a dark figure with the sun behind it, so high atop that mountain that it was nothing but a silhouette. It circled up and down, up and down, back straight, arms and hands waving as they kept the rhythm, long legs moving to the music, buck dancing.

~

The next morning, I found a five-dollar bill in my apron pocket. When Harley came down to breakfast, I could tell he had something on his mind, that he was somewhere else. He said, "We'll talk about money in a little while, Velva Jean. Just let me eat and take care of a few things first. I got some things to think about," and I knew the five dollars wasn't from him.

When the table was set and the food was ready, I stepped onto the back porch to call Levi, who was asleep in his favorite chair. I stood and watched him for a minute—hat drawn over his face, chin on his chest, bony hands folded on top of his stomach, feet crossed at the ankle—and then I leaned in and kissed him, light as I could, on his head. He stirred a little and then pushed his hat back. He opened one eye. "What is it?"

"Breakfast," I said.

TWENTY-FIVE

The word spread fast through the valley—Johnny Clay was back. I heard it first from Butch and then from Lally Hatch and Sweet Fern. He had been gone two months, working toward three, but it had seemed like forever to me. I'd been worried that Johnny Clay had really left me for good this time, gone off like Daddy and Beachard. When I heard he was back, I dropped everything I was doing and ran all the way up to Mama's, but there was no one home.

The newspapers were yellowed and curling off the walls. The *Grier's Almanac* still hung on a nail by the fireplace. Mama's old cross-stitch, the one she'd done as a young bride, hung on the wall in a wood frame: "Bless Our Home." Behind the glass, the cloth was fading, browning a bit at the corners. I thought about Mama's fingers making each stitch—a young bride's hopes and dreams and happiness fading on the wall.

From outside I heard a familiar rumbling. Then there was barking and a long whistle. I ran out of the house.

Johnny Clay looked wonderful. It was like the gold had rubbed off on him—on his skin and on his hair. He said, "Velva Jean, what do you think? I'm rich as hell." He slid out of the yellow truck and slammed the door. He was holding a package—a big, white box tied with string. "Guess what's in here? A zoot suit. Fanciest thing you ever saw. I look like something out of a Fred Astaire picture in this suit."

"What on earth do you need with a suit, Johnny Clay?"

He wasn't listening. He was walking ahead of me, whistling. Hunter

Firth was at his heels, jumping up now and then, trying to get his attention.

"So you got to the vein before anyone else."

He waved his hand. The palms were blistered, the knuckles scraped. A miner's hands. "That vein was all dried up. I found something better. Tracked it down myself. I'm a gem miner now. Garnets, rubies, topazes, sapphires."

I said, "Johnny Clay, you are crazy. You're a gold miner. You can't change just like that. You can't just become a gem miner."

He said, "There's no more gold, Velva Jean. We've mined it all. But these mountains are packed full of gems. When I got to Toxaway, there wasn't nothing but a few sad miners drinking and fighting and turning around for home. But I'd come that far and I wasn't about to go back empty-handed. I climbed to the top of Toxaway to see what I could see, and up there I found a trail winding along into the horizon, disappearing into the clouds. Well I ain't never been saved, Velva Jean, but I figure that was the closest I'll ever come. I just started walking to see where it would take me, up along the top of those mountains. I must have walked thirty miles, and when that trail came to an end there were the men working on the Scenic. I wound down through the trees to the valley below, and a man there told me I was on Mount Pisgah. Just like Moses when he first saw the promised land. I said, 'What can you tell me about this mountain?' And the man said, 'It's made of garnets and rubies and sapphires.' He was a retired miner so that's how he thought of the mountain—what it was made of. He let me stay with him and his wife and he taught me how to mine. Gem mining's harder than gold mining. It's more dangerous."

His eyes lit up at this. He held his hands out, spreading the fingers so I could see the nicks and cuts that went right up his arms. "I went into the mountain, down deep in the dark, and hit that vein so wide open, you'd a thought someone left it there just for me." He fished something out of his pocket. "I brought you one. It's a sapphire. It ain't as dark as the others I found. To me this one looks like the blue of Mama's eyes or the sky over Sleepy Gap just after it rains."

I held the stone and turned it in the light. It was rough but in the sun it shone a clear, bright blue the color of asters. I thought of the emerald Daddy had brought me long ago, still rugged and uncut in my hatbox.

Johnny Clay grabbed my hand. "I got to show you something."

"Don't pull me so hard," I said, but my heart was pounding. I was so happy to see him, so happy to be home, I thought I might start crying.

He yanked me around the yard and toward the barn. "You won't believe it," he said.

"This better be good, the way you're pulling my arm right out of the socket."

He dropped my hand and dragged open the barn door. The light was dim and I blinked, trying to adjust my eyes. He pushed me inside. "Go on," he said.

I could make out two headlights, a grill, a silver bumper, a dark red hood. "What have you gone and done?" I said.

He laughed and took my hand, guiding me. He opened a door and sat me down and then he sat down next to me and threw the package in the back and turned on the engine. I felt the wind and sun in my hair as we drove out of the barn. "There's no top, Johnny Clay!"

"It's called a convertible." He laughed again. The car was smooth, not bumpy and loud like the truck. He drove it this way and that around the yard. It was beautiful—creamy insides, dark red outsides, the color of skin and blood, only inside out. Skin on the inside, blood on the outside. It was fancy and shiny and sleek. "It's a Nash LaFayette," he said. "Get out and I'll show you something."

He turned off the car and we walked around back and he opened up a little hatch. "That's called a rumble seat," he said.

"That's the cutest thing I ever did see," I said. And it was. "Johnny Clay, how on earth did you afford this?"

"I told you. I'm rich. I reckon I'm richer than anyone else on this mountain next to the Deals. I told you I was going to make something of myself."

"You're ridiculous," I said. "How'd you get home?"

"Butch came and met me and drove the truck back. I rode on the Scenic, Velva Jean. It ain't close to being done, but it's the most incredible thing I ever saw. You ride across the mountaintops just like you're in the clouds."

"Did you see Beach?"

"No. But you wouldn't believe it. There were people driving on that road, people from around the country, here to see these mountains—our mountains. You could see the whole wide world up there."

He was climbing in and out of the rumble seat. He was telling me about something called a travel bed, where the seats folded down and window screens could be slid into place and attaching tents could be purchased for added living space, but I had stopped listening. I was staring at Danny Deal's truck and wondering what he was going to do with it.

"Velva Jean?" he said. He knocked me on the head with his hand.

"Sorry."

"You want to go for a ride?"

"Sure."

"What's wrong?"

"Nothing's wrong. I was just wondering." I tried to keep my voice casual. "What are you going to do with the truck?"

He looked at the yellow truck. He shrugged. "I don't know. I guess I could give it back to Sweet Fern."

"She don't want it," I said. "She told you she never wanted to see it again."

"Well hell's bells, Velva Jean, I don't know. Do you want it? If you want it, it's yours," he said.

I looked at that yellow truck. There were little dings in the doors and scratches in the paint. It was still in good shape, but it looked its age. Johnny Clay had promised Danny to take good care of it. I thought: If he could see his truck, Danny Deal would roll over in his grave.

"Yes, I want it." I wanted it more than anything. I wanted it almost as much as I wanted Harley, even more than I wanted Nashville, which

I never thought much about anymore anyway. Sometimes I loved and sometimes I hated that part of myself that was like my daddy, that couldn't be content to sit still and quiet and be happy with the way things were. If I had that truck, I could go anywhere. I could get out of Devil's Kitchen and go to Alluvial or come up here to Fair Mountain to see Granny and Daddy Hoyt. I could even go to Hamlet's Mill. But you can't drive, a voice inside me said. What on earth are you going to do with an old yellow truck?

Johnny Clay handed me the keys. "Just so you know," he said, "I ain't giving it to Harley or to you and Harley. I'm giving it to you."

I nodded.

He said, "What am I giving you the keys for? You can't drive. I guess I'll have to drive you home now. Just hold on a minute while I put the Nash back in the barn. Then we'll drive that truck up to Devil's Kitchen. We'll take the Nash out some other time."

"Is it hard—to drive, I mean?" I said.

"It ain't bad," he said. "I been doing it for so long. The instruction manual's in the visor. It tells about how to run it, about the care and operation and all that." He climbed back into the Nash and turned on the engine. He grinned at the sound. "You hear that?" he said. "Like music."

"If you drive me, you'll have to walk home," I said. I was already thinking about that truck, about how I was going to learn to drive. I would teach myself. I'd already decided.

"I don't care," he said. "I'm so goddamn happy, I feel like I could fly." He was already aiming the Nash toward the barn. He yelled, "One thing I learned when I was up there on that skywalk and up there on the Scenic, crossing all those mountaintops—there's a great big world out there, Velva Jean. It's so beautiful and big, it made me cry. What we got up here is only a little part of it. It's a good part, but it's just a little part."

~

Harley said, "That's real nice of you, Johnny Clay. But we already got a car."

Harley was sitting on the front porch, making notes in one of his notebooks. He had the Bible open on his lap. I stood next to him. My feet were practically dancing with excitement. The yellow truck looked even better from up on the porch.

Johnny Clay leaned out the window of the truck. He was tapping his fingers on the outside of the door, waiting. "Where should I put it?"

Harley sighed. He stood, picking up his notebook and his Bible and setting them down in his chair. "Park it over by the barn, out of view of the house." Just like Sweet Fern, I thought. He turned to me, "What is this about, Velva Jean? We can't have that bright yellow truck up here for all the world to see."

"Why not?" I said. "I think it's beautiful."

Johnny Clay drove the truck behind the barn and left it there. He got out and walked toward the house. I noticed that he kind of swaggered now like a movie star or a cowboy, like someone with money. I thought, heaven help us all.

I said, "You want to come in and have supper?"

Johnny Clay said, "No thanks. I got to be getting back. It's a long walk home." He came up the steps and handed me the keys. "Remember what I said, Velva Jean. I'm giving this truck to you."

"I remember," I said.

Johnny Clay hugged me hard and fast and then took off down the porch steps, long legs flying. He bounded off down the hill, outrunning the dying sun, hair shining like gold.

"What did he mean by that?" Harley said.

"Oh," I said, "he wants me to have that truck."

"That's silly," said Harley. "You don't even know how to drive."

"I know," I said. But I'm going to learn.

TWENTY-SIX

The truck sat by the barn. I walked by it. It seemed to be looking at me. I looked at it. I walked by it the other way. The truck seemed to be watching me go past. I stood in front of it and stared. We sized each other up.

I walked over to the window and stood on the running board. I rubbed the dirt and the dust off the glass and looked inside at all the gears and the knobs. I tried the door handle. The door opened. I set one foot inside and then pulled myself up and sat down behind the wheel. I sat up straight and tall because I had no choice, because that's the way the seat was made. The windshield was right up near my face. The windshield frame was hinged at the top and could be swung out toward the hood. I opened this up and let some air in. I put my hands on the wheel. It felt cool and big and slick.

I reached across the seat and pulled the *Ford Truck Instruction Book* out of the visor. I opened it to the page that read "Owner's Responsibilities."

> The Ford truck has been designed and built so that it will furnish a safe, comfortable, carefree, and economical means of transportation for many thousands of miles.

Comfortable and carefree sounded good to me. I kept reading. What followed were suggestions to assist in the operation of the truck, such as:

Avoid driving with your foot resting on the clutch as this may cause the clutch to slip, causing premature wear of the facings and clutch release bearing.

Depress the clutch pedal while starting the engine, particularly in cold weather.

Wheel and axle shaft nuts must be kept tight at all times.

Check the oil level every 100 miles when operating under high speeds or heavy load.

Do not add cold water to an overheated cooling system.

Avoid racing the engine while it is cold.

I tossed the book aside. "Comfortable" and "carefree," my left eye, I thought. I might not learn to drive after all if there were that many things to remember. I put my hands back on the wheel and twisted it back and forth. I set my foot on the gas pedal, which looked just like an upside-down teaspoon with the widest part at the bottom. I moved the long-knobbed bar that came up from the center of the floor, the gearshift lever, and rested my foot on the brake, which looked like a little round rubber target. I pretended I was going for a drive.

I rolled down the window and let my hair down, just like it was blowing free. I thought of the people I would pass. I would speed up when I went by Alice Nix and Rachel Gordon. I looked in the rearview mirror and imagined their faces, staring at me.

I would wave at the people as I went by them. "Hello, Sister Gladdy!" "Hello, Sister Dearborn!" "Hello, Sister Oderay and Sister Pernilla!" Their mouths would pop open in surprise and shock. They would run to tell Harley: "There goes Velva Jean Hart Bright. Just look how fancy." I looked at my reflection in the rearview mirror. Some lipstick would go with this truck, I thought. A nice shade of red. Magnet Red. And maybe a pantsuit. That would really get the women talking. Then I thought: I could drive this truck all the way to Nashville. Just like that. I don't know what made me think it.

Somewhere along the way, I'd stopped planning for the Opry and I'd stopped saving my money. I wasn't exactly sure when or why it happened. I sat there and tried to think where the framed picture was that Johnny Clay had given me of the Opry stage, all those years ago. Was it at Mama's? Had I brought it with me to Devil's Kitchen? I couldn't remember.

I stopped steering. I picked up the instruction book and put it in the visor. I pulled the windshield frame closed. Then I rolled up the window. I opened the door and climbed down, shut the door, and walked back into the house. I stood inside at the kitchen window and looked out, staring at that truck. I stood there for a long time before I let the curtain fall and started fixing dinner.

~ 1941 ~

Oh who will come and go with me?
I am bound for the promised land.

—"Promised Land"

TWENTY-SEVEN

Damascus King, famous evangelist preacher, came to Alluvial on February 22. This wasn't like the Glory Pioneers dragging their circus tent from one little mountain holler to another. This wasn't like Reverend Nix or Reverend Broomfield leading camp meeting or even Harley preaching to the congregation in the Little White Church. This was the biggest name in religion since Billy Sunday. This was a man so charged with the power of the Lord that he had once saved fifty thousand people in a single night in a revival meeting in New York City.

When Damascus King came to preach in Alluvial, there weren't fifty thousand people to turn out. There were maybe five hundred. We walked down the mountain, Harley and me, with the Harridays and Sister Oderay, and sat in the front row, so close you could feel that man's sweat as it flew off his brow and see the lines of his muscles underneath his fancy white suit. After the sawdust had settled and the shouting had stopped and Damascus King had claimed to save each and every one of us, we walked home, me behind, listening to Harley and Brother Jim and Sister Gladdy and Sister Oderay talk about what a great man Damascus King was and what a great and dutiful woman his wife, Julia Faith, was and what a great and momentous day it was, how it had changed their lives.

I was worried that just being close to Damascus King had undone my being saved all those years earlier in Three Gum River. I was worried that being "saved" by him had somehow taken away the time I was really and truly saved when I was ten. I had been praying ever since Damascus King took my hand and held it and then pronounced me saved before winking at me just like one of the Gordon boys or Hink Lowe when they were trying to get me to go off into the woods with them. For the first time in my life, I just wanted to get back up to Devil's Kitchen, that place I couldn't stand.

I would never forget his words. After he got done cursing the moon-shiners for turning men drunk and the prostitutes for turning men blind from venereal disease, he said: "The Lord himself has told me that the time of Revelation is coming. The sun will turn black and the seas will turn red with blood before they dry up and vanish forever. I saw Alluvial burn to the ground and all the drunkards and the whores and the sinners run crying in the streets. I saw these mountains crumble to the earth and all the smokers and the bootleggers and the back-sliders fall."

And then everyone dropped to their knees, eyes closed, cheeks stained with tears, hands raised toward the sky, knees pressed into the earth—men, women, children, old people. I'd never heard such a sound. Those people were howling and crying and wailing while Damascus King shouted over and over again, "Repent!"

I had kneeled like everybody else, staying silent while Harley and the Harridays and Oderay Swan wailed. All around me was the sound of great despair, of hundreds of people in mourning, crying for their souls. I thought Damascus King was a horrible man to do that to them, to make them feel so fearful.

That night, after we got home, Harley locked himself in his mud-room. I stood outside and knocked on the door and said, "Harley, you'll wear yourself out. You won't be worth anything tomorrow." He didn't answer. I said, "How are you going to give a sermon if you don't get any sleep?" When he still didn't answer, I went upstairs to bed.

~

The next morning I sat on the front row at church, just as I always did, but that was about the only thing that felt the same about Sunday's service. Something had come over Harley. He was filling up that little church with enough pomp and bluster to run a steam train from here to Asheville.

All of a sudden, in the middle of his sermon, he marched right down the aisle and out the door. Everyone started buzzing and craning their necks around, trying to see where he'd gone. Butch Dawkins leaned up from the pew behind me and said, "Are we supposed to follow?"

I turned around and stared out the open door. Harley was nowhere to be seen. He was probably standing out there waiting for us. I said, "I guess."

I got up and walked down the aisle and Butch and the Harridays followed. Soon everyone came blinking out into the sun, and there was Harley, his pants legs rolled up, wading into the waters of Panther Creek. He held his arms out to his sides like he was carrying something we couldn't see. He said, "Come on in. The water's clean. I feel so healed and new. God loves us! Praise Jesus! Hallelujah! Praise the Lord!"

We all stood there on the banks, dressed in our Sunday clothes. I thought: I am not taking off my shoes and going into that cold water. Brother Jim sat down on the ground and started rolling up his trousers. He pulled off his shoes and socks and set them aside and then waded in next to Harley.

Harley grabbed hold of Brother Jim and splashed his forehead with water. He said, "We baptize our brother, Jim Harriday, in the name of the Father, in the name of the Son, and in the name of the Holy Ghost." Harley splashed him again. He closed his eyes and began to speak in tongues. It was a wild sound, like an animal unleashed in the woods.

Sister Gladdy, standing next to me, burst into tears. She ran right into the water without taking off her shoes. Harley grabbed hold of her. He splashed her on the forehead. She cried and cried and waved her arms and praised Jesus and began to wail.

Sister and Brother Dearborn and Sister and Brother Armes and old Brother Marsh and Brother Finch and Sister Turner, who was a widow, all ran into the water. Clydie Williams scrambled up and down the bank, speaking in tongues and praising the Lord. He looked just like a rabid dog. Just like something you would shoot if you didn't know better.

Butch and I stood back, away from everyone, and watched all this happen. In front of us, the boys from the Scenic whispered to each other and one of them laughed. At that moment, I hated them, these strangers. I caught Butch's eye and looked away.

Pernilla Swan moved over beside me, watching. Her eyes were so pale they were barely a color. Her eyebrows faded right into her skin. Her hair peeked out from under her hat—wisps of strawberry yellow that curled against her face. We were getting sprayed by the people in the water. She moved back a step. "Someday I'll be saved," she said. I couldn't tell if she was talking to me. She was staring at the water and at the people and at Harley. Her eyes were all lit up. Harley was walking up and down, saying: "Thank you, Lord, for this beautiful day! Thank you for helping us to see the light!"

From somewhere behind us, Pernilla's mama started calling. "Pernilla! Come help me. Where did you get off to, girl? Ungrateful child. Get back here."

Pernilla Swan said, "Someday. But not today."

~

Early the next morning, Harley drove off in the DeSoto without a word about where he was going. In the afternoon, I was working in the chicken house, singing Butch's blues song, the one I'd heard at Deal's. I was making up my own words and dancing while I cleaned the cages, when all of a sudden I felt someone watching me. Harley stood there with a funny look on his face.

He said, "That sounds sexy."

I said, "Thanks."

He said, "Did you write that song?" There was a strange sort of smile on his face, a baiting sort of smile.

I said, "No." I thought it was a silly question because he must have recognized the song from that night down at Deal's.

"Sometimes you sound real sexy when you sing, Velva Jean," but the way he said it didn't sound like a compliment. It sounded like something to be ashamed of. It made me feel just like one of those Atlanta harlots Granny was always talking about. He turned around and walked out.

I thought: Oh no. Here we go. I followed him. He stood in the yard, leaning against the porch. The sunlight beat down on him and I could see he was dressed in an ivory white suit. It was a three-piece suit with a vest. It looked like it was cut for him.

I said, "Where'd you get that suit?"

"Do you like it?"

"It looks good." I thought: It looks like something Damascus King would wear.

"It's a Palm Beach suit. The color's called Barathea white. I went down to Hamlet's Mill to L. B. George & Company. I need to start thinking about how I look."

"How much was it?"

"You let me worry about that."

"We can't afford it," I said.

"I bought it on credit," he said. "I'm supposed to have this suit, Velva Jean. Little White Church. Little white suit. It was the only one on the rack, the only one in the whole goddamn store. And it was my size. I told the man I wanted to try it and he said, 'Mister, I don't know if that's going to fit you.'"

Harley looked like a god of some sort, come down from heaven, with all that dark waving hair, and his green eyes like emeralds, and his white teeth, and that ivory suit. I felt my heart skip a beat in my chest—literally like it was jumping over a fence. Suddenly, I could smell myself. I smelled just like chickens.

I said, "It fits."

~

After supper Harley and I sat on the porch, just the two of us. He had taken off the white suit and hung it upstairs in the chifforobe next to my old dresses. We sat in the rocking chairs, side by side, looking out at the night. Harley lit a cigarette and said, "Velva Jean, our lives are about to change." His voice was low and serious.

I said, "How so?"

He said, "I'm going to pick up this church and carry it with me on the road to salvation, on the path to glory, on the journey to the glory land. I got a lot to do and I'm going to need your help."

I said, "All right."

He said, "Something is building in me and I can't explain it."

I said, "All right." What I didn't—couldn't—tell him was that something was building in me too, and I didn't think I could stop it. I had the need to move, to go. Harley was standing still and I was standing still with him. I stood still in the yard, hanging the laundry, looking out over the mountains. I stood still in the canning room, putting away the jars, looking out over the top of the world. I stood still on the hill near our house, singing songs to myself where I could be heard. I stood still at the kitchen window as I washed the dishes, staring out at that yellow truck, which stood still waiting for me. Even when I was praying for people and looking after the sick and running after loose and injured cows and leading the circle meetings, I was standing still.

Sometimes I took the truck keys out of my hatbox and held them in my hand, pretending I could go out there to that truck if I wanted to, that I knew how to drive. And then I'd picture myself driving down the hill, my hair flying out the window. Sometimes I sang my thoughts out loud because there was no one around to hear them. I tried to dig out my deepest feelings, just like Butch Dawkins had in his song that night at Deal's. *I'm going down to town in an old yellow truck*, I'd sing. *Going to teach myself to drive it one day, even though Harley says to park it by the barn. Guess he wants to park me by the barn, park me up on this hill forever.* The songs didn't rhyme and they weren't pretty. Sometimes they were messy and sad and lonely and mean, but they were all my thoughts and they were filling me up so full that I had to get them out. I didn't know what else to do with them.

On the porch beside me, Harley was still talking. He said, "I can be better. I got to make a difference, Velva Jean. I got to give back, and with this church I finally have that chance. But I need to know you're with me."

I wasn't sure about the way he was talking. Something about it made me nervous deep down. I thought he was losing track of himself.

I looked at Harley now and said, "Just promise me one thing."

He said, "What is it?"

I said, "Promise me you won't forget the moonshiner's son who married the orphan girl and took her to Balsam Mountain Springs Hotel on their honeymoon." As I said it, I heard a voice, from somewhere deep inside myself: What about the little girl who planned to wear a costume made of rhinestones and sing at the Grand Ole Opry? Did you forget? What ever happened to her?

~

The next morning, two dollars appeared in my apron pocket and we were good for another week. That evening I pinned my hair back and put on my church dress, one that Harley had picked out for me. I stared at myself in the mirror, trying to recognize the girl I saw in there. The navy of the dress washed me out, chasing all my colors away. My skin looked pale underneath my freckles. My hair looked dull pulled back like that, like the life had gone out of it.

Harley and I walked to the Little White Church. In the moonlight, he shone beside me in his Barathea white suit. I barely recognized him either. He moved in the darkness as jaunty, as fluid as a panther cat, standing out as the only bright thing against the black of the earth and the trees and the sky. The moon sent down its light and caught him in it, and his suit reflected light back to the moon like Harley and the moon seemed to have an understanding. I felt jealous and admiring at the same time, clomping next to him in my black pumps and my dowdy blue dress, the pins poking into my head. I felt like a girl playing dress-up, pretending to be someone she wasn't, walking beside her glorious husband who was carrying on a secret conversation with the stars.

TWENTY-EIGHT

Aunt Junie left the Alluvial Valley for good on March 8. The day before she moved, Harley and I walked up the mountain together, to where she lived with her sheep and the bees she kept in a little log cabin covered with trumpet vines and wisteria. Roses, tiger lilies, dahlias, and larkspurs grew wild.

We stayed an hour. The cabin was plain inside—just a stove and a bed and a table and chairs and vases of wildflowers in the windows. Bees buzzed in and out. Two sheep slept curled up in one corner. Junie served us tea with honey and fresh honeycomb, which tasted sweet and warm.

"Where will you go?" Harley said. He was glaring into his teacup, his face dark as a storm cloud.

"To Flower Knob, high up where my sheep can graze and where I can be left alone," she said.

He said, "How are you getting there?"

"I'm walking it with my sheep and my bees and everything I own on my back." It was a far way to Flower Knob. When Harley offered to help her, she waved her hands and shook her head once and said, "No. Thank you. I don't want what I can't carry myself." Then she looked around at her house and said, "I've never spent a night outside of this house. I was born here. I was married here. My husband died in that bed. We slept in this house all my married life. I've never known another place."

Harley said, "You can't leave."

She said, "I'm afraid that's not a choice I have."

Harley got up, set the teacup down with a bang, and walked outside.

I said, "But can't you cast a spell or turn the government men into goats?"

She stared at me and then her eyes grew wide and she threw her head back and laughed. She said, "Oh, child, I wish I could."

I pretended like she hadn't just laughed at me. I said, "What will happen to your house?"

She said, "Maybe they'll keep it, turn it into some sort of history site. The home of the devil's witch." She smiled and the lines of her face shifted and changed so she suddenly looked much younger than one hundred. I thought, she's magic.

~

Three days later, on a Monday, Harley announced that he was going down to Alluvial and that he wouldn't be back until nightfall. He gave me a kiss and then he walked out of the house like he was already somewhere else. He had been angry and distracted for days. I stood in the doorway and watched him as he climbed into the DeSoto, legs folding under the dash, and drove off.

I couldn't imagine what business he had down there. Since Damascus King's revival, he had been spending each day at the church and each night locked in the mudroom, hard at work on his sermons, most of which preached against the evils of the Scenic. He walked through the house bleary-eyed and pale, looking like a ghost.

Arizona Rayford and his brother Terry came that morning like they did three days a week. When I walked outside to give Arizona the week's pay, he pointed at the yellow truck and said, "Someone ought to drive that truck. It's just a shame to see that truck sit there."

I looked at the truck. It was covered in leaves from the fall, which no one had bothered to brush off. Weeds had grown up around the tires. Pine needles poked out of the windshield. There was a splatter of bird droppings on the front window. The yellow of the paint was dusted a faint brown from the Carolina soil. That poor truck looked a sight.

I said, "You're right, Arizona. At the very least, someone ought to clean it."

"You want us to wash it today?"

"No," I said. "You all got enough to do. I'll take care of it if I find the time." I tried to sound casual, like I might get around to it, like the idea wasn't burning a hole in my brain. Just looking at that truck made me feel guilty. How could I have abandoned it? How could I have forgotten it? Wasn't that just as good as forgetting Danny? If it was the last thing I did, I was going to march into the house right now and tear up some old rags and get some soap and water in a bucket and come right back out and wash off that truck.

~

I sang as I washed. I sang the song I had written about the truck, for the truck.

> *Yellow truck coming,*
> *Bringing me home again,*
> *Yellow truck going,*
> *I'm on my way*

Outside the barn, Terry Rayford stopped what he was doing and listened. Inside the chicken house, Arizona came to the door and leaned against the doorway and closed his eyes.

> *Yellow truck coming,*
> *Bringing me joy again,*
> *Yellow truck going,*
> *Taking me home . . .*

I was standing in the truck bed, bucket at my feet, dressed in one of my old, faded dresses, with the sleeves rolled up past my elbows. I had my hair pulled back, but here and there it kept escaping and I stopped now and then to blow it out of my way. I was washing the roof of the cab. It was all that was left to do. I had washed the tires and the windows and the hood and the sides and the bumpers and the fender and the grill and the wheel wells. I had even washed out the bed. My arms and shoulders ached and I was hot, even though it wasn't yet spring and winter still hung in the air, and wishing for some overalls like the ones Arizona and Terry wore.

I finished the last line of the song with the last rub of the roof. I stepped back to look at my work. The sun hit the cab and made it shine. The yellow truck caught the reflection and beamed it back to the sun, like they were talking, having a discussion, trying to decide who was brighter.

"She looks real pretty," Arizona said from the chicken house. "She's just shining like a dime."

I nodded. I couldn't speak. Something in me was filling up and for just a minute I thought I might cry. The sun was so hot and bright, beating right down on this very spot, like this was the only spot on the whole of the earth that it was choosing to shine on. The truck seemed to glow. I picked up my bucket and my rags and walked to the edge of the truck bed and hopped down onto the ground, sloshing the water onto the dirt, turning the red-brown soil into little rivers everywhere.

~

Three hours later, the Rayfords were gone. I watched as they walked up the hill and then cut through the trees toward the house they shared with their mama and daddy and their nine brothers and sisters. I waited till they were out of sight and then I went upstairs to the bedroom and from the back of the chifforobe I pulled out my hatbox and opened it up.

There were the pictures of Carole Lombard and Buddy Rogers, now starting to yellow. There were the painted thimble, the silver whistle, my Little Orphan Annie secret decoder ring, the fairy crosses, and the clover jewelry Mama and I had made. The little singing girl given to me by the Wood Carver, her mouth still open in prayer or in song, I couldn't be sure which. Daddy's emerald. Johnny Clay's sapphire. My Nashville money. I opened up the handkerchief and counted. $15.56, after what I'd had to spend for the groceries and pay the Rayford boys. I whistled. Not bad. I put the money away and told myself I just might start saving again. I took out the keys to the yellow truck.

I slid the hatbox into the back of the chifforobe, behind my clothes and my mandolin. Then I pulled Mama's brown suitcase out from under the bed. There, mixed in with a couple of old dresses that didn't fit me anymore, was my framed picture of the Opry.

~

"Okay," I said. "All right."

I put the key in the engine. I turned it. The engine sputtered and shook, coughing like Levi on one of his early morning jags. Then it smoothed out and steadied and it kind of hummed like Linc's old tractor or like Mama's old cat, Percy, when he purred. I sat there, not steering, listening to the hum, feeling the rumble, the unfamiliar power of it.

I rolled down the window and let the day in. Then I leaned across the seat—across the framed picture of the Opry, which sat propped up next to me—and took the owner's manual from the visor. I sat there and read the book from cover to cover. When I was finished, I slid the book back in the visor and said, "That was no help at all."

What I needed was a driver's manual, but Johnny Clay didn't have one of those. I studied the dash. I put my hand on the gearshift. It rattled and shook with the engine. I yanked my hand away and laughed out loud. I put my hand back and held on to it this time. I put my foot on the brake.

"Clutch, brake, gas." I tapped each pedal. I knew which one was which from the manual. "Clutch, brake, gas." I tapped them again. I pretended to shift while I tapped them. The heat came up from beneath the floorboards and through the firewall. I thought I would melt into the seat. I tried to get the feel of the truck. The engine growled and hummed. I did this over and over and over again.

Then I rolled up the window and turned the key until the truck went quiet. I am going to learn to drive this truck, I thought. And the thought was real, like it came from somewhere else, someplace other than me and my own mind and heart. I shivered. I climbed down from the cab of the truck and shut the door. I leaned there for a minute, feeling the heat of the sun and the heat of the truck. Someday. But not today.

~

The noise came from the woods. I woke up and reached for Harley, but he wasn't there. I pulled the covers up around me and listened. It was a bright night—a full moon. The sky was lit up. In the distance, from up in the woods, I could hear the gunshots. One. Two. Three. I slipped out of bed, the floor cold and hard. I found a robe and pulled it on and saw from the clock on the wall—the one that had belonged to Li'l Dean's mother and her mama before that—that it was just past midnight.

I put my ear to Levi's door but I couldn't hear anything from inside. I cracked the door and looked into the room, but his bed was made and there was no one in it.

Now I was starting to get scared. Was I alone in the house? I went down the stairs, one at a time, pausing on each step to listen. I made my way through the front room to the kitchen to the back porch, but Levi wasn't there. Harley's mudroom was dark—the door open, the desk tidy.

The nearest neighbor was Floyd Hatch, a quarter of a mile away. I went out onto the porch and wrapped my arms around myself and listened to the night. I said out loud, "Are you there, Lord? It's Velva Jean. I don't know what's happening, but someone's shooting up in the woods. Harley and Levi are gone. I'm here by myself. I don't know what to do."

Suddenly, Harley and Levi appeared from the woods above the house, rising out of the dark like a couple of spooks. I almost screamed, but then Harley ran for me, damp and laughing. He kissed me hard on the mouth. Then he kissed me softer and took my hand.

I said, "Where do you think you've been, Harley Bright? Did you hear those gunshots? What on earth is going on?"

We went into the house and Levi came in after us. In the oil light, I could see their hands and arms were scratched bloody and smeared with dirt.

"What have you been doing?" I said. Harley went into the kitchen to wash his hands. Levi scuffled up the stairs one at a time, talking to himself.

Harley walked back into the room, drying his hands on a towel. "Let's go to bed," he said. He had a look in his eye—a mean, happy look. It was the same look he'd had years ago when he was leading the bad Barrow gang. In spite of myself, my knees went weak.

I said, "Where have you been? Are you bleeding? Why are you so dirty?" But I let him lead me up to our room.

In bed he was rough and urgent. Butch's song started up in my mind. I couldn't remember any of the words, but I could feel it running inside me. Harley couldn't get close enough to me, like he was trying to crawl up in me and through me and across me to the other side. Something had gotten him all stirred up. At one point, he pulled away from me and said, "You'd better be thinking of me, Velva Jean. Only me. I don't want you ever thinking of anyone else." And he sounded both angry and sad when he said it—his voice far away and lost.

I said, "Honey, what are you talking about? Of course I'm only thinking of you." I tried to block out the song. I said, "I love you, Harley Bright," but by then the moment had passed and he was back and focused, his eyes wicked and laughing, and then wide open and full, and he said, "I love you, too." And then he collapsed on top of me and I rocked him gently, gently till he fell asleep. For the rest of the night I lay there, wide awake, wondering what on earth had got into him and where on earth he'd been.

~

The following afternoon, Sheriff Story came up the mountain on behalf of the National Park Service and the federal government and went from house to house, asking everyone questions. He said that twenty-three trees had been cut down and piled across the fresh-carved scenic roadway, along with logs and other garbage. So far no one would say who did it. When I heard this, my stomach turned over. Suddenly, the night before made sense—the gunshots, the blood and dirt on Harley and Levi's hands. I tried to push it out of my mind, to tell myself they couldn't have been involved in something so horrible.

The sheriff and I stood looking at each other. He was a nice and decent man. He had taken care of my daddy many a time, cleaning him up, keeping him out of trouble, making sure he got home safe. He had taken care of Levi.

He said, "The government is thinking of hiring park rangers to protect the Scenic. I just don't understand who would want to cause such damage to a road, especially one that ain't even built yet. Just because some folks don't believe in it, don't mean they have the right to ruin it for the rest of us. I ain't been many places in my life or seen many things, but I figure that road might give me the chance. I don't appreciate whoever did this trying to take that chance away." The sheriff was watching me close. He said, "You know what I mean?"

For nearly a full minute I couldn't say anything. After all this time, I had never once thought about it that way. Not even once. When I finally found my voice, I said, "Yes. I think I do."

~

Later that day, after the sheriff was gone, I tiptoed out of the house and down the porch steps and across the yard. Harley was at the church. Levi was up in the woods at his still. I was all alone as usual, stuck up on that hill.

I got into the yellow truck and turned the key and brought that old engine to life. I hit the starter pedal, letting it go. I put my hand on the gearshift and my left foot on the brake and my right foot on the clutch. I downshifted and felt the truck lurch, and then I took my foot off the brake and hit the clutch and moved my right foot to the gas. I thought: I have no idea what I'm doing. Yellow truck, show me the way.

The truck started moving backward and I hollered. I hit the brake and moved the gearshift and then eased up on the brake and tapped the gas, and this time I moved forward just a little. I hit the brake. I tapped the gas. I hit the brake. I tapped the gas. I hit the brake. I did this over and over again, my head jerking back and forth, until I had inched past the barn and the chicken house and out toward the front yard. I stopped the truck and adjusted the rearview mirror. I looked at myself. I said, "Look what you've done, Velva Jean Hart Bright. You just drove this yellow truck."

Then I backed up, one inch at a time, until the truck was back behind the barn, right where it started. Where no one would know it had ever been driven at all.

TWENTY-NINE

In one week's time, the twenty-three trees and the garbage and logs were cleared off the Scenic and construction began on the stretch that wound from Devil's Courthouse to Buckeye Gap. Miles away, to the west of us, over the ridgeline, crews moved in toward the Indian nation around Soco Gap and down toward Big Witch. We felt surrounded. The road was now closing in and coming at us from two sides. Aunt Junie was already gone from her land, and one day Buck Frey and his family were gone, too, followed by the Toomeys.

After the damage done to the Scenic, the outlanders stuck to the top of the mountain. For a little while, they didn't come down to Alluvial, and Butch and the other boys stopped coming to church. Harley was back at work, back to preaching, just like nothing had happened. We never talked about what went on that night. He never offered, and I never asked.

~

Janette Lowe was saved on a Sunday in the middle of May. She was born again in the waters of Panther Creek. One minute Harley was talking, not even trying to save anyone—he hadn't even got up to steam yet, hadn't even hit his stride. The next minute, Janette went tearing out of the church and was dancing up and down the banks of the stream. She passed over quicker than anyone I'd ever seen, dancing in the Spirit, with love and joy and a fire so pure and wild it could make a doubter believe. "Just like her mama," Sister Dearborn said. We all stood watching her, especially Harley, who I could tell by the look on his face was wondering what went wrong.

Janette Lowe danced by me and suddenly I wanted to join her. I thought how silly it was that we just stood staring at her while she rejoiced, like she was something to be watched, like a carnival show. I wanted to rejoice along with her. For the first time, Janette Lowe didn't seem worried about how dirty she was or how poor she looked. She didn't seem to care who watched her dance.

As she spun by me, she brushed my arm and I grabbed her hand. She looked surprised and then she took hold of my other hand and together we started dancing. I heard Harley call, "Velva Jean." I caught a glimpse of his frowning face as we spun around and around in happy circles—dizzy, laughing, spinning madly. We laughed and yelled and jumped up and down, and I started to sing. We splashed through the creek and back up on land and our feet moved up and down and didn't rest.

~

On the way home, Harley said, "The two of you looked like fools."

I said, "Only to you maybe, but not to the Lord."

"To me and the rest of the congregation," Harley said. "I didn't even save that girl. How did she know she was saved?"

I said, "When you're saved, you know it. You don't need anyone to tell you." I thought Harley was being awfully possessive of Jesus these days, just because Jesus had given him a church.

He didn't say anything for a minute. Then he said, "You could make 'Nearer, My God, to Thee' sound sexy, Velva Jean." I could tell he didn't mean it as a good thing.

The hem of my skirt, where it was still wet from the creek, smacked against my leg and stuck to it. I focused on that feeling—smack, stick, smack, stick—and in my mind I put myself back in that creek, dancing with Janette, so that Harley couldn't bring me down.

~

The day after Janette Lowe was saved, I sat on the porch in Daddy Hoyt's rocking chair and thought about the joy in her face as she danced. That joy made me want to sing everywhere, all the time. But suddenly I was fed up with the songs I knew. I had probably sung every song there was to sing on the radio and every hymn and murder ballad at least five times. My own songs seemed silly. I wished I could write a song like the one Butch Dawkins played down at Deal's—a real song with real feeling, one that would stir people up. Except for the thoughts that I sang to myself now and then, it had been a long time since I'd tried to write anything. I thought: It's time to change that.

I stood up and went inside the house, right over to Harley's office. I looked at the neat stacks of paper, the notebooks where he sometimes wrote his sermons because he was too insecure to just let the Lord lead him, the sharpened pencils that he kept in an old milk bottle. Quiet as I could, as if someone might hear me or see me—even though there was no one home but me—I reached out and picked up a pencil and then I opened one of Harley's notebooks and turned it to the back where the blank pages were. I tore out a page, neat as possible, and then put the notebook back.

I had never written down any of my songs before. Outside, I sat back down in the rocking chair and looked at the paper and wondered how to begin.

~

The next day, after Harley left to go down to the church, I sat out in that rocking chair and I kept on writing. Suddenly I realized how much I had in me—all these words I'd saved up. I started on a song about a boy named Old Mule who loved a girl called BeeBee, about how she sang while he buck danced on a mountain that was named for her and how they lived happily together until the day he broke her heart and left her there to die. When I finished it, I cried for half an hour. Then I took out a new sheet of paper and wrote another song.

The words came fast and easy, but the music was harder. I got out my mandolin and fiddled around with the strings and tried to put the melody that was in my head down onto the paper. I could read and write basic notes—Mama had taught me—but when I wrote them down, they stopped working together. On the page, they split apart and went their separate ways and when I tried to play back the tunes, they sounded different from the way they sounded in my head.

At the end of the week, on Friday afternoon, I sat there in that rocker and looked at the stack of papers in my lap. All I had was words and a few notes. I was trying to remember the melodies and keep them in my head where they sounded good, where they worked. Something in me had been stirring around for the past few days, ever since I'd started writing songs. It felt great big, much bigger than me, and it made me feel small but worthy at the same time. I felt just like Janette Lowe, dancing in the Spirit.

That night I lay in bed, wide awake, curled on my side, waiting for Harley. Just before midnight, he slipped into the bedroom. I heard him undressing and I felt the bed sink as he sat down on it, and then he slid his body between the sheets and I could feel the cool of his pajamas and the heat of his bare chest as he moved behind me and wrapped his arm around me and breathed in my ear.

There was a song that I'd been singing all day. It was a song I'd written about him, about when we'd first met. I thought I might try to sing it for him. As I lay there next to him, I felt the hard, cold knot start to melt a little—the one that had been building in my chest ever since he wrecked the Scenic. I let my body shift into his, but I kept my back to him. I went over the tune and the words, trying to get it right in my head.

He tightened his hold on me. The tune started going away from me a little. I tried to get it back.

"I'm sorry I'm away so much, Velva Jean. It's just that there's so much to do. I'm tired, honey. Sometimes I just want to get back on that settee, listen to the radio. But I'm needed there." His voice was getting blurry, drifting away.

I said, "You're needed here."

Harley yawned.

I opened my eyes and stared out into darkness, nothingness, out toward the wall with Harley's little boy picture and the pictures of his three dead brothers and his mean, dead mama. Every day I meant to take those pictures down and put them away somewhere so I didn't have to look at them. Every day something happened that made me forget to do it. *I ought to put my Opry picture up on that wall where I can look at it all the time,* I thought.

I said, "I wrote a song today. About us when we first met." *I'm writing lots of songs. I'm teaching myself to drive.* I had the tune in my head. It was waiting. When he didn't say anything, I said, "Harley?"

His breathing had shifted and he was asleep, his arm around me— weighing me down, pushing me down like it weighed one hundred pounds—his breath heavy on my neck. I lay there the rest of the night, warm and uncomfortable, and too disturbed to sleep.

THIRTY

Two weeks after Janette Lowe was saved, I walked to Alluvial to do the shopping with what was left of the money I had saved from my apron fund. The first thing I noticed was that the boys from the Scenic were back. I saw them hanging around on the porch at Deal's and rocking in the chairs at Lucinda Sink's.

I looked for my daddy, to see if he was with them, but he wasn't. And then I looked for Butch, and I didn't see him either. After I did the shopping, I went to call on Mrs. Dennis and Dr. Hamp. I sat with them and had tea out of the little rose teacups that Mrs. Dennis was so proud of, the ones that had belonged to her grandmother.

I left with a stack of books from their library—*The Motor Girls on a Tour*; a collection of stories on auto journeys (including one about Alice Ramsey, the first woman to drive coast-to-coast in 1909); and Emily Post's *By Motor to the Golden Gate*, telling about her motor trip from New York to San Francisco in 1917 and her tips for driving across country by automobile. I also left with two manuals: *How to Drive* and *Man and the Motor Car.* I figured if I was going to learn to drive, I was going to do it right.

As I came out of Dr. Hamp's house, I saw Butch sitting on the steps of Deal's. He was tuning his steel guitar and drinking from a bottle of root beer. When he saw me, he waved me over. He said, "What you got there?"

I said, "Just some books."

He nodded. He kept tuning, his hands sliding up and down the guitar, working the strings.

I said, "Have you had any sings lately?" I missed hearing about them.

He squinted up at me. "We're having one tomorrow night. You should come."

I said, "I don't think so." What I wanted to say was, "I'll be there." I shifted under the weight of the books. They were heavy in my arms. I wanted to ask him about the music I was trying to write, but I didn't know how. I said, "I been writing songs."

He said, "Words?"

"Mostly. Something happens when I try to put the music down. The notes get scattered."

He nodded. He put the broken bottle neck in his mouth and played a few chords. He took the bottle neck back out and twirled it in his fingers before sliding it into his pocket. "You want me to help you?" He had this look about him like a cat that just swallowed a bird. It was a look he wore a lot, like he was thinking things to himself—dangerous things or racy things or things that only he knew—that he wasn't about to share with anyone else.

"Yes." I said it without thinking.

"You got any with you?"

"No."

"I'll come up to the house then. But I don't want to see Harley. Nothing against you, but I got nothing to say to him." I thought about the Scenic, about all Harley had done.

I said, "He's got a meeting at the church tonight. I don't have to go with him." My heart sped up. What would Harley say if he knew I was telling Butch Dawkins to come up there while he was gone?

Butch said, "I'll see you then."

~

I went home that afternoon and finished my work, and then I took the books outside to the truck and set them on the seat next to my Opry picture. I sat in the truck and, one by one, picked up the books and flipped through their pages.

Alice Ramsey taught herself to drive her husband's car, one he had never learned to drive himself. She had already driven it six thousand miles, in the summer of 1908, before she ever drove it across the country—which she did without even using a road map. She once said, "Good driving has nothing to do with sex. It's all above the collar."

I read parts of Emily Post and parts of the Motor Girls book, and then for a while I studied the driving manuals. They both said the same thing—do not learn to drive without a teacher. According to the books, not only couldn't I drive a car without a teacher, I couldn't possibly drive a car until I understood the engine and all of its "mechanical possibilities" and "limitations." I was supposed to know how to read the water temperature gauge, the oil pressure gauge, and something called the ammeter. There were words like "throttle valve," "crankshaft," "choke valve," "flywheel," "differential pinion," and "combustion chamber."

There were five steps to starting the engine. After that there were seven steps to putting the car into drive. Then the steering began.

There were five steps for stopping the car from low gear; four steps for shifting from low to second gear; five for shifting from second to high gear; three to stop from high gear; five to shift from high to second gear; seven when turning around; and six when parking on an angle.

I was so confused by the time I was done reading that I wondered how on earth I had ever even got the truck started. I thought I would just put the books away and never open them again and that maybe I would give up driving. I threw the books onto the floor. When I did, *Man and the Motor Car* fell over and opened to a page in the middle.

As I leaned down to pick it up, I read, under the heading: "Are Women Worse Drivers Than Men? According to available statistics, the answer is No. The average man is four times as likely to have an accident as the average woman, and five times as likely to have a fatal accident."

"Maybe men are the ones without sense," I said out loud. Then I hit the clutch, flipped the ignition switch, released the starter pedal, and pressed my foot on the gas as I downshifted and started steering myself forward toward the front yard. My heart was pounding. I got scared and stopped, jerking forward so hard that my head nearly hit the wind- shield. I started over again. Brake, clutch, gas, shift, steer. The truck pulled to the right and I steered to the left to make up for it, and all of a sudden I was sailing right past the house. I turned the wheel as hard as I could so that I could go around the side. My arms ached. I forgot what to do with my feet. I jerked to a stop again.

I was breathing hard. Sailing past the house was exhilarating. It was like hanging upside down from the chinquapin trees or spying on the Wood Carver and feeling like I was about to be discovered and killed only to find out I was being saved instead. It was like singing in front of strangers and having them clap for you. It was like writing the words to a song and seeing them on paper for the first time.

I sat there trying to catch my breath and then I started over from the beginning. I steered my way around the other side of the house. I made it all the way around without stopping, and then I started at the front of the house and circled it again. I thought: I'm "harnessing the engine!" It was something I had read in one of the books.

I drove around the house five times in all, and each time it got eas- ier; each time I stopped and stalled less. Finally, on the last trip, I made it all the way around without stopping. I put that yellow truck in gear and set my foot on the gas and laid my hands on the wheel, and I just sailed around the house, finding the rhythm of the clutch when I needed to shift gears, feeling the rhythm of the truck, the rhythm of the land beneath the tires. I thought: Driving is like music. You just have to feel it. When you drive there's no such thing as counting steps or worrying about money or feeling alone.

After I made it all the way around once without stopping, I thought I should quit while I was ahead—let myself end on a high note. I told myself that next time I would go around the house five times without stopping. And then I would drive down the hill. One day I would drive down to Alluvial and maybe even as far as Hamlet's Mill. But I thought:

That's enough for now. You can stop here. You don't have to do it all today.

~

Half an hour after Harley left for church, Butch came ambling up the hill, guitar over his shoulder. I met him outside on the porch and we sat in the dusk, side by side on the steps—just like Harley and me years ago when he used to come calling. Butch laid his guitar down beside him and took his time rolling a cigarette. Even in the fading light, the guitar gleamed. I wanted to ask him where he got it and how much it cost. I wanted to hold that guitar and play it myself. When he was done, he offered the cigarette to me, and I shook my head.

"How long you been smoking?" I said. I was nervous. I had a nagging feeling I was trying to ignore, like I was doing something wrong having him up here with Harley gone. I wanted to make conversation. He had me on edge. I thought: I don't know anything about this boy.

He said, "I can't remember." He put the cigarette in his mouth and lit it, taking a drag. He shook out the match and said, "Show me what you got written down."

I brought out my papers even though I didn't want to show him. I felt shy. I thought: What if he laughs at my words and these sad little notes that are running all over the page? The notes looked like they wanted to escape, like they couldn't wait to get free. I thought he might tell me I was crazy for trying to write my songs down at all.

He took the pages and thumbed through them. He wore a large silver ring on his left hand. It was shaped like an eagle. On his right wrist he wore three strings of beads, the color of the earth, and on his left wrist he wore a band of old, worn leather. Around his neck, he still wore those beads of burned red. Harley didn't wear any jewelry except for his wedding band. Sitting close to Butch, I smelled the heavy green smell of woods and the smell of tobacco, sweet and bitter. I tried not to think what Harley would do if he came back and saw me sitting here like this, even though I wasn't doing anything wrong. After all, Butch was a friend of Johnny Clay's, even if I didn't know much about him.

I said, "Who's coming to the sing tomorrow? Is that man that picks the guitar with his teeth going to be there?"

He said, "I'm not done reading."

I got quiet. Finally, he was finished. He tapped the papers against his leg so that they stacked back up and then he handed them to me. He said, "These are good songs. You write exactly what you know, which is what you should do. You write the truth, Velva Jean." I didn't tell him that one reason I did was because of him, because of the song he'd played at Deal's. "The words are there. But the notes aren't working for you. I want you to close your eyes right now and sing me one of these songs. Just pick one. Don't look at the page. Don't worry about the words. If you can't remember them, just sing anything that comes to mind. It doesn't even have to be a real word—just sing *la* or *so* or sing *stump weed* over and over. I just want you to think about the music."

I sat there and didn't sing because I was embarrassed. I wasn't about to sing anything in front of him, much less anything as ugly as "stump weed."

He said, "What are you waiting for? I'm not going to laugh at you, girl. I'm here to help."

I said, "If you laugh at me, I'll kill you."

He laughed and held up his hands. I thought how nice he looked when he laughed, even if his teeth were uneven and not straight like Harley's. "I'm not going to laugh at you. I swear. Go on." And he rearranged his face so it was serious.

I took a breath and began to sing. It was a song about living up on Devil's Kitchen, all closed up and quiet, about how I used to go places like my daddy but now all I did was hang up the laundry and serve the food and dream of riding that road of unlimited opportunity, when I dreamed at all. I didn't think it was very good.

When I finished he was staring at me. I said, "What?" He was making me nervous.

He said, "Your brother's right. Your voice is something special, Velva Jean. I wonder if you know how good it is. Song's good, too. Now let's put it down on paper."

I could barely breathe. I said, "But I don't know how."

He said, "Yes you do. You felt it when you sang it, didn't you? You just got to put those feelings on the page. Don't worry about the notes."

He set the cigarette down, its end burning off the porch, and took the paper and pencil from me. He said, "Sing." I sang. While I sang, he drew. He drew big sweeping lines and low lines and soft lines and hard lines, all following the ups and downs, crests and valleys of the melody. When I was finished singing, when he was finished drawing, he held it out to me and said, "You can put the notes in later. But this right here? This is your song, Velva Jean."

I looked at the paper and he was right. I said, "How did you know to do that?"

He said, "It's just something I taught myself. Sometimes you got to not overthink things. Sometimes you got to just feel, especially when it comes to music. Notes, scales, they can just get in the way." He leaned toward me and for one minute I thought he was going to touch my chest, right over my heart. I stopped breathing then. He gave me one of those cat-swallowing-the-bird looks. I couldn't read him at all. Then he sat back and picked up his cigarette and stuck it between his lips. He took a smoke. He knocked himself lightly in the chest. He said, "This is where it comes from. The trick is getting it from here," he tapped himself again, "to here." He touched the paper.

We worked a while longer and then he stood to go, picking up his guitar.

I said, "Did you ever know a man who worked on the Scenic name of Lincoln Hart?"

He leaned against the railing. "The name ain't familiar. Why?"

I gathered up my papers—my songs. "No reason," I said.

~

It got to where I couldn't wait for Harley to leave and for Levi to leave and for the Rayfords to go on home after they were done with their work. I would watch them walk off and then I would write down my songs. I covered pages and pages with words and lines. When I was done, I would run for the truck.

I drove backward and forward and over the hills and around the trees. I drove round and round the house. I bumped and bounced all over the meadow, mowing down the flowers. I felt bad about that, but the field was perfect for driving. It was flat and wide and open. I drove in straight lines and circles. I backed up and drove forward again and again.

I got to know that truck like the back of my hand. I learned that once it got going, you almost couldn't hear yourself think for all the wind noise. I learned to be careful turning corners because you could catch your pinky between the steering wheel and the door. I learned that the truck had a tendency to wander from side to side if you weren't careful because the kingpins on the front axle were worn down. I learned that if you got to going above twenty miles per hour, it took on a real serious shimmy.

The one thing that had stuck in my head from the driving manuals was that I needed to know how the truck worked. What if I was out somewhere on the road by myself and something happened? What if I had to change a tire or change the oil or the radiator fluid? I decided to teach myself about the engine. So I studied the books. I took *How to Drive* with me when I crawled underneath the truck to learn about what went on down there. And I propped it up next to me when I opened the hood and studied each and every spark plug and connecting rod. I laid it on the ground while I took off one of the tires and put it back on again, just to learn how.

I sang while I worked on the engine and I sang while I drove. I sang old songs but I also sang the new ones I had written myself. Sometimes on days or nights when Harley had a meeting, Butch would come over to Devil's Kitchen when he wasn't working, and we'd meet up on the hill where I liked to go and sing—the one where I could really hear myself. There, he would help me put my songs down on paper and we would sit and talk about music, about what it meant to us. I tried to ask him questions about where he came from, about where he was going, about his family, his work on the Scenic, his guitar, his tattoo—but he never answered. Instead he sang me songs he had written and taught me to play the blues on the mandolin. I taught him to pick the guitar like Maybelle Carter and showed him how to buck dance. Sometimes he sat beside me in the truck and played me a song while I drove us around and around. Sometimes we sang together.

Emily Post said, "Is there anything more exhilarating than an automobile running smoothly along?" By now I knew exactly what she was talking about except that I would have added "and writing and playing your own music" to that, too.

It was hard not to mention my driving or my music to Harley. At supper we talked over our days and I listened to him go on about the work he was doing over at the church, about Brother Harriday and the revival they were planning or the homecoming they were planning or the money they were trying to raise or the cow they had rounded up for Berletta Snow.

When he asked me about my day, instead of telling him I had taught myself to drive the truck in reverse or to turn the truck around without stalling or that I had learned to change the oil—something I was especially proud of—or that I had written a new song and learned a mean, low-down blues riff on my mandolin, I told him about doing the shopping or working in the barn or mentioned that it was almost time for a new broom, that the bristles were wearing down on our old one.

THIRTY-ONE

By the second week in June, the heat was all anyone could talk about. No one could remember it ever being so hot in our mountains, especially so early. Harley said we were being punished for something, that something was brewing and we were all paying the price. It was the Lord's way of reminding us who was in charge.

The Rayfords worked with their shirts off and I tried not to stare. I thought: So that's what it's come to. You're as bad as Lucinda Sink. You might as well go down there right now to the Alluvial Hotel—if only you had the energy to move—and ask her if you can just come live with her and start up business.

I turned on the radio, bored with the heat, bored with my life. I sat on the porch with the mending and rocked and fanned myself and I thought about what Ruby Poole had said about how she would live in a tree as long as she could be with Linc. I wondered now if I could live in a tree with Harley. I could barely live in a nice house with him lately, what for the heat and the feeling so stuck and alone.

Lately, since the heat spell, I had been having horrible thoughts along the lines of: Well. I suppose this is it. I will spend the rest of my life up here on this mountain all by myself. There is nothing else to look forward to. I will just live out my time driving that old yellow truck around this house and talking to myself and singing along to the radio, as long as the battery works, and looking after these men who don't pay any attention to me and taking care of this farm and writing my songs down on paper. Every once in a while I will see my family, but it will never be long enough, and maybe one day Harley will decide we should try to have a baby, so then at least there will be someone else to talk to up here, even if it will be a while before it's able to hold a conversation. And then I will raise the baby by myself while Harley is off at church and Levi is off at the still, and then that baby will go off somewhere and leave me behind here in this house on this mountain, and then I suppose I will die. Yes. I guess that is how it will go.

I was too hot to even pick up a pencil and write down my songs. I was too hot to even think of any. That is what the heat of June and living in Devil's Kitchen had done to me.

To make myself feel better, I had started playing a game. It was a way to make myself feel more linked to the outside world, like I belonged in it and wasn't trapped up here in Devil's Kitchen. I started with Troublesome Creek, which ran just past the house and then fed into Panther Creek, which fed into Three Gum River. I liked to think of how Three Gum River then emptied into the Pigeon River, which flowed into the French Broad River, which merged with the Green River and then with the Broad River, which eventually flowed into the ocean. When I sat on the porch and looked out at Troublesome Creek, running right through my front yard, and thought how that little bit of water ended up feeding into the great big ocean, I felt easier.

"Darlon C. Reynolds has come all the way from Nashville via New York City to find the best hillbilly talent off the mountains," the radio announcer was saying. "For the next five days, he's taken up residence in the Waynesville Grand, an old vaudeville theater in downtown Waynesville, hearing anyone who can pick or fiddle or sing."

I didn't like the term "hillbilly." I thought it sounded mean. I wondered who Darlon C. Reynolds thought he was to come here and call people that.

"If you can sing and play," the announcer said, "Darlon C. Reynolds wants you to come make a record."

I pricked my finger over and over. There were little red dots where the blood kept springing out. I set the mending on my lap. I hated sewing. I thought sewing was one of the stupidest things a person could do.

"He'll pay fifty dollars per record to the best of the bunch."

I threw the mending down and went into the front room and stared at the radio. Fifty dollars was a fortune. What did Darlon C. Reynolds mean coming down here and offering up that kind of money?

The train ran from here to Waynesville or we could take a car. I knew Johnny Clay would go with me if I asked him. After all, he wasn't working regular now that he was so rich—just panning for gems here and there when it suited him, and driving around in his convertible. But I could never tell Harley. Harley wouldn't like it one bit. "How would it look, Velva Jean?" he'd say.

"Get yourself down there to Waynesville," the announcer was saying. "Get yourself down there right now."

~

It was far enough to Waynesville that Johnny Clay thought we should spend the night, but I told him that was impossible. Harley would never stand for it. I didn't plan for him to know I'd even left the Alluvial Valley. I got up before the rooster, up before Harley or Levi. I fixed the breakfast and left Harley a note. It said: "I've gone to Granny's. Back before supper."

The birds were awake and singing. The sun was just starting to creep into the sky, which was colored pink and gold and blue. There were clouds off in the distance, off toward Sinking Mountain, but overhead it was clear. I walked down the hill, all the way to the bottom, carrying my shoes. I carried my mandolin in the other hand. I wanted to wear my dress with the bolero jacket, even though it was hot as the devil, but I didn't want to take the chance that Harley would see me. So I was wearing Mama's old flowered dress. My Magnet Red lipstick rattled in the bottom of one of my shoes. I picked a flower and stuck it in my hair.

Johnny Clay met me at the bottom of the hill in Alluvial. By the time I reached him, the sun was up and the sky was blazing white and blue. The sun warmed my skin, turning it pink. I could feel it freckling already. Johnny Clay was sitting in the car with his head tipped back against the seat, eyes closed, sun lighting up his face. I climbed in beside him and said, "Well. Let's go to Waynesville."

~

We were a mile past Hamlet's Mill, speeding along in the Nash, wind blowing our hair, when the words started running through my head: "Who can find a virtuous woman?" It went on, getting louder and louder. *Who can find a virtuous woman?*

I began to talk, hoping that would put a stop to it. "How many people you think will be there?"

"Hard to know." Johnny Clay was holding the wheel with one hand and reaching over the seat with the other to check on his guitar, to make sure it was secure on the backseat and wouldn't fall onto the floor. He'd brought it along because he said he might play something himself.

The Nash bumped along the dirt road curving down the mountain to Waynesville. We wound up and down hills, the car bouncing so much we could barely talk. All the time, the sun beat bright overhead. Johnny Clay was a wonderful driver. He could fly over those mountains. I was holding my mandolin in my arms like a baby. I thought I would go black-and-blue from swinging against the sides of the car.

Who can find a virtuous woman?

I began to speak louder, "I don't know what I'm going to sing. What if I forget the words?"

Johnny Clay gave me a look. "What're you shouting for?"

"I just didn't think you could hear me over all the noise." I was trying not to think of Harley up at the church. I was trying not to think what he would do or say if he found out about this.

I pictured him coming home and asking me what I did today. I pictured lying to him, to his face. He would kiss me and it would be done and I would have to live with it, carrying the lie around inside myself until it grew heavier and heavier.

"Who can find a virtuous woman? For her price is far above rubies. She will do him good and not evil all the days of her life."

I thought of the time I ran away from Sweet Fern and got chased by the panther. Years later I still had a scar down my leg. It had faded some, but Daddy Hoyt said I would probably always have it, the scar I still wore for lying and running away.

I said, "Stop the car." We were driving round a high hill, closing us off on both sides. There was no room to stop. The sun disappeared and there was only the hill, looming over us, shutting out the sky.

"What's wrong?" Johnny Clay kept driving.

"I can't go," I said.

"What?"

"I can't."

His grin faded and then he sighed. "Harley?" I nodded. He rubbed at his jaw.

"I been hearing this voice in my head ever since we started down." I thought of Darlon C. Reynolds and his recording machine, but mostly I thought about Nashville and the Grand Ole Opry. I'd brought along the words to some of my best songs, like the one about the yellow truck and another about an orphan girl who runs away and becomes a famous singing star, and I'd painted my lips with lipstick and then rubbed them with Vaseline so that they shone. "Harley would kill me."

"Well." He waited till we were past the high hill and back on the open road, and then he stopped the car completely. "Shit."

"I'm sorry, Johnny Clay. You go on."

He looked down the road and then back at me. "I'm in love with Lucinda Sink," he said, all of a sudden. We sat there looking at each other.

I said, "What did you just say?" I thought maybe I'd heard him wrong.

He said, "You heard me. I'm in love with her. I always have been. Ever since I was thirteen years old and Daryl Gordon dared me to go knock on her door. I want to marry her. I keep asking her, but she keeps saying no."

I said, "You could have any girl on Fair Mountain or Devil's Courthouse or Witch or Bone or Blood mountain. You could have any girl in Asheville or Atlanta or even New York City. Why do you want her?"

He said, "Because I love her. She's my life's dream, Velva Jean. Just like singing's your life's dream."

"She's not your life's dream. Gold panning's your dream. Or gem mining. Or being a cowboy. Or a pilot. Or a spy. Or an adventurer." *Or my hero.*

He looked off toward the distance. The sun was beating down on us. My hair was starting to curl up. I was starting to feel hot from the inside. I wanted to feel the wind again. I wanted to go.

He said, "Those are just things I want to do. But they don't mean much when you get down to it. I only chased that gold vein and mined those gems and bought this car to make something of myself, so she'd see I was serious, so I could take care of her. 'What will it take, Lucy?' I said to her. 'What will it take to get you to marry me?'

"'There's nothing you can do, honey,' she said. 'You're too good for me. I'm too old for you. Too used up. You're young and beautiful and have places to go. Your whole life is ahead of you. Get out of here while you can.'"

I said, "I don't understand it." I folded my arms up around my mandolin and looked away from him. The more I sat there, the hotter I got. I wanted to punish him for loving Lucinda Sink when he should have loved someone nice and normal, someone we all could have approved of.

He said, "I only told you because I thought you, out of anyone, would understand."

I didn't say anything.

He said, "Let me ask you something. You still want to be a singer at the Opry?"

I didn't say anything because I wasn't speaking to him.

"Answer me, Velva Jean."

"Why you asking me that, Johnny Clay?"

"Because I sure as hell haven't heard you mention it since you met Harley Bright."

"Johnny Clay, what do I want to be famous for? I'm a married woman." I shot him a look and then turned away again and stared out the window. I said it to punish him, to make him angry. What I wanted to say was, yes, I do. I still want to wear rhinestones and stand on that stage and sing my songs for everyone. I just forgot for a while, but now I remember. The only thing is I don't know how to make that dream come true anymore because I am planted just like a tree up there in Devil's Kitchen.

"I ought to make you get out and walk home." Now he sounded mad.

"You wouldn't."

"Oh, but wouldn't I? All your life, all you've ever talked about was the Opry, till Harley came along. And then suddenly it's like you forgot you ever spent your whole life planning to go there one day. You should just get out and start walking home right now." He turned his face away and looked ahead, his hands on the wheel. His hands were broad and tanned and nicked up with scars around the knuckles. We didn't speak for a long time.

"I been working on songs," I said. I was so mad at him. I wished I had all my songs with me so I could throw them in his face. "I'm writing them down this time. Music and words. You wouldn't believe how many I've written. Good ones too. Ones to stir people up. I can even play the blues some."

He looked at me. "Where'd you learn to play the blues?"

I said, "Butch Dawkins taught me."

He stared at me but didn't say anything. He said, "I hope you know what you're doing."

I said, "Don't you talk to me. Don't you try to make this cheap." You, in love with a whore-lady, I thought. I turned away. "Lucinda Sink," I said. "So what now? You think you can make her change her mind?"

"I don't know. I hope so. If I can't, I just don't know what I'll do." He rubbed at the steering wheel, back and forth, back and forth. He closed his eyes and leaned his head back in the sun. The light caught him and lit him up all over and showed only what was best and good about him, and I thought, Lucinda Sink is the stupidest woman that ever lived.

I turned around and looked back up the road to home. It wound so much that you couldn't even see where we had come from. I couldn't tell which of the mountains was Fair Mountain. It just blended in with all the rest. *Who can find a virtuous woman?* I looked at the road in front of me. *Darlon C. Reynolds is looking for musical acts—fifty dollars per record to the best hillbilly talent he can find.*

I looked at Johnny Clay. I looked down at my daddy's mandolin, and then at my wedding ring. I looked up at the trees, at the sky, at the sun. And then I said, "Let's just keep driving."

~

Waynesville was beautiful. It sat at the bottom of high mountains that swept away and upward from its downtown. Main Street was one long block of storefronts and churches with steeples that reached up toward the mountains. The theater was on the corner of a downtown street. Folks spilled out of the double doors and onto the sidewalk, winding down the street through town. They carried instruments and some of them were dressed like they were from Atlanta or New York, in fancy clothes bought at department stores. I wished now that I'd worn my dress with the bolero jacket after all. I felt silly in Mama's homely, worn-out dress, and Johnny Clay in his overalls. We looked like hillbillies. We looked like exactly what they were expecting.

"There are so many of them," I said. We were cruising down the street, past the line of people. There were young people and old people and people in between. They came in buggies, on horseback, in automobiles, on foot, carrying their guitars and fiddles and banjos. Suddenly, I wanted to turn around, but we were here and we had come a long way and Johnny Clay was parking the car and we were staying.

~

After an hour waiting in line—wet and freckled from the blazing sun—I said to Johnny Clay, "I don't think we're going to make it. This line moves so slow and there's more folks waiting inside, and at this rate we'll never get in there. I can't be late home or Harley will have a fit."

Johnny Clay was standing behind me with his guitar slung over his shoulder, his arms crossed over his chest. He narrowed his eyes at me and then at the line ahead of us. Then he grabbed my hand and said, "Come on," and he stepped out of line and dragged me around toward the side of the building.

"Johnny Clay! Now we lost our place!" I watched as the people behind us moved up.

He said, "Come on, Velva Jean."

There was a door on the side of the building. Johnny Clay kept one hand on my arm and tried to open it. It was locked. He pulled me with him and went around back. There were some rickety, rusty iron steps and a door at the top. He let go of me and sprinted up the steps, which made a sound like a saw waving back and forth—a spooky, metal sound of wind and rattle. He tried the door and it opened and he waved at me, "Come on."

"No," I said.

"Get up here."

"I will not. I don't want to do this the wrong way, Johnny Clay. I only want to do this the right way."

"Who's to say this ain't the right way?" He shifted his guitar. "You want to sing, don't you? Or do you want to get back in the car right now and drive home and think for the rest of your life about what might have happened if you'd just walked in this door?"

I was standing in the middle of a tall patch of weeds, on a mound of red clay. All around me back there was nothing but weeds and overgrown grass and red spots of earth. The paint on the sides of the theater was crumbling. It looked like it hadn't been used in a while, like maybe it had sat abandoned till Darlon C. Reynolds came along and decided to pack it full of hillbillies. That was how I felt up on the mountain sometimes, like I was sitting empty, my voice going to waste. I set my foot on the bottom stair and my hand on the railing and climbed up after my brother.

~

We came out in the second-floor balcony. Down below on the stage were three girls and a boy. Two of them had guitars and the boy had a banjo, and the three girls were singing "Cotton-Eyed Joe." It was just awful—slow and flat and out of key. There were two men running the recording machine and a round man, with round glasses and thin brown hair, sitting in the front row.

Johnny Clay and I stood still as we could till the bad singers were done, and then we moved down to the edge of the balcony. I fanned myself a little and held my hair off my neck and then fanned my neck before I dropped my hair back down. The round man didn't stand up. From his seat he said, "Thank you. But I'm afraid we can only use original tunes."

The boy said, "We got an original tune. One I wrote tother day." The boy's voice was halfway between a bark and a wheeze. He sounded like he had the croup.

The man said, "I'm afraid we can't use you. Thanks for coming in though."

Suddenly, a woman appeared—also with glasses and light blond hair piled high up on her head. She was wearing a smart green suit and green high-heeled shoes. She smiled and guided the singers off the stage. Johnny Clay's guitar shifted then and bumped against the balcony railing and the round man looked up. He said, "What are you doing up there?"

Johnny Clay said, "That line was too long. We got to get home soon and you need to hear her before we go."

The man said, "You have to wait in line like everyone else." He stood up and stretched his arms and rubbed his neck. He was short with only four or five strands of hair combed over his head. Underneath that hair, his head shone just like he had rubbed it with a cloth. He said, "I'd be in a fine mess if everyone decided to cut in line."

Johnny Clay looked around. The theater was empty except for us and the three men. Johnny Clay said, "Yeah you would. But you're not because we're the only ones that are doing it."

The round man crossed his arms and leaned with his rear end against the seat back. He looked at the other two men, a look that said watch me mess with this hillbilly. He said, "Let's hear her then. But stay right up there. Don't even bother coming down. I may need to send you out as quickly as you came in."

Johnny Clay looked at me and said, "Well. Go ahead."

I said, "What do you mean 'go ahead'? Why don't you go ahead?"

He said, "You're the one he's waiting to hear."

Down below, the men started laughing to themselves. That made me mad. I was mad at them and mad at Johnny Clay. I pulled out my mandolin and started playing. I played the song I'd written about the panther because that was one of the maddest songs I'd ever written. After I was done, I looked at Johnny Clay and said, "I ain't speaking to you anymore today."

The men were standing up and staring. They were all three looking up at me. The round man said, "Young lady, do you have any more songs like that one?"

I said, "Yessir. All I got is songs."

~

The song I ended up singing on the front side of the record was "Yellow Truck Coming, Yellow Truck Going." The one I sang on the back side was "Old Red Ghost," which I'd rewritten some with Butch's help.

I stood right up next to the microphone and directed my voice into it, and on "Old Red Ghost" Johnny Clay stood at his own microphone and accompanied me on guitar and sang harmony.

When we were done, the round man, who turned out to be none other than Darlon C. Reynolds, said, "I'd like you to stay over for a couple of days and record some more songs. I'd like to give you a recording contract."

I said, "I have to be getting home. If I'm not home tonight in time for supper, my husband will pitch a fit. He thinks I'm at my granny's right now."

Darlon C. Reynolds looked at me like he couldn't understand a word of what I'd just said. He said, "I will pay you fifty dollars per song. I want to put you on the radio."

I said, "I have to get home to cook supper."

Mr. Reynolds looked at Johnny Clay like he wanted some help. Johnny Clay just shook his head. He said, "You'd have to meet her husband to understand."

I said, "Will you be paying me now?"

Darlon C. Reynolds smiled. He nodded at Lesley Hall, his secretary, the woman in the green suit. She brought out a checkbook and a fancy black pen. "What is your full name, dear?" she said.

"If it's all the same," I said, "I'd prefer cash. I don't have any place to put that check."

Miss Hall and Mr. Reynolds looked at each other and he nodded. She said, "Of course." And then she counted out one hundred dollars and stood up and handed it to me.

"Thank you," I said. I handed twenty-five of it to Johnny Clay for his half of "Old Red Ghost."

I said, "Can I have a copy of my record?"

Mr. Reynolds said, "Of course. You give me your address and I'll have it sent to you." Then he said, "You ever come to Nashville or New York, you look me up. We could use someone like you—someone with actual talent. We'll make more records. There's no telling what we'll do." He handed me a card. I looked at it and there were all sorts of numbers and his name in slanting letters, just like Harley's on the little white cards he liked to carry around and leave for people.

I said, "Thank you." Then I sighed. For one afternoon, I'd been a singing star. I had let myself think of rhinestones again. I had pretended my worn black shoes were high-heeled cowboy boots and that Mama's old dress was a satin costume.

Then I shook Darlon C. Reynolds's hand and asked to borrow a pen and paper. I wrote down my name "c/o Deal's General Store, Alluvial, Fair Mountain, North Carolina." I handed it to Miss Hall. Then Johnny Clay and I picked up our instruments and walked out of the theater and into the sunlight, which blinded us for just a moment after being inside for so long. Then we ran for the car, fast as we could, past the long line of people still waiting to be seen.

~

"How was your day, Velva Jean?" Harley asked that night. We were sitting on the porch after supper. It was still so hot out that the tree frogs were barely humming. I had gotten home late, in a panic that I would be found out. But Harley got back just after me and Levi after that. By the time they walked in, supper was on the table.

"It was fine," I said. "Hot."

"Yeah," he said. "This heat is bound to break sometime."

"You would think," I said. I wondered when I had stopped talking to him or wanting to try. I wondered when I had started keeping everything inside of me. I wondered if it was his fault or mine or if it was both of ours.

We sat there for a while in silence. He had already told me the latest news of the Scenic and the fact that he was pushing the revival from August to September. He said, "I think I'll go on up to bed. Are you coming?"

I said, "In a minute."

He stood up and kissed me on the head and then he went inside. I sat there, staring out into the dark across to the mountains—to my mountain, the one named for my family—and thought about my actual day, not the one I'd told Harley about. The first thing I'd done when I got home was open the family record book and write it down in there: "Velva Jean records her songs." I never wanted to forget it. I thought it was just about the best day I ever had.

THIRTY-TWO

Suddenly, all I could think about was Nashville. And rhinestones. And high-heeled cowboy boots. And Hawaiian steel guitars. I was letting myself dream about the Grand Ole Opry again. I carried Darlon C. Reynolds's little white card around in my apron pocket and took it out when no one was around and stared at it. "Darlon C. Reynolds, Decca Records, New York, New York; Nashville, Tennessee." I memorized the numbers that were printed there, and sometimes, when I was down at Deal's doing the shopping, I thought about asking Mr. Deal to use his telephone. I imagined placing a call to Mr. Reynolds himself to tell him I was on my way to Nashville, that I would see him soon so we could record more songs. I would just leave the grocery bags with Mr. Deal and hop the train and go. Or, better yet, I'd go back up the hill and climb in that yellow truck and drive to Nashville myself.

It was getting harder and harder to sit still. On the morning of June 20, Harley was at the church and Levi was up in the woods. I climbed behind the wheel of my yellow truck and headed to Alluvial. I could make it ten times around the house now without stopping and I figured I was good enough to drive down the hill.

I felt such a thrill that I could hardly breathe. I thought Harley might kill me if he found out. I thought Sweet Fern might faint if she saw me. Heaven knew what people would say. But I didn't care. The thought of shocking everyone only made it more exciting. It was my truck and I was going to drive it.

I changed my mind the minute I started down the hill. It was too soon. I still didn't know how to drive. I wasn't ready to leave the yard. Going downhill was a lot different from driving on flat ground. But once I got started, I couldn't stop. The truck went faster and faster, picking up speed till I couldn't feel the ground anymore. I kept slamming my foot on the brake, but that truck just took off like it had a mind of its own. It acted like it couldn't wait to get back down there to Alluvial, back to where it used to live. I closed my eyes and prayed to Jesus to let me live to see the bottom. Then I opened my eyes and saw the blur of trees and sky and green, green, green go flying by.

I shouted, "Old truck, you are not in charge here!" There were too many things in charge of me. I was not about to let some truck be in charge of me, too. I grabbed hold of that wheel and started wrestling with it. I grabbed on to the gearshift and pumped the brake and finally the truck slowed down.

I came to a stop just outside Deal's, the breath knocked out of me. I turned the truck off and put the keys in my purse and climbed down to the ground on shaky legs. A few of the boys from the Scenic were standing outside Deal's, loading up with some sort of supplies that I guessed they were taking back up the mountain. A couple of old-timers sat on the porch, chewing tobacco and reading the paper. They stared at me like they had never seen a yellow truck before or a girl driving.

I walked past them, trying to make my legs go straight. One of the Scenic boys whistled and another boy called out to me, but I ignored them too and went right into Deal's.

Jessup was stacking boxes toward the back. He was wearing a blue shirt that turned his green eye almost blue, almost the same color as the other one. "Hey, Velva Jean," he said. "You just missed your brother."

"Which one?" I said.

"Johnny Clay."

I looked out the window. There was his Nash parked in front of the Alluvial Hotel. I picked up a basket and pulled out my list and began to collect things. I walked very calmly, like I hadn't just driven all the way down the mountain in a truck, and like my own brother wasn't at the local whore-lady's house in broad daylight for everyone to see, probably just this minute getting a venereal disease that would leave him blind.

I paid Jessup for the groceries and walked out of Deal's. I meant to go back to my truck and back up to Devil's Kitchen, but I was barely down the steps of the wide-open wooden porch when Johnny Clay and Lucinda Sink came out of the hotel. They were carrying suitcases, which Johnny Clay threw into the back of the convertible—powder blue suitcases with white trim. Lucinda was wearing a green satin dress with high-heeled shoes and a hat. She was wearing white gloves, just like a lady. Johnny Clay held the door open for her and she climbed into the car. He leaned down and kissed her and she kissed him back.

I threw the groceries down in the back of the truck and started right over to him. He wasn't even around to his side of the car before I was there, beside him. I said, "Where are you going?" I didn't look at Lucinda Sink, even though I could feel her looking at me. "Where are you going, Johnny Clay?"

He said, "We're getting married, Velva Jean. We're going down to Hamlet's Mill to the courthouse and then we're leaving on our honeymoon." He picked me up and spun me around and then he put me down. "Sorry I didn't come up to tell you. We been so busy. Velva Jean, this is Lucinda. Lucinda, this is my favorite sister, Velva Jean."

I looked at her then—the whore-lady. Her skin was so pale you could almost see through it and was lightly dusted with freckles, like she had sprinkled them there with powder. Her hair was more of a deep cherry brown than a red, and her lips were painted to match. She had blue eyes and long lashes and little lines around the corners of her eyes where her age was showing. She was softer and prettier than I'd expected. She leaned over and held out her hand and she said, "How do. It's nice to meet you." Her accent was foreign to me—southern, but like no accent I recognized. It was an accent that sounded like sea air and swamps and the low country.

I told myself to take her hand. Johnny Clay was watching me, a grin on his big dumb face. The sun was catching his hair and lighting him up from the outside, and love was lighting him up from the inside. I didn't think I'd ever in my life seen him look happier, which only made me mad. I kept hearing his words from when we were young: "I'll never leave you, Velva Jean. Don't you ever worry about that."

I said, "If I hadn't come down here when I did, you would have been gone without ever telling me. You're rotten, Johnny Clay Hart."

I had never in my life been so mad at my brother. I could have killed him. Instead I turned on my heel and walked away. He shouted after me, over and over, but I walked right back to Deal's, right back to the truck. I slammed in behind the wheel and turned the key and started on up the hill before I even thought about it. I didn't know how on earth to drive uphill. I didn't have the faintest idea. I just put my foot on the clutch and my foot on the gas and my hand on the gearshift, and I climbed right up the mountain. I was so mad that I didn't even stop to think about what I'd done until I got home. I went all the way up that hill and then I came to a stop back behind the barn and I sat there and thought: Look at what you've done. You just went to Alluvial. You just climbed up that hill all by yourself. You just got yourself back home.

I marched into the house, up the stairs, into my bedroom, and opened the family record book. I took a breath. I calmed down. And then I wrote: "June 20, 1941: Velva Jean learns to drive."

~

I lay awake all night. It was too hot to sleep covered up, so Harley and I slept flat on the bed with the blankets and sheets folded down at the bottom. Every now and then he'd throw an arm across me and I'd pick it up by a finger or wrist and give it back to him. It was too hot to be touched. I could barely stand my own body heat, much less his.

"Can't you sleep, Velva Jean?" he said at one point, his voice muffled and his face against the pillow.

"No."

"Don't worry," he said. "He'll be okay. You'll be okay. He loves you."

I was surprised—but grateful—that Harley was being so nice about

Johnny Clay, considering how he felt about him. I lay there listening to him breathe and I stared at the ceiling, at the way the moonlight moved across it, and I thought about my brother and That Woman, as I was calling her in my head. I tried not to think about how pretty she was or how happy he'd looked or the way they'd gazed at each other.

I wondered what Mama would say. She'd always had such a soft spot for Johnny Clay. He could always make her laugh, even when he was driving her to distraction. I called up the image of Mama, of her cornflower blue eyes with the sunflower centers. I felt her hands rocking me, holding me, soothing me, making things better, heard her voice singing me to sleep until eventually I drifted off for just a little while.

The next morning, I was still stewing over Johnny Clay and Lucinda Sink. When I came downstairs, I heard unfamiliar voices. Harley stood out on the porch with a man of about fifty, built thick like a washtub. He wore little spectacles and a brown Stetson felt hat, a blue button-down shirt with the sleeves rolled up to the elbows, and blue jeans rolled up over rubber work boots.

When he saw me, the man took off his hat. He had a thick head of hair, one of the thickest I'd ever seen, and a no-nonsense face that had seen too much sun.

Harley said, "Velva Jean, this here is Getty Browning from the Scenic. He's come to invite me to go up top to Devil's Courthouse and see what the boys are doing."

Mr. Browning said, "We thought someone like your husband might be a good influence in the community and might help the people understand the benefits of this road. We've had some trouble and we're anxious to put that behind us."

I looked at Harley and lifted one eyebrow, but Harley wasn't looking at me.

Mr. Browning said, "We've asked some of the preachers and community leaders from the surrounding valleys. Reverend Bright's name came recommended."

Harley was beaming like he'd been asked to meet the president. I said to him, "Are you going to go?" After what you did to that road?

He said, "Of course."

Mr. Browning was looking at me. He said, "I know your daddy. Before there ever was a road or a plan for a road, back when we were still trying to figure out what we were doing and where we were going, I walked these mountains with him. He was very helpful."

I didn't say anything because I was remembering a long-ago conversation on my old front porch: "I walked from there to Virginia, across the top of the mountains, with a man who's building a road. He's building it right across the mountains, right across the tops of them. That road is going to reach from Virginia all the way down here, right down through these mountains we live in. It's going to be the greatest scenic road in the world. A road of unlimited horizons."

Mr. Browning said, "He's a good man. I'd like to see him again, to thank him for what he did."

I said, "He's not here anymore. He hasn't been here for a long time." I thought of the man I had seen at the CCC camp, the one with the long legs that danced and the way he'd walked away from me even after I'd called to him.

He said, "I'm sorry," and I could tell he thought that Daddy had died. I felt bad about this, but I wasn't going to correct him because to me it felt like the truth.

~

Before he left, Harley kissed me and said, "I won't be back till late. You be good." He smiled, dimples flashing, and something came over me— a wave of love and longing, and a homesick feeling that started in my throat and made it hard to swallow. When he walked away I ran after him. He turned and I threw my arms around his neck. He said, "Velva Jean? What's this?"

I kissed him and hugged him. I said, "Nothing. I just miss you, I guess."

He laughed. "I'll miss you, too. But I'll be back before you know it."

Then he folded himself into the DeSoto and winked at me and spun off in a cloud of red dust. No, I thought, I didn't say *I'll miss you,* as in just today. I said "I miss you," as in every day.

I went into the house and did my chores and fixed the lunch and set it out for Levi. Then I went outside and climbed into the truck and waved good-bye to Terry Rayford, who was on his knees in the vegetable garden, and drove down the hill—slow and steady this time. I was driving to Hamlet's Mill. I'd decided it the minute Harley told me he was going up to the Scenic. I was going to drive through town and then turn around and come back home. I was going to look for Johnny Clay.

I rolled down the window. I let my hair blow. I sang:

> *Yellow truck coming,*
> *Bringing me home again . . .*

I passed through Alluvial, waving to Elderly Jones and Dell Haywood and Mrs. Armes and Mr. Finch and Sweet Fern, who was sitting on her front porch with Coyle Deal, watching the children play in the yard. Sweet Fern's jaw dropped as I drove by. She yelled something but I couldn't hear it because I was singing so loud.

> *Yellow truck going,*
> *I'm on my way . . .*

I drove past the Baptist church and the school and the Alluvial Hotel and then I bumped on over the cattle road, banging my head against the windshield every time I went over a rut or a rock. I slowed down and took my time and dipped down the hill and tried to keep to the faded old trail that ran through weeds and bramble. I felt brave and daring like Constance Kurridge or Carole Lombard. I thought of each of their faces as I drove by—Sweet Fern, Coyle, Mrs. Armes, Mr. Finch, Dell Haywood, Elderly Jones. I supposed Mrs. Armes and Mr. Finch would report this back to Harley. I supposed he would have something to say about it—something about me turning him into less of a man and about a wife doing her husband good and not evil all the days of her life.

~

Hamlet's Mill was quiet. Hardly anyone was out. The trees were green and full, and the phlox and coneflowers and lilies and sunflowers and fairy wands were blooming in the center square. I drove around the square and through the three blocks of town. I drove past L. B. George & Company and the movie theater, the drugstore, diner, bank, grocer, and the two churches. I looked everywhere for that Nash convertible but I didn't see it. I stopped in front of the Hamlet's Mill Inn and then pulled into the parking lot and circled around and looked at all the cars, but I didn't see the Nash anywhere. I pulled back out onto Main Street.

I drove to the very end of downtown, to the very last building, to where a sign stood saying: "Now leaving Hamlet's Mill. Knoxville— 112 miles."

I slowed the truck down. I looked at the sign. I thought: I could just keep going. I could go all the way to Knoxville. I could go past Knoxville. I could keep going till I run out of gasoline. And then when I do, I could just buy more and keep on going again. There isn't any place I can't go.

I looked on up the road, past the sign, up toward where Knoxville must be. Then I turned the truck around and headed home.

~

I knew something was wrong the moment I headed back into Alluvial. I was coming up past the Alluvial Hotel, up near the school, getting close to the Baptist church. The first thing I saw that was wrong was Reverend Broomfield standing outside the church, dressed in a jacket and tie. Now what is he doing here? I thought. He should be up on the Scenic with the rest of the community leaders. Then I saw Mr. Deal walk out of the general store, pick up a case of Coca-Cola, and walk back inside. Why isn't Mr. Deal up there on that road? He should be there, too.

How long was I gone? It couldn't have been more than an hour or so. Maybe two at the most. I looked at the clock on the Baptist church and realized with a heartsick feeling that I had been gone close to three hours. And then I saw Mr. Getty Browning. He came out of Deal's, nodding and talking, hands in his pockets, hat on his head. He stood there a minute and called back to someone, and Harley joined him on the porch.

I swerved a little but kept my hands on the wheel. I thought: Just keep driving fast as you can. Just speed up and maybe he won't notice this bright yellow truck going past him up the hill.

I slammed my foot on the gas pedal and the truck sped up and I could see in my mirrors the dust flying behind me. I was passing the church and passing by Deal's when I saw Harley turn and catch sight of me, saw him clear the steps and run past Sweet Fern's and disappear from my sight. I was starting uphill now, and I prayed I could get home before Harley got there. I prayed maybe he hadn't seen me after all, that maybe he'd taken off after a sinner or a squirrel, instead. But then suddenly there was Harley, big as day, right in front of the truck, standing just feet in front of me. He was smiling. It was a waiting kind of smile. I took my foot off the gas. The truck started rolling backward. I pressed down hard on the brake.

We stared each other down, him smiling and me not smiling. I kept my hands on the wheel and the engine on. Finally, he walked over and patted the hood and leaned in the window and said, "What do we have here?"

I said, "I taught myself how to drive."

He said, "I can see that."

I said, "All by myself."

He said, "Why?"

I said, "Because this truck needs to be driven. It was just going to waste."

He pulled off his hat and fanned his face and turned to look over his shoulder. Most everyone we knew was gathering around in front of Deal's.

I prayed for the earth to open up and swallow me whole right then and there. Harley turned back around and said, loud enough for everyone to hear: "'Drive, and go forward; slack not thy riding for me, except I bid thee.'"

I said, "What?"

He said, "Velva Jean, I don't want you driving."

Someone—I'm not sure who—called out, "If the good Lord had meant for women to drive, he would have given them some sense." I wished now I'd memorized that passage about men being worse drivers than women. I would have leaned out and yelled it at them right then and there.

I started rolling up the window. Harley pulled back. To the right of me, Sweet Fern came out of her house. She was standing on her porch, watching. "Let's see what you can do, Velva Jean," Harley said. "I want to see you drive." Shorty Rogers climbed onto Deal's porch, like he was hurrying to get out of the way; like "Oh no, here comes Velva Jean! Best get up on the porch!"

Harley stood in front of the truck, hands on hips, grinning like a fool. I had never been so mad at him. He was so puffed up and full of himself, telling me what I could and couldn't do, and in front of all these people, even Mr. Browning, a stranger. I released the clutch and pressed on the gas and downshifted and the car jumped forward and then stalled, which caused a few of the men to laugh.

I leaned in close to study the gears. Suddenly, I couldn't remember how to shift or what to do with my feet. The truck was making short, jerky starts and stops. I was trying to concentrate on the pedals but I was only getting them confused. I kept seeing Harley out there in front of me, standing so smug and self-righteous. The Reverend Harley Bright in his Barathea white suit. Hurricane Preacher. Brave preacher of the rails. Saver of souls. Mean Harley. Spiteful Harley. I lurched forward and banged my head and Harley just about died laughing. That did it. I thought: What if I had hurt myself?

I narrowed my eyes in his direction. I popped the clutch and smashed the gas pedal and shifted gears and headed straight for him. Harley scrambled out of the way, stumbling over his feet, nearly landing in a bush. When I was two inches away from him, I slammed on the brake.

Harley was white as a sheet. He shouted, "Goddammit, Velva Jean!"

I sat there in shock. One by one, I released my knuckles from the steering wheel. I gave Harley a little shrug and a smile—the most that I could muster—as if to say, "Sorry," which I wasn't. Not one bit.

~

That night at supper, Harley didn't say a word to me. I thought he was acting like a baby, that I was the one who should be mad. He said, "Daddy, did you know that in some places they use thirty-five thousand drills to make that road? In some places, as much as one hundred thousand cubic feet of solid rock is drilled and blasted."

And then I learned the real reason Mr. Browning had taken Harley up there to the Scenic. "They want to build a tunnel through Devil's Courthouse," Harley said to Levi. "Right through the mountain, below the summit. Just right through."

I sat straight up and threw my fork down. I said, "So suddenly you like this road and think it's a good thing?" I wasn't so much mad at the road as I was mad at Harley. I couldn't stand the way he was pretending I wasn't even there.

Harley took a bite of food and then washed it down with the water he was drinking. He leaned in toward Levi and said, "I can't imagine another feat of engineering as miraculous as the Scenic."

I thought Mr. Browning's plan had certainly worked. Harley was impressed. When I tried to say so, Harley talked over me to the old man. He said, "Maybe I can take you up there to ride on it, Daddy, as soon as it's done."

Levi said, "You'd better not." He looked angry at the thought of it.

I wanted to say, "Take me. I'll ride on it." I was already imagining driving on it. But I didn't say anything because Harley wasn't talking to me.

Later, as we undressed and got into bed, I said, "Are you still sore at me for almost running you over?"

He said, "I don't want to talk about it." Then: "You didn't almost run me over."

Because I couldn't leave well enough alone, I said, "Actually, I almost did." He didn't say anything to this. I said, "It's just that you made me so mad. Do you know how hard it was to learn to drive? How proud I am of myself for learning? For teaching myself without any help? And then you came along and laughed at me, Harley. In front of all those people."

I got into the bed, under the sheet, and pulled it up. I pulled up the blanket even though it was summertime and warm out. I always got cold when I argued with Harley—so cold that my teeth practically chattered.

Harley sat down on the other side of the bed, right on top of the sheet. He said, "I'm old-fashioned. I can't help it. I don't want my wife driving." His voice was hard but there was something else behind it that almost made me feel sorry for him, and this also made me hate him a little.

I rolled on my side, away from him. I waited, hoping he would come after me, but he didn't. He just sat there until I finally went to sleep.

~

The next day, Harley sat me down on the settee in the front room. He sat down beside me and took my hand. He seemed calmer, like maybe he had forgiven me. He said, "Velva Jean, you're a leader in the community. You're my wife. We got to set an example for people to live from. I got a responsibility."

I said, "I know that."

He said, "We got to have some new rules around here."

I thought: Oh no. Not more of them. How many more rules can there be?

I said, "I don't know how I can do more. I'm already leading the circle meeting and calling on the sick and going to the funerals and sitting in the front row at church. I'm leading the prayer groups and giving suppers and making quilts for the needy. And when I'm not doing that, I'm trying to keep this house and the farm in working order for you and me and your daddy."

Then he looked me deep in the eyes with his green eyes, the color of Three Gum River, the color of emeralds—like the one my daddy had brought me years ago—the color of the greenest green on earth. For a minute, I saw only his eyes and his warm skin and the little lines in his face, the scar above his eyebrow that he'd got in the railroad accident, the dimples on either side of his mouth, the full lips, the waving dark hair. I wanted to lean in and kiss him, to remind him of us as we used to be, of him as he was when I met him. I wanted him to smile and breathe and let go of all the tightness inside of him that was making both of us cross and unhappy.

He said, "I don't want you driving off this property. I don't want you driving at all."

I said, "What?"

He said, "I don't want to hear about you driving anywhere or see you driving anywhere. I don't know why you even feel you have to, Velva Jean. I don't know any women that drive up here. I think you should just give me the keys."

"I'm not giving you the keys, Harley Bright."

He frowned at this and moved his mouth around a little, like he was chewing something. I could tell he was trying to think just how much to fight with me on this one. He said, "Well, then, you have to give me your word that you won't drive anymore."

I didn't tell him that now that I knew how to drive there was no going back. I couldn't very well teach myself how *not* to drive. I said, "I can't promise that."

He said, "You're going to need to." He winked at me and flashed me a smile. He was charming Harley now. But his voice was firm. Then he said, "You're going to need to promise me something else. You know I think you got a pretty voice. Prettiest voice in the world."

I waited. He was saying nice things the way someone did before they told you something bad about yourself.

He said, "But, Velva Jean, sometimes it sounds sinful when you sing."

For a minute, I sat there wondering if I'd heard him right. Then I said, "What?"

He let go of my hand and sat back a little. "It sounds sinful when you sing. Sexy. I mean I like it, I do." He winked at me again. "I love your voice, but you're a preacher's wife. Not just a preacher's wife, you're *my* wife. I think it's best that you don't sing." He leaned forward and patted my knee.

I could tell he was waiting for me to say something, but my throat was starting to close up. My chest felt tight and empty at the same time, like my heart was both too big and too small for it. I didn't know what to do with my hands. They felt miles away from me, way down at the ends of my arms, heavy and useless. They lay crumpled in my lap, palms up, as if holding some great weight.

"You mean when we're out somewhere or with people?" My throat felt tighter and tighter, like someone was squeezing it. I was thinking about my songs, all the ones I'd written. I was thinking about my trip to Waynesville. I was thinking about the Opry and the framed picture in my truck and the money I'd been saving off and on ever since I was little that was tucked away safe in my hatbox. There was ninety dollars and fifty-six cents, counting the money I'd earned making a record for Darlon C. Reynolds.

"I mean, I don't want you to sing at all." He was already up and moving toward the kitchen, stretching, yawning, searching for something to drink in the icebox.

I watched after him and thought: I should have run you over when I had the chance.

THIRTY-THREE

Three days after he had left to get married, Johnny Clay was back. I heard he was home from Lally Hatch, who heard it from someone in town. She said the wedding never happened, that Lucinda changed her mind at the last minute, and that they had come back up to Alluvial in the middle of the night and he had dropped her off at the hotel with her powder blue cases and hadn't been back since.

I waited for him to find me and tell me himself. But days passed and he didn't come. "He's stubborn," Sweet Fern said, "and embarrassed. He'll come eventually."

I couldn't stand it. I didn't like the thought of Johnny Clay off somewhere and hurting. But I wasn't about to go to him myself. I hadn't forgiven him yet for going off and leaving me and not even trying to say good-bye. I thought he owed it to me to apologize.

Instead of feeling relieved, I was feeling just like I felt before a storm. I was cold right down to my feet—even though the thermometer on the side of the barn read eighty-eight degrees—and I had a feeling of dread way deep down in my stomach. Something was getting ready to happen.

On the afternoon of June 23, I stood on the porch and looked up at the sky, as if I would be able to see the storm clouds coming. It was blue and clear. The sun was shining. You couldn't tell, to look at it, the trouble that lay ahead.

~

On the last Friday in June, I was in the yard, cleaning out the milk buckets, washing them, scalding them, and hanging them in the sun to dry. I was trying not to look at the yellow truck because every time I did I felt guilty for not driving it. So far I hadn't so much as started the engine, but I missed the feel of the wheel in my hands, of the pedals under foot, of the rumble of the motor, and the way I still felt it run through me even after I had turned it off.

Jessup Deal whistled as he came up the hill. He could whistle louder than anyone. It was the kind of whistle that hurt your ears. He was grinning when I turned around. He had the mail bag he sometimes carried slung over one shoulder. "There's a package here for you, Velva Jean."

"For me?" I hung up the last of the buckets and then I dried my hands. I tried to imagine who would send me a package.

He held up a wide square wrapped in brown paper. The label said: "Velva Jean Hart Bright c/o Deal's General Store, Alluvial, Fair Mountain, North Carolina."

"Are you expecting something?" he said.

"Oh," I said, "I don't know." I didn't want to tell him that I was waiting for something every day—that Johnny Clay and I had gone to Waynesville and a man had recorded my voice and paid me money and I had been waiting ever since for him to send me the record of it. "It's probably some handkerchiefs I ordered."

I waited till Jessup was gone, watching as he walked away, back through the trees, and then I went inside the house and shut the door and sat down on the settee. I tore open the brown-paper wrapping and there it was—my very own record. Black, round, with writing in the middle. On one side, "Yellow Truck Coming, Yellow Truck Going" by Velva Jean Hart, on the other, "Old Red Ghost" by Velva Jean Hart. They had left Harley's name completely off it.

There was a note inside from Darlon C. Reynolds. It said:

Dear Mrs. Bright,

Here is your record! It was one of the best ones I recorded in my search. I only wish we could have recorded more songs. I hope you haven't lost my card because I would love the chance to record you again. Please get in touch with me.

Sincerely yours,
Darlon C. Reynolds

P.S. Sorry we had to leave off the "Bright," but we didn't have room.

I ran my fingers over the grooves—lightly so as not to hurt anything. I couldn't wait to hear it. My voice. It was on here, captured on this flat, round disc. I had sung into a microphone and this was where it ended up. I thought it was a miracle. I put the record on the player and cranked it up and there came my voice, wheezing out, crackling and spinning, sounding higher than normal, and not at all like I thought it did in real life.

I listened to it twice through. Even if I did sound funny, I thought it was just about the best thing I ever heard. The only thing that would have made it better was if Mama was there to listen to it with me.

After I played it the second time, I picked up the record and put it back in its wrapping and closed up the phonograph cabinet. And then I sat right down on the floor and cried.

~

I walked over to Sleepy Gap to show Johnny Clay. The house was empty when I got there. I ran all through it, calling his name, but got no answer. Hunter Firth came barking from the woods, and then I heard a shout from Linc's house. I ran in that direction and found Linc and Ruby Poole working the field while Russell crawled in the shade.

We, all of us but Johnny Clay, gathered in Daddy Hoyt's parlor, around the old Victrola, to listen to the record. When I asked where he was, Daddy Hoyt said, "Your brother needs time. He's been off by himself ever since he got back. He'll come around to you soon."

I tried to be satisfied with this, to focus on the record and listen to it with the part of my family that was there. I kept saying, "That's not how I sound. I don't sound like that." But everybody kept shushing me. Granny was sitting with her hands folded in front of her mouth, her feet tapping, her head shaking back and forth. Her eyes were wet and she was barely breathing. Daddy Hoyt was sitting tall and proud.

They made me tell the story, from start to finish, about how we'd gone to Waynesville, about the theater, about sneaking in through the balcony, about Darlon C. Reynolds, and about singing on the stage into the microphone. I even told about how Mr. Reynolds wanted me to stay for a few days to keep making records, but how I'd told him I had to get home in time for supper. I missed Johnny Clay even more after I told the story. He would have told it better.

Daddy Hoyt said, "Your Mama would be proud of you, Velva Jean. No matter what happens, this record will always exist."

I liked the sound of that. On the walk home, I kept it close to me, pressed against my chest. I had wrapped it up carefully so that it didn't get too hot in the sun. This is something no one can take away from me, I thought. I hadn't decided whether or not to tell Harley. I knew he wouldn't be happy about it—especially about Velva Jean Hart having a singing career all on her own without his name, and cutting records behind his back. But I wanted to think that a part of him, somewhere deep inside, could be happy for me because it was what I loved to do and he knew it was what I loved to do, no matter how much he didn't want me to sing.

No one can take this away, I told myself as I climbed up the hill toward Devil's Kitchen, as the house came into view. I was already thinking of ways to slip the record into the house past Harley, of places to hide it, and of how I would keep it in my hatbox with all my other secrets.

~

That night at supper Harley was in a good mood. Afterward, as I sat up in bed, watching him pulling off his shirt, pulling on his pajamas, I thought of the record lying in my hatbox in the chifforobe nearby. All I had to do was stand up and walk over to it and bring out my hatbox and say, "Look, Harley. Here it is. I made a record. Can you believe it?

An actual record. Let's go downstairs and listen to it." But I couldn't imagine Harley thinking that was a thing to be happy about.

So I let him climb into bed next to me and turn out the lantern light and kiss me good night. I didn't say anything. And I lay next to him as he put his head on the pillow and started drifting off into sleep, his body twitching slightly, his breathing growing deeper. And still I didn't say a word.

~

The next morning, after Harley was out of the house, I picked up my record and hiked to the top of the mountain. The Wood Carver was sitting on his stoop, staring out toward the horizon, concentrating. He didn't have a phonograph or a Victrola, but I wanted to show my record to him. He had always believed in me, even when no one else had the time to. He had seen the little singing girl before anyone else, except Mama.

I sat down next to him and said, "They're working up on this mountain, over by Tsul 'Kalu's cave."

He said, "Are they?" But the way he said it told me he already knew.

I said, "Everyone up here has had to leave but you. You're lucky the road just missed you." He had always been on top of this mountain and I hoped he always would be, no matter what kind of tunnel they blasted or what kind of road they built.

The Wood Carver didn't say anything to this. Instead he pointed to my record and said, "What do you have there?"

I said, "You won't believe it. I made a record. Two songs, one on each side." I unwrapped the paper and held up the disc. The sunlight grabbed it and held it and made it seem shinier than it was.

The birds were singing. The butterflies were floating from flower to flower. The air was warm and cool at the same time, a combination of sweet and grassy smells, and if you breathed in deep it made your head spin. It was the most peaceful place I'd known since my mama died. And in the middle of it sat the Wood Carver, looking a part of it, like some ancient woodsman, working his knife in a piece of wood.

He laid his knife down and took the record from me and turned it back and forth. He studied it close, every groove. After a long time, he nodded. "That is some record," he said. "Since I can't hear what's on there, why don't you treat me to the songs?" He picked up his knife again. He continued carving.

I sang "Old Red Ghost" first and then I sang "Yellow Truck Coming, Yellow Truck Going."

Afterward he didn't look up, just kept on carving. I watched the way his hands held the knife, the way his fingers felt the grain and knew how to cut and where to cut. He said, "Did you write those songs?"

"Yes."

"Velva Jean, you must never stop singing."

I thought about Harley telling me not to sing, and then, before I could stop myself, the words came out. I said, "I'm not sure I married a good man. I sometimes think he's changed from the man I married, that he's gotten off course since then and become someone else, that he's lost himself along the way, and because of that he's lost me and us. You'd think that when he found Jesus it would have helped, but somehow it only made things worse—made him worse. But then I sometimes wonder if he just wasn't very good to begin with—or if he wasn't as good as I thought he was and hoped he was, the way I colored him to be in my mind."

The Wood Carver sat there and listened, as he always did, his hands working the wood.

"When I first married him, there were all these different Harleys, and it was exciting, even if I didn't like every single version of him. But now there seems to be just one version—the one that stands still. The one that's tired and busy and rooted to the Little White Church and Devil's Kitchen and doesn't ever have time for me or us or to remember the old Harley anymore. I'd rather be married to the bad Barrow gang Harley than this one. I'd rather have him tipping over privies and stealing moonshine and getting into fights.

"Each night I wait for him to come home and I think, 'This will be the night that he'll be like the Harley I remember. The one I thought I was marrying.' But then he comes in the door and he's this other Harley, the one who's serious and tired and who doesn't have time for me, who can't be bothered because his mind is on other things, who wants me to behave myself and not trouble him and just make things easier for him at the end of a long day. And then I wish he hadn't come home at all because it's better when he's away. Because at least when he's away I can think of him as he was, and at least when he's away I can breathe."

I pulled my knees up to my chest and wrapped my arms around them. I hugged myself tight. "It's like this time I accidentally killed a lightning bug. I didn't know it was a lightning bug. I thought it was a beetle. I picked it up in a piece of paper and I squeezed it and then its light went off. It was already dying, but it couldn't help flashing its light. I had no choice because I'd already hurt it—I had to kill it all the way, and before I did, it flashed its light again." I started to cry—big, rolling, silent tears that plopped onto my legs.

"I don't think I've ever felt so horrible in my life as when I killed that lightning bug. I watched its light go out. I put out its light." I looked at the Wood Carver. He had stopped carving. He had laid down his knife and was sitting with his wrists hanging off his knees. I said, "I'm afraid I'm like the lightning bug and Harley is like me. I'm afraid he's starting to put out my light."

I didn't wipe my eyes, but let the tears roll. The Wood Carver didn't say anything. When I had cried myself dry, we sat for a few minutes, not speaking. Then the Wood Carver tilted his hat back on his forehead and pointed the knife at the dogwood tree.

"Do you see our old friend there?"

I looked at the lean black trunk, the heaven-reaching limbs. "Yes."

"Remember when the tornado came through in 1935, taking down half the trees up on this mountain?"

"Yes." That was the year of the Alluvial Fair, the one where I'd sung by myself for the first time.

"I had to chop down the trees that were broken in half and replant where I could. But this tree," he pointed at the dogwood, "remained standing. Why do you think that was?"

Because it's a magic tree, I thought. "Because it has good brace roots?"

"No," he smiled. "Because instead of standing rigid against the wind, trying to fight against it, this tree bent with it."

I looked at the tree, looked at him.

"The strongest trees are the ones that bend with the storms, Velva Jean. Those are the trees that remain after the storm is gone. At the same time," he said, "the tree knows not to give itself up. It stands its ground. It bends, but it doesn't break. And it's still there."

It's still there.

I suddenly felt like hugging the Wood Carver and laughing and crying at the same time. Who are you? I thought. What is your real name? Where did you come from? I know even less about you than I do about Butch Dawkins, but you know everything about me. You always have. Instead I said, "I should get going."

"Yes, you should, Velva Jean. You have many things to do." The way he said it made me look at him funny. His eyes were dark and hard to read. He had the darkest eyes. There was barely any light in them at all.

This time he walked with me through the laurel thicket and down a ways, for about a half mile. Then he stopped, gazing beyond the ridge as if there was a boundary only he could see. "I have to be getting home. Good luck, Velva Jean. I would say that your light is never in danger of going out."

I watched his back, strong and broad, as he hiked up the trail toward his cabin. I watched him walk away, with a slight limp, till the woods swallowed him and I could no longer see him, and then I made my way down the hill toward home.

~

I walked home singing. I sang funny little songs that I had made up and songs Mama had taught me when I was a girl. I was happy in the sunshine, feeling like it had somehow reached inside me and was filling me up, feeding me like it fed the plants and the trees and the flowers.

The nearer I got to Devil's Kitchen, the slower I started walking. My chest started to close up. It got tighter and tighter. I didn't want to go home to that house where I felt locked in by four walls and a ceiling and the woods that surrounded it, where I lived like a treed raccoon, all alone and shut off from everyone except for someone who told me no and told me not to sing and not to drive. I didn't want to go back where someone would try to squeeze my light out and press it down till it didn't exist anymore and kill it till it was gone.

That was one reason I loved that yellow truck. Because it could take you anywhere, away from those four walls and the woods and that tree. And it was bright and lovely and no one could take that brightness away, unless they painted over it, and even if they painted over it, it would still be bright underneath. No one could stop it from being bright, like Harley was trying to stop me.

But there was nothing to do but go home. "It's a great big world," Johnny Clay had said. I couldn't very well live in the woods and I couldn't go back to Mama's. I couldn't live in a tree or in a cave, and I couldn't live at the top of the mountain in a house I'd made with my own two hands like the Wood Carver. So I would have to go back.

When I finally got there, dragging my feet all the way, the DeSoto wasn't in the yard. When I walked into the house, I called Harley's name and waited. I called it again and went to the mudroom and upstairs, just to be sure, but he was nowhere and neither was his daddy. Then I went into the front room and turned on the record player, the one Harley had bought me when we first got married, and put on my record. I turned the volume up as loud as it would go, and then I danced out onto the porch and into the yard.

> *Yellow truck coming,*
> *Bringing me home again,*
> *Yellow truck going,*
> *I'm on my way . . .*

I just danced and danced and sang along at the top of my lungs, like mountain trash, like some kind of wild and wanton woman, like one of those harlots down in Atlanta. I danced until my feet hurt, and even after they started hurting, I kept right on dancing. You are not going to put my light out, Harley Bright, I thought. I am not going to let you.

~

"Where were you today, Velva Jean?" Harley's voice came out of the dark and nearly made me jump out of bed. I had thought he was sleeping. He said, "Lally Hatch saw you go up the mountain this afternoon. She said you came back down sometime later and that she heard you singing."

I lay still and quiet, trying to think of what to say. He said, "I been trying to think who's left up there now that the Toomeys and the Freys and Aunt Junie are gone." He leaned up on one elbow and looked at me. "Did you go up to the Scenic? Were you visiting someone up there? That friend of Johnny Clay's maybe?"

I said, "Of course not. I went up to see the work they're doing and then I came back home. I guess I just forgot myself and sang along the way. The day was so pretty." I prayed that would be the end of it. I closed my eyes and finally he fell back against the pillow. We lay side by side, not talking, not touching. I said, "Harley?"

He said, "Good night, Velva Jean."

THIRTY-FOUR

Johnny Clay stood in back at Daryl Gordon's funeral, dressed in his work pants, the ones with the holes in the knees, and one of Daddy's old shirts with the sleeves pushed up. His feet were bare. His hair had grown long and hung in his eyes, and every now and then he shook his head hard so he could see.

Harley and I stood right up at the front. It was a simple service—just the Gordons and Lou Pigeon holding Rachel's hand and Alice Nix on her other side, and Johnny Clay and the Lowes and Daddy Hoyt and Granny. Harley said we needed to be there, that it was good in a time like this to show our support.

It was a snakebite that killed him. By the time Lester found Daryl, he was barely breathing. Daddy Hoyt said it was most likely a rattlesnake, that their poison killed the quickest. Mr. Gordon talked about what a good hunter Daryl was, how he could shoot a deer at two hundred yards and never miss. Mrs. Gordon cried and Rachel cried and Alice Nix cried and Janette Lowe, standing by her family, cried and offered up prayers for Daryl and the rest of his family.

Afterward, while Harley was shaking hands and passing out his little white calling cards, I ran after Johnny Clay. He was already headed home, beating a pathway through the grass with a stick. I fell into step beside him.

"Listen," I said, "I'm sorry. I don't know what happened between you and Lucinda Sink, but I'm sorry it didn't work out."

He said, "You could have shook her hand."

"I guess I should have. But I was mad. You were going off and leaving me without even saying good-bye."

He beat the grass hard with the stick. Then he stopped suddenly and said, "I was wrong to do that." He was blinking up at the sky. His skin was tanned, his nose freckled. His hair fell down into his eyes again and he left it there. "I love that woman, Velva Jean. I love her with my whole heart. I wanted to marry her and make her life easy. I wanted to take care of her and make her happy. She was going to marry me. I'd finally convinced her, after all these years." He looked at me and smiled. "But we got down to Hamlet's Mill and she said she couldn't do that to me. She said I have my whole life ahead of me and she'd never forgive herself for holding me back. She said, 'I've made my choices and I have to live with them. People can't change that much. They have to own up to who they are.'"

His eyes grew wet and he rubbed them hard with the backs of his hand. "She made me bring her back up here. She wouldn't even let me touch her. She wouldn't even look at me. I brought her back here and dropped her off and I haven't seen her since."

"What are you going to do?"

"Nothing *to* do." He started walking again, beating the grass as he went. "Just go on, I guess."

We were almost to Mama's house. I laid a hand on Johnny Clay's arm. "I'm glad you're home," I said. "I missed you."

"I missed you, too," he said, but I wondered if it was true.

We walked on in silence. I thought how right it felt to be back in Sleepy Gap, how good and familiar. I knew that place better than any other place. I knew its sounds and colors. I knew the feel of the earth and the slope of the land and the shade of the trees and the pattern of the light as it slanted through the leaves and then hit the ground. I knew every trail and every cave and every stream and flower. I was home. For a few minutes, I could believe that I was Velva Jean Hart again and Mama was still alive and Daddy hadn't left and Beachard wasn't off somewhere. Johnny Clay wasn't twenty, almost twenty-one, and I wasn't eighteen, almost nineteen. We were young and our hearts were fresh and innocent. No one had touched them or hurt them. Any minute now we would play spies. He would be Red Terror. I would be Constance Kurridge. We would go on our next daring mission.

"My record came," I said.

"How about that? Does it sound any good?"

"Not really. I don't think so, but everyone says it's good."

"You'll have to play it for me," he said.

I was so glad he was home. Now that he was back, I didn't know how I ever stood him being away.

"Guess what I did?" I said. "I taught myself to drive that yellow truck."

Johnny Clay whistled.

"I drove all the way down to Hamlet's Mill and back." I didn't tell him that I'd come down there looking for him.

He threw his arm around my neck. "Well now that's fine," he said. "That's about the finest damn thing I ever heard."

~

The next day, I was under the hood of the yellow truck, going over the engine—checking the oil and the radiator fluid. I wanted to make sure the truck stayed in good working order since it wasn't being driven. Suddenly, there was the crunch of rocks and the honk of a horn. And there was Johnny Clay in his Nash convertible. I jumped ten feet and banged my head on the hood. He hollered, "Come for a ride, Velva Jean!"

We left the Alluvial Valley on the old cattle road, heading out toward Hamlet's Mill, and then we cut across to the brand-new dirt road that Johnny Clay said had been made by the government for the Scenic workers. The access road cut up Silvermine Bald, which was just one ridge over from Devil's Courthouse.

The trees grew heavier and fuller the higher we climbed, a dark midnight green. Here and there, a splash of bright yellow lime. In just three months the leaves would catch their glory and the colors would come alive and the mountains would look completely different. As we drove, we sang "Keep on the Sunny Side" and "Girl on the Automobile" and "Red River Valley."

As we made our way to the Scenic, we came out onto a wide-open space, half a mile long, curving along the top of Silvermine Bald and Devil's Courthouse. There was nothing soft about the land here. The high, sheer faces of the mountains were craggy and clifflike, and they seemed wild and overgrown, like no person had ever set foot here before. We could see where the workers had blasted through the mountainside and started work on the Devil's Courthouse tunnel. The trees were cleared and the earth was cleared and for part of the way there was a road.

Johnny Clay said, "Welcome to the Blue Ridge Parkway, Velva Jean. The road of unlimited horizons." He pulled the Nash onto the road and we drove as far as it was paved. At the end of the pavement, we sat and looked out over the valleys and the mountains that lay beyond, layer on layer. I wanted to hate that road for all it had done to us—for the worry it had caused, for taking Daddy away, and for changing the lives of people like Aunt Junie and the Toomeys and the Freys, who just wanted to stay in their homes and not be bothered.

I looked to the west, over toward the Indian nation, where I knew the road was reaching. I looked to the east and to the north, and the road wound up and onward, as far as the eye could see. I looked directly to the north—just below me—and tried to pick out my mountain, to see Alluvial and Sleepy Gap and Devil's Kitchen. Sitting up on that road, with the whole world spread out around me on all sides, I couldn't hate anything.

And then it hit me. I said, "This was what Mama meant when she said to live out there."

~

Johnny Clay drove me home just before dark. The convertible top was down and the air was fresh and cool. The crickets were humming and the night was alive. Johnny Clay was back—the storm had passed. Maybe that would be it. Maybe that had been all there was ever going to be. Maybe I had worried for nothing.

"Let's keep driving," I said. Harley would still be at the church. He wouldn't be back for hours. I wasn't in any hurry to get home. Suddenly, all I wanted was to run away like we had when I was twelve and Johnny Clay was fourteen.

My brother was quiet as we passed through Alluvial. He kept his eyes straight ahead as we drove by the hotel and didn't look back once, but I could feel him thinking and churning and I could feel his anger. You always knew Johnny Clay's anger was there, even if he didn't show it.

"Where you want to drive to?"

"Anywhere," I said. "Anywhere in the world."

"What about Nashville?"

"Nashville's as good a place as any." Yes. Let's go to Nashville. Let's go.

"Used to be it was the only place."

I got quiet then. I didn't know what to do about Nashville. What if Johnny Clay was right all those years ago? What if I really couldn't be Mrs. Harley Bright and be a singing star too? I was beginning to think that maybe you couldn't do both. But who said I needed to? I had an actual record with my name on it—Velva Jean Hart—even though Harley had made me promise not to sing. If I never did another thing, I thought that was something. Besides, I was happy driving my truck and writing my songs. Maybe that could be enough.

"I been thinking about what to do. I might sign up for the army," Johnny Clay said.

I said, "What?"

He said, "I can't stay here all my life. I think I might be a paratrooper and jump out of airplanes."

I said, "Johnny Clay Hart, why would you go away from here?" It was one thing to dream it—it was another to do it. In my head I thought: Why would you leave me again? You only just got back.

"There's nothing for me here. I need to get out there and see what I can find. It's a great big world, Velva Jean."

"You sound like Daddy," I said. I meant it in a bad, mean way.

He said, "That's about the one thing Daddy was right about. I don't plan to stay here on this mountain for all my days and only know the same people and the same places."

I looked away from him. I tried to pretend he didn't exist, that he had already gone.

"Okay," I said after a while. "Let's go to Nashville."

"Velva Jean," Johnny Clay said, "if I thought for one minute you were serious, that you really and truly meant that like you used to, I would pack up all my money and my zoot suit and you and me would hit the road right now. I'd forget all about the army and turn this car around so fast your head would spin. And Harley Bright would be out of luck and out of a wife for good."

I tried to picture myself in Nashville, wearing my rhinestone suit and playing my Hawaiian steel guitar. For some reason it seemed funny now, just a funny little faraway dream.

I said, "Or we could just go to Asheville."

Johnny Clay sighed. He said, "Hang Asheville," and started up the hill toward Devil's Kitchen.

~

Toward the end of July, I spent nearly every day at Berletta Snow's, leading a prayer circle for her wayward daughter Merry Ashley, who had run away from home to join the Mormons. I came home one afternoon—worn out, sick and tired of Berletta Snow, Merry Ashley, Jesus, and myself—to find Butch Dawkins sitting on my front porch, smoking a cigarette, guitar by his side.

I sat down beside him.

He stood up and shook his head. "Uh-uh." He stuck the cigarette in his mouth, picked up his guitar, and held out his hand. "Come on."

He led me up the mountain to the Devil's Tramping Ground, that barren circle of earth where no plants grew, where the devil himself was supposed to walk nightly, forming his evil plans. Butch said it was an inspiring place for a blues musician always searching for good material. He said the tramping ground was almost as inspiring as the crossroads in Rosedale, Mississippi, where bluesman Robert Johnson had sold his soul.

I had only been here once, years ago with Johnny Clay, and it was a place that still terrified me. But I pretended to be brave as we sat on a dead log and Butch plucked at his guitar, and sang some of a new song.

> *You down in the valley,*
> *You down by the stream,*
> *You down by the river, seems just like a dream.*
> *You just like a vision,*
> *When I need it most,*
> *Moving here beside me, Father, Son, and Holy Ghost.*

The song was blistering and sexy. It made my mouth go dry just hearing it. He said, "That's all I got. The words aren't coming out right."

I said, "Who are you writing this for? Some girl back in Louisiana?" For some reason I hoped not.

He said, "It doesn't matter."

I said, "It does. You need to know who this is for. If you don't know who the words are about, how do you expect to find them? No wonder you're having trouble."

He said, "It's for a girl I know. She's about the loveliest girl I ever met. She's as loving and loved as she is lovely. But sometimes I think she's got no idea. I want to write a song for her."

Something about the way he said it made my heart race a little. After a moment I said, "I like myself best when I'm writing songs or singing. I like the feeling of being lost in the words and the music. Anything can happen because I can make it up. I can go anywhere— far away from Devil's Kitchen—I can be anything, not just me."

Butch was quiet. He picked out a melody on the guitar. He strummed a few chords. Then he said, "Johnny Clay told me you're going to Nashville. Or you were. He wasn't sure which."

I could have killed Johnny Clay. I thought about Darlon C. Reynolds and my songs. Then I thought about Harley and Levi and the Little White Church. "Things change. Now I'm not so sure." I sighed because I was remembering what it felt like to stand in front of the recording microphone.

Butch played a little more then stopped, his hands resting on the guitar. "I've been on the road a while now. Before that, I sat at home for a long time and waited for something to happen to me, but nothing ever did—not the big things I expected or wanted. I knew what I wanted my life to be, but it wasn't turning out that way. Then I figured it out—if my destiny wasn't going to come to me, I had to go to it."

I said, "So now you're on a journey." Something about this made me sad. He would finish his work on the Scenic and move on one day, maybe to Chicago or New York, some place far away from Devil's Kitchen.

He didn't say anything, just played a few more chords. Then he handed me the guitar. He said, "Why don't you play me something?" The guitar was heavy—it weighed a good ten pounds. I opened my arms up wide and rested it on my knee. It felt big and awkward. I plucked the strings and tried to pick out a tune. "The music's in there, same as in your mandolin," Butch said. "It just feels different at first."

And then I started to play. I played "Yellow Truck Coming, Yellow Truck Going," and I did it without a broken bottle neck or pick. When I was done, I handed the guitar back to Butch, and it looked right on him—it fit him like that white suit fit Harley. I could still feel the pulse of the strings deep inside my fingers, still feel the thump of the guitar on my legs, against my chest. I thought: I can't wait to get my own just like it.

"Maybelle better run like hell," he said. He played a lick. The guitar sang for him in a way it hadn't for me.

I handed him my record then, wrapped in the brown paper it had arrived in. I didn't say a word as I passed it to him. I watched his face as he opened it.

He read first one side and then the other and then he looked at me. He said, "When did you do this?"

I told him about Darlon C. Reynolds advertising for hillbillies and about going to Waynesville with Johnny Clay. I told him what Mr. Reynolds said about wanting to make more records with me but how I told him I had to be home for supper. We laughed at this and then he looked at the record again and whistled. He said, "Girl, you up to somethin'. You going in search of your destiny yet."

Then he set the record down and stood up and held out his hand. He helped me to my feet. He spun me around and pulled me close—so close the breath almost knocked right out of me and I could feel the medicine beads he wore around his neck pressing against my chest— and we danced there on the Devil's Tramping Ground while Butch sang my yellow truck song in a get-down-in-the-gutter blues style. I rested my hand on top of that tattoo—"The Bluesman," it said—and held on to him hard and fast.

Suddenly, there was the sound of leaves underfoot, of twigs snapping. We both turned. There was no one there, no one I could see, but I let go of Butch and stepped away, my back as rigid as Hunter Firth's when he got to tracking. I picked up my record and wrapped it up tight. I said, "I'd best get on home." I almost whispered it. We walked back down the hill, not talking. I walked far away from Butch, putting as much distance as I could between us.

~

Harley was quiet during supper, barely saying a word. After the meal was over, he followed me upstairs to the bedroom and watched as I washed my face and pulled on my nightgown. He leaned against the closed door, his arms crossed over his chest. He looked wired but worn out, like he hadn't slept in a week.

When he spoke, his voice was calm and low and it sent a chill right through me. He said, "Do you have something to tell me, Velva Jean?"

I got into bed and sat up against the pillows. I said, "What do you mean?"

He said, "I need to know what's going on with that Indian friend of Johnny Clay's." I felt a cold panic rising in my chest. "Because I'm hearing things that I don't like, and I'd rather not believe them. I'd rather

hear what you have to say before I go making up my mind about this."
He sat down next to me. He was smiling a little, but it was a dangerous
sort of smile, the kind he smiled when he was trying to protect himself.

I didn't say anything because I didn't know what to say. I had sudden flashes of Butch and me at the Devil's Tramping Ground or down
at Deal's or here at this very house—Harley's house—working on my
songs. Had someone seen? But there was nothing to see. We're just
friends. Just friends.

Harley said, "I don't want you seeing him. I don't even want you
thinking about him." His smile was gone. He said, "I know you
wouldn't betray me, Velva Jean, that ain't in your nature, but I don't
want you thinking about that man and I don't want you seeing him
when I ain't around."

I finally spoke. I said, "Who's saying these things? Where is this
coming from?" My voice sounded far away. I could barely hear it.

Harley said, "That don't matter. What matters is that I don't want
that man coming around here anymore."

I opened my mouth and closed it. I told myself to tell him he was
wrong about all this. But nothing came out.

He said, "I don't want to know why he's coming around, but I can
imagine. On his side at least. I'd like to kill him, and don't think I
haven't thought of it." He smiled again, a horrible smile. He stood up
and walked to the chest of drawers. He picked up my hairbrush, my
comb. He played with the hair ribbons that lay there, the few pieces of
jewelry I had. "I want to trust you, Velva Jean. And I do. But part of
the trouble with you is that you trust other people too much. That can
be a fault. Too much of anything can be a fault."

I said, "He's my friend. Nothing would ever happen. Nothing could
ever happen." I suddenly felt ashamed and silly and stupid, like a little
girl. What had I been thinking, having Butch up here while Harley
wasn't around?

He sat back down on the bed. He said, "I don't aim to share you,
Velva Jean, not even for a minute." He touched my head. "Even in
there."

When I could find the words, I told Harley he was crazy to talk that way. I heard myself saying all the things you were supposed to say—"I love you. I only love you. I only think of you." But I felt upset and unsettled, like he had somehow seen into my private thoughts. I didn't like it. And what did he mean, "part of the trouble" with me? I burned hot on the inside and prayed it didn't show in my face. The truth was, I didn't know how I thought of Butch, but I did get excited working with him on a song and I liked being with him. I liked talking to him about music because he understood what it was to put yourself down on paper and because he listened. Did this make me a bad wife? A bad person?

Harley moved in close then, kissing me so hard and holding me so tight that the breath went out of me. I thought about that first time, on our honeymoon, when we were just like a couple of animals rooting around in the bushes. He was like that again, reaching for me, like he couldn't quite find me. I kissed him back, my eyes closed, not because I wanted to but because I felt like I owed it to him for causing him so much pain, and then Butch's song started up in my head. I opened my eyes, trying to stop the song, and instead of Harley, with his green eyes and dimples and straight white teeth, there was Butch's face—the dark eyes, the high cheekbones, the crooked, gap-toothed smile. I felt the medicine beads against my chest. I heard him sing, *Moving here beside me, Father, Son, and Holy Ghost.*

I blinked hard and there was Harley again. He said, "What? What's wrong, Velva Jean?" I wrapped my arms around him and held on.

~

That night, while Harley slept, I lay in bed and thought about Butch. He was just my friend. Only my friend. He and I never talked about anything outside of music. And with Harley there was more than that. When I was sick, it was Harley I wanted. When I was scared or sad, when the ghosts of my daddy or mama got too much to bear, it was Harley I needed to send them away because he had been there from the beginning.

How dare Harley make me feel bad about Butch and make me

doubt myself and accuse me of being too trusting, like that was some sort of sin he needed to wipe out of me. Butch cared about my talent and my voice. Butch had helped me write down my music when Harley wouldn't even listen to it. Harley told me not to sing, but Butch was helping me write down my songs.

And then, because I didn't want to think about any of it anymore— Harley or Butch or my own mixed up self—I thought about the Scenic. Instead of picturing myself up on it in Johnny Clay's convertible, I put myself there in my mind in my yellow truck. I was driving and there was no one in that truck but me. No Harley, no Butch, no Johnny Clay. Just me. The entire road was paved, from Big Witch Gap near Cherokee on up into Virginia. I drove the length of it, along the mountaintops, the whole world spread out below me.

THIRTY-FIVE

On August 19, the day the trouble happened, a dozen of the boys from the Scenic came down the mountainside for the afternoon, including Blackeye and his brother and some of their friends. At first no one looked twice at them, except me, hoping to see my daddy. We were used to the Scenic boys hanging around in the late afternoons or weekends, sitting or standing on the steps of Deal's, smoking and drinking, flirting with girls, rocking on the porch of the Alluvial Hotel.

The day started with a sing in front of Deal's. Some of the boys were drinking, and Butch was playing his steel guitar. A few of the others had banjos or guitars or harmonicas. A colored boy was singing. I came down to do the shopping, to pick up some salt and sugar and a new pair of work boots for Harley. When Butch saw me, he waved me over. He said, "Come over here and sing with us, Velva Jean," and kept on playing.

I said, "I got shopping to do." My heart was speeding up and my cheeks had gone hot. I was happy and nervous at the sight of Butch Dawkins and feeling just like a sinner. I couldn't get Harley's words out of my head, and I couldn't forget the feeling of those medicine beads— real and imagined—against my chest.

I went into Deal's and saw Dan Presley and Corrina poking around at the candy display, just like Johnny Clay and me all those years ago. Sweet Fern was sorting through a box of dress patterns, and when she turned I had to look at her twice because she was wearing lipstick, a bright and rosy shade of pink. Before I could say anything, she said, "Don't tell me I shouldn't wear it because I'm a widow. I know I'm a widow. Everywhere I go I hear, 'There goes the Widow Deal.' Or, 'Good morning, Widow Deal.' The Widow Deal. It's horrible. It sounds like a gruesome old haint tale Granny would tell to scare us to sleep. Well, there's more to me than that. I didn't stop being Sweet Fern just because my husband died." Her cheeks were as pink as her lips.

I thought: Who said anything about your being a widow? It's strange enough that you're plain old Sweet Fern wearing lipstick.

I bought the sugar and the salt and picked out the work boots and tried not to listen to the music from outside. I wanted to start dancing all over the floor and out the door. Coyle Deal looked at me and said, "What's wrong with you, Velva Jean? Are you sick? Your face is red like you have a fever."

I said, "No, it's just this heat," even though the heat had broken and it was cooler now.

I took the bag from him and walked outside. Butch sat there, brown-black hair shining in the light, head bent over the guitar, beads on one wrist, leather band on the other, silver ring on his finger, legs splayed out, feet planted on the ground in dusty work boots. I thought of Harley's new boots wrapped up in the brown-paper bag I carried. The top three buttons of Butch's shirt were unbuttoned and you could see the medicine beads thumping against his chest as he played. He was singing the song he'd played me up at the Devil's Tramping Ground, the one he wrote for a girl he knew. He said, "Come on over here, Velva Jean Bright, and help me."

I stood there like a dummy, like one of those mannequins in the windows of L. B. George & Company down in Hamlet's Mill. Some of the men snickered. Butch started singing.

I know a girl from high on a mountain,
Who's lovely and loving and loved . . .

I walked out and set the bag down and stood beside Butch where I could look at him. He was beautiful, I thought. I didn't know why I hadn't seen it first off. Gold-brown skin. Dark eyes. Wide cheekbones. Crooked smile, with a gap between the two front teeth.

I started singing harmony. We sang loud, our voices soaring, his low and mine up high, and then meeting in the middle, blending, merging just like they were one voice so you couldn't tell whose was whose, and those boys got quiet, not a one of them snickering now.

After the last chord, Butch looked at me and I looked at him and it seemed to last a minute or a week, the way he stared right at me and I stared back. I wanted to just keep looking at him. Then he said, "You want to sing another? How about the one you wrote about living up in Devil's Kitchen? Or the one about the yellow truck? Or one of those you wrote about your mama or your daddy?"

And then I realized what I'd done. This man here knew all my innermost thoughts. He knew the music in my heart and every word inside my head, and there wasn't anything he didn't know by this point. He knew more about me than Harley did. I didn't know a thing about him, like how long he was staying or where he was going next or did he have any family or was he married or had he ever lost anyone close to him. I didn't even know when and where he'd got his tattoo. And now I'd sung a song with him in front of everyone, a song we wrote together. I felt like I was suddenly stripped naked for everybody to see, most of all him. Singing with Butch was worse than kissing him. It was the most personal thing I could have done with a man who wasn't my husband.

I said, "No. I'm done." I picked up my bag and started for the truck.

Butch stood up. He said, "Velva Jean?" I could hear him start down after me and then stop. I didn't turn around. I didn't want to see him.

I reached for the truck door and that's when I saw Harley. His car was parked in front of Sweet Fern's, and he was halfway up the walk. He was standing with his hands down by his sides. They just dangled there like they were dead and forgotten, and he was staring at me. The look on his face told me he'd been there for a while. Without moving his face away, he turned his eyes toward Butch, then back to me. I started toward him.

It was that exact moment that Blackeye stood up and rambled over to the hotel. Someone yelled at him, "She ain't answering the door."

Blackeye stopped and looked back toward Deal's, where the yelling had come from. "What d'you mean?"

"She's closed for business," one of the boys said. "Ever since she gone away all those weeks ago to Hamlet's Mill and come back."

Blackeye narrowed his eyes and looked at all of us looking at him. He said, loud enough for everyone to hear, "She's going to open the door for me. I'm going to go over there and make the whore come out."

I saw Blackeye go around back of the hotel and disappear. A minute later, he came back around front and climbed up on the porch and whistled to his friends. Four other men joined him—his brother Slim, the German, a towheaded boy I hadn't seen before, and a boy I thought I recognized from a nearby valley—and they started banging on the windows and the front door, hollering things at Lucinda and yelling at her to let them in. When this didn't work, one of them picked up a rocking chair and threw it off the porch and into the dirt, and another one picked up a chair and threw it at a window. There was the sound of glass breaking.

Harley and the Deal boys and Butch and Mr. Deal were in the road. Some of the other Scenic boys were standing around outside the general store, smoking and drinking, looking like nothing much had happened. Elderly Jones stood on his front porch, praying to Jesus as loud as he could.

Harley and the Deals were up on that porch in a heartbeat, swinging over the railing and grabbing hold of Blackeye and the others that were causing the trouble. My heart jumped. There was a crash and swearing and shouting and another crash and, from inside the hotel, a woman's scream. I started running for Lucinda. Butch caught me half-way there, grabbing me round the waist and pulling me back. He said,

"You stay here." The he joined the others on the hotel porch just as Harley and the Deals came down off of it, dragging Blackeye and Slim and the German and the other two. Harley looked mean and happy. He was grinning and his eyes were wild. There was a thin, red line on Blackeye's cheek where he was bleeding.

Harley said, "You get out of here. Go on. Get back to Silvermine Bald. And don't you come back here again."

Behind Harley, up on the porch, hovering in the doorway, was the outline of a woman. I couldn't see her clearly, but I caught a glimpse of red hair just before she turned and went back inside, shutting the door. I heard the click of the lock being turned.

The German spat on the ground and blood came out along with one of his teeth. Slim sat right down on the ground until the towheaded boy kicked his boots and then pulled him up. Blackeye didn't look back at Harley. He held his head up and pushed through the crowd and walked over to the train tracks and started walking along them. Then he cut across them and over them and disappeared into the woods, followed by his friends.

~

Harley got home ahead of me, racing his DeSoto up over that hill so fast I thought he was going to fly off the mountain. I parked the truck behind the barn and came into the house just after him and stood outside the closed door of his mudroom. "Harley?" I said. I knocked. I held my breath. "I'm sorry. Please open the door. We got to talk about this."

He didn't answer. There wasn't a sound from inside the room.

Finally, I went to the kitchen to fix the supper. Levi was on the back porch, sleeping off a late-night whiskey run. I could hear him snoring as I moved around, making the biscuits, pouring the tea, pretending we were a happy family, all in its place, that Harley wasn't trying to freeze me out, that I wasn't walking on eggshells. I was scared to death of what he might do.

We hadn't been home an hour when there was a pounding on the front door. The door to the mudroom flew open and Harley appeared.

He walked right past me, my arms full of silverware and plates, on my way into the dining room to set the table.

From the hallway, I heard Johnny Clay's voice. He was yelling. I ran into the hall and stood there. Johnny Clay said, "Did they hurt her?"

Harley said, "They never got to her. We stopped them in time."

"Did they have a knife? I heard they had a knife."

"That don't matter, Johnny Clay. They weren't ever able to use it," Harley said.

"Did they have a knife?" Once he got something in his head, Johnny Clay was like a dog with a bone. He just would not let it go.

"Maybe one or two of them did."

Johnny Clay was down the steps at this point. Harley went after him.

"Don't do anything stupid," he said. "Don't make it worse than it already is."

I could tell Harley was getting madder. I put my hand on his arm and pulled on the muscle. I said, "Don't." Then, to Johnny Clay, I said: "She's okay. They didn't hurt her. Harley and the Deals got there before they could do anything."

"Why didn't you tell me, Velva Jean?" I'd never seen Johnny Clay look like that—equal parts upset and sad and hurt and mad.

I said, "Harley took care of it. Lucinda was fine. He chased them away."

Johnny Clay said, "Who was it?"

I said, "Those boys from the Scenic."

He said, "Which one started it?"

I didn't say anything at first. I knew if I told him, he would go after him.

"It was hard to tell. It was all of them," I said finally.

"I'll just find Butch and make him tell me."

I waited, hoping he might let it go, but knowing that he wouldn't. I sighed to let him know I wasn't happy about telling him. "It was that one they call Blackeye."

Johnny Clay said, "Chasing him away was for me to do, not Harley."

I said, "You weren't there."

This shut him up. He stood glaring at the ground. Finally, he said, "He had a knife?"

Harley said, "You're welcome." He had his arms folded across his chest.

I said, "Go in the house." I said it loud and sharp, like I was talking to a dog or a child that wasn't listening.

Harley looked at me in surprise, but he went into the house and closed the door.

Johnny Clay was staring off at the woods, his jaw set, his eyes fixed. He was madder than I'd ever seen him, so mad it curled my blood. I said, "Johnny Clay? What are you going to do?" When he didn't answer, I felt the fear rising up in my chest like the thing he was going to do—whatever it was—was already done. "Johnny Clay?" My voice came out high and loud. "Answer me."

He said, "That's not for you to worry about."

I said, "Don't be stupid. If you go up there to the CCC camp, you're going to get yourself killed." I knew how his mind worked. I knew what he was thinking.

He said, "Not if I send Red Terror instead." He winked at me and smiled, but that smile was ice cold. Then he got into his car and slammed the door. He sat there for a minute, looking down.

I called out, "Johnny Clay? Why don't you come back up here? Why don't you come inside?"

He didn't say anything. He started the car and drove away.

～

I told Harley we needed to go see Daddy Hoyt right now, right this minute, that there was no telling what Johnny Clay might do, but Harley would not be hurried. He wanted to finish his supper and eat every bite.

Long after Levi and I were done eating, I watched Harley scrape the crumbs off his plate and wipe up the last bit of gravy with his soda biscuit. I watched him drink it down with sweet tea and then wipe his mouth with a napkin. I knew now he'd want an after-dinner cigarette, even though he liked to pretend he didn't smoke. He'd stand out there on the porch and stare off at the mountains and he'd drift off to some-place else in his mind and there would be no talking to him for a while.

"Harley," I said, after he threw down his napkin, just as he was standing. "Let's go now." I wanted to see if Johnny Clay was home or if he had gone off, like I was worried he had, to the CCC camp.

"I got to digest first," Harley said, which meant he wanted that cig-arette. He looked at me, cold and hard, before walking away from the table.

Just then there was a banging on the door and I thought for one minute it might be Johnny Clay—that he had come to his senses. But when Harley opened the door, it wasn't Johnny Clay at all but Mr. Har-riday and Sister Gladdy. Sister Gladdy was crying. Right away, she moved past Harley and came into the house and threw her arms around me and just heaved and heaved, her enormous bosom moving up and down. My first thought was oh, my Lord, Johnny Clay has got himself killed.

I said, "What is it?" I looked right at Brother Jim.

He said, "Preacher Bright, there has been a tragedy up at the church. Sister Janette Lowe was up there laying flowers at the pulpit. She was all by herself." He pulled the glasses off his face and started fussing with them, rubbing at the lenses with a handkerchief. He wiped his eyes quick with the back of one hand. His head was bowed. He said, "Someone came after her. They found her up there alone. He had a knife. He held it to her throat. She began praying and he said, 'It's all right if you pray, but don't pray too loud or I'll kill you.' She said it was her prayers that saved her."

Harley was saying, "Who found her? Who came after her?" His face had gone white. Levi was standing in the doorway to the dining room, his mouth working like he was talking to Jesus.

Brother Jim said, "Sister Lowe didn't know the man. She said he was an outlander. Preacher Bright, that man attacked her."

Harley said, "As preacher of that church, you can be sure I'll get to the bottom of this. I'll find out who did it. I've got some ideas. That man Blackeye or one of the other Scenic boys."

I said, "You can't blame all the Scenic boys just because some of them are rotten."

Harley looked at me. He said, "How do you know not all of them are rotten, Velva Jean? Since when can you speak for each and every one of them? Or is it just one in particular you're concerned with?"

I didn't say anything to this. I didn't trust his expression, the meanness in his eyes.

Brother Jim said, "Hink Lowe and her daddy and her uncles and the sheriff are on the hunt for that man right now. We thought you could come with us. There's fixing to be some trouble in town. This has got folks worked up. We need you."

Harley said, "Velva Jean, I want you to stay inside and lock the door. Daddy, you're not to leave her. That man could be anywhere."

Levi was already heading up the stairs, muttering under his breath. I knew he was on his way to his room to fetch his Luger.

I waited for Harley to kiss me, but instead he just walked through the door and went with the Harridays out into the night.

~

In my dream I heard hammering, like someone pounding a nail. Then the hammering got louder until it felt like it was in my head, and I woke up and heard the knocking at the front door. Harley still wasn't home. I felt a moment of panic. What if it was the outlander? The one that attacked Janette Lowe? I lay there in bed, my heart beating wildly. The hammering continued.

Slowly, carefully, I raised myself up on my knees and peered out the window. There, down below, was Johnny Clay's Nash convertible parked in our front yard.

I slipped out of bed and found my old bathrobe and ran down the stairs. He was banging on the door now, just as loud as could be, slapping his whole palm against it.

I threw the door open and said, "You're going to wake the entire holler. Are you drunk?"

He looked drunk. His hair was messy and his clothes looked like he'd thrown them on in a hurry. He was acting like he had the fidgets, looking over his shoulder and glancing all around. He leaned one hand on the doorframe and said, "Velva Jean, I got to go."

I said, "Go where? Why're you waking me up in the middle of the night?" I leaned in to smell his breath.

He pushed me away. He said, "I want you to listen. I didn't kill him, but I hurt him good. They'll be after me."

I said, "Who did you hurt?"

He said, "Blackeye."

I said, "Why would you do something so stupid?"

He said, "Because he tried to hurt the woman I love."

I said, "Is he dead?"

"No. And he ain't going to die. But he's as close to dead as I could make him without killing him, although I wanted to kill him. And you better believe they'll come after me. That's why I got to go."

I said, "Where? Where will you go?"

"I don't know," he said. "Maybe New York. Maybe California. Somewhere I can get lost. I'll send you a postcard, let you know where I end up."

I was standing there, in my bare feet, trying not to cry like a baby. "You can't leave," I said. I knew that if he left the most important part of my world would be gone. I knew that if he left nothing would ever be the same again.

He said, "I got to, Velva Jean. I did a bad thing, but it was a thing I had to do. No one's got the right to touch her if she don't want them to." Standing there, he looked like the best of our mama and daddy. He looked gold even in the moonlight. He said, "I brought some things to give you. I been saving them for you." He handed me a green box, the kind you put recipes in, and a folded road map. He said, "This should get you where you need to go."

Then, before I could stop him, he pulled me close and hugged me tight and then pushed me away so that I went spinning into the door and had to throw out my arms to catch myself. He was gone then, in a cloud of dust, one arm waving like the queen as he disappeared from my life and into the night.

~

I sat down in the front room with the things Johnny Clay had given me—the map and the green recipe box. I opened the box and looked inside, but it smelled so much like Mama—like lavender and honeysuckle and lye soap—that I closed it right back up again. Opening that box made me want to cry, and I was already wanting to cry over Johnny Clay leaving. But I wouldn't cry. I knew that if I started I might not stop.

I picked up the map. It was an Esso gas-station map. I unfolded it and there was the state of Tennessee with part of North Carolina next to it. I found a little dot that said "The Alluvial Valley." Johnny Clay had circled it. From there, he had marked the route to Nashville along the only road that came anywhere near us—the Blue Ridge Parkway.

I put my head down and started crying, and I didn't stop for an hour. I cried so hard that my eyes swelled almost shut. All the while, I rocked myself back and forth on the settee, my arms wrapped tight around my knees. Finally, when I had cried myself out, I lay back and tried to breathe. I thought how strange it was that you could cry like your heart was breaking and then all at once feel like stopping, even when you were still so sad and lonely that you weren't sure you would ever be happy again. I held up that map and looked at the route and tried to figure out how long it would take to drive from here to Nashville.

THIRTY-SIX

The next morning, just after breakfast, Brother Jim came to the house to talk to Harley. There were other men with him—I couldn't hear who they were. Harley was needed in Alluvial and while he was itching to go, I could tell he didn't think he should leave me. I was still lying in bed, long after the rooster crowed and the sun had rose over the mountains and into the sky. I didn't want to be awake, because being awake meant that I would have to face the day for the first time since Johnny Clay had gone for good.

Downstairs, the men argued with Harley. When he came upstairs to check on me and bring me some water, I said, "If you need to go, go. Don't worry about me. I'll be safe." I was beginning to get tired of lying there, but I felt so heavy and worn down that it was hard to get up.

Harley studied my face. He had taken to doing this lately—taking it in with long looks, not saying a word, as if he was trying to get to the bottom of things, as if he didn't quite trust what he saw there. Downstairs, Brother Jim coughed and cleared his throat impatiently.

Harley was a hundred miles away from me. Finally, he said, "All right, Velva Jean."

~

As I lay there, I made myself stop thinking about Harley and Johnny Clay and I thought instead about Janette Lowe. I thought about the first time she came to the Little White Church and about the day that she was saved. I thought about dancing with her after she'd received salvation, about the way the two of us danced up and down the shores of Panther Creek.

The more I lay there, the guiltier I felt for lying there and feeling sorry for myself after what had happened to her. So I got up out of bed and got myself dressed. I washed my face and brushed my hair, and then I walked into the canning room at the end of the hall and chose three of my nicest jars of fruit. I put them into a basket and tied the handle with a bow and then I walked down the hill toward Alluvial.

~

The Lowes lived way up in Sleepy Gap, up past Mama's and Daddy Hoyt's. There was a trampled-down path that wove under the tree cover. I picked my way over and through this and about six hundred yards or so later I came to the house, which was set back in the trees so you could barely see it. The house looked like it might fall down any minute. It had the look of being just barely propped up. Here and there in the yard lay wide rings of leaves and tree limbs and animal bones and the gray-black dusting of ashes, leftovers from the fires Hink and his brothers liked to burn.

I had only been here once before, long ago with Johnny Clay. Fifteen people lived in that little house and not all of them were right. The only one with any sense was Hink's second sister, Praise Elizabeth, who had gotten out years ago by marrying a traveling salesman and moving to Tennessee. She had never once come back.

There were at least three Lowes hanging off the porch, staring at me. There was another one in the front window and two more that ran around back. They were just like rabbits, Granny always said. They just multiplied before your eyes.

I walked up onto the porch. The floorboards creaked and I thought I might fall right through. I knocked on the door.

"Daddy ain't in there," one of the Lowes on the porch said. He was filthy—small and mangy with hair that stuck up all over.

"Where is he?" I said.

"He gone off after a bear." The three Lowes came creeping over.

They stood around me. One of them was chewing on his thumb. The other one was smoking even though he wasn't any older than nine. "We think the bear probably killed him. We think he's probably dead somewhere, chewed up by an animal."

"Is your mama home?" I said.

"Mama's in there lying down," the oldest boy said. "On account of what happened with Janette."

Actually, Mrs. Lowe was always lying down. She was either resting in bed because she was just getting ready to have a baby or because she was just getting over having one. "Can I see her?"

There was a shuffling sound and Javeen appeared at the door. She was fourteen or fifteen, but she was taller and fatter than Janette. She hollered at the boys on the porch, "Get down offa there and go away. Janny's trying to rest."

I said, "Javeen? Can I come in please?"

She looked me over and then nodded. She said, "She won't want to talk to you."

I followed her into the room inside where Mrs. Lowe lay on one bed and Janette lay on another, turned on her side, face to the wall, a thin brown blanket pulled up over her shoulder. There were six or seven other beds—wide enough for just one person—all around, and another room beyond with more beds.

I looked right at Janette, then at Mrs. Lowe, who was staring at me from her pillow. I said, "Ma'am, I didn't mean to disturb anyone. I came to see Janette."

Mrs. Lowe said, "She ain't up to company."

I said, "I'm so sorry to hear about your trouble. I want you to know that I'm here to offer any help I can. I care about Janette. She's my friend. I'm sorry she was hurt, that anyone would hurt her. I'm sorry that someone would do such a thing in this world." I started to cry even though I hadn't meant to. I said, "I want her to know that I'm here for her if she needs anything or if you need anything at all."

Mrs. Lowe was crying now. Javeen sat down and held her mama's hand. Mrs. Lowe said, "That man attacked my daughter. He's going to pay for it. My husband and my brothers and my son have gone to find that man and make sure he gets what's coming to him."

I glanced at Janette, still lying in her bed. She hadn't moved since we came in.

I said, "Does she know the man who did this?"

Mrs. Lowe said, "She never seen him before. She said he was a stranger. She called the one that did this the outlander. The sheriff come up here last night after Hink found Janette. The sheriff and Frank and Hink, they took off toward Cherokee. They figure that boy is going to try to run through down there to the railroad, and then to Bryson City or on over to Tennessee."

I thought: The storm isn't over. It's only just coming. Heaven help us all.

~

From the Lowe's house, I climbed the rest of the way up our mountain to Old Widow's Peak. Standing there, I missed Johnny Clay all over again. I felt the familiar homesick lump in my throat and for a while I couldn't swallow. There at the top of the peak, I had a good view of the Scenic. No one was working—no men, no guards—which was strange for the middle of a weekday.

I stood there for a little while longer, looking out past the new road and over the valleys and the mountains that grew up one after another as far as the eye could see. I wondered where Johnny Clay was, if I could see him from where I stood. I wondered about Beachard and Daddy. And then I turned toward home.

~

I heard Harley before I saw him. The train was stopped in Alluvial, the doors to the boxcars standing open. A crowd was gathered beside the tracks, outside Deal's. Not just a crowd—there were at least a hundred people, maybe more. It looked like everyone had come down off our five mountains, like they were gathered for the Alluvial Fair.

Harley was preaching about something, but I couldn't make out the words. Dusk was coming; the sun was moving lower in the sky. Lightning bugs were beginning to appear, flickering on and off here and

there. The crickets were starting to hum, like fiddles just warming up.
Men stood with arms folded. They leaned on shotguns. Some of the
boys from the Scenic crowded together in groups, surrounded, gathered up around the boxcars, guns pointed at them. There were miners
and boys from the band mill staring out from inside the train. I saw
Burn McKinney and his family, and Burn looked mad as a hornet.
Then I saw Mrs. Dennis and Dr. Hamp, and Mrs. Dennis was crying.

The first person I recognized in the crowd was Coyle Deal, standing outside the store, arms folded. From the back, he looked just like
Danny, sandy blond hair, sturdy shoulders. For a moment, you could
almost believe he was Danny. He turned and then he was Coyle again.
I ran to him.

"What's happening?" I said. Beyond him I could see everyone I
knew—everyone from the mountains. Harley stood at the front of the
crowd, up on the back of someone's truck.

"Harley's preaching against the outlanders. Everybody's calling for
blood. There are a lot of people who want them gone, Velva Jean—
anyone who isn't from here—and Harley's leading it. He's talking
about casting the demons out."

"Demons?" I said, too loudly. A couple of people—Ez Ledford,
Shorty Rogers—turned and gave me nasty looks.

Jessup walked over to us and said, "If you ask me, there's more than
one demon needs casting out here."

Coyle said, "They've rounded up the boys from the band mill and
the boys from the CCC camp, the ones that aren't local. They're sending them south on the train, out of Alluvial, out of North Carolina."

I felt light-headed. The air started swimming and I thought I might
have to leave or sit down with my head between my legs. I said, "Why
doesn't anyone stop them? What about the men who run the band
mill? The men who run the camp? What about whoever it is that's in
charge of building that road?"

"They couldn't plan on anything like this happening. These men
went up there like an army and took what they wanted."

"Where's the sheriff?"

"On the manhunt, trying to find the outlander, the one that attacked Janette Lowe. He and Deputy Meeks and the Lowes are in Murphy. They sent word that they've got a lead on a man down there."

"What are they doing with the McKinneys? With Mrs. Dennis and Dr. Hamp?"

"They're outlanders, too. They're not from here so they're making them leave."

"They can't do that," I said. "Where's your daddy? He can stop this. Where's Daddy Hoyt?"

"Trying to stop your husband from making matters worse," Coyle said. "They been fighting this thing all day. They been shot at and swore at and pushed out of the way."

Jessup said, "Someone even came after Ruby Poole because she's from Asheville, but Linc threatened to kill them, and everyone knows he'd keep his word."

I was trying to understand everything they were telling me. I felt like the air had run out of my head and like my brain had shut off and like I couldn't understand anything at all, no matter how I tried.

Up on the back of the truck, Harley was barnstorming. He had shed his white jacket and was standing only in his shirtsleeves and vest. There were damp circles underneath his armpits. There were little drops of water winging off the ends of his hair. "We need to ban together," Harley said. "We'll flush them out of their hiding places. They'll have to face us. And then they'll see the light. We'll make them see it. They'll pay for what they've done. And then we will be free—not only the souls of those they've harmed, but those of us that are left here to mourn them. We will be free once again in our homes."

Harley was completely carried away with himself, and he was carrying everyone else away with him. I watched as now and then they raised their hands and said: "Tell it, preacher!" "Come on, preacher!" "Amen!"

I strained to find Daddy Hoyt or Linc or Mr. Deal in the crowd. I stood on tiptoes and peered above heads and shaded my eyes and studied faces. I pushed my way through the people, row by row, trying to find someone else to explain this to me, someone to put a stop to it.

Harley's eyes were closed. His hands were held up to the sky. He said, "The kingdom of heaven was snatched away by violence. 'Vengeance is mine; I will repay, saith the Lord.' We need to cast out the devil that's entered our house. Now that this road has come through, that devil is free to come and go. We need to find the devil and cast him out and make certain that he can never enter our house again."

"Praise the Lord!"

"Amen!"

I made my way toward the front of the crowd, pushing against people, bumping into one person after another. The crowd got thicker and tighter the nearer I got to Harley. Folks were trying to get closer to him, trying to hear him and see him. I was reaching for Daddy Hoyt, who was standing to the side, by the railroad tracks, with Mr. Deal and Reverend Broomfield and Reverend Nix and Linc and Uncle Turk. I pushed my way through until I reached them.

"Why is no one stopping him?" I said when I did. Daddy Hoyt held out one arm and pulled me close.

"We're outnumbered," said Mr. Deal.

Daddy Hoyt said, "As soon as they heard that an outlander attacked Janette Lowe, that was all the excuse they needed. They went up Blood Mountain and pulled the miners from their shacks, and then they went up there to the CCC camp and the band mill camp to round up the outlanders and send them off this mountain."

Butch. I looked but didn't see him anywhere.

"Mr. Deal called the sheriff's office in Hamlet's Mill and they're sending someone up here," said Linc. "They're calling the police chief in Civility to help us out."

"'A house divided against itself will collapse.' Are we divided?" The sun was disappearing over the trees, behind the mountains. Up on the mountain it would still be light, but down here in the valley, darkness was coming fast.

Some shouted, "No!"

"'Every house or city that disagrees with itself shall not stand.' Do we disagree?"

More people: "No!"

"'The house that remains standing is the one that stands together.' Do we stand together?"

Everyone: "Yes!"

"'Whosoever is not with me is against me.' Are you with me?"

"Yes!"

Something was happening in this valley, in the faces of these people I had known all my life. There was a hunger as they leaned in close for Harley's every word. He was feeding them. There was a strange, unsettling energy in the place that made me want to leave, except that I couldn't turn away from it.

Listening to Harley, I thought that this was maybe his greatest moment, that he had finally broke free of his mama and Damascus King and his own low and wicked past—a past spent searching for direction and vision and purpose. He had even broke free of Jesus. Harley Bright had finally arrived. But instead of thrilling me and making me love him, it made me hate him. I felt something turn in me and a coldness come over my heart like a door closing or a wall building fast, brick by brick, where there wasn't one before. I saw him as a poisoned person, like someone filled up with snake venom. I thought: What if the poison starts to work on me, too?

Then I thought: Quick. These are the things to feel joyful about:

> my family
> my music
> my truck
> my hatbox
> making a record
> writing down my songs
> Butch Dawkins
> the Wood Carver
> the Grand Ole Opry
> Nashville

But none of it helped. I could see that Harley Bright, standing under the lantern lights in his Barathea white suit, eyes ablaze, was alive with the devil. It was shining out of him just as strong as could be.

And then, just when I thought it couldn't get more horrible, Harley said, "There's another outlander that's been living on this mountain for some time, trespassing in our home. He's been haunting us, spooking us. But he's just a man. He's got fingerprints, just like you and me. He's got a heart that beats, just like you and me. He's got blood that bleeds, just like you and me. He stays up there on Devil's Courthouse. He's a runaway murderer. It's time we round him up and send him home with the rest of them."

~

After Harley was finished, there was a great buzzing and everyone tumbled about and pushed forward, trying to talk to him and to each other. The men gathered together while the women, clutching their shawls and their children, moved out into the night. They went up toward home in groups of three or four: close together, looking over their shoulders, and jumping at the night sounds they knew so well—the same night sounds they had always heard since they were babies.

Mrs. Dennis and Dr. Hamp were rounded up and forced onto a train with the McKinneys and the boys from the Scenic and poor old Elderly Jones, who someone decided at the last minute was a threat just because his ancestors must not go back quite as far as some of the rest of us. And then I saw Butch, standing in the crowd next to Dr. Hamp, steel guitar across his chest, silver ring glinting, corners of his mouth turned down. I wanted to see that lazy, crooked smile. I wanted to look in my direction. See me, Butch, I thought. I'm over here. Over here. Look my way. Here I am. I'm not a part of this. This is Harley's doing, not mine. Please don't think I have anything to do with this. Please look at me.

Look at me.

Look at me.

Look at me . . .

He stared straight ahead and didn't once look my way, this man who had listened to my words and my music, who had given me my songs. And then, just like that, he was gone. The doors to the train were closed with the help of men I had known all my lives. Men with faces that were changed and strange. Men I didn't recognize anymore.

The mob was forming, swarming, heading up Devil's Courthouse. Harley suddenly brushed by us, walking quickly ahead. Daddy Hoyt shouted, "Velva Jean!" I ran away from him into the night, away from the lights and the noise and the crowd, up the mountain after my husband.

~

Harley was moving fast through the house. He went up the stairs two at a time and into his daddy's room and pulled out the dresser drawers, rifling through the clothes.

He said, "Velva Jean, I want you to stay here." He got on his knees and looked under the bed and then moved to the old army trunk and threw back the lid. He worked fast, shuffling through every paper or boot or hat. He slammed the lid shut and stood up and crossed the hall to our room, a flash of energy, of electric white.

I was after him. I said, "What are you doing?"

He said, "You need to stay here and promise me not to leave this house." He was reaching into drawers, turning them upside down, and then back into the chifforobe, back behind the clothes. He pushed aside my hatbox and knocked it onto the floor so that it opened up and the things inside went everywhere. He said, "I know Mama kept a pistol."

I grabbed his arm and I said, "Harley," sharp and loud, just like I'd slapped him. He stopped and looked at me. I took his hand. I got down on my knees beside him, right down on the floor, and I said, "Look at me."

"Velva Jean . . ."

"Look at me."

He sighed a little. His other hand stopped working in the back of the chifforobe. "What is it?"

"I want my old Harley back. The one I could believe in. The one I married. The one who rode up to Sleepy Gap in his shiny blue car and swept me off my feet and counted stars with me and never could get the dirt out from under his fingernails and worked an honest living and bought me a radio so I wouldn't be lonely and gave me a wall of windows so I wouldn't have any more darkness and wouldn't let me be till I married him. I want the man who saw right into me and promised to love me and swore he'd be true to me forever."

Harley sat back, leaning against the door of the chifforobe. He rested his arm on his knee. He looked like he'd had the wind knocked out of him. His green eyes were sad. He looked like a little boy, like a young-old man, lost and unsure. Seeing him like that touched my heart. I wanted to put my arms around him and tell him it was going to be fine.

Instead I said, "I miss you. I want you to come back to me. I want to go back to the beginning, back to the way it was. I want to get back to us, Harley. Somewhere along the way we got derailed, just like a train—just like the Terrible Creek train—and we need to get back on track. I know we can, but I can't do it by myself."

Even as I said it, I wondered if I believed it. What if there was too much between us now? Too many silences, too little said, too much said? My songs? My driving? Butch? Things I could never forget or go back from. I picked up Harley's hand and put it on my heart. I laid my hand over his and through it I could feel my own heart beating.

He said, "You know I love you, Velva Jean. I love you more than anything."

I said, "I love you, too." I could feel the stinging behind my eyes that meant I was getting ready to cry. I wanted to believe that we could be like ourselves again, just Velva Jean and Harley. Velva Jean Hart and Harley Bright forever. Forever and ever. Happily ever after. The end.

He said, "I'm sorry if I've let you down. I know I ain't been around much."

My heart swelled and I suddenly felt like it was going to be okay. The tears came then, slipping down my face one at a time. I tasted one as it ran into my mouth.

He wiped a tear away with his thumb. Then another. He said, "But I got to see this through."

I sat back a little. *No no no no no.* "See what through?"

"This. All of it. I been given a gift, a calling, a purpose. You know that. You were there to see it. Sometimes I don't want it, Velva Jean. It's making me tired. What they did to Junie—that road. The responsibility of it all. Sometimes I just want to lie down and give up and go to sleep, not ever go back to that church, just get back out there on the rails and preach—or not. Just do something else altogether. Maybe lie back on that couch and listen to the radio again. Listen to *The Lone Ranger*. But I wouldn't be here if I hadn't been chosen in some way. I'd be dead like Straight Willy Cannon and the others, and I'm not. So I got to see this through."

I said, "What you did to the Scenic—when you went up there and caused all that damage—you did that for Aunt Junie, didn't you?"

He nodded. "For Junie, and for all of us." He said, "I won't have Satan, destroyer of all that is good and just, upset a part of my home." He looked right at me and his voice turned hard. "Or anyone else for that matter."

And then he stood up and he gazed down at me and it seemed like he was doing so from a long, long way away. Suddenly my tears were dry. And then, at the same moment, we both of us saw my record lying on the floor: Velva Jean Hart, "Yellow Truck Coming, Yellow Truck Going." Harley stooped down and picked it up. He held it in his hand and studied it. He turned it over and looked at the other side. Then he looked at me—a look full of hurt and sadness and blame.

I said, "I can explain."

He said, "I ain't interested."

I said, "I was going to tell you, but I didn't know how you'd react. I wanted to play it for you, but I didn't know if you'd want to hear it. I gave them my full name, but they left it off, not me. They said it didn't fit."

Harley wasn't listening. His eyes had glassed over and he was looking at me, but looking past me, too.

I said, "We can go downstairs right now and I can play it for you. Harley, I want to play it for you. I'm so proud of this record. You're the person in this world I most want to share it with."

He said, "I wonder if that's true."

Then he stared down at the record and kind of tipped it back and forth in his hands. I thought for a minute he was going to break the record in two. But instead, he handed it to me—just handed it over like he couldn't bear to touch it anymore—and walked out of the room.

~

I ran after Harley down the stairs. Right before my eyes, I could see my life going away from me and there was nothing I could do. I was thinking: Harley Bright, if you walk out of this house, there is no telling what will happen. I think that will be it for us, so you'd better not leave. I felt helpless to stop him, helpless to do anything, and I felt terrible and guilty over my record. At the same time, I wanted to kill him for trying to spoil it for me, my one and only record that I had made and that was supposed to be forever, something no one could take from me, not even him.

THIRTY-SEVEN

In the distance, I could hear the voices of men gathering. The night was a warm one, the kind Harley and I should have been spending on the front porch, holding hands on the swing, looking up at the stars like we used to. The crickets were humming so loud that the air was vibrating. I usually loved to hear them, but now it sounded like they were building toward something dark and horrible.

I picked up my skirt and I ran up the mountain, following the men up the hill as close as I dared. It was clear they didn't know where they were going. They just knew they needed to go up toward the very top of the mountain. It was Lester Gordon and his daddy, Dell Haywood, Clydie Williams, Lou Pigeon, Ez Ledford, Shorty Rogers, Marlon Day, Floyd Hatch, Root Caldwell, Brother Dearborn, Brother Armes, Brother Marsh. There were others—too many. I never saw if Levi was there. He may have been. So many were there, but some weren't. Most were, though. That was the unsettling thing. Harley was nowhere to be seen.

Floyd said, "The outlander is up by the giant's cave. He built a cabin near there. I know where he is. We'll go up there to get our bearings, but I know where he is."

I broke off from them as quiet as I could, and I cut through the woods. I would get there first. I would warn the Wood Carver. I stopped every few feet to listen, thanking God and Granny for the Cherokee in me that helped me track a trail in the dark. I tried not to think of panthers or bears or convicts or haints. I thought only of the kind, peaceful man who was my friend.

~

I got there just before them. I found him standing on his front step, hands on his hips, staring out toward the horizon, as if he knew what was coming. His hat was pushed back on his head. His knife was in his pocket. He stood completely motionless, like Hunter Firth when he was tracking something. He didn't even look at me.

I said, "A girl was attacked by an outlander. Now they're on the hunt for other outlanders. They are coming. You need to leave. I'll go with you. I can't stay here."

He said, "I'm not going anywhere."

I said, "These men have blood on their minds. They've turned vicious. My husband has helped turn them that way." I felt like spitting after the word "husband," just like Johnny Clay did whenever he swore.

He said, "I'm not going because I'm not guilty of attacking that girl. I am not going to run from something I didn't do."

I was starting to get angry. I said, "They don't care that you didn't attack her. What matters to them is that you're an outlander. They want them all gone. They have guns. They'll kill you!"

He crossed his arms in front of his chest. He was dark against the porch, against the sky. "It's not your fight, Velva Jean. Go. Fly. And remember—there is a difference between running *from* something and running *to* something. Never run from something, if you can help it."

~

I went to fetch Daddy Hoyt as fast as I could, my feet flying over earth and clay and leaves and grass. Suddenly—halfway down the mountain—there was a beam of wavering light and Linc appeared at the other end of it, and over his shoulder Daddy Hoyt. Then I saw the Deals—Mr. Deal and Coyle and Jessup, carrying their rifles. And beyond them Reverend Broomfield and Reverend Nix and Uncle Turk and his Cherokee wife, Nomi, and Granny, who was riding Mad Maggie and clutching her handheld ax.

We headed up to the Wood Carver's house together. Daddy Hoyt didn't ask me how long I'd been coming there or how I had found the Wood Carver or why it had started. What he did say was, "What do you know about the Wood Carver, Velva Jean?"

I said, "I know that he's my friend. And I know that for as long as I can remember, he's been up on top of this mountain."

Daddy Hoyt walked in silence. I could hear him breathing harder than normal as we climbed. He said, "I remember when he showed up. Ten, maybe twelve years ago. I don't think anyone knows his real name, but there have been rumors, of course."

I said, "People say he's a monster that walks on all fours. They say he breaks into their houses at night and steals from them."

Daddy Hoyt said, "People will always invent stories about things or people they don't understand. It makes them feel better about not understanding."

I said, "Who do you think he is?"

"Henry Able," said Granny.

Daddy Hoyt picked up a large stick and used it as a cane, letting it work him up the mountain. We were moving fast, the Deal boys and Linc up ahead of us. Daddy Hoyt said, "Henry Able or Hank Able. From up near Spruce Pine. Young man working in the mines there about fifteen years ago. Fought with a fellow name of McAllister after McAllister tried to seduce Able's wife." Daddy Hoyt fell silent as he caught his breath. I didn't say anything, just waited for him to continue. "After May Able rejected him, McAllister tried to kill Henry Able, but he fought him off with a knife, hit an artery, and McAllister bled to death. Able disappeared into the woods, turning up later in Kentucky and then Chicago. Tried to return for May, but she was gone and he was a wanted man. She lives down near Pinhook Gap now, right by Bee Tree Fork, just over the ridge there. She never remarried. I think he came up here so that he could look out for her, so that he could see her."

"How do you know all that?" I said.

"Most of it was in the newspapers. He's still a wanted man. The McAllister family had influence."

"But what makes you think it's him?"

"Something I read—just a line. Hank Able had a hobby. He liked to work with wood." I listened to his breathing. We were almost there. Daddy Hoyt said, "I could be wrong, of course. I think, more than anything, he is a man in need of forgiveness. I think he came here to this mountain to seek it. Who do you think he is, Velva Jean?"

I thought about Janette Lowe, about her thin face and her hand-me-down dress and the way she had danced in Panther Creek the day she was saved. I thought about her dirty feet and her dirty hands and the way she carried her head, like she was a lady. I thought of her brother and her daddy and her uncles, searching for the man who had done this to her—who had attacked her. I thought of the people I knew and loved—my husband most of all—who were suddenly turning on strangers just because they were different, just because they weren't from here.

I said, "I think he's my friend."

~

From a half mile away, we could see the flames. The fire inched high into the sky, over the tops of the trees, red and orange fingers reaching for the stars and the moon. We started to run.

They were throwing things into the fire—his beautiful things. Canes, birdhouses, dancing men. Harley stood next to the fire in his ivory suit, flames lighting up his face, casting shadows. Something shone from his belt. He'd found his mama's pistol. "Put everything in," he said. "Every false idol. He's bewitched them all." Men were coming from the cabin, their arms filled. As they fed the fire, the blaze grew brighter and bigger, climbing into the sky. The Wood Carver stood apart from it all, watching, his eyes black. Dell Haywood, Ez Ledford, and Lou Pigeon stood around him.

Clydie Williams walked through the madness, shoving his way through. He was pointing his pistol. He said, "Let's just shoot him."

Mr. Deal said, "No one's shooting anyone."

Clydie's eyes flickered over to Mr. Deal, to the rest of us. He said, "This don't concern you."

The men gathered around tight. Linc and the Deal boys stepped up till they were face-to-face with the others.

A figure appeared out of the smoke and the darkness. "Go back," it said. Lou Pigeon made a move and Linc made a move and the figure held out its arm and pushed Linc back. It said, "You'll end up getting more people hurt that way."

The figure was lean and weathered. It belonged to a man with long hair and a deep voice. He wore a beard, not long like the Wood Carver's, but short and clean. There was a knife in his back pocket. The way he stood was confident, like he was sure of his own two feet. I felt my heart do a little jump and my palms went clammy. It had been six years, almost seven, since I'd seen my daddy, since he'd come back and I'd sent him away. It was three years since I'd seen the man at the CCC camp who may or may not have been him. I used to wonder where he was—if he had made another family or if he was long gone or if he was dead. But gradually I'd stopped wondering. Sometimes days passed before I even remembered to think of him at all.

Then the figure came forward, and the smoke cleared, and it was Beachard, looking older than when I'd last seen him, looking more like Mama than Daddy, with his narrow Cherokee face and his gray-blue eyes.

The Wood Carver let himself be led past the fire, past the dogwood tree that stood stark against the red backdrop. He was pushed and tripped and it was then I saw that he was bleeding from the left shoulder. I started to follow him, but Beach took my arm and stopped me. "No," he said. "This mob will tear you apart, Velva Jean."

The light from the fire lit up the Wood Carver's face. It was a good face. He stood taller than the rest of them, looking over their heads, which only seemed to unsettle them and make them madder. They buzzed around like ants, throwing things in the fire, organizing themselves.

Root Caldwell walked around behind the Wood Carver. He was staring at him. He kneeled down and looked at his legs. He said, "How does he stand on two legs? I thought he had to walk on all fours at night."

"I thought he changed with the moon," said Lou Pigeon. He pointed up at the sky. "It ain't full. Maybe it has to be full for him to walk on all fours."

Root Caldwell stood up. He pushed the Wood Carver a little. Daddy Hoyt said, "We need to be reasonable. We need to be calm." His bass voice boomed, louder than usual. Root pushed the Wood Carver again. Root laughed. He was leering up into the Wood Carver's face, looking every bit like a weasel. He stared at him for a long time and then he spat at the Wood Carver. The hackles on my neck stood up. Beside me, my brothers tensed. Granny was still sitting atop Mad Maggie, her ax gripped in her hand. Her eyes were fierce. She looked like a drawing I'd seen of her granddaddy, a great Cherokee warrior and medicine man. The Deals leaned on their rifles, careful not to point them yet because pointing them would have sparked off a civil war. The fire was reaching up toward the sky. I thought: The sun is turning black. The seas are turning red. The storm is finally here.

Daddy Hoyt stepped forward. He said, "This man hasn't done anything to anyone up here."

Floyd Hatch said, "Except for when he wanders down the mountain to break into our houses."

"Or snatch babies from their beds," said Ez Ledford.

Daddy Hoyt said, "This man never leaves this house. He keeps only to the woods surrounding. He doesn't come down the mountain."

Clydie said, "All the outlanders got to go. There's been nothing but trouble since they came here. We're never going to have another in our valley."

In the midst of it all, in the black of the night, Harley stood out. In his white suit, he was the only one you could see clearly in the dark, on his own, apart from the fire. He said, "Let's take him down the hill. There'll be a midnight train coming through. We can put him on that. Make sure he leaves the valley." *If you change your mind, there's a midnight freight that's passing through on its way to Alluvial.* I thought of the dirty moonshiner's boy and of the runaway orphan girl he had told that to all those years ago.

Beach said, "You're not taking him anywhere."

Clydie said, "Then we'll kill him right here."

Beach said, "Well you can just kill me too." He walked over to stand beside the Wood Carver.

Granny jumped down off Mad Maggie. She walked right up to Clydie Williams, standing over him like she was looking down on a child. She said, "And me also." And then she went over to stand in front of the Wood Carver. Linc and the Deals followed her, gathering close around him. Then came Uncle Turk, Nomi, Reverend Broomfield, Reverend Nix, and Daddy Hoyt.

Harley was staring at me. He said, "Velva Jean."

I said, "I guess you can just shoot me too, Harley Bright." I joined my family.

The muscles in Harley's jaw were twitching. He was mad—oh, was he mad. Everyone was looking at him and at me, at him, at me. I knew he needed to save face and fast. He said, "No one's shooting anyone. But we are sending this man off this mountain." His voice had turned cold. He wasn't using his preacher voice anymore, the one he used as much for himself as for other people because he liked the sound of it. Then he said, "'But, behold, the hand of him that betrayeth me is with me on the table.'" He looked right at me when he said it.

Brother Harriday said, "Amen, preacher." I looked for him and there he was in the crowd, dressed in a white shirt, his black-rimmed glasses catching the light of the fire. I thought: Brother Harriday? Not you too.

Harley said, "'In my name shall they cast out devils.'"

Daddy Hoyt said, "Marlon Day, your mama comes from Franklin, doesn't she?"

Marlon said, "What?"

"Doesn't your mama come from Franklin?"

"Yessir." Marlon looked confused.

Daddy Hoyt nodded. He rubbed his chin. He said, "So that makes you one-half outlander."

Marlon stood there, shotgun in his hand, trying to make sense of this.

Harley said, "'Get thee hence, Satan: for it is written, Thou shalt worship the Lord thy God, and him only shalt thou serve.'"

Daddy Hoyt said, "And Dell Haywood, your mama's people came here from Tennessee, as I recall, just one generation back, which means you've got some outlander blood yourself."

Harley was watching Daddy Hoyt, watching the men. He said, "'The people which sat in darkness saw great light; and to them which sat in the region and shadow of death light is sprung up. From that time Jesus began to preach, and to say, Repent: for the kingdom of heaven is at hand.'"

Daddy Hoyt started pacing, walking from one man to another, peering in their faces, like he was studying them. "Ez Ledford, you may not know this, being so young, but neither your mama nor your daddy was born here. They was born right over the mountain, right over by Civility. They came over here to give you a better life, to raise you and your brothers and sisters in this nice valley. But Wrongful Mountain is definitely not one of our mountains, which means that you, my boy, are a full-blooded outlander."

Ez looked like he wanted to pass out, right there on the ground.

Before Harley could open his mouth to say anything, Daddy Hoyt stopped in front of him. He was taller than Harley. Daddy Hoyt stared down at him, looking Harley right in the eye. He said, "Harley Bright. Your mama was from here. Her people go back a ways, it's true. But the Brights—now help me remember." He rubbed at his chin some more. "Your daddy grew up here, but his daddy and mama came from somewhere else. I want to say it was somewhere over by Bandana or Celo, but no, that don't sound quite right. Somewhere around the Toe River Valley."

Daddy Hoyt waited for an answer. Harley had his eyes fixed on him. They just stared at each other, neither one blinking. Finally I said, "They were from Kona."

"Up in the Black Mountains?"

Harley didn't say anything to this. Daddy Hoyt just nodded. He said, "So that makes you part outlander, too."

"What's your point?" said Clydie.

"My point," said Daddy Hoyt, "is that you should know yourself before you pretend to know someone else. You have to be careful when you're labeling folks, saying he's this, she's this, and deciding to send people away based on something you say they are. Because you just might be that same thing. Who are you to make the rules? To play God? Who's to say where to draw the line? You sent Elderly Jones away, but he's more of a native to this place than a lot of you: more than Ez here, more than Marlon, more than Harley Bright. Elderly goes back at least a generation on both sides of his family."

Daddy Hoyt stood, hands on hips, in the middle of all the men that were gathered and staring at him. He said, "Maybe my family should be the ones deciding all this. After all, we were here before any of you. We came here and named that mountain long before you all ever set foot here. To us, you're all outlanders. But you don't see us rounding people up, just because one outlander did a horrible thing to one of our own. You don't see us blaming every stranger for the sins of that devil." He turned in a circle, gazing from one face to another. He was giving each man a good, long look. For a moment, I thought he was finished, that he had said his piece. Then he said, "You got to be careful before you send people off on trains. Because just as easy, it could be you."

It was over then and we knew it was over. A few of the men drew back. Shorty Rogers and Dell Haywood stood there like they were frozen. Ez Ledford looked mad enough to spit. Marlon Day wiped at his eyes so hard, I almost thought he was crying. I stared at him and then he looked down at the ground and wouldn't look up again.

Daddy Hoyt stood tall—taller than all of us. He looked like a man ten years younger. His eyes shone out and he stood straight and not bent. Behind him, the Wood Carver disappeared into shadow, becoming a part of the woods and the night. The men stayed in place, looking stunned, angry, hurt, lost, the half-light of the moon hitting their faces.

Brother Harriday sat down on the steps of the Wood Carver's house and began to cry.

Harley stood there, the fire blazing up behind him. He was white against the night, against the flames. He scanned the crowd and finally his eyes settled on me.

I watched as the men faded away down the mountain, one by one, two by two, grumbling, cast down, heartbroke, some still hungry for blood.

Daddy Hoyt and Mr. Deal and my brothers were trying to put the fire out. They were dragging things from the ashes and trying to save them. On her knees, Granny was repeating an ancient Cherokee prayer that her granddaddy had taught her. Reverend Broomfield stood to the side, tears running down his face. Reverend Nix was singing hymns.

Harley walked over to where I was standing. He said, "Let's go home, Velva Jean." His voice was flat. He barely looked at me. The fire caught his face and made it glow. I thought how handsome he was, but that it didn't mean anything to me, that it was like looking at a picture in a movie magazine or a lipstick down at Deal's. It was something outside myself that I could see was pretty but that didn't touch me in any way. He reached for my hand. He rubbed his finger over my wedding ring. He said, "I been neglecting you."

I thought: Don't you try to make nice with me, Harley Bright, just like you do after you don't get your way. Just like you do when you need to get your footing back. Now you decide to listen. Suddenly you pretend to understand. I don't believe it for a minute. He was looking at me in a way that used to buckle my knees. He had his hand on my face. His eyes were calm now—like Three Gum River after a rain. There wasn't any sign of the devil in them. He said, "I love you."

I thought—

Just that.

I thought nothing.

I said, "Harley, I'm tired. I'm going to help Daddy Hoyt clean up and then I'm going to go home with them so I can see Beach. I'll be back tomorrow." I knew he wouldn't argue with me. He stood back a little. He looked hurt. But he didn't argue.

He said, "Okay, Velva Jean. Whatever you need to do. I'll see you at home then." He leaned in and kissed me, first on the forehead and then on the lips, very light, almost like he was nervous to touch me. Then he straightened and smiled and it was a sad smile but a real one. He said, "Prettiest face on Fair Mountain. Fair Mountain or anywhere."

Tears sprang to my eyes. I couldn't help it. And then he vanished into the woods.

~

"'And when I passed by you, and saw you weltering in your blood, I said to you in your blood, Live, and grow like a plant in the field.'" Daddy Hoyt held his hand on the shoulder of the Wood Carver as the Wood Carver sat up behind his house, on the rock face that hung out over the mountain like a stone porch. Daddy Hoyt had filled the wound with soot and cobwebs and then made a tourniquet out of a rag and a stick.

"I'm not a blood stopper," he said. "I'm not a faith healer like Junie. But that's a phrase she taught me, and I think it should work, along with these other things."

With his dark eyes, the ones that barely let in light, the Wood Carver stared at my granddaddy. He looked tired and weak. It was strange to see him look that way. He said, "Hoyt Justice. I made you something."

"Rest," Daddy Hoyt said. "We'll be right here."

"A crutch for your rheumatism, carved out of balsam wood." The Wood Carver gazed out past us, at nothing. He said, "I'm sure they burned it with everything else."

I was staring at Daddy Hoyt. I said, "You've been here before. That's how he knew me. That's how he knew my family."

The Wood Carver kept his face still but turned his eyes to look at me. He held up the fingers of the hand on his good arm. I took them without thinking. He squeezed my hand, just slightly. His eyes went back to Daddy Hoyt and then back to me. "Good brace roots," he said.

~

I sat with the Wood Carver and for a long while we didn't speak. Then, when he felt strong enough, the Wood Carver stood, face to the sky, staring out over the mountains. I looked at his eyes and followed them and saw that he wasn't staring at the mountains at all, but south into the valleys—Pinhook Gap, Bee Tree Fork—that lay below.

I said, "Do you ever go down there? To see her?" I pointed toward Bee Tree Fork. When he didn't answer, I said, "I hope she's forgiven you and that you can be together someday."

He was quiet. I tried to think of what I could say to him to make up for all that had happened, all we had brought upon him. I said, "They've almost got the fire out. The Jesus tree is fine. I guess it will take more than a fire." Then I said, "I am so sorry."

He shifted a little. "It wasn't you," he said.

"You can carve more treasures," I said. "You can start again. I'll help you. You can carve more dancing men and more birdhouses and more canes."

"Don't you see?" the Wood Carver said. "They've violated the sanctuary of my home. They've violated the spirit of who I am. There's no going back, Velva Jean. This place will never be the same."

I said, "Are you worried about the road coming through here?"

He said, "It's more than that now."

I heard my name from down below, somewhere in the distance.

"Go," he said. "And remember what I told you, about running *to* something."

I didn't want to move because I was afraid if I did I might never see him again. I stood there beside him, not saying anything, listening to my name being called over and over. I wanted to ask him about May. I wanted to know where she was, if he ever planned to go to her, to be with her for good.

But instead I looked out over the mountains, out toward Tennessee and up toward Asheville. Somewhere below, a train was carrying my friends out of this valley—Elderly Jones, Dr. Hamp and Mrs. Dennis, Butch Dawkins. I wondered where Butch would end up, where his journey would take him next. I supposed this was just a part of that journey, just another part of his destiny. I supposed I was just a small part of it, too. I imagined him landing in some other valley, in some other town, writing songs with some other girl.

In the distance, up on the ridgeline in the glow of the half-moon, I could just make out the new road that was being forged across the Blue Ridge. I lowered myself over the side of the rock face and dropped to the earth.

~

I rode on Mad Maggie, up behind Granny. I wrapped my arms around her birdlike waist, thin yet strong. I rested my head against her back, and turned away from the fire and the crowd. I closed my eyes. Harley had brought those men up here. Harley had just as good as killed the Wood Carver.

Granny turned Mad Maggie around and let her lead us home. I felt us going down, down, down the mountain, away from the little cabin and the dogwood tree and the laurel thicket. The smell of smoke began to fade. Soon it was just Granny and me and my brothers, walking behind us, and the night. The hoot of an owl. The rustle of a creature in the underbrush. And somewhere in the distance, the high, lonesome cry of a panther.

THIRTY-EIGHT

Long after everyone else had gone to sleep, Linc and Beachard and I sat out on the porch of Mama's house, just like we used to, looking at the stars and watching Hunter Firth walk around in the yard, sniffing at bugs. He moved slow, like his bones hurt, like Aunt Bird or Elderly Jones. I guessed he was getting old. I think he missed Johnny Clay like I did.

Beach told us that after he finished his work on the Scenic he had roamed up to Kentucky. He had gone into Virginia and Tennessee. He had worked on the railroad and traveled by rail, and he had written on trees and rocks and barns and walls wherever he felt like it. He was in Del Rio when he got the urge to come home. He said he somehow knew we needed him.

He found his way at first by the train and then by the trees he had marked: "Jesus Weeps." "Jesus Mourns." "Jesus Grieves." Before pushing on through the woods toward home, he took time to carve another: "Jesus Heals." That was when he heard the voices and saw the fire. He said that from far away it looked like Devil's Courthouse was burning.

When he got done telling us all this, I said, "There's one thing I don't understand. Where was Daddy?"

Linc said, "What do you mean, 'Where was Daddy?'"

I said, "I thought I saw him once when Harley and I went to the CCC camp to preach. I didn't get a good look, but there was a man there that looked like him."

Beach said, "Daddy was here. But now he's not. I reckon Daddy's down at Soco Gap now or maybe up in Virginia. There are some parkway sections starting work up there soon."

"Why didn't he come home?" I said. "All that time he was up here."

Beach said, "He came as close as he could. Why do you think he wanted to work on this particular piece of the road, Velva Jean?"

I thought of Daddy nearby, all that time—how long was he here before he'd left again? And then I thought of Daddy off somewhere, walking on those mountaintops. I pictured him buck dancing against the sun.

When morning came, we walked over to Granny's for breakfast— eggs and bacon and grits. Aunt Bird brought fried pies, and Aunt Zona brought mint jelly, and the twins and Ruby Poole made cinnamon rolls that fell apart in our mouths. Sweet Fern—her lips painted a rosy pink, a flower in her hair—came up from Alluvial with the children. For the first time in a long time, we were all together, all but Johnny Clay. It was like Thanksgiving or Christmas.

~

Afterward I walked up to the Wood Carver's house. He was gone just like I knew he would be. It was like he had never been there at all. There were just four walls and a dogwood tree that had survived a tornado and would survive much more.

Inside, the little cabin was bare. His books were gone: burned in the fire. The bed was stripped bare; the shelves emptied. Only the little camp stove remained to remind me that anyone had been there. I stood in the middle of the room for a minute, listening to the great silence, feeling the emptiness of the space, which weighed down on me until I couldn't breathe. And then I walked outside and closed the door behind me.

I picked through the ruins of the fire, but there were only bits of wood—scraps that used to be a cane or a carving or a dancing man or a birdhouse. In the ashes, something glinted—a flash of silver. The only knife I had ever seen the Wood Carver use. I picked it up and rubbed the blade clean on my skirt. I polished the handle. I worked that knife over till it shone like it was new, then I laid it on the step where he used to sit, where I'd first seen him all those years ago, just in case he ever came back.

~

The sun was up and blazing by the time I came down the mountain. I stood on the shores of Three Gum River and heard my mama's voice.

Oh, they tell me of a land far beyond the skies . . .

I walked into the water until it covered my ankles and then my calves, washing up over the scar where the panther had got me, and then my knees. My skirt pulled me toward the bottom but I pushed on till I was standing waist deep in the river. The water felt cool and calm. The sun beat down from the great wide sky. I opened my arms as if I could take it all in, as if I could hold it and carry it and pull it close. There was blue but no clouds. The storm had passed.

I fell backward and let myself float. My skirt billowed up around me and then filled with water and sank back down. My hair sailed out around my head like seaweed. I was a mermaid. I was a girl captured by the cannibal spirits, made to live below the water, looking at the world from my watery home.

Floating, I felt like I was ten years old again. I could almost hear and see the people on the shore—Johnny Clay thumping his guitar, Linc and Beachard clapping, Sweet Fern standing up the bank with Danny, Granny dancing like a wild bird, Daddy Hoyt and Clover and Celia Faye. I could feel Reverend Nix sending me under and pulling me up again, the snakebite scars on his hands and arms. I could see my mama's face and hear her voice as she sang to me.

I went under. I wanted the water to make me feel fresh and new, like I did when I was ten years old, back when I was saved the first time, before anything bad had ever happened. I wanted to come back up and see my mama and Danny Deal and Butch and Aunt Junie and the Wood Carver, standing off in the distance, and my daddy too. I wanted to see Johnny Clay standing there with his arm around Lucinda Sink while Janette Lowe danced up and down the shore with

Daryl Gordon and Straight Willy Cannon. I wanted Harley to be there, his face dirty from coal dust, pinching the end of a cigarette and wrapping it up in his handkerchief for later.

I held my breath as long as I could. When I could no longer breathe, I came up to the surface and filled my lungs as quick as I could, short and gasping at first, and then taking long, deep breaths until I was breathing normal again. The shoreline was empty. I was alone.

I smoothed my hair back off my face and waded out of the water, feeling heavy from the weight of it, but peaceful and clean.

~

I went back to Devil's Kitchen and tried to act like nothing had happened. Harley greeted me at the door. He took me in his arms and held me and kissed me on top of my wet head. He said, "I missed you, Velva Jean. I'm glad you're home."

I sat with him in the front room and listened to him while he told me things would be different. "My eyes are open now," he said. "I'm going to be better and more deserving. Calling or no calling, Jesus or no Jesus, I'm just an ordinary man. But there's nothing ordinary about you. Sometimes that's hard on a person. That ain't your fault, though. That's not what I'm saying. I just got scared. I just lost track. Like the Terrible Creek train. I think you got off track, too, but mostly it was me. I'm willing to own up to that. Well I'm back on track now. I'm here. And I may be ordinary, but I'm going to try to be as good as I can be for you. Just know this, Velva Jean. No man on earth will ever love you like I do."

I listened and I tried to feel something. I felt bad about Butch Dawkins and bad about getting derailed myself, but mostly I thought: Why didn't you say this to me months ago? Why are you saying this to me now? Why does it feel like—nice as those words are—I'm still being accused of something, like you're blaming me for what's wrong with you and us? Why should I believe you now, when you've let me down so many times? And what do you mean no man on earth will ever love me like you do? Why does that sound like a warning rather than something sweet and true?

Later that morning—the Thursday morning after the Wood Carver and the outlanders were run off the mountain—Harley went down to the church to talk to Brother Jim. They were thinking of holding a new revival, of traveling to neighboring cities. Harley said he missed life on the road. He said he thought things would be better if we went back to the way it was, just him and me, traveling like we used to, taking our music and our ministry to the people. He was all fired up about it. It was a Harley I hadn't seen in a while.

I thought: Finally. It's about time. I've been waiting for this, for you to take me out of here. Then I thought: But you waited too long. We've hurt each other too much. There's too much built up between us. It's too late now. And besides, Harley Bright, it isn't enough to stay here and just drive my truck and write my songs. I do want more than this.

I spent the next two hours trying to do the same things I always did every single day of my life. I did my chores and I pretended that nothing had changed, that I was the same Velva Jean as before, and that Harley was the same Harley.

When I couldn't stand another minute of it, I got into the yellow truck and drove to Sleepy Gap. I went first to Daddy Hoyt. I found him, as if he was waiting for me, on his front porch. He was sitting in his rocking chair, but he wasn't rocking. He had his feet flat on the floor and his palms resting on the arms of the chair. His face was set in grief.

I stood on the step and said, "Where's Granny?"

He said, "Hiram and Betsy Lee are having their baby."

I said, "I was thinking about something the Wood Carver said, about how they've violated the sanctuary of his home and the spirit of who he is. I can't get those words out of my mind. All I can think is that's what's been done to me. That's how I feel. All I can think is that I must be an outlander, too, because unlike Harley and the rest of those people, I see that road as going out, not just coming in." Down in Alluvial, I could hear the sound of a train whistle—a sound that made me lonely down to the very bottoms of my feet. But it was also a sound of possibility. I said, "I can't stay here."

Daddy Hoyt stood up. He touched his hand to his back where his rheumatism was bothering him more and more. He went into the house and then came out a moment later and handed me a coin purse.

"What's this?" I said.

"It's to help you on your way."

I opened it. There was twenty dollars and fifty-five cents. I said, "I can't take this."

He said, "It's yours to take. I've been entrusted with it."

I said, "I'm not taking your money."

He said, "It's not my money, child. It's your money. Your daddy sent it to me to put aside for you, just like all those years he sent Sweet Fern money to pay for things for you children. I got some here for each of you and that right there is yours. But if it's not enough, Reverend Broomfield offered me one hundred dollars for one of my fiddles. Clydie Williams offered me one hundred fifty, but I'd sooner sell to a snake. I'm thinking of taking the reverend up on his offer. I could go to him today, Velva Jean."

"I won't let you do that. No more than you would ask me to give up my own music."

He sighed and rubbed the back of his neck. "Promise you'll let me know how to find you if you ever want for anything. There are always more fiddles."

I threw my arms around him and hung on. He was like a tree— solid and sturdy. But he was warm and I could hear his heart. I kept my ear against it, listening to the beating of it, trying to memorize it, trying to memorize the smell of him—cedar and pine and oak and the forest with a hint of Granny's lye soap thrown in.

He put his hands on my shoulders and gently pushed me away. He patted me on the back. He cleared his throat. He said, "You let us know where you are when you get there."

I didn't say anything because the lump in my throat was too big. The tears had filled my eyes. All I had to do was blink and they would fall. I kept them there, blurring my vision, keeping my cheeks dry just a second more. Then I blinked, and down came the tears and I couldn't stop them. I ran away from Daddy Hoyt, my throat so sore I couldn't swallow—and I was afraid I'd never be able to swallow again.

~

By the time I climbed into that yellow truck and drove back down toward Alluvial, the lump in my throat felt permanent. Daddy Hoyt was going to say good-bye to everyone for me. The fewer good-byes I had to say, the better.

I held the money in my skirt. Twenty dollars and fifty-five cents. I couldn't get over it. Money from my own daddy. Money he'd earned and sent for each of us over all these years.

The train had pulled into Alluvial. From every door, boys came down off the steps and lined up together—the boys from the Scenic— and this time there were guards with them. Men with guns to make sure no one hurt them or got near them. I sat and watched as the boys finished spilling off the train, as they grouped together and stood glaring at Deal's and at the locals who were there, and then as they started marching up the mountain, up to the camp at Silvermine Bald and back to their work at Devil's Courthouse and beyond, guards surrounding them, protecting them from us. Butch Dawkins was nowhere to be seen.

I leaned out the window and called to one of the boys I recognized, a colored boy who'd come to church with Butch once. "Hey," I said, "Did Butch Dawkins come back?"

The guards moved in closer to him, protecting him from me. The boy yelled, "Nah. He's long gone by now."

I sat there watching those men march up the mountain, wondering where Butch was, wondering if wherever he was he was playing his steel guitar and singing our song, my song, the one he wrote for a girl he knew. I wondered who was singing it with him. I hoped, wherever he was now, that I had mattered to him. Somehow that was important to me, to know that I had meant something—even a little something— that I wasn't just another stop on his journey, just another person he'd met along the way.

I looked down at the books I'd borrowed from Mrs. Dennis and Dr.

Hamp, the ones I still had on the floor of the truck. I wondered what would happen to their library, to their home, and if they would be allowed to come back, too.

As I drove past Sweet Fern's, I slowed the truck. For a moment, I thought about stopping. After all, she had raised me like her own. She was as good as my own mama. She had been my mother almost as long as Mama had. Sweet Fern was standing on the porch. Dan Presley and Corrina were playing in the front yard, running round and round, being chased by Justice and little Hoyt. I almost stopped the truck and got out. Then Coyle Deal walked out onto the porch from inside the house and stood next to Sweet Fern and she smiled up at him with her painted pink lips and he smiled down at her. He wasn't as lean as Danny. He was more solid and square. But he looked at Sweet Fern the same way Danny had. And she looked right back at him.

I kept on driving.

~

The house was quiet. Levi was gone. Harley was gone. It felt like no one had ever lived there. I let myself in and went up the stairs to the bedroom. The lump had settled in my throat—it was still there, but not as big. I could swallow now. I had to. I had to be able to think and to plan. I reached into the chifforobe and pulled out the green recipe box that Johnny Clay had given me. It was just a small box—an old, green *American Home* recipe box. I sat on the bed and held that box in my lap and opened it.

Suddenly the room was filled with lavender and honeysuckle and lye soap. *Mama.* Inside was a handkerchief and two little hair combs that Mama had worn—Bakelite with pale blue stones. And then Mama's wedding ring and two folded pieces of paper. I slipped the wedding ring on the ring finger of my right hand. It fit perfectly. I opened the first piece of paper. It said:

Dear Velva Jean,

Daddy left this in the message tree by Mama's grave. He's come back now and then over the years, I guess to check on her and us, only he never wanted us to know. Did you ever feel like you was being watched? That was probably him. It was him that killed the panther that chased us, that twisted its neck till it died. Him that found Danny's blue hat in the train wreck. I saw him out in the woods one night and caught him and he said the ring was for you. I'm going to give it to you sometime when the time is right. Whenever that is, I guess it's now because you're reading this. Don't be too hard on him. He's been working on the new road that's coming into the mountains. So you see, depending on how you look at it, I guess he's done at least one good thing in his life. As Daddy Hoyt likes to say, it's an incoming road, but it's an outgoing road too. Anyway, the ring is yours. Daddy looked exactly the same as ever, just older.

Love,
your brother,
Johnny Clay

P.S. I found these other notes hid in the house where Sweet Fern must have put them years ago.

I folded the note away and put it back in the box. Then I opened the other notes, which were folded together. The first was crumpled and the writing was faded and hard to read. It was written in pencil in a loose, slanting hand.

Dear Beebee,

I am going up the mountin to git som work. Don't you wurry. Soon you will be in the Hospitial and on the mend and gitting along all right. You will see. I'll be home wen I can.

Yurs furever,
Old Mule

The other note had writing on both sides. On one side, in neat printing, it said, "July 29, 1933. Dear Uncle Lincoln, Enclosed please find the sixty dollars. I hope Aunt Corrine feels better soon. Your nephew, Toss Bailey." On the other side, in my daddy's slanting hand, was the following:

July 16, 1933

Dear Toss,

I hope you are well. I shur am having a time. I don't know hardly what I will do. Corrine is sick and poorly. I think she needs to go to the Hospitial so that she can get on the mend. If she does, hir bill will be about $200 if she gits along all right. I can pay $50 on it. Linc is getting me $25 mor tonight tho he don't know what it's for. Corrine don't want the family to know. She don't want anyone to wurry. Now I am going to ask you to send me $60 and charg me with enerst. If you need the $60 before then I can pay it. I am taking Beach out of school and he is helping me. We both make $9.50 per day so you know we can pay you back most any time. I am taking a job in Weaverville also, leeving next week. You can male the money to Sleepy Gap c/o my oldest son, Linc Jr. Don't say why you are sending it. Just say it's for me.

Your uncle,
Lincoln S. J. Hart

I read it over three times and then I reread his note to Mama. I read both letters again, searching for the answer to Mama's sickness, for the reason I was sitting here on this bed right now, getting ready to leave my husband and my home. There was so much I hadn't known back then. Mama sick and needing a hospital. Daddy going to earn money to make her well. Beach leaving school. Linc giving them money.

Daddy writing to a nephew to borrow money to help Mama get better. And then—later on—Daddy sending money to Sweet Fern and to Daddy Hoyt to keep for me.

All those hours and weeks and months I had worried about that note and blamed my daddy for killing my mama. All those years I'd put into hating him for making her sick and then leaving her to die. After all that, Daddy had been trying to save her. And I had sent him away.

I crumpled up the notes and stuffed them into the box. I was crying angry, hot tears. The lump in my throat was loose. It was sliding away. I was so mad, but there was no one to hear me—no one anywhere.

~

That afternoon I stood in the yard outside the house, a knife in my hand, and thought I should mark the trees just in case I ever needed to find my way back. I was thinking about the Cherokee who were forced to leave their mountain home for the Trail of Tears and how they bent and shaped the trees along the trail so they could find their way home someday and how they called them "day stars" because they could see by them.

I looked at the old oak where Beachard had carved his message. "You Are Loved." In my mind, I walked past this to the field where I taught myself how to drive; past the trickling end of Panther Creek where Harley had saved Janette Lowe and where Johnny Clay and I had once collected fairy crosses. I saw my way down to Alluvial and Sweet Fern's house, past Deal's and Lucinda Sink's, up the hill to Sleepy Gap and home—a place I would never forget as long as I lived, a place I would never need any help finding.

I decided my trees were already marked. I had plenty of day stars to see by.

~

For supper that night, I served fried chicken and angel flake biscuits and stewed tomatoes and for dessert we had half-moon pie. Harley was in a good mood because the sheriff and the Lowes had caught the outlander—the one they called the German—coming out of a house just outside of Murphy. Harley said the Lowes had wanted to string him up right then and there, but the sheriff had sent him to Butcher Gap Prison for safekeeping. Harley said, "He'll be kept under heavy guard so nothing happens to him." Harley called this a waste of time. He said everyone knew the boy would get the chair.

When he was finished eating, Harley had to undo the top button of his pants. He said, "That was some meal, Velva Jean."

Afterward, when we were getting ready for bed, I felt sick to my stomach. I didn't know if I could go through with leaving. I looked at Harley, standing in the moonlight. He was still in a good mood from the meal and the day. He kept saying we were turning over a new leaf, making a fresh start. A lot of people thought he was a hero. To folks who had been down to see and be healed by Damascus King, he was better than that—he was a savior. Harley had cast out the demons and, at the same time, rescued everyone on the mountain. It didn't matter that the outlanders were back at work on the Scenic. They had been warned and the one that had attacked Janette Lowe had been caught.

He was my husband. His wedding ring flashed in the light. He took off his shirt. He was wearing the bottoms to his pajamas but not the top because it was so hot outside and inside that you couldn't get away from it. He lay down on the bed and he bent one elbow underneath his head on the pillow. He flexed his muscles a little.

I said, "Remember when you first found the Little White Church, back when it was just getting started? Remember when you talked to them about making choices and keeping the faith, about the Lone Ranger and fighting a good fight?"

He closed his eyes. "'For I am now ready to be offered, and the time of my departure is at hand. I have fought a good fight, I have finished my course, I have kept the faith.'" He opened his eyes again. "Why?"

I said, "I just wanted to see if you remembered."

I got into bed and lay down next to him for the very last time. He lay there, smiling up at the ceiling, every now and then flexing his arm muscles. I turned on my side, facing him. I said, "I want you to know that I have truly loved you."

He turned his head to look at me. He grinned his big white grin. He rolled on his side to face me. He said, "I love you, too, Velva Jean. We got us a fresh start." He pulled me close, wrapping his arms around me. He started singing: *Come take a trip in my airship, come take a sail among the stars . . .*

I could feel his warmth. I could hear his heartbeat. It beat strong and fast. I breathed him in. I was wide awake for a long time after he went to sleep.

~

Early the next morning, I got up and fixed the breakfast, pitted Levi's prunes, stirred his oatmeal in a bowl, and waved good-bye to Harley as he walked off toward the church. As soon as he disappeared into the trees, I tore off my apron and dropped it onto Daddy Hoyt's rocking chair and flew down the porch steps, over to the truck.

According to *How to Drive*, there were five things to make sure of before you took your car on a journey:

1. There is gasoline in the tank.
2. The radiator is filled with water.
3. There is enough oil in the crankcase.
4. The tires are inflated to the pressure prescribed by the tire manufacturer.
5. The lights are working—if you are to make a night trip.

I knew that there was enough gasoline because I had already filled up the tank. I lifted the hood. I checked the level of the water. It was low, so I added more. I checked the oil, and it was fine. I walked around the truck and studied each tire. Also fine. And then I checked the lights. Fine.

Afterward I crossed the yard, back to the house. I picked up my apron and went upstairs and dressed. I pulled the only clothes I wanted from the chifforobe—Mama's flowered dress and my old dresses that were my very own (not the ones Harley had picked out for me) and the suit with the bolero jacket that Harley had bought for me because that one I liked. Then I put on my black shoes with the bows across the top and I packed away my clothes—all my underthings as well—into Mama's old brown suitcase. And, at the last minute, I put the apron in too, because it had belonged to Mama. As I did, something fell out of the pocket and onto the floor. I picked it up and unfolded it—a ten-dollar bill. My eyes started stinging and then they went blurry, and for just a moment, I thought I would have to sit down on the bed and cry.

Instead I took the hatbox and mandolin out of the back of the closet and I put Mama's little keepsake box inside my hatbox along with my record and the ten dollars. Then I set my wedding ring on the dresser.

Harley would be at the Little White Church now, surrounded by Brother Jim and Sister Gladdy and the rest of them. He would be working on his next sermon, trying to decide who to save next or avenge next or condemn next.

I pulled out the family record book and opened it and read over the last few entries—there was Mama's death, Daddy's leaving, the first time I was crowned Gold Queen, the first time I sang by myself at the Alluvial Fair, the time Johnny Clay and me ran away from home, the panther, my marriage to Harley Bright, the Balsam Mountain Springs Hotel, the Terrible Creek train wreck, the death of Danny Deal, learning to write my music, my first recorded songs, learning to drive, Janette Lowe, Johnny Clay leaving, Butch leaving, the Wood Carver going away. I thought: There is my life. All summed up in those few lines. There it is, captured right there.

Beneath it all, I started to write: "August 22, 1941: Velva Jean . . ." And then I stopped myself because I wasn't sure what to put next. "Leaves home"? "Sets out for the Promised Land"? "Goes in search of her destiny?" I didn't know what was going to happen next, so I decided to just leave it for now. I would fill it in later, once I found out for myself.

I packed the book into my suitcase. Then I picked up the suitcase and my hatbox and my mandolin and I walked down the stairs. Levi was sitting at the table, eating his oatmeal. He looked at me over his spoon and I looked at him. He looked down at my suitcase and my hatbox. Then he looked back at his paper and kept eating. I started to walk away and then I turned back around. I went up behind the old man and leaned right down and kissed him on his head.

I walked outside and threw the suitcase into the bed of the truck and climbed into the cab, setting the hatbox and the mandolin down on the seat next to me. I sat there for all of a minute, staring up at the house, at the window of Li'l Dean and Levi's old bedroom on the second floor where Harley and I had slept.

Then I turned the key in the ignition and started the yellow truck. When it sputtered and shook, I prayed that Harley wouldn't somehow hear it all the way over at the Little White Church. I glanced back up at the house. The curtains in the bedroom window blew a little in the breeze, but otherwise they didn't move. There was no one there to bother them. I put my foot on the gas pedal and headed down the hill.

I passed the field where I had taught myself to drive and where I sometimes drove with Butch, singing my songs. And then I came down into Alluvial one last time and I passed Sweet Fern's house and then Deal's and the old school and the Baptist church and the Alluvial Hotel, where Lucinda Sink sat rocking on her front porch. As I drove by, I waved and she waved back. I passed the road up to Sleepy Gap and Daddy Hoyt and Granny and my family and my home. My heart lurched and I felt the lump in my throat grow back.

I gathered up speed through the valley and didn't stop to wave to anyone else who happened to be out this early and who called to me, wondering where Velva Jean Hart Bright was off to so early on a Friday, hair flying out the window, lips painted Magnet Red, and singing loud enough for everyone to hear.

> *Oh, they tell me of a land far beyond the skies,*
> *Oh, they tell me of a land far away . . .*

Then I left the valley on the bumpy old cattle road, which wasn't even a road—just a narrow line between two high mountains—and headed outside my world to the one beyond. On the way to Hamlet's Mill, I met up with the access road that cut up toward Silvermine Bald. I wound around the mountain, up to the top. I prayed the truck would go all the way and get me there.

> *Oh, they tell me of a land where no storm clouds rise,*
> *Oh, they tell me of an unclouded day . . .*

I reached the Scenic, up where the road twined across the mountain like a gray-black ribbon. I waved to the workers—the outlanders who were a part of this place now, like it or not. There were guards standing over them, walking nearby, making sure that no one bothered them.

There was one long section of the road just finished where it was paved and smooth. I turned up onto it and drove as far as I could. The truck floated. It soared. It practically flew. Then, too soon, the road went bumpy and rough and gravelly, and then it was dirt and barely a road at all, but I kept driving anyway because it felt so good to be up there, on top of the mountains, with the great wide world spread out on all sides. From up there, I could see everything—not just North Carolina and Tennessee and South Carolina and Georgia, but Johnny Clay and Nashville and Butch and the Wood Carver and Daddy and even Mama, just over a cloud, so close I could almost reach her.

> *O they tell me that he smiles on his children there,*
> *And his smile drives their sorrows all away . . .*

I thought: Look at me, Harley Bright. I'm singing *and* driving. The map was spread out on the seat beside me. The tank was filled with gas. I thought: I am running *to* something, just like the Wood Carver said. I am running to something just as fast as I can.

I wiped the tears off my cheeks as I went round the bend that would take me toward the highway, the one that came up and across Wagon Road Gap and intersected the Scenic. Down there on Fair Mountain—my mountain that had been in my family for generations—sat my mama's old house. Down there on the hill above it stood the cross Daddy had carved out of his pain and grief, keeping watch over Mama's grave.

And they tell me that no tears ever come again,
In that lovely land of unclouded day.

I was still crying as I drove over the mountains above Hamlet's Mill, where Johnny Clay and Danny Deal and I had driven up and down in this same yellow truck, waving like the queen of England.

Oh the land of cloudless day
Oh the land of an unclouded sky
Oh they tell me of a home where no storm clouds rise.
Oh they tell me of an unclouded day

I was ten years old when I was saved for the first time. I was fifteen when I was saved for the second. But I was eighteen before I was found. All it took was eight years, a panther cat, a tent preacher, a blues singer, a murderer, an old yellow truck, and a road that could take you anywhere.

I pressed my foot on the gas pedal and sped along the mountain-tops, heading up the road to "off somewhere," out into the great big world. Only this time it had a name—Nashville. I thought it sounded beautiful, like music. I didn't know anyone in Nashville. I didn't have a place to stay and I didn't have a job—not yet. But I had plenty of gas and a map and $121.11, most of which I'd earned myself.

The truck started climbing higher and higher. The world was spread out before me. As I reached Wagon Road Gap, my voice grew stronger. By the time I got to the highway, I was singing louder than I had ever sung before.

"Yellow Truck Coming, Yellow Truck Going"
(words and music by Velva Jean Hart)

The Mean Devil Blues,
they're the worst kind of blues,
the kind that won't leave you alone.
They smack you down
and hold you fast
and chill you to the bone.

Over in Asheville
there lived a man
struck down by the Mean Devil Blues.
He drove a dark truck
and dressed all in black
from his hat down to his shoes.

The Mean Devil Blues
had him down on his knees
out of fun, out of hope, out of luck.
"I've gotta change something
or die," he said.
"I'll just start with this old truck."

He painted that truck bright—
yellow like the sun,
and then he started to pray;
and before he knew it
bad luck changed to good
and chased those blues away.

Then a boy named Danny
drove into town,
hoping to find good luck;

money changed hands
and Danny drove home
proud of his new yellow truck.

Danny was a family man—
loyal and loving,
good, kind, and true.
He died a hero in
the Bone Mountain wreck,
saving people he never knew.

Before Danny died
he gave his truck keys
to a boy named Johnny Clay
who was made of
gold and magic dust
and drove that truck away.

You can see that truck coming,
see that truck going.
Yellow truck coming,
bringing me home.

Even though Danny's gone,
that truck is still with us,
yes, even after he's gone.

Johnny Clay drove
that bright yellow truck
to the promised land above,
mining for garnet
and rubies and gold
to win the woman he loved.

Then the truck sat cold
and empty and dead
until his sister came along.
Velva Jean learned to drive
in that yellow truck,
teaching herself while singing a song.

Yellow truck coming,
bringing me home again.
Yellow truck going,
I'm on my way—
on my way to tomorrow
and dreams come true,
leaving my yesterday.

Velva Jean drove
over holler and hill and
through the valleys and streams,
to the tops of the mountains
and then through the clouds
on a road forged from dreams.

Yellow truck coming,
bringing me home again,
Yellow truck going,
I'm on my way.
Yellow truck coming,
bringing me joy again.
Yellow truck going, taking me home.

ROOTS

Of my great-great-great-grandfather, Samuel McJunkin, had not had a stormy first marriage, divorced his tempestuous Cherokee wife, become an Indian fighter, and then married a serene and pretty young woman twenty-five years his junior, I would not be here. That quiet second marriage produced his last son, Samuel James, a blacksmith like his daddy, who died young of typhoid, leaving his wife to take in boarders and finish raising five children alone. One of those children was my great-granddaddy, Samuel Jackson, whose fondness for alcohol and tendency to run wild drove his poor mother—a strict disciplinarian and devout teetotaler—to distraction. Samuel Jackson (called Papa by our family) was hard-drinking, hard-loving, and hard-working. And he loved to buck dance.

In February 1902, when he was twenty-two, he married Florence Fain on the North Carolina–Tennessee line, just four days after her twentieth birthday. Afterward they moved to Murphy, North Carolina, to live on Fain Mountain, named for her family. They raised ten children there when they weren't following Papa's blacksmithing work over to Copperhill, Tennessee, or Ducktown, Tennessee, or up to Woodfin near Asheville, North Carolina, where he helped to forge Beaucatcher Tunnel and sculpt the andirons for the great fireplaces in the lobby of the Grove Park Inn.

My Granddaddy Jack, their sixth child, was—by his strong, take-charge, confident nature—the family leader. He grew up in hand-me-downs. He and his brothers and sisters were turned loose on the mountains that were always a part of their lives in some way, whether they were living on Fain Mountain or in the Smoky Mountains of Tennessee or in the Black Mountains of Asheville. When Granddaddy was older—when I knew him—he dressed impeccably, in beautiful, expensive, tailored clothing. He was the only one of his siblings who went to college, something the family, to this day, is still immensely proud of. He was a fine athlete and a successful businessman. He married a glamour girl from Florida—my grandmother, Cleo, with red hair and lots of va-va-voom. She was a city girl, part Italian, part Irish. She was one of ten children herself and—her in-laws said in hushed tones— "came from money." My father, Jack Jr., their only child, was born in Manhattan. But Granddaddy never forgot his Appalachian roots.

I didn't know most of this until I started writing this book. Velva Jean herself was first born in a short story of my mother's. From the short story, she evolved into a short film I made, in 1995, while a graduate student at the American Film Institute. I knew then that I wanted to develop her story into something more, but I had to wait to do so until I knew what that story was.

North Carolina and the mountains have always been a part of my life. I divided every childhood and teenage summer between my Niven grandparents in Waxhaw, a tiny town outside Charlotte, North Carolina, and my McJunkin grandparents in Asheville. Each year one of the highlights was driving the Blue Ridge Parkway with Grandmama and Granddaddy McJunkin, who told me some of its history. Granddaddy's brother Sam had worked to help build the parkway. I always felt at home with my grandparents, at home in the mountains. But while I felt I knew everything there was to know about the Niven side of my family—the story of where they had come from, of how they happened to settle in Waxhaw—I knew little about my McJunkin ancestors.

As I began writing this book, and as I became more and more immersed in the culture and world of the Carolina mountains, I became more curious about those mysterious McJunkins. They were my Appalachian link, my mountain people. Although he and my grandmother eventually settled in Asheville, Granddaddy talked little about his roots. I never knew his parents because they died before I was born. My own father was never very interested in family history. Granddaddy died in 1987, Grandmama in 1995, my dad in 2002.

In late 2006, I dug through a box of old photographs that had belonged to Granddaddy and found a single picture of his mother—Mama, as the family calls her. She never drove an automobile, but in the picture she sits in a rocking chair up on Fain Mountain—her family's mountain—a car in the background. My father and grandfather were very into cars. They loved old classic cars, fancy cars, fast cars. That was my granddaddy's car in the picture. He had driven it up there to show Mama. She thought it was beautiful. But she didn't want to ride in it. She did, however, agree to have her picture made in front of it. That picture sat on my desk while I wrote this book.

By the time the photograph was taken, Mama had raised ten children and lost one. There was an eleventh child, a boy, born in 1926, who died a few days after delivery. Mama was in the hospital then. Papa nearly lost his mind. He loved her more than anything (he called her BeeBee; she called him Old Mule). He was barely literate and had no real education. There is, as far as we know, a single handwritten letter that survives him. In it, he is trying desperately to care for the woman he loves—the one he sometimes had to leave, the one he sometimes had to uproot and unsettle and upset by his very nature—to find a way to help her and protect her and make her well again. It is this letter I have quoted in part when Lincoln Sr. is writing to his nephew Toss Bailey.

I discovered all of this when I discovered my family history through wonderful cousins, nieces of my granddaddy, who found me through my Web site and led me to the rest of the warm and sprawling McJunkin clan.

But the eerie thing was that so much of what they helped me find mirrored what had already been written, by then, in these pages. I just came along afterward and filled things in a bit. We have a friend who describes it as "bone memory," a way of remembering and knowing something that is deep in your blood and in your bones—the places and people you come from—even if you haven't yet consciously learned about those places or people or experienced them. That is what this novel is for me, even though it is, for the most part, a work of fiction.

It is Velva Jean's story, first and foremost. I owed it to her to finish what I started. It is something I promised her years ago. She has waited a long time. But it is also a story of bone memory.